HOLDER OF SECRETS

PART THREE
UNREPENTANT

BY

MARGARET GREGORY

Cover designed by msgdragon
Cover images: © Can Stock Photo / heckmannoleg (girl)
© Can Stock Photo / andreykuzmin (record)
Pixabay/Nico_ma1 (wall)

Also by Margaret Gregory
TYMOREAN TRUST SERIES:
Book 1 - Power Rising
Book 2 - Great Ones
Book 3 - The Return to Earth
Book 4 – Earth Mission
Book 5 – Alien Contact
Book 6 - Invasion
ATAPI SORCERESS SERIES:
Prequel – Korvu: The Beginning
Book 1- The Wild One
Book 2 – Atapi Sorceress
THE THIRD GENERATION SERIES:
Book 1 - Wanda: From Bad to Worse
Book 2 - Wanda: Choosing Crime
Wanda – Early Days (anthology) Book 1 and 2
Book 3 – Wanda: Risking Life to Live
Book 4 – Erin: The Forcing of Wisdom
Book 5 – Wanda: A New Life Part 1 – Hidden Secrets
Book 6 – Wanda: A New Life Part 2 – First Mission
Book 7 – Wanda: Full Circle

For permission requests, address the request to the author c/o
Permissions,
C/o TAT Indie Publishing
PO Box 2728
Rowville, Victoria, 3178
www.tatindiepublishing.com.au

Holder of Secrets
Unrepentant

Chapter 1

The sergeant arrived after Wayne Carson had started his performance. McMasters, concerned for his back-up singer, met him at the door and the two of them spoke softly for a while. Then the policeman exclaimed, more loudly, "How did you find out about the call?"

Peg stood up, took off her beanie, and said, "Why else would they do this to me?"

"Why didn't you mention this earlier," was the immediate question as the policeman scrutinised her.

"Then, I didn't think it was intended to do more than humiliate me. Probably because they believed I helped that kid in Bathurst. Since then, I heard what you told Mac, and I found a plastic bag of, what I assume is stolen, items in my drawer."

Peg picked the exact moment when the policeman identified her, and was surprised when he didn't challenge her. Instead, he asked, "And can you explain why the only fingerprints we could identify in the laundry belonged to a Peg Jessup?"

She smiled grimly, "I think you have already figured that out and I am not denying it. However, I did not do this to myself, and the two men I described probably didn't know not to mess with me."

"And why is it that you are here when your brother is due to be returned to Goulburn?"

"Ask Mac. It is the first I knew about it. I told Stan to give himself up."

"You should have told the police," the sergeant lectured.

"I did." She didn't say it was well afterwards. "Anyway, Stan isn't dangerous. Not like Devlin. And it's not consorting to talk to your own brother."

Her attitude wasn't endearing her to him, nor was her posture and the deliberate stare. She was being like her friend and former co-internee, Les Shaw, once again. For survival.

"I need to ask you to come with me Miss…er, Jessup."

"Ready when you are. Don't you need to find the evidence? "

He took her arm and let her lead the way.

"Second drawer, at the front. I touched the outside of the bag, since I didn't know what it was in the dark."

The policeman took the bag by a corner, and placed it on the bedside cabinet until he could take out another bag to put it in. He released her for this, but kept watching her, expecting her to run.

"Can I ask you a favour?" Peg hoped the man would listen.

"You are in no position to ask," was his reaction.

"What happened to innocent until proven guilty?"

"What is it then?"

"Don't mention my name to the media."

"Which name?"

"Either."

"Why?"

"Most people think Megan Arthur has long black hair. The only people who know this look are the two guys and whoever sent them. It is likely they will start rumours about Megan, but I don't want them to know they got Peg Jessup."

"As far as I know, the media aren't involved."

"Don't count on it."

Chapter 2

"So, you decided to report in again," Eugene Taylor greeted Jack when he was given the phone.

Jack wasn't sure if his step-grandfather was being the former Chief Superintendent, or teasing him.

"Yes, Sir. How is Uncle Justin?" Jack was trying to sound meek.

"His pride is his worst injury, even though he was given a good going over by King, and warned. However, I chose not to tell him who tipped us off, so, if you decide to return, you should be safe from his foul mood. Have you found anything that I need to know?"

"Just interesting facts. Ida Jessup purchased her house from the estate of a Sylvia Lomax. That family have deep roots up this way. The only child of the widow Lomax, died ten years earlier. Her name was Mathilda. I haven't found any proof here, but I think she married Luke Simmons."

"Was it a cash transaction?" Taylor asked.

"Yes. The council took over the place and accepted an amount that covered the unpaid rates from when Mrs Lomax was put into care."

"Do you have dates?"

"Sale went through in March 1945."

"Good work. One wonders how Ida, or Adelaide, got the money to buy it."

"I don't know that, Sir. But there was another thing we found by a fluke."

"Yes?"

Jack told him about 'The Fielder's Inn' a motel in Mansfield with a notorious unit 13. His grandfather fell silent, probably thinking back over the years.

"I don't recall such a case. I will ask about it. You could mention it to Sergeant Maddern in Matlock. He might have a record. It is indeed an interesting find. Don't discuss it generally, and ask Maddern to call me after you tell him."

"Yes Sir. Can I ask if you got Ida Jessup's deed box open?"

"That, yes."

Jack waited.

Taylor finally admitted, "The missing share certificates that David Blair was after, were in there, along with a document, formally endorsed, transferring them to Megan Blair. The documents were never registered, but they are still perfectly legal, and binding. "

"What will happen to them?"

"If you are asking 'Will I let Blair have them', then no. They are evidence. The document specifically referred to the daughter of Margaret Blair. They are dated in 1955. This is proof that Margaret Blair did give birth to a live child."

Jack suggested, "It occurred to me that the child might have been sickly, or early. Perhaps the delay in the transfer was to wait and see if the child survived."

"Yes, that was my thought too. Now, your story of the motel becomes pertinent. I think the baby was born there, and the Blair girl died. Somehow, Ida Jessup got the body and the baby away."

"Mike and I were discussing that. Our best guess is that Harry King helped her. We both reckon he also dumped the two bikers in the same waterhole, and also tried to dump Peg there."

"Tell me your thought processes there, Jack."

Jack complied, adding the information about the phone call Peg had partly overheard.

"We need to get that man out of circulation," Taylor thought aloud. "What else do you think you can find up that way?"

"I don't quite know, Sir."

"Why don't you keep on as you have been? Looking through local records."

"Okay."

"What's your number there?"

Jack told him and his grandfather rang off. It was only then that he wondered again about the deed box. His impression of it had been that it was full of papers, since nothing moved when he'd shaken it. Had there been anything else in there?

Since they were back in Matlock, Mike Scott, had gone back to his job at the café, to listen to the local gossip. Jack was at a loose end. He could go to the library until it closed at five, but it would be wasted time if he had no idea of what to look for. He decided to go for a walk and think about all he knew so far, and was in the process of finding a jacket when Mrs Church, the owner of the boarding house, told him he had two visitors.

Partly alarmed, partly curious, he went to the Church's lounge room. His alarm faded. He instantly pegged the two as detectives, and from Peg's descriptions, they were Maddern and York.

"Jack Dawes?" the older, thicker, dark haired man asked.

"Yes, that's right. How can I help you?"

"We had a call from Ex Chief Superintendent Taylor," Maddern explained. "He suggested that you had some information that we should hear."

"Right!" Jack rolled his eyes in annoyance. He'd hardly had time to go to them yet. "Just let me get my notebooks, then if you prefer, we can go back to your office."

The younger man grinned. "Should I go and invite Mike Scott back too?"

Jack relented and grinned back. "If you want. He went back to work at the café to pick up the latest gossip."

He hid his concern about how much his grandfather had told these men about him. Surely he wouldn't bring up old scandals.

Mrs Castle was hovering as he headed for his room. He didn't explain his visitors, but she was probably wondering about him.

York casually answered it by asking Jack, "I believe you are related to the Chief Super."

Mrs Castle heard him say, "Yes, I inherited the old guy when my mother married one of his sons. He has become quite human recently."

Jack glanced her way, but she was returning to her kitchen, satisfied no doubt, that he wasn't being arrested.

Before agreeing to answer questions or volunteering any information, he asked to be able to ring his grandfather and check what he could and could not discuss. He listened to his grandfather, getting the feeling that several operations were being planned. Yet the overall advice was, "Use your discretion". If he did not want to reveal his sources, his grandfather would back his decision. The basic information to pass on was the old motel case, but he might have to touch on Ida Jessup's murder, and the shares. He'd have to think before speaking.

Once settled in a chair, Jack asked first, to know who he was speaking to. He nodded to each introduction. He did have the names right, but, well, they should have said who they were earlier.

"Well, you probably already know a bit about me," Jack began. "The pertinent part is that my otherwise idle hands have been put to work in the land registry archives, the BDM office, as well as the immigration records and other places."

"I am aware that Ex Chief Superintendent Taylor is working closely with the Organised Crime Task Force," Maddern revealed.

"Then you will excuse me if there are some things I am not able to discuss at this time," Jack added. "I do have some leeway."

"Why don't you start with what you can tell us – something about an old murder case?" Maddern suggested.

"Ok. I have been looking at land transfers related to particular significant people. My reason for coming up this way was to find out information about the property Ida Jessup owned. She is known to have been in close association with some of the OCTF's principal suspects."

At the mention of Ida Jessup, Jack saw both policemen lean forward.

"My car gave trouble in Mansfield and I had to wait there overnight for a part to come to fix it. So while we waited, Mike and I did some delving into old newspapers. I hoped to find what I wanted that way, and I did, but I also came across an old news article that I believe is important."

He explained what he had read, and at Maddern's probing questions, summarised the potential importance, and how it may link to two of their current unsolved cases.

Maddern glanced at York, "Go bring Mike Scott here, would you."

"So, you are alleging that Ida Jessup was killed because of some shares in Blair Holdings," Maddern summarised. "And the same killer killed the two bikers and the woman we found in the dam?"

"Well, as I said, I think the person dumped the woman at least."

"Do you know who the killer is?"

"I have a damn good idea, but no proof. That is something the OCTF is working on."

"What about Peg Jessup? Do you think she is still alive?"

Jack tried not to react, but Maddern's faint smile told him he had failed.

"My official answer right now is that I hope she is alright. But to answer the question you didn't ask, Peg saw the person I can't discuss, with another man, at Ida's house. She'd been knocked around and tied to a chair.

Peg walked into it, managed to get away from the house, but didn't have a chance to call for help. Someone caught her and knocked her out."

Maddern's face had changed, as if he sensed what was coming.

"When Ida Jessup couldn't or wouldn't tell him about some shares, the bastard who killed her began to work on Peg – even though she was unlikely to know. He beat her, raped her – again I might add, and tossed her in the dam. She was lucky though."

"Was it you who found her?" Maddern asked, with sympathy.

"Not then," Jack corrected. "If you must know, Stan Jessup had come back – intending to see you and turn himself in. He saw it happen, didn't know it was Peg at first. He took her to Jack Casey's place."

Maddern was nodding.

"And yes, I helped her get away on the bike Stan had used to come back. Trouble is, she came down with a very high fever. I finally had to have her lying in the river to bring it down. After that, we split up. As far as I can tell, and hope, the guy thinks she is dead."

Mike had arrived during the telling and nodded. "That's about it," he confirmed.

"So, what does your grandfather expect of us?" Maddern asked.

Jack didn't exactly know, so he used his discretion. "If you still have, or can get hold of, reports of that investigation that you look over the file and maybe what I told you will provoke new ideas. Probably any witnesses will be long gone. Also, do you have any reports involving Ida Jessup since she has been up here?"

York chuckled. "We have lots of them. The Jessup boys were allowed to run wild." Then he sobered. "And some recent ones when Peg was trying to straighten Ida out."

Mike grinned, he'd heard about the latter ones. "I assume Jack meant reports about Ida herself."

"Anything else?" Maddern asked.

"There are a number of things I need to find out about, but first – you oversaw the removal of stuff from Ida's house, did you leave much?"

York listed what they had left. None of it sounded important.

"I still intend to have a look around there," Jack announced to see if they had any objections. When nothing was said, he went on, "There are a number of people around this town that I need to get answers from. If they won't talk to me, I may need you to ask them officially."

"What kind of people," York asked.

"Bank managers, solicitors," Jack told them.

Mike broke in. "Jack, it might pay to explain about the keys."

Maddern queried that. "Keys?"

Mike sat on the front edge of York's desk. "Back when Peg disappeared, I wasn't completely forthcoming with you. She told me where she had stashed some stuff and asked me to keep it safe. It is down in Melbourne and the OCTF knows about it." He mentally added, Most of it! "Peg had two keys, one she found in Stan's wardrobe after those bikers kicked its door apart. The other was one Ida gave her just before…she died. The task force is trying to identify the keys. We think Ida Jessup has been hiding things from dangerous people."

"She had a deed box that we now know had the missing shares in it," Jack inserted. "I think there might have been other things, but I haven't been told."

"I am surprised that Taylor has been making use of a pair of green investigators." Madden looked at both young men.

Mike answered that, as he was more at ease with the two Matlock detectives. "In the scheme of things, we are doing grunt work. Stuff that has to be covered, but may not prove important. We are just two young hotheads, being kept out of mischief."

"Vengeful hotheads?" York suggested.

"Very," Mike agreed.

"So, what is Peg Jessup to both of you?" Maddern asked suddenly.

"A friend," Mike said at once.

"My wife," Jack admitted, betraying that he did know where Peg had gone.

"And I think she might be my sister," Mike added.

He and Jack grinned at the looks of astonishment on the detective's faces.

Maddern began to nod. As if the little he had been told had explained some questions. "Obviously, there is a lot more than what you have said. I'll let you look around and ask your questions," Maddern agreed. "All I ask is that you keep us up to date. Not so that we can take over, just so that there is a record of what you discover in case anything happens to you."

Jack told himself, It won't, but only nodded.

Mike took Jack up to Ridge Road and showed him the house where Peg had grown up. The remains of the police tape was still on trees and poles, but it had been torn away. The house itself was already beginning to look derelict, with several of the windows now broken.

Inside, too, showed the detritus of uninvited visitors, both animal and human. In places, the floor had been ripped up.

Jack murmured, "The police found a hiding place under the floor in the lounge. Seems somebody found out and word spread. Let's look under the house. I have a torch in the boot."

The half door leading under the house had been partly ripped away. It now hung by only one hinge. Without even going under, the torch light revealed a multitude of slither trails. More than one person had been under there.

"Give it a miss?" Mike suggested.

"Yeah. We should have come earlier," Jack agreed. "I don't suppose you have heard any rumours of recovered treasure?"

"No," Mike confirmed. "What now?" He glanced to where a dog was yapping. "Maybe we should talk to Mrs Bernstein, the neighbour."

"The one who tried damn hard to convince the police that Peg killed her aunt?" Jack growled.

"Yep, but she probably thought she was being a good citizen."

"Then why didn't she see King and my uncle?" Jack retorted. "What's your point?"

"Only that Ian said she'd been a busybody since she moved in there – umpteen years ago."

"Did he talk to her?"

"I think so. Didn't say about what."

"Do you really think we'd get anything more, now?" Jack asked.

"We might be able to provoke useful memories. If she is the bitchy type, she'd want to know the dirty secrets."

Pretending to be journalism students, undertaking an investigation for a final year project, they soon had Elvira Bernstein talking.

She had claimed, "I'm only telling you this now because she's dead. I wouldn't if she were still alive."

However, what she told them didn't add anything to what they knew. Ida had always had lots of male visitors, though the neighbour couldn't describe any of them. Her comments on the Jessup boys were scathing, and the returned Peg didn't escape her criticism. They let her talk, took occasional notes, and tried to push her mind back to the time when Peg was a baby.

She confirmed what Stan had said, about how the baby had cried, almost endlessly, for weeks. She had wanted the baby taken away and was still indignant that it hadn't been.

"I got social services to come out," Elvira told them, "But they still let her keep it. Seems it was her brother's kid, an orphan, and the mother had been a dope addict. There wasn't much the doctors could do for it, but comfort it and let it cry. I'm surprised that slut Ida Jessup didn't smother it. There weren't as many men coming then, and if they did, they didn't stay."

That last memory caused the old gossip to chuckle. "That whole family got what they deserved."

Extricating themselves finally, Mike and Jack drove back to town, each thinking on the dirty secrets, not just about Ida Jessup, that they had learnt.

"Glad I don't live in a country town," Jack summarised. "But at least we have confirmation that MB's child was an addict at birth. We can ask Maddern to get the official records of that. As for the rest…."

"Food for thought," Mike decided. "She didn't mention that Ida was related to the Lomax family. Peg's aunt must have kept quiet about that."

"And a lot of other things," Jack agreed. "Do you want to go out for tea?"

"Why not? The pub seems to be another good place for local gossip."

"I hope we aren't turning into a couple of bored old women," Jack joked.

"Someone I know, would not like that," Mike retorted.

"Les, you mean?" Jack asked casually.

"No, I meant Peg, but…yeah. Her too."

The mention of Jessup on the pub's overhead TV, caught Jack's attention. He wished he could hear the commentator better. He nudged Mike and they both listened. They saw an image of a crashed van, and police cars. When the report ended, the occupants of a nearby table added their own ideas.

"Jessup won't come back here. Nothing for him now."

"Showed more guts than he used to have."

"Nah, his mates did the hard part."

Mike leant closer to Jack. "They were returning him to Goulburn, and the van was ambushed. They will assume he was complicit in it and hang him out to dry."

Jack shook his head. "I think they were expecting this. I wonder if they had reasons to let it succeed."

"With three blokes in hospital?" Mike argued.

"Probably not, but Costa was behind the first escape. He needs Stan for something. I wish I knew what."

It was one more mystery to think on.

"Stan won't want to do what the guy wants," Mike predicted.

"Too bad. He will just have to tough it out. We have other priorities."

They left the pub at ten, but neither had drunk more than one beer. They wanted to keep their minds alert. At the boarding house, they entered quietly, not wanting to disturb the Castle's, but it seemed that the phone had already done that.

Mrs Castle told the caller, "He has just come in." Then she pointed to Jack. "For you." After handing the phone to him, she went off muttering, "Damn late hour to call someone."

"Hello?" Jack spoke tentatively. He wondered who would be calling him this late.

"Is that Jack Dawes?"

"Yes. Who is this?"

"Wayne Carson. I have a message for you."

Jack's heart began thumping harder and his gut felt like the beer and the food were fighting for space. "Hello Mr Carson. This is unexpected."

Mike's eyes widened and he moved closer to try to hear the conversation.

"You can call me Wayne."

"Okay. What's up?"

"Not good news. Oh, Megan has got over her accident yesterday, or will do. I expect you know of that?"

"Yes."

"And what she thought was the reason for it?"

"Yes. What else has happened?"

"The local police have identified Peg Jessup's fingerprints at the scene of the incident."

"Ok…ay. And?"

"Someone planted some stolen items in her room here. They also ensured that there were some eyewitness reports of a person with bleached blond hair."

"Damn. I told her to be careful."

"Mac and I can alibi her time, particularly here. I don't think they will charge her. Mac went to the police station with her. Hang on…"

In the pause, while Carson had his mouthpiece covered, Jack whispered, "Peg's been picked up. Someone set her up. Likely they thought of her only as Megan Arthur. It's got to be payback for helping Jimmy B. However, the police now know she's Peg Jessup."

"Are you still there?" Carson asked.

"Yes."

"Megan is going to be taken to Melbourne. She is going to be met by the OCTF. They won't say why. Perhaps you know?"

"Yeah, I have a fair idea. Does this mean that she is finished with you?"

"No. I do think she needs time to sort things out. If you can talk to her, let her know that."

"I will. Thank you."

Jack hung up the phone. He was pale, but then he announced, "I'm going to Melbourne."

Mike grabbed him before he could move more than a step. "What did he tell you?"

"The OCTF guys are going to take her to Melbourne."

The phone rang again, and Mike released Jack to answer it.

"Castle residence, Mike speaking."

"Put my grandson on the line."

"For you," Mike said, then mouthed the words, "Your grandfather."

"Sir."

"You are to listen to me and listen well. You are to stay where you are. You are not to come haring down to Melbourne. Do you understand?"

"I heard you," Jack acknowledged.

"The woman will be perfectly safe."

"As safe as Stan Jessup," Jack retorted.

"That is not related to this, lad."

When Jack didn't reply, because he was trying to think of a polite way to tell his grandfather where to go, Taylor spoke again. "Jack, I am giving you an official police order. If you disobey, you will be picked up and detained."

"Bastard! She's my wife!"

The silence indicated that he had surprised the old man. "That can't be allowed to change things. There is more going on …"

"Yeah. Yeah. I have that up to my eyeballs."

"Put your friend on, Jack."

Jack thrust the phone at Mike and began to pace the room.

"Sir?" Mike said more respectfully.

"See Jack stays where he is."

"May I ask why, Sir?"

"No, but you will find out soon enough. We will be keeping Maddern updated."

"Okay, I will do my best, sir."

"Good lad. Good night."

Jack stopped pacing and demanded, "What did he say?"

"He told me to make sure you stayed here."

"No way, mate."

"He said we'd find out soon enough."

Jack looked away and returned to pacing.

Mike suggested, "Perhaps she is not going to Melbourne?"

Jack stopped again. "Why not? Where else would they take her?"

"Here? Maddern still needs to talk to her. Everyone will think like you that Melbourne is logical."

The nearest chair sagged as Jack collapsed into it. "The old man has known that Peg was alive for a while. He just never spoke of it. He didn't know we were married though, until I just told him."

Mike chuckled. "I bet that did surprise him."

"Doubt it will make any difference."

"No, but maybe he suspected something anyway."

"Whatever!"

"Go to bed, Jack," Mike suggested.

Chapter 3

Peg hadn't slept well. Not surprisingly, as she was a guest in the Goulburn lock up. The locals only knew that she was wanted on a Victorian warrant. They had not added any charges, although it had been a close thing. The deciding factor had been the reply from Melbourne about the identity of the two men she had described to the sketch artist.

Both men had recently been released from Pentridge. Both men were known to have gang associations. Neither could have met Peg prior to the attack.

Until then, the sergeant and one of the local detectives had been at her about the robberies – asking her to confirm her movements in both Bathurst and Goulburn.

She did, citing that her manager was strict on routine, and although she had a habit of going out and walking around, it had only been at night. They tried to imply that she had time to go out between getting up in the morning and rehearsals, or between that and the show.

They told her times and places and implied that she could have got there.

Peg had calmly pointed out, "I have rehearsals from two until four. Ask my manager if I was missing. I start getting ready at seven, the show is at eight. How could I be in the centre of town at that time? I can't just rush in, put on a wig and bounce onto the stage. Besides, how would I have known where to go?"

It made her feel elated that Mac had confirmed her words. If he hadn't been sure of her, would he have been so persistent?

Still, the police couldn't let her go. She could have denied being Peg Jessup, but they would have found her out anyway. Hadn't Jack said, "Truth was better?"

And she had told Stan to give himself up. Should she do less?

Part of her still wanted to run, and hide, but she didn't want to have to do that all her life. She wanted to have a normal life, with Jack. Without the threat of Harry King and the shadow of Gianni Costa. She wanted to have status enough to tell David Blair where to go and rot.

During the night, her resolve had stiffened. She'd do whatever she could to get Harry King put away. She fantasised about him being on the run, hiding from shadows, being caught, resisting, being shot…It still wouldn't be enough.

Then there was Costa. He was still alive – living the high life. It was past time he was made to suffer. If she could, she would see to it. How many lives had he ruined? How many people had died because of him? Too many.

King and Costa wanted her out of the way, because she might have learnt things from her aunt. Did they even suspect the truth? That she really was David Blair's illegitimate grandchild. Her very existence was dangerous to them…they would learn.

Morning came and she was joined by two women who at first glance, might have been prostitutes. One was in a black two piece track suit and had her hair bleached like Peg's had been. The other was in slacks, with a western style shirt, and had long black hair.

Peg gaped. The blond showed her a police ID.

"The OCTF want to talk to you. We are to see that you get there without trouble. We've got make up to hide that bruise, and a brown wig to hide the bleach job. I am going to add a flashy white bandage to my look in a minute."

"How will all that help?" Peg asked. "If anyone sees you both together, they will believe the police have got me."

"If they think that and want you, then the non-descript brown haired woman will be overlooked."

"Okay, then. I will play your game," Peg agreed. I don't have a choice, anyway.

Things did not play out as she expected. The two women, handcuffed and escorted by uniformed officers, went off without her. Later she learnt that it had been in separate police cars. She left an hour later, handcuffed, but now clad in blue pants and tunic top, looking like an escaped prisoner. Surely no one would thing she was Megan, or Peg.

All the way south, she relaxed and dozed, noticing in her wakeful moments that the driver and his partner kept watching for followers. Once she heard the radio, something about a car being shot at. The shooter had been caught, not expecting the plain car escort. She wished that she knew which car it had been – the one with the fake Megan, or the fake Peg.

When they stopped to give her a rest break, it was at a trucker's rest stop. There had been no trucks there to give her concerns. After that much needed stop, she dozed the rest of the way to the border.

There, Victorian escorts took over from the NSW ones, and she was transferred to an unmarked police car. By then, she had rested enough to stay awake and take note of the route. They had told her they were taking her to Melbourne, but she realised they weren't.

At Benalla, they escorted her into the police station and into an interview room. She had not been there long, when her two escorts withdrew and two other men entered. One was Steve York. The other was a stranger who needed a walking cane.

Both men studied her, but York spoke first. "What are you calling yourself, Peg?"

"Megan. It is actually my real name."

"Megan then. This is ex-Chief Superintendent Eugene Taylor," York introduced. "He is part of the OCTF."

"I know."

"Why don't you sit down, young lady?" Taylor invited, gesturing to one of the chairs at the table.

Deciding that the request was as much for his own benefit, as for hers, she did so without fuss, allowing York to help move her chair. Hard to do while handcuffed.

Taylor sat on the other chair, and placed his walking cane on the table. "You know who I am?"

"Yes."

"Young Jack told you, I suppose?"

Peg nodded.

"I believe you have been providing him with useful ideas."

"Maybe. I don't exactly know."

"Why have you been running away?" Taylor suddenly challenged.

Peg found herself glancing at the neutral face of Steve York, reluctant to speak. Taylor also glanced that way, and the York took something from his pocket. He held a key and then proceeded to undo the handcuffs. Peg rubbed her wrists, wondering what the gesture meant. She looked back at Taylor, as he was obviously the one in charge.

"I expect, that to get you to trust me, I should speak first. I know some of what happened to you round the time your aunt was killed. I would like to hear it all from you. Your aunt was a person of interest to the task force. We should have brought her in, but as so much time had passed, and with her living away out in Matlock, it never seemed urgent enough."

Peg studied her hands, while forcing her face into neutrality, as she recalled that time. She had thought she had put it behind her.

"Do you think I killed her?"

"Circumstances to the contrary, your friends do not believe it."

"I asked you! Do you think I killed her?"

Put on the spot, Taylor felt he understood her unspoken question. He did not blame her for not trusting him.

"No. I am aware that my son was there and he helped you escape. He did not see your aunt killed."

"He was obeying that bastard, Harry King. Did you know that?"

Taylor nodded, and waited for the girl…no, for the woman, to answer. He wasn't going to make excuses for his son.

"Tell it from the beginning," Steve York advised quietly. He had stayed standing, just to one side of the older man.

The beginning?

Peg wondered how much Steve had told the guy about her and her aunt.

"My aunt, who I now know for sure was not any blood relative, had been having lots of male visitors while I was away. They were still coming when I got back home. I didn't want to go back to Meredan, so she needed to clean up her act. I knew what she was up to."

"How often did you spy on her visitors?" Taylor interrupted.

"Only once."

"My grandson proposed a rather interesting suggestion. Was it based on that instance?"

Peg nodded.

"I will come back to that. Go on with your story," Taylor encouraged.

She told of events as if that had happened to someone else, and looking at her hands, not her audience. Her voice grew hoarse when she spoke of what Harry King had done to her, and for a while, she couldn't go on. Then she glanced at Taylor. His face was neutral, so perhaps he already knew most of it from Jack. Steve though, well she could read his sympathy.

Steve inserted a question. "Are you sure that your Aunt was tied to the chair when you saw her?"

"Yes. It looked to be with some of her stockings. Why?"

She wasn't answered, and considered asking another question, but said instead, "I was lucky. I wasn't conscious when King discarded me. He must have thought I was dead, or almost and would drown. He took off, and Stan found me."

"Her brother," Steve said quietly.

Peg went on. "He took me up to Jack Casey, and he patched me up a bit and lent me some clothes."

"And my grandson and his friend helped you to get away," Taylor ended the story.

"Yes."

"Did you get all that, Senior?" Taylor asked.

"Yes, Sir."

"Megan, thank you for that. I know it was hard. I am going to get Senior York to type that up. I would like you to sign the statement. Will you?"

Peg nodded.

"Now, I would like to get your opinion…Do you think it was the matter of the shares that set the events in motion?"

Peg considered that point, then spoke slowly, "Harry King wanted them, yes, and Aunt Ida wasn't telling him. He can't have expected me to know, but that was just his excuse. He is a right bastard, even if he is the father of Ned and Jasper. He used to molest Stan when he was much younger and he raped me when I was barely 15."

Again, she had shocked York. "Why didn't you tell me this?"

"Steve, he would have killed me sooner if I did. I knew if I did as he said, he'd let me be – more or less. And, before I was sent away, I was a kid! No one in that town would have believed me."

"A doctor would have known," Steve said.

"I was a kid."

Taylor studied her in silence for what seemed like a long time.

"And now?"

"Now what?"

"If King were here now, what would you do?"

"Give him to you with bows and ribbons," Peg said, acerbically.

"What do you mean?" Taylor asked.

"If I had my wish, I would have him turned into a girl."

Most men blanched at that idea, but not these two. Steve smiled faintly.

Peg went on, "Since this state no longer has the death penalty, that's the next best thing…"

"I would like you to work with us," Taylor invited. "Will you?"

"If it gets King locked up for the rest of his life, and his boss Gianni Costa too, you bet I will. I know Jack and Mike have been already, but I was too scared to stick around."

"Excellent! It is my belief that co-opting those two young hot heads was the best idea I had. At the time, I had no idea what an important piece of the puzzle you were."

"Huh?"

"David Blair's grandchild," Taylor summarised.

"Oh, so you know that? Your son thought I was some hussy that Jack had picked up."

Taylor chuckled. "I won't say that my son has always made the right decisions, but calling you that was the best of protections at the time. Would you agree?"

"Maybe. But now it is sure to get out that you have me somewhere."

"That we have Peg Jessup somewhere," Taylor corrected.

"Same thing."

"Not the way I want to play it," Taylor began to explain. "I want you to stay in Matlock. I have told my grandson that I would have him locked up if he left there."

Taylor smiled, seeing Peg's face light up at the thought of seeing Jack. "Word will get around that we have Peg Jessup in Melbourne."

"Do you think that King will try to have a go at the supposed me?"

"Perhaps. It is one possibility. They made an attack on the car taking your brother back north."

"What? Do you mean they freed him again?"

"Yes. However, he is co-operating with us. Your friend Jack Casey is his advocate. He will be trying to help us isolate King and flush out Costa, in exchange for a reduction of his sentence."

"He doesn't want to work for Costa," Peg blurted. "What if he has to commit crimes for him?"

"We are aware of that possibility. He is a grown man and has made his choice. I want you to consider your own situation, and let the task force oversee that plan."

"Does that mean that you are going to cause those two skunks a lot of distractions?" Peg asked.

Taylor nodded. "So your part…. I want you to tell Maddern, or York here, every little thing you can think of that might open new avenues of investigation. I will say, that since you met my grandson, we have made great progress in our investigation aimed at finding Costa."

"Okay. I can do that."

"Later on, I will have one of the task force officers brief you, in outline only, about our investigations to date. I hope that might help provoke memories or ideas that might help."

"You should have questioned the old lush," Peg told him. "She was Gianni Costa's favourite whore, before she came up here. And the fact that he still kept coming to Matlock occasionally must mean something."

"Until you came back, we didn't know that."

"And he doesn't know, I know!" Peg gave a malicious grin.

"And that is why I need to learn everything you can tell us," Taylor finished.

Taylor stood, retrieved his cane, and left Steve with Peg.

"Ready?" York asked her.

"For what?"

"Going to Matlock."

"Are you going to buy me lunch?"

"If you want," York agreed with a smile.

"Pleeease! And can I get out of these ghastly clothes?"

"That can be arranged. Someone packed your stuff for you. Have you decided how you intend to look?"

"Well, if Jack can get more of that stuff to colour my hair. I will try to look like a boy," Peg decided. "This bleach job is even brighter than the one I came home with, and my performance persona had long black hair. This wig isn't bad, but it is too like my natural look. Some people might remember how I looked before I went away."

"You have changed a lot since then," Steve York commented, appraisingly. "For the better, I might add. I don't think many people who see you will think Peg Jessup right away."

"Maybe. But then, I have been getting lessons in performing."

As they drove to Matlock, Peg was only thinking of being back with Jack. York had other thoughts.

"I don't think that I can recall the time that King must have hurt you. I am amazed that you didn't let it affect you."

Peg commented, "By that time, my self-esteem had already been pecked to bits, and I had learnt that betraying hurt increased the pecking."

"And now?" York probed.

"What do you think?"

York considered that question. "I think you have learnt a lot from Les Shaw, and she has absorbed some of you?"

"You met her recently, then?"

"I did."

"I heard that Libby F tried to take a peck at her and choked."

"You have an interesting way with words. Though it seems that some others your age have had to learn new attitudes too." Steve glanced at Peg, wondering if she would comment.

She wasn't going to admit to anything about her little reprisals.

"My return must have been an example – this could have happened to you."

Chapter 4

Jack didn't appreciate Maddern arriving mid-afternoon and taking him from the café. He did think perhaps the detective might have had things to tell him, but it seemed more like he was some kind of offender being arrested.

"Do you need me too?" Mike asked, ignoring the intent listeners at the nearby tables. He was working as well as keeping Jack distracted.

The girls were ignoring Jack, who hadn't shaved in a week, was as twitchy as a druggie needing a fix, and totally disinterested in the female scenery. Mike sensed their relief when Jack was 'removed' from the café. The girls then went back to trying to irritate him.

"You know something, ladies?" Mike said, turning back to them. "My dad is a music journo in Melbourne. And I know someone who will be performing here in, oh, about six weeks. If you don't totally piss me off. I might even tell you who it is."

They tried to call him back when he walked off.

Maddern took Jack out to his car, but did not head back towards the police station. Instead, he went past the town centre and pulled into a driveway of a house a block down from the main street.

"You will be staying here now," Maddern told him. "I will get Mike Scott to bring your things around."

Jack suddenly knew why he was there, and who was there. He was out of the car and at the door before Maddern had stopped the car engine. The three people watching the reunion had huge smiles, but the two who had flown together like attracting magnets, were oblivious to anyone but each other.

A polite cough, distracted them enough to glance around. Peg blushed, but Jack Casey was still amused. "Well, you look much better than when I saw you last."

"Um, yeah. I guess. Except for the bump on the head." Peg tried to be nonchalant, but she still had Jack's hand in hers. "Um, yeah! I guess you guys want to quiz me some more. As if I haven't had enough talking today already."

With the policemen and Casey sitting in lounge chairs, and Peg and Jack cuddled on the couch, Maddern started speaking. This wasn't to be an interrogation, but a briefing. Casey being the OCTF representative sent by Eugene Taylor. York however, was ready to take notes.

After listening to what Casey had to say, Peg had the first question.

"Mr Casey, did you know those crooks would try for Stan?"

"Why so formal?"

"Okay, Old Jack. Did you?"

"Yes. We kept him in Pentridge until we were ready."

"So he agreed to be abducted, did he? He didn't want to work for Costa."

"A deal was made, young one. And perhaps you haven't considered a particular point. That is if Costa, who ignored Stan until now, wants him so badly, then he must be desperate, or the matter is someway vital to him."

"But what if Stan can't or won't fill the role they have in mind for him?"

"Let us worry about that. Why don't you try to consider what this move might be about? You can bounce ideas off us, even if you think them silly."

Peg hadn't expected such a request, but no one interrupted her thinking until Jack asked the policemen, "Do the police have a file on Reg Costigan?"

Maddern deferred to Casey.

"One is being compiled. We know his record as a V8 driver, and he has had a couple of warnings about drinking before races. There has been several complaints from women about him, but I think most of those are because he dropped them. He is most often been seen with well-built women, but lately there have been rumours that he is homosexual. We are looking into his earlier years, financial records, and all that."

Jack sat up straighter. "Homosexual? Really?"

"They might just be rumours," Casey warned.

Peg spoke, glancing at her husband. "You know, Aunt Ida was Gianni's full time whore when she had Stan. Then a couple of years later, he tells her he is married and his legal wife is going to have a kid. I told you that, didn't I, Jack?"

"Yeah. That would have been back in 1939. But your aunt didn't buy that place on Ridge Road until 1945."

"I don't know why she moved up here," Peg said. "But since then, she didn't see Gianni very often. Anyway, I think Gianni Costa and John Costigan are the same person. In which case, the resemblance Jack saw between Stan, and Reg Costigan, is because they are half-brothers."

"Megan," Jack used that name deliberately since they were with other people. "I definitely found records of two different people. John Costigan can't be Costa."

"But nothing on Costa after 1938," Peg poked him to remind him of that point.

Maddern interrupted, "How can Costa be Costigan?"

"Have you ever seen Costa?" Peg asked. "Recently?"

"That's the point. No one has," York told her.

"I have! And I told old Taylor that too."

"What point are you trying to make," Jack Casey prompted.

"I'm not sure, but it is almost like Aunt Ida and Stan and all came here to be out of sight. What if part of the reason was so no one would chance upon the resemblance between Stan and Reg? He might not have trusted Aunt Ida to keep quiet about Stan's parentage. Everyone would still think he was Bertie Jessup's kid."

"You and Stan found his name on Stan's birth certificate," Casey recalled.

"Maybe Costa hadn't had ideas then, or he didn't know she had put him there?" Peg suggested.

"Can you remember the man you believe to be Costa, well enough to do a photofit with us?" Maddern asked.

"Uh huh. I can do it for King, too. The NSW guys were impressed by the sketches they got of the guys who gave me this bump."

Peg didn't touch it. The area was still very tender.

Casey was grinning. "What did I tell you, Vic?"

"Megan, how did you get to be so devious and…" York began, but was interrupted.

"Malicious?" Peg suggested, a sickly sweet smile on her face. "Well, you and your mate over there sent me to this training place, and well, I learnt more than basic reading, writing and sums."

Neither detective took issue with her remarks, so she went on. "And Les. If there was a nasty light that could possibly be cast on a situation, she would. I used to be rather naïve."

"Obviously not anymore," York commented. "We will get one of the sketch guys up here."

"Yes," Maddern agreed. "I see why the ex-Chief Super wanted you debriefed."

Jack inserted. "Even if we are wrong about Costa being Costigan, the other possibility is that they are cousins."

"Nah!" Peg insisted. "I reckon Costa did away with the real Costigan."

Just to see what she would say, Casey asked Peg, "How would you find out if you are right?"

"I don't have to. It's the task force's job. They are getting paid for it."

"But, if it was your task?"

"You'd have to dig into Costigan's early life. Maybe he had broken bones of funny teeth or something. I don't know. Then compare the records to recent ones."

"What about finding out if Reg is homosexual?" Casey persisted.

Peg was feeling more relaxed now, that it was obvious that York and Maddern were not going to charge her with anything.

"Hmm, if I had the power, I would set Les onto him," was the polite part of her answer. "She always said she could smell a ----- "

Her crude term caused Casey to frown and receive a smug smile back.

Maddern heaved himself up from the deep arm chair.

"Steve will come back later with your earlier statement to sign. He will also write up what you have told us, to be sent to Melbourne. I want you to stay here – inside – at least for the next few days. If you have to go out, I want you to ask us first."

Peg nodded, and Jack said nothing. Steve York took the hint and rose to follow his superior, but he glanced back with a grin on his face, just before going out the door.

Casey was about to get up as well, when Peg turned her attention to him.

"What's this about you being the brother in law of that arrogant so and so David Blair?" she demanded. "Did that have something to do with you coming here? And does that bastard know who I really am?"

"Who are you really?" Casey asked. He seemed perplexed.

Peg glanced at Jack, who shrugged. "I did tell my grandfather, but he must have kept that info to himself."

"Well," Peg quietened. "If you are Blair's brother in law, you were Margaret Blair's uncle, so that makes you my great-uncle."

Casey's face went totally blank with shock. "My God!"

Alarmed by the sudden pallor of the older man's face, Jack asked, "Can I get you a cup of tea, Sir?"

"No, lad, I'll be fine." Colour came back to his face. "It's just a shock. I never agreed with David about kicking his daughter out. And I had been relieved when she hooked up with Ian. He was older than she was, but steady."

"Blair hated musos," Peg said. "Probably felt vindicated when Ian got arrested."

"Yes, but can you be absolutely sure?" Casey asked. "It was a shock when I heard Margaret had birthed a child."

"Yeah. I am sure. And I am a shocker, aren't I? Are you sorry you ever met me?"

"No, no. This is just so unexpected."

Peg turned to Jack. "I reckon he looks like Mike must have when he figured out about Ian," she commented. Then she returned her attention to Casey. "Now, I did not tell you that because I want to make lovey-lovey with David Blair. Fact is, as far as I am concerned, I have cut him out of my family tree. I will just keep you if you still like me."

"Oh, child! Of course I do."

"Warts and all?" Peg asked, and she grinned as Casey echoed it.

"Good! Now, if you don't mind, I have had a very tiring day, and didn't sleep last night. I want to find a bed and invite my husband into it."

Chapter 5

Stan, controlling a fury that had risen the instant that he saw Harry King, shoved the man with a strength he rarely showed.

"I don't want anything to do with you, or some figment that you claim is my father. I am not a naïve child anymore and I owe no favours to a bastard who never did anything for me all my life."

Stan hadn't tried to moderate his voice, and was waiting for a reaction from King. "I don't owe you anything either. You never did much for your own sons either."

King snarled. "I should have freed them instead! They like me."

"You think? Well I set them straight," Stan raised his voice further. "They know all about you now. As for the kid, they know what you did to her, too."

"She was just some whore's trash. Wasn't worth anything more than to be one too."

Stan shoved King again. The older, solider man may have been off balance the first time, but he wasn't anymore. He just laughed into Stan's face.

"You know that the little bitch killed your mother," King alleged. "The police finally picked her up. Nobody is going to believe she is innocent. I have witnesses."

Stan was sure King wanted him to completely lose his temper, but he controlled himself.

"If you really want to, boy, I will let you help free her."

"Right," Stan snarled. "And get me caught again, and increasing my time even further. You didn't abduct me just for that, you bastard."

"No, he didn't," a sharp authoritative voice lashed the air.

Stan turned and stared. "Who do you think you are?" he greeted the fat man. He knew though, for he remembered seeing the man a few times, but never up close.

"I am the person who wanted you out of prison," Gianni Costa stated.

"Well, no one asked me! And if you are trying to convince me that you are my father, you are thirty years too late. You have never done anything for me. You dumped my mother, married who knows who, just to get a legitimate heir, and I was what? Trash?"

Stan wondered what the man would say to try to convince him otherwise.

"I saw to it that your mother had money for you and the rest of her ill-conceived brats. If she chose to waste it on drink and whatever, it is just one more reason why she was ill suited to being my acknowledged wife. The bitch was addicted to sex, would have cheated on me at every turn. Even so, I never stopped loving her."

"Well, I don't owe you anything."

"Do you really like being in prison that much?" Costa demanded. "It won't be a place like Goulburn you go back to. It will be Longbay. The prisoners there would eat wimps like you."

"If that's what you think of me, why am I here?" Stan retorted.

"I would like you to meet someone." Costa gestured to someone behind Stan.

A younger man, a leaner version of Costa, strode into view. All the hairs of Stan's neck prickled him. The man didn't blatantly exude the air of a homosexual, but Stan had met some in prison – the dominant ones. This was one.

"Do you know who I am?" the newcomer demanded.

"No. Should I? Why don't you tell me?"

"I drive V8 cars. Fast ones," Reg Costigan proclaimed. "Ever wanted to do that?"

Stan had, for a time, but he didn't say so. He just said, "So? Is that supposed to tell me who you are?"

"I am someone that you are in a unique position to help with a delicate problem. And if you do, I can arrange for you to try out one of the racing V8 cars."

"Unless I get caught first," Stan stated the obvious.

"That isn't the intention," Reg Costigan promised. He outlined the reason why Stan was there.

Stan shut his mouth which had begun to gape open like that of an idiot. "You've got to be joking! How are you going to get the girl to agree with that?"

"You leave that to me," Reg assured him, slapping him on the shoulder.

"You want me to f… your fiancée? Is there any reason why you can't?"

Reg's face twitched. "Unfortunately, I had mumps a few years ago. It has made me sterile. My fiancée's Daddy is a sick man, and he wants proof of the next generation before he goes off."

"And you want Daddy's money, huh?" Stan began to smile, as if deciding he liked the plan. "What's in it for me?"

"What do you want?"

Stan pretended to consider it, but doubted that he would see whatever they promised.

"Two hundred thousand dollars, a new identity and a ticket to America." Personally, he thought his demand outrageous. "If you are so determined on this idea, it must be worth heaps to you."

"If that is what it takes," Costa spoke again, and Stan looked at him. "But at that price, there must be absolutely no word of this to anyone."

"I intend to look after number one," Stan said intensely. "I don't aim to be shot. However, I can't see that he is all that like me. How did you get your claws into him anyway?"

Reg still hadn't introduced himself, so Stan was playing dumb.

With a laugh, Reg explained, "I have a few vices that my father doesn't approve of, and your old man is helping me overcome."

"The two of you are like enough," Costa stated. "Of course, you need to be fed up a bit. We will arrange proper clothes for you, and grooming. Then I will get you some training in how to please a woman. Nothing illegal."

"What if this girl comes to decide she likes me better?" Stan asked, testing the attitudes of the two men.

"She won't," Reg said flatly. "She's in love with the motor racing me. Fast cars and all that."

"It doesn't matter who she prefers in her bed," Costa said. "If she wants a brat to please her daddy, she'll have you. But she is marrying Reg."

Stan nodded, as if just identifying Reg Costigan. "That's good. I don't want a woman dragging me around. Okay, so when the bitch is pregnant, I get the 200 grand, the ID and the ticket out of here."

Costa nodded, but Stan didn't assume that was confirmation.

"Fine. I'm starving and I need a bath!"

Costa left the room, but someone else entered.

"Hi Jessup," Mick Devlin greeted. "Glad you're here now?"

"Go to hell!"

Devlin only laughed. "Trouble with you yokels, you think small."

"Mind your mate, Dev," Harry King ordered. "Where's the bitch?"

"Down in the bar, eyeing the card players."

King strode from the room, followed by Reg Costigan.

He returned a short time later with two bottles of beer, and Les Shaw who had four glasses.

"You!" Les exclaimed, identifying Stan.

"Give him a beer, Shaw," Mick ordered. "Can't you tell the guy is parched?"

"I don't have to do what you say," Les retorted. "He can pour his own. Want a glass old man?" Her last question was aimed at King.

"Later!"

Stan found Les moving uncomfortably close to him. He moved back and King laughed.

"The bitch is in heat, and I don't have time for her. You can use her if she is so keen to be laid."

"I could wash your back," Les cooed, and both King and Devlin left the room as she said, "Lighten up Jessup. I know you've just got out of the pig pen."

As soon as the door closed properly, she whispered, "Pretend I am still all over you."

Stan watched as Les went to a cupboard and pulled out a tape recorder. Amazed, Stan nearly stayed silent, then he said the first thing he could think of. "Hey, I'd rather have the stink off me first. What about that beer?"

Les quietly ejected the tape, and inserted another that she took from her pocket. When the tape recorder was back in its hiding place, she put the used tape into her pants before going to open the bottle.

"Haven't got the hang of that," Les said, when beer froth flowed over the lip of the glass.

"Drink up," she continued in a normal voice, then in a much lower one, added, "Don't drink too much of this. King has it specially bottled. Be a bit dopey later, okay?"

Stan grabbed Les's wrist and asked very softly, "What are you doing here?"

"Same as you, farm boy. Making a stash to get away with."

Having seen what she had done, he realised that she was playing a deep game too. He gave her a faint smile. He wouldn't be giving King a reason to give her trouble.

Later, after hiding the tape in a place that King never went, Les sensed him coming up behind her. She was ready for his vicious tweak of her breast, and caught his ball in one of her own.

"Are you ready to play, old man, or are you past it? It's been a week since you could do it last."

Such slights to his maleness, always made King want to prove himself. Once he made her hurt, he enjoyed caressing the hurt before slaking his lust. This time, Les pretended to enjoy it, but her mind was concentrating on her act of revenge. The trouble was, her attempts to get his fingerprints had failed, so far. The bastard was careful by habit.

This time, she had made plans. She had a way that ought to make him near mindless. The whore who told her of the ploy had provided an aromatic oil that had an aphrodisiac mixed in, and which would also numb her skin to a small degree. The woman had also provided a hand paddle for King to use on her, instead of his hand. The whore had this very technique used on her, and she claimed it had been the best sex she'd ever had.

Les liked the idea, and hoped that the smell would begin to make King extra ready, and to use the oil, he would need to remove the skin tight gloves he usually wore.

What he wouldn't know, was that she had two of the paddles and would swap them. He wouldn't know that she had also doped her after sex lemonade either. He usually pinched it and left her to drink some of his doped beer. He usually fell asleep after slaking his lust, so he would not think it odd that he did. He would just be more deeply asleep that usual. She herself, would be out until morning.

Les wasn't surprised to wake up to find King gone. That was normal. What wasn't usual was the fat man sitting in a chair watching her. Figuring that he had seen everything she had, she wasn't coy about doing a reverse strip while he watched.

"Am I supposed to be impressed by your attention?"

"You should be," Costa told her.

"So, why are you here?"

"Peg Jessup."

"Heh? What's the little bitch to me? Isn't she dead?"

"Perhaps not," Costa suggested.

"I went looking for the bitch when I got out. The cops implied she'd done her aunt in, even though the bitch deserved it. Then they implied she'd done herself in."

"I have been hearing rumours that she has been found alive."

"Won't be if I find her," Les promised. "That pathetic wimp promised to help me when I got out."

"If she is alive, I want her," Costa said, with menace in his tone.

"Okay, but if you want me to find her, I'm not going to go near any cops."

"No. I expect she will be well guarded. See what you can hear from that boyfriend of hers. The cop's nephew."

"Why are you even interested in her? She was a pathetic tagalong before I taught her to spit back at people."

"Did she ever tell you anything about her family?" Costa asked.

"You mean her brothers, or the whoring lush she called her aunt?" Les asked. "None of them were very smart."

"Her aunt?" Costa pounced on that. "I thought she was another of Harry's brats."

"She reckons she wasn't since he left two of her brothers alone and molested Stan and raped her."

Costa didn't seem to be the least bit shocked by that revelation. Had he known? Or did he not care? "Did that shock you?"

"If that was all that happened to the kid, she was lucky. So why is she so important if she is not a ghost?"

"Why is no concern of yours. I need to know if she is alive and with the police, or if it is a ruse."

"Can't you ask your police flunky?"

"No. His old man has him bound and gagged." Costa seemed unmoved. "Why don't you find his nephew and bring him here?"

"Okay," Les agreed. She needed to see the guy anyway. "Do you have his address?" She already knew it, but she didn't want this creep to know she did.

Costa gave it to her and then she asked, "What can he tell you?"

"Like I said, he's got a thing for the Jessup girl. And he has been doing stuff for his uncle. He may have heard something. His uncle reckons he went haring up to Matlock when he heard she was in trouble."

"Wouldn't he be a bit old for her?" Les asked.

"Just find him and bring him to the pub," Costa instructed as he rose to leave. "You will be well rewarded."

Les figured that King didn't know she was aware of the young guys he usually sent to watch her. Whenever she did an errand for him, she wandered idly until she had spotted them. Usually there were two, this time there were three. Probably in case she did actually find Lover Boy and he proved to be difficult. They would be disappointed. She knew that he had hot footed away when the police had found Harry's pet captive. Still, it needed to look like she was doing his majesty's boss's will. He had been too busy to care that she had nicked some coke cans and chip packets to take with her. They were a reason to have a backpack with her. He hadn't been around when she had added the other items to the pack. Maybe she could give him the flick soon.

After hopping on a tram to get her closer to Lover Boy's flat, she walked the rest of the way to give her minders time to find her again. They must have had a fourth guy with a car who probably knew her destination anyway.

One of the weedy teens was practically breathing down her neck when she reached the building where Jack lived. That was fine. He could report that no one had been at home. She went up to the second floor and found the door with 22 on it. One glance was enough to tell her that someone had been there before her. The lock was broken. She pushed on the door with an elbow and spoke loud, "You here, Lover Boy?"

Not expecting an answer, she went in anyway, looking around as she muttered curses that would reach the ears of the teen who had followed her up the stairs. She didn't speak at more than normal conversational loudness, as she opened and shut drawers and cupboards.

"So where the hell are you, Lover Boy?"

She used the sleeve of her long sleeved jacket to lift the phone. The line was still connected.

"Okay, maybe your mate knows where you are."

Using her body to block the view of the phone, and the number she was dialling, Les called the Matlock number of the place where Mike usually stayed.

"Why aren't you here, Church Boy," she greeted, relieved that it was Mike who answered, and not his landlady.

"Why should I be," Mike retorted.

"Because I heard that Lover Boy's light of love was in Melbourne."

"Apparently," Mike agreed.

"Well, shouldn't he be here? Personally though, I'd settle for you."

"I have to stay where I am," Mike told her.

"Okay, I've got that. When will you be back?"

"Les, I don't know. What's the problem?"

"I'm looking forward to giving you what you wimped out on last time."

Les waited, hoping Mike would start picking up on her cryptic hints. "Is someone listening?"

"Now you start to get it."

"You want Jack to come to Melbourne?" Mike guessed then.

"Not him! You! Though I have heard his rat of an Uncle is restrained right now. He might take up an offer of taking me back to that pub where we met. For conversation and who knows what else."

"Is that a warning?" Mike guessed again.

"Uh Huh. Like I said though, it's you I'd like to see."

"Okay. I'm a couple of hours away. Where are you?"

"Well, I went to Lover Boy's place. The door was already open so I went it."

"Shit!"

"Thought I ought to hang around until you guys get back."

"Am I right? Someone wants Jack? Are you meant to set him up?"

"My offer won't last for ever," Les said, aware of the listener at the flat door.

Mike was silent for a while, then said, "Tell whoever that Jack got sent somewhere and told if he returned to Melbourne that he would be picked up and locked up. That was by his grandfather who is older and meaner than his uncle."

"Yeah, I'll do that."

Les hung up, hoping that Mike wouldn't waste time. She some things to give him before any of King's pack rats found them on her. However, the little twerp who was practically getting off listening to her conversation needed to be fixed first. He would be easy. After finishing the job he was doing on himself, he could take a message back to King. And he probably wouldn't recall anything she had said on the phone. Then, in the few minutes it would take him to go down and send one of his mates up, she could hide stuff.

Chapter 6

Mike, who had just been about to go around to the rented house to have another talk with Casey, Maddern and York, put the receiver down thoughtfully. If he understood Les's cryptic conversation correctly, King wanted Jack. He probably wanted to know how the police found Blair, or were there other questions? It didn't matter. Jack had to stay in Matlock – not that he would leave Peg now they were back together. Or maybe, they were trying to find out if the Peg Jessup in Melbourne rumours were true.

Les wanted him in Melbourne though. It sounded urgent.

He quickly dialled the rental house and had York put Jack on.

"I need to borrow your car," he said first. I think Les has something for me, and I think she is meant to set you up for an appointment with King."

In the background, he could hear Jack passing that information on. Casey came on the line.

"Is there anything else?"

Mike quickly mentioned about Jack's flat having been broken into, and his hope that Les had managed to get King's prints on something.

"Pick me up on your way," Casey told him. "I will come with you."

"Five minutes," Mike said in agreement. Les might complain, but, too bad.

At the flats, Mike encountered the manager who knew him by sight.

"There's a lady waiting for you in your mate's flat. Said she called you? Had some youths hanging around as well."

"Les, yes. Said she thought that the lock had been broken. Had you noticed that?"

"No mentioned it to me," the manager said. "Do you want me arrange someone to fix it?"

"If you could. Jack is tied up with work and can't come," Mike told him. "That's why I came when I could get away."

While Mike was talking, Casey looked around and had noticed several youths come in and go out as if checking on them.

"Stairs or lift," Mike asked Casey.

"I'm not so old that I can't manage a few stairs," Casey growled.

On the second level, the watching youth didn't quite duck out of sight soon enough.

Casey spoke quietly. "Watch what you say. I will stay near the door."

"What's with bringing the old guy, Church Boy?"

"He's a friend. I needed to get a lift," Mike said in his normal voice, then lowered it. "He's Peg's friend."

Mike saw Casey checking the passage and said, "Tell me what's up, quickly."

Les told him. "It's some guy who reckons his name is Costa, who wants Jack. He wants to know if the cops really have the kid. And I have something with King's prints on. And a tape."

Mike gave a huge grin as Casey, from the doorway, said, "Get them, quickly."

Les saw Mike nod, and fetched them from where she had hidden them. When he saw the plastic wrapped paddle, he gave her a questioning look, but Les just stared back at him.

Casey gestured Mike to the door, and came over to take the items. The tape went into the pocket in his shirt, and the paddle into a pocket of the overcoat he had worn to come to Melbourne. It had large inside pockets.

"We will need to get a statement from you," Casey told her. "It will be very important to have a line of ownership of these objects."

"How are you going to do that?" Les hissed. "King has three or four young guys hanging around, watching me and for Lover Boy. I'll be dead if he thinks I went to the cops."

"Mike, why don't you get the manager on the phone and ask him to call the police to report this break in? Then have a look around to see if anything is missing. I will go down and check his mailbox. Does he lock it?"

"No."

"I will wait downstairs for the officers."

Casey knew that someone had crept back to listen, even if Mike hadn't heard him. He figured that a mention of the police would see that they went off. His presence down near the mail boxes would be a further deterrent. He considered Les Shaw. He had heard of her from Peg, and more from various enquiries that he had made. Today, her attitude had been as he had expected. Her body language though, that hadn't fit. She was moving carefully, not arrogantly. He considered how Maddern had described her in relation to the Miss Falconer episode – the obvious bruising, versus the Falconer girl's claim she had done that to herself. He considered that to mean that she would endure pain, to achieve something she wanted.

Although he had not said anything to Peg, he had doubted the wisdom of her having more to do with Les. Yet, Shaw had taken on a dangerous role to help her friend. She was a woman who had survived a horrendous childhood, and whose adolescence had been a series of violent outbursts and it seemed that her only friend, was more important than…than what? It now seemed to him that Shaw was more honest than the spoilt and pampered Falconer girl.

The police arrived quickly. Casey intercepted them, introduced himself by showing his OCTF credentials, and didn't care if the young loiterers heard him mentioning the break in.

He manager must have mentioned those lads hanging around, for one of the officers went off to talk to them. The other accompanied him up the stairs, and listened to his request that a statement be taken from a witness about some vital evidence. He didn't say what evidence, but his request to have Eugene Taylor brought to the local station, emphasised the request.

When the policeman walked in the door, Les moved closer to Mike, but flinched when he put an arm around her. She saw his unvoiced look of concern, but just shook her head. He didn't need to know what she had let King do to her. The bastard must have done more of it to her after she had been asleep – before he had nicked off. The bottle of oil and the other paddle had gone from the room too.

Eugene Taylor walked into the room where two detectives were taking the report of the break in at Jack's flat. Les saw them stiffen, the seated one stood, and both nodded at the new arrival. She twisted around.

Mike whispered. "It's all right. He is not out to get you."

One of the local detectives announced, "We will get this typed and you can sign it before you leave."

Both local detectives left the room, and the newcomer took the seat behind the desk, and placed a cane on the top of it.

Casey made introductions, "Les Shaw, Eugene Taylor." He explained who Taylor was and added, "He is very keen to hear about Costa and King.

Anything you can tell us."

Les reverted to her usual abrasive tone. "It true that you've Peg Jessup stashed somewhere? I heard she'd done herself in."

Taylor didn't react to her tone, but merely said, "We do indeed have her in protective custody. She is helping us in our enquiries."

"The kid didn't kill her aunt."

"We are fairly certain that you are correct. However, it is a useful reason for us to want her."

"Okay then," Les grumbled, toning down the attitude. "What you want from me?"

"I understand you were meant to set up my grandson."

"Lover Boy, yeah. That's what the fat man wanted."

"Describe the fat man," Taylor requested.

Les did, with spiteful accuracy.

"Did he give you his name?"

"He didn't exactly introduce himself, but I reckon he's his majesty's boss."

"Who?"

"Harry effing King. I reckon the fat guy was giving old Harry orders."

"Tell me about when you met him. Had you seen him before?"

"Seen him? Yeah. Day before. I was kinda listening in on a conversation he was having with Stan."

"Stan Jessup?"

"Yeah."

"Where were you?"

"Right next door. Harry doesn't think I know about the peephole and the hidden microphone. When I heard they were going to get me to do something, I quickly nicked back down the stairs."

"Go on. What did you hear?"

Les told him all she had heard and what she'd been told to do. Then, "The fat man left first, Harry went later, and he sent Mick up to make sure Stan behaved."

"Mick Devlin?" Casey asked.

"Yeah. He's acting like King's flunkey these days."

"Go on," Taylor urged.

"Anyway, I got left alone with Stan. Didn't ask him about his business with his majesty. I'd heard enough, and King don't like nosy people. I took the opportunity to pinch a tape I had running in there, and to put a new one in the machine."

"Wasn't that dangerous?" Taylor asked mildly.

"So's living, mate. Anyway, they put the recorder there in the first place, but I figured that wouldn't be a conversation they'd want a record of."

"Where is the tape now?" Taylor asked.

"Your mate here has it." Les pointed at Casey.

"Indeed. Continue."

"Well…" Les seemed to take a deep breath before going on. In fairly crude terms, she told them that she'd been letting King have sex with her, and that he liked to rough her up. That she had been trying to get something with his prints on. "But he's too bloody careful by habit. But, I kept trying because Lover Boy and Church Boy thought it would help."

"And did you?" Taylor leant forward, intent on the answer.

Her smirk spoke volumes. She told them how she had tricked King, with King thinking he'd tricked her.

Taylor considered all she had said, and then began to probe for more details, by asking provocative questions.

During this, Casey had taken over the role of note taker. He now said, "You will need to have the fingerprint guys go over the other things she gave me."

"Yes. I will arrange that before we leave. I will want that information typed as a statement so that Miss Shaw can sign it."

"Ain't sure I want to stay here much longer," Les said, starting to squirm on her chair. She stood up. "King had a pack of young guys following me in case I found Lover Boy."

Casey nodded confirmation. "I can get her signature later. All we need now is her to sign over the items to me and for me to sign them over to you."

Taylor waved an agreement to Casey, and spoke to Les. "So, you'll be saying that you just reported the robbery and the police were slow typing it up. Do you think you can convince your watchers of that?"

"Let me and Church Boy leave by ourselves and go back to Jack's place."

Mike, who had kept silent throughout, simply passed the car keys to Jack Casey.

"And if they insist hard enough that I tell them where Jack is, I will say that Maddern and his mate took him off somewhere. Meanwhile, Les will be trying to find out if I know more than that." Mike managed not to blush by telling himself they were really just going off for a coffee.

Chapter 7

Peg, answering to Megan while around others, was not to answer the phone if it rang and she was alone. So when Mike rang, she knew it was him when it went to the answering machine. She really wanted to talk to Mike, but would have to let Jack go out later and find out what he wanted. Jack had just gone out to fetch whatever he had decided tea would be, and to call his grandfather.

Over the past couple of days, she had done her best to recall oddments of information from conversations with her aunt. These details were passed onto York and then to Maddern. However, on its own, the information didn't seem useful. She needed to think of it in light of other events. She had actually suggested to York that he check on the man Dunstan – the guy her aunt had tried to blackmail. In her turn, she promised to think overall she recalled and see if other ideas came to mind.

When she heard the key in the front door, she went to the kitchen to get plates out. Being in the same place as Jack, seemed like heaven.

"I hope you weren't wanting tea for two," Jack called out as he came in. "Steve's going to be here tonight and I invited him to tea. Told him the fee was information."

"I hope it's worth it. I haven't heard anything since Mike and Jack Casey left. Mike rang ten minutes ago,"

"Well, we can hear what Steve has for us. It won't be much, because the OCTF only give out what they think we need to know."

When the three of them had finished eating the packaged pub meals, Peg was inpatient for news.

"So, Steve, what do you know?"

York told them of the break in at Jack's flat, which had him scowling. Then he mentioned that Les had managed to tape a conversation between Costa, King and others, and also achieved another goal she had worked for. Steve didn't say what, but Peg guessed that she had finally got King's prints.

She hoped that was so.

"And do you think Les should still hang around King?" Peg asked.

"I think that she decided that she would. She is hearing useful things," Steve told her.

"Yeah, but, she has seen Costa." Peg tried to express her fear. "No one has seen him for decades."

"It seems your brother spoke to him too."

"But he knew the risks," Jack pointed out. "How did you find that out? Les?"

"Obviously. I am not privy to a lot of details," Steve admitted.

"I will go give my grandfather a call. He may tell me more," Jack decided.

"And Steve," Peg put an innocent smile on her face. "I know I'm meant to stay in here. But since I am back in Matlock, there is stuff I ought to be seeing to."

"Not reacquainting yourself with old school mates," Steve grinned.

"No. Why would I?" Peg made a face. "I am supposed to be seeing to the legal stuff related to Aunt Ida's will. Probate stuff, whatever that means."

"At the moment, Ida Jessup's house is still a crime scene," Steve pointed out.

"Hardly secure," Jack said pointedly. "Oodles of people have been there recently."

Steve grimaced. "It might be better if we approached Ida's solicitor and got him to handle it."

"Fine," Peg didn't argue that idea. "I also want to go back to the house."

"Like Jack said, the place has been gone over thoroughly, and not just by the police."

"Did you look under the house? In the roof?" Peg asked.

Steve nodded.

"What about the garden?"

"Why there?" Steve was suddenly intent.

"Something Stan told me. He said there used to be a chook shed, but only a slab was left now. Somewhere in all that overgrowth out the back."

"It might be better for someone else to go clear that stuff. I might have a word with the council. The growth is a fire hazard."

"And you called me devious," Peg said, shaking her head. "But it would save me some work. And the stuff from inside the house. I heard that was taken somewhere. Can I look through that?"

"I'll ask," Steve promised. "Why?"

"Nothing particular. Just that I never had a proper chance to go through all of Aunt's stuff. Like all the stuff in her room."

"I will talk to Vic, but you may have to wait to do that."

The moment that Les returned to the North Melbourne pub, she felt the tension shared by many of the patrons. It didn't seem to affect the casuals, but those that were regulars were huddled over corner tables, talking low and always looking over their mate's shoulders.

She could go and join one group or other, but they'd not tell her anything. To them, she was still a casual. Next best thing was to sit at a nearby table, and listen.

The group she sat near, were all approaching retirement age – old lags and age weakened bashers. If they were afraid, what had happened?

With the press of other patrons, and their chatter, Les only heard occasional words, but some seemed important – bodies, St Kilda gang war, and other places. She stood and went to the bar.

"Why's there all these long faces?" she asked the barman, and shoulder shrugged to the group in the corner.

"Keep out of it," the barman advised in a very low voice, meant only for her. "And avoid your friend."

"His majesty in a snit is he?"

The barman gave her another glass of lemonade. "Six of the old timers got taken in."

"Huh?" Les snorted. "What would they know? They're practically senile."

She wondered if it were a good time to get a message to King, and if she should say that the cops did have Peg Jessup in Melbourne. Her gut instinct was that they had her somewhere else. The old cop wouldn't have said anything to her unless he hoped it would be passed on.

"Hey, Freddo. If I had a message for him, could I leave it with you?"

"Business or personal?"

"Business. I doubt he's ready for personal again, yet."

Freddo smiled slightly at that insult to King. "Stay here, I will ring upstairs."

The barman moved to the far end of the bar, to a phone hidden under the counter. I was an internal line only.

He returned and told her, "You can go up, but for your sake, I hope it's good news you have."

Les strode up the stairs with her usual pose of arrogant unconcern. She was met by Hanson, one of King's lesser cronies. Interesting. She'd expected Mick, but if the cops had been around, he'd have jumped into the nearest dark hole.

"What you want?"

"Got word for old Harry."

"What about?" Hanson demanded.

"The Jessup girl," Les told him. "That's all you need to know."

"He's still busy, in there." Hanson shrugged. "Where will you be?"

"Down with the marks, if you are too scared to tell him I'm here. He said to come up."

The door opened, and King edged out. One glance at Hanson had that one trotting down the stairs.

"Well?"

Les took in the flushed face, and didn't needle him. "I couldn't get to the worm's nephew. Just to his mate. But I reckon they do have the little bitch. Lover boy was all set to rush back from the bush, but the local cops got him before he got anywhere. Told him to stay put. Guy didn't want to. He had that option or that of being locked up. Order came from his uncle's old man."

King's expression eased to a smirk. "The little bitch should have stayed dead. Now I can give her another lesson."

"Not until I've had a go at her first, mate," Les retorted. "She ran out on her promise to me."

Les relaxed when King's smirk became broader. He pulled his wallet out and gave her two hundred dollars, or rather shoved it down the front of her crop top. "Make yourself scarce for a day or so, and keep your mouth shut."

When he had returned into the room and shut the door, Les considered for a moment going to listen at the peep hole. Her sense of 'way too dangerous' kicked her down the stairs. As much as she wanted to know the full story, she decided to return to her digs…on foot…to check if King still had his rat pack watching her.

The rat pack had returned to their holes. Perhaps that was because there seemed to be a lot more cruising police cars. Seeing one was unusual, but she had seem three already. They didn't worry her, but they made her wonder if the arrest or picking up of the old timers was a ruse. Maybe the police were planning to raid the hotel? That idea caused her to smile.

She smiled even more when a car pulled up just ahead of her and Church Boy stepped out from the driver's seat and gestured to the passenger side.

Chapter 8

Jack didn't say anything when he came back in, and Peg, seeing his thoughtful expression, didn't question him until they were alone.

"Grandfather didn't give me details, he said some of it would be in the papers tomorrow. He'd just had a further report from Mike. From what he said, I'd say that the OCTF has a series of unpleasant shocks planned. Today, they picked up a bunch of old lags and one time bashers who worked for Costa, way back. One of them was, I think, an OCTF mole."

"Old gang members? Whatever for?" Peg mused.

Jack shrugged. "Possibly in relation to the six bodies dug up by an excavator at Blair's St Kilda properties."

Peg's eyes widened. "Do you think that was why Costa wanted that land? Could they be tied to anyone after all this time?"

"Possibly. I don't know what the police can do besides try to identify them. They may have some ideas of who they are already. Les went to tell King that you must be in Melbourne because I tried to rocket down there. While she was waiting to get to see him, she heard mention of bodies, some old gang war and 'other places'."

"Well, I hope the task force have fun. Those bodies aren't our worry."

"No, but I have been thinking on the idea of other places and keep coming back to those five other places still in Costa's name."

"Are you doing more about that?"

"Not at the moment," Jack told her. "It is just possible that Grandfather is going to throw another problem at Costa and King."

"Oh?"

"Have Costa declared dead and have those properties confiscated. Turf out the tenants etc."

"Interesting. Costa won't be able to do anything. Not if he wants to stay hidden. He'll be livid."

"Mmm," Jack indicated agreement. "Especially after losing Blair."

"I guess that now will not be a good time to go look at the Aunt's stuff that Mike took away for me."

"Going to town? No. Mike could bring stuff here. What do you want? There's lots of saved letters to go through."

"Might do that," Peg agreed. "Did Mike tell you any more than York told us?"

"Just that Les reported Costa, King, Stan and Reg Costigan getting cosy at the pub. She got a tape of the meeting."

"Yes!" Peg hissed. "I was right!"

The finding of the six bodies in the St Kilda development site took up all but a tiny square of the front page of the Melbourne papers. Most of the report was an expansion of the details Jack had told her. The find was linked to an infamous gang war, back in the early fifties. The victims had, it was believed, failed in an attempt to take over another organised gang of criminals. Police were, reportedly, interviewing old criminals who had been active back then, trying to link it to the time. Costa's name was not mentioned. Only hints to various known criminals of that time who had disappeared were mentioned.

Peg decided, that whether or not the police knew the ideas as fact, Costa should be getting worried if he had been involved.

However, the small corner of the front page not on that subject, was of equally great interest. It pointed to a small article on page three that reported the recapture of Mick Devlin. Reference was made to Stan Jessup, at large again, and the belief that Devlin had masterminded his second escape.

Such nuggets of information on the task force progress, were sporadic. Neither York, nor Jack were told everything. Peg, herself, was already bored with the house seclusion. Jack at least got out when he went for food, called his grandfather, or was 'checking things'.

She had exhausted all she could recall from her aunt.

At the end of the first week, Jack came in grinning. Not quite hidden behind his back was a guitar case.

"Got a delivery. Had it sent to Benalla PO." Jack saw recognition in Peg's eyes. "Got something else too." Jack's grin grew wider as Peg snatched the brown paper wrapped parcel, addressed to Megan Arthur, from his hand.

"Put that on the chair," Peg told Jack, referring to her guitar. "When did you speak to them?"

"Who?" Jack pretended innocence and failed.

"Wayne Carson!"

"Oh, him? Well, I figured you needed something to do."

"I did! So what did he tell you that you didn't tell me, you rat?"

"He had to talk to your manager. But he suggested that you practice your songs. I assume the outcome of the talk is in that parcel."

"I need a tape player," Peg announced, when she saw the three cassettes in the parcel. She began to scan the letter that came with them, and then saw that the rest of the folded pages were music scores. "He's put music to the two songs I was working on and created a duet line to one of the others. He wants me to practice them all and play them on time to what's on the cassettes. He is hoping I can still make the recording date in Sydney."

"When is it?" Jack asked.

"In about two months," Peg told him after checking the letter.

"I don't know," Jack said, hating to dampen her delight. "We will have to see if you can be got there anonymously. Things are starting to get dangerous in certain circles."

"And likely, the powers will still not have won by then," Peg agreed, her spirits drooping. "What else have you heard?"

"It is what I didn't hear that worries me," Jack admitted. "Grandfather said for us to keep a very low profile, and even though he would like to use me to find information, it wouldn't be safe."

"Not since King got a look at you," Peg said with a shudder.

"Probably," Jack agreed. "But I don't like it. I assume Costa and King will be out to get anyone who might know something about them."

"Does that mean that your uncle had better watch out?"

"The old man had better lock him in a dungeon," Jack proposed.

Peg was teaching herself one of the new scores, later that evening, when Steve York arrived. One look at his face told her he had news, and it wasn't all pleasant.

Jack took himself to the kitchen and fetched a cold can of Coca cola. He returned and passed it to Steve.

"You look like you could use a drink. Sorry it's not beer."

"It's fine. I'm still on duty." Steve did drop into one of the arm chairs, and asked, "What are you playing, Megan?"

"Some music Wayne Carson sent. What are you trying not to tell us?" Peg went straight to the point.

"They have identified one of the bodies found at St Kilda," Steve began. "A known enforcer who disappeared twenty years back. The guy had a pin in his leg. The rest are likely to be identified shortly."

"My grandfather mentioned some old lags that were picked up," Jack prompted, when Steve seemed not to be about to say more.

Steve grimaced. "They were no help. All they admitted was that they knew the man had worked for some crime boss, but that person had disappeared about when WW2 started. Everyone assumed the crime boss had been drafted."

"And?" Jack persisted.

"The old guys were released. Four of them were travelling together in a taxi. A truck deliberately ran into it, killing the four men and the taxi driver."

"Shit!" Peg said quietly.

"I guess it isn't unexpected," Jack said then. "But would that mean that those men may have known something? Or those dead men – something about them – might be a weak point for Costa. I have to believe he was behind that truck attack."

"At least they can't blame us for that revelation," Peg said with a shudder. "Can they?" Jack shook his head.

"Indirectly, they might. I did find a reference to them, but the actual deeds were in that box of your aunt's – with the share documents."

"That woman definitely had a death wish!" Peg said, once the information sank in.

"I don't think Grandfather will let on where he got the info from," Jack assured her.

"I sense a but…."

"It may be unrelated, but Avery, one of the OCTF, was beaten up last night," Jack told her and then he glanced at Steve York, who hadn't mentioned that.

Peg guessed that Steve hadn't wanted her to worry. "Is there anything else you two haven't told me?"

"The only other thing I was going to mention," Steve inserted smoothly, "was that Vic and I found a reference to that motel incident. The investigating officer is still alive, but couldn't add any more detail than what he had in his report. The main important point was that the room had been booked by a Miss Simmons."

"Bingo!" Jack said. "Anything else?"

"Just that it seemed that a lot of blood had been incompletely washed away and the bedding had been taken."

"So have you passed that information on to my grandfather?"

Steve nodded. "He will keep it in mind, but he can't see how it will help in the main task."

"Do you know how it is helping?" Peg said, putting her guitar aside and standing up. She went over to Steve and poked him in the shoulder. "That motel incident…when likely I was born, has led to one very vengeful bitch, aka me." She poked again for emphasis.

Steve countered with, "I know that. But do you want certain people to pay any more attention to you – in any of your guises?"

Her shudder was answer enough.

"So, any more new ideas today?" Steve asked.

"No. Any word about when they might clear out the jungle from the aunt's place?"

"Later this week," Steve told her.

"Well, if that's all the news. I will sort out tea," Jack decided.

The following morning, after they were up, but before they'd had breakfast, the doorbell rang. Steve went to check who was calling, and immediately opened the door. Voices from the hall brought Peg from the kitchen.

"Les!" she exclaimed, greeting her friend from Meredan with a hug that Les didn't expect.

"You were meant to be here when I got out, bitch, not got yourself in more trouble."

"Yeah, well, it wasn't my intention this time," Peg pointed out. "Besides, I like how it confused certain people in town."

Les gave Steve York a glance. "Yeah, the bitch deserved what she got."

Meanwhile, Jack was greeting Mike and they were in a huddle.

"Hey, no secrets," Peg called to them.

Les said in a bland tone, "Maybe Church Boy and Lover Boy are comparing notes."

Peg elbowed her. "Have you and he….?"

Les answered with a smirk. "Had to have my fun somehow. His majesty, who has an inflated view of his own eminence, told me to nick off for a few days."

"I read that Mick got nabbed," Peg commented.

"Couldn't happen to a more deserving bastard," Les remarked, then added, "Actually, it could. His majesty has had things his way far too long."

"Yeah," Peg agreed.

"So kid. What's this I hear about you getting chummy with that guitar hunk?"

"Purely business, and temporarily on hold. Did Mike mention what happened to me in Goulburn?"

"Some, but they were being cagey and making out that you weren't the singer. They on your side now?"

"I think so. Steve and Mr Maddern don't think I killed my aunt."

"Them's smart then," Les said, mollified. "So why are you being kept hidden?"

Steve interposed a comment. "Because she is a thorn in the plans of a few people you seem to know."

"Put her and me together, we'll be an effing briar patch," Les promised.

"Good," Steve agreed. "You can be more protection for Megan."

"Megan. Right. Nothing new in that except her name," Les agreed. "Too bad Church Boy is insisting on going back to Melbourne."

Chapter 9

Peg reminded Steve York of her request to look through the stuff taken from her aunt's house, using the idea of, "It might help me think of other things."

"You do recall that they really don't want you to be seen?" he reminded her.

"Ah, but if Les and Jack are seen, I can sneak off to look."

"Megan, if you think everyone will mistake Les for you, then others may think you are up here…and you are!"

"Ah, yeah. I didn't think of it that way. Damn!"

"What say I ask if you can, and then work out how? The stuff is still here in Matlock."

"Wasn't it going to be shipped to Melbourne?"

"It was going to be, but then we were told to hold onto it."

Later, Peg, Les and Jack were told, "Vic has agreed to let Megan look through the stuff we put into storage. However, he doesn't want Megan looking like any of her normal selves, and he did like the idea of Les walking around with Jack. Last time she was here, it caused confusion. If people think she is Peg Jessup, they won't be looking anywhere else."

"As soon as she opens her mouth, they'll know," Jack retorted immediately.

"I'll keep quiet and pretend to be all lovey-dovey," Les countered, beginning on an impersonation of a love sick girl.

Peg elbowed Les, but grinned – appreciating her friend's ability as a mimic, even if the person she was aping was herself.

Steve also grinned. "However," he warned, pausing to be sure he had their attention, "keep alert for anyone who seems too interested in you."

"Lover Boy here is paranoid by nature, I reckon," Les said. "I will look out for anyone I have seen in Melbourne."

Jack nodded at that. "Good thought!"

"And I will pinch some of Jack's clothes to wear and put a beanie on." Peg had, by then, redyed the bleached hair to black. "I can be some scruffy runaway you nabbed."

"Won't be the first time, Kid. Anyway, you can have that if you think it's fun. I prefer to go with Lover Boy."

Steve left first, after telling Peg to go out the back and cut through to the next street, where he would pick her up. He gave no reason, but Peg wondered if he thought someone was watching him.

Jack and Les went out next, and Jack found he needed to increase his stride to keep level with his companion.

"If someone thinks I'm Peg, I will be quiet like, otherwise I'll be me, okay Lover Boy?"

"Confusion," Jack murmured. "I like it. What say we go to the café where Mike works when he is around?"

"That will get the gossips going," Les agreed.

Peg observed the street for a while before heading out the back. When she left, she made sure the doors were locked, knowing Steve had keys. In the next street, after jumping a fence and sneaking along beside the house, Peg began a slouching walk along the street.

She was on the lookout for Steve prowling in his official car. Anyone observing when he suddenly saw him swerve to the kerb, would think she was being nabbed.

Within a couple of minutes of driving with Steve, Peg asked, "Do you think we are being followed?"

He glanced in his rear vision mirror for the sixth time before answering. "Just being careful."

"Where are we going?"

"The Harris place. On the Wilga Road," Steve told her. "Jack Casey recommended him. Said he was a nut about security. I'd say obsessive, but that's all to the good."

Harris certainly scrutinised her when Steve arranged for her to look through the stored boxes. He told her to get busy, and ask Harris to call when she was ready to leave.

By contrast, Jack was soon aware of covert interest as he and Les moved along the street. It was even more obvious when he sat down in the café. He wasn't sure if it was the people who thought Les was Peg, or something else. By prior agreement, they didn't give any hint that they were aware of the watcher or watchers. In low voices, they spoke between mouthfuls of coffee and cake. Jack got Les talking about Meredan, while he shared some of his experiences from his year in Maldon.

They were finishing up when Les's attention went to someone entering the café. Jack didn't turn, but asked, "What is it?"

"Tall guy. Knocked up a bit. I've seen him, at the pub in town. Don't know his name."

Jack took that as being the place where he had met King for the first time. For a moment, he thought it might have been his uncle, but the man who pulled over a chair and sat astride it, uninvited, was not.

"Avery," Jack greeted.

The man ignored that and said, "Dawes, Jessup. I didn't think you two were meant to be seen around."

In turn, Jack didn't answer Avery's innuendo. "Why are you here?" He made no comment about the black eye, grazes, and several sutures decorating Avery's face, though his eyes flicked to each in turn.

"Added security. Squizzy didn't think you'd behave."

"Squizzy?" Les asked, in what was for her, a subdued tone.

"Grandfather," Jack said quickly before prodding the senior policeman. "Looks like it was you who needed the extra protection. What happened?"

"Nothing that need concern you, boy. Though I believe Jessup here has several keys that might open up things up here. Have you had any success talking to the people you needed to see?"

Jack's instincts, or his paranoia, were fully on the alert. He didn't think his grandfather was going to tell anyone where Peg was, or anything about her activities. Avery might have heard his grandfather telling him to stay up here, and not being able to locate Peg in Melbourne, come up here on a hunch.

That bit about the keys and looking for what they unlocked, was odd. Eugene Taylor had seemed satisfied to have the local cops follow that up.

"Ah, no. Peg doesn't actually have the keys. I had to send them to my grandfather, since just the pictures I gave him first weren't good enough. I thought he was going to send them to the local cops. Do you want me to find out?" Jack offered. "And let them know you need to find out if they've made progress?"

Avery considered that. "Okay, if you would."

Once Jack had gone to the phone, Avery turned his attention to Les, thinking her Peg Jessup.

Les spoke first. "So who are you then?"

"I'm with the OCTF."

"Another of those! Obviously not important enough for me to meet when they had me in Melbourne. I told those flunkeys all I knew then. So, why are you here?"

"Like I said…"

"Yeah. I don't need extra security. You are like a big, big arrow saying Peg Jessup is here."

"What do you know about the five properties Gianna Costa owns?"

"Huh?" Les told herself to be careful. She had to stick to what Peg had told her, not what she might have learnt herself. "The old bitch might have thought the sun shone out of his arse, but the subject of property, his, hers, or anyone's, never came up. I was surprised to find out she actually owned the house on Ridge Road."

"Yeah, I've been there. Place is being knocked around. Emptied."

"You cops did that. Didn't you know?"

"Must have been the locals, not the OCTF." Avery sounded arrogantly superior.

"Cops is cops," Les told him, relieved to see Jack was on his way back. She watched him approach.

Jack sat and said, "Maddern is on his way around. Talk to him." To Les he asked, "Want another drink?"

"Nah. I'm good."

"Coffee?" he suggested to Avery. The policeman shook his head. Jack decided to test Avery and asked some questions that he already knew the answers to.

"You know I can't discuss OCTF business, Jack."

"Ah, come on, Avery. I put in hours in the archives. It'd be nice to know if any of what I found helped."

"Did you find out about the properties Costa owned?"

"Not directly," Jack lied, but he kept meeting Avery's gaze. "I did suggest that someone should check the cross indexes. I didn't have that much access."

Avery didn't comment. If he wasn't in Eugene Taylor's full confidence, that would seem to be the truth.

"Obviously, my idea paid out. What happened?"

Avery chuckled. "Costa hasn't been seen for over thirty years. No tax return, no mention in the electoral rolls. If we hadn't been hearing on going rumours, you'd think the guy was dead. Squizzy got the court to declare him dead, and for his property to be impounded by the State. The current tenants were evicted and were questioned about the owner."

"And?" Jack prompted.

"Tut, tut, Jack. Police business." Avery shut up again.

"Is that how you got that shiner? One of the tenants gave it to you?"

Jack saw Avery's face muscles twitch and beyond him, Maddern entering the café. He didn't say that, just let the local detective greet his city based superior.

"Perhaps we should talk back at the station, Sir," Maddern suggested respectfully.

Avery nodded and stood up, noticing what he took to be a glare that Maddern was giving Jack and the girl. They both got up in a hurry and went to pay and leave.

Once outside, Jack set off at a fast walk, but not directly back to the house. "I rang my grandfather first. He didn't send Avery here. He's meant to be on sick leave. We have to pack our stuff – Peg's and mine, and get out of the house. He can't be sure the place hasn't been compromised."

"Reckon that cop is on his Majesty's payroll?"

"I didn't want to think so, but since Uncle has been taken off the case, he would need someone else on the inside. Costa must be getting worried."

"I'm surprised that he didn't recognise me," Les said. "I have been around when he has been talking to his majesty."

"I am and I'm not," Jack said as he gestured for Les to turn into a lane on their right. "If he saw you in town, he wouldn't expect you to be here. And he might have heard that you could be mistaken for Peg."

"What, with the hair job?"

Jack considered. "No, if Costa was behind that, it would be Megan Arthur who was given it. Grandfather made it look as if Megan and Peg are two separate people, and getting Peg was a fluke."

"How will we let Peg know what's up?"

"I told Maddern that Avery wasn't sent officially. He was going to send Steve to pick her up. When we have our stuff, we are to slip out and meet Steve near the station."

Peg looked at the stack of boxes and wondered where to start. Then she noticed the boxes were labelled according to the room where they were packed, and she sorted out those from her aunt's bedroom. Boxes that were also marked clothes, she ignored. The stuff from the wardrobe and drawers took her attention first.

A lot of the stuff was junk, but it must have meant something to her aunt, maybe memories from an earlier time. None of it roused any thoughts of possible uses now, decades further on. She wondered who had packed the boxes, and if they or the police had kept anything aside. Maddern hadn't said anything about that. She came to an old biscuit tin, and opened it. An involuntary, "Ahh!" escaped her.

The box contained photographs, mostly black and white. She looked closely and saw photographs of her younger self, and younger versions of her foster brothers. Some were posed, others taken when they were playing. Under all were photos taken at school – class photos and individual ones. All this time, and Peg had never known her aunt had kept them. She had never been one for framed family photos. Perhaps so that people would not see how different she and Stan were to Ned and Jasper and each other.

Jasper, already tall in the most recent photo, was already starting to look like Harry King. Stan, well, she knew who he took after. As for herself, she didn't have a good enough photo of her mother, or one of her father to decide. She put all the photos back in the tin and kept it aside.

She had gone through four more boxes when she heard the door open and looked up.

"Steve? What—"

"Grab anything you found and come on."

"Why?"

York just gestured her to hurry. She did, sensing trouble.

After casually thanking the Harris guy, and letting him know they might need to come back again, Steve opened the passenger door for her, making everything seem routine. Only when he didn't turn back towards town, did she start to ask questions.

"What's going on, Steve? I thought I would have longer."

"Orders. I don't know. All I was told was that I had to go and pick up that kid again, and pick up some stuff that used to be about the old miner's place."

"So, I am that kid," Peg said aloud. "I don't get the rest."

"I am going to drop you near Jack Casey's place, after checking it out. Then I have to go and bring your friends up. It will just be overnight, or until we work out another place."

"Why?"

"I really don't have details. Vic didn't want it mentioned over the air."

"Someone must have figured where I was," Peg decided. "Damn! I'm tired of having to keep ducking out. Why can't the OCTF get their act into gear and round up Costa, King and all their crowd?"

"Vic told me that since you came on the scene, they have made a great deal of progress."

"Not enough though. It would be nice to know they are about to arrest the lot of them."

"Patience, Megan, You know we will need airtight proof to make the case stand up in court. That isn't going to be easy after thirty or more years."

"Yeah, and no doubt a lot of the stuff aunt knew relates to stuff older than the statute of limitations."

"Unfortunately, that's true," Steve agreed. "But even if we can't charge Costa with old crimes, it is building a picture. And he has shown himself recently. That is promising. You don't want to give up now, do you?"

"Hell no. I just wish it were over."

"I do understand. But, don't forget, there is no time limitations on murder."

"And finding proof from thirty years back won't be easy," Peg said with a sigh.

She stayed in the car while Steve checked out Casey's shack, and the mine.

"All seems clear, but if you think anyone is around, hide."

Peg sensed his concern. "I'm good at that, don't you know?"

"I do. You and those brothers of yours. I'll be back with Jack and Les as soon as I can."

"Oh, before you go. I didn't find anything useful, just some old photos of us Jessup kids. Ones Aunt took, or from school. The later ones of Jasper, sure remind me of Harry King."

"Really?" Steve commented. "Do you want me to look after them?"

"You might as well," Peg decided, handing over the old biscuit tin. "If I have to duck out again, I don't want to have to lug it with me."

<h1 style="text-align:center">Chapter 10</h1>

Two weeks of forced inactivity had not improved Justin Taylor's demeanour. For almost all his working life, he had believed he was making a difference – keeping crooks from becoming like the unlamented Squizzy Taylor. It was always ironic that he shared a surname with the gangster. Yet, as his adopted nephew had pointed out, and his idle time in the past two weeks had allowed him to consider, all that time he was being used. He could see it now.

His father, when he had still been an active force member, had encouraged him to be friendly with the crims, to make contacts and informers. That is mostly what it had seemed to be. Until King had approached him two decades ago.

That had been a shock. The man had known of the shameful thing he had done, and threatened to tell his superiors in the force of it. Even if it was never the cause of formal charges, it would ruin his career. If it did, he would end up in jail with all the angry little crooks had had put away.

In his favour, he had told his father everything about that time of shame. At least he had been heard and cleared of complicity in the girl's disappearance. His former fiancée's disappearance. He had been particular in reporting everything his informants and contacts had told him, and the questionable things King had asked of him. Those questionable acts had been increasing in the past few years, but what was asked of him was also of value to his superiors, or related to ongoing investigations. Like the missing shares that David Blair had asked him to investigate.

The worst of his troubles had really started when Ida Jessup's name had begun to be mentioned. King had suggested she might have taken the shares.

Ida Jessup, formerly Adelaide Swan, had been Gianni Costa's one-time whore. He'd met the woman, many years before when he had been looking for Blair's daughter. He considered her a brainless wench, considering her choice of career. Now he wondered how much of that had been an act. Costa, as her pimp, wouldn't want her to be smart.

When he'd had a call from her, out of the blue, he had been fool enough to ask King about her. He'd not seemed concerned, but suggested that he see her if he wanted to. It had been more of an invitation to bed the bitch.

His own instincts had suggested that she had to have been worried about something. It had seemed a good opportunity to ask her more questions about his one-time fiancée – Blair's daughter.

He hadn't had a chance to ask about her. The old whore was babbling about someone trying to blackmail her. She had a name and a photo. Only because he wanted the old whore to trust him, did he agree to talk to the man. He had thought, that when he reported back to her, she might talk of other things.

The photo was a new print from a negative taken twenty years before. Ida Jessup didn't look like that now, and in his mind, she had nothing to lose by it coming to light. He knew from King that the shadowy person that was Costa still sent clients her way. King had laughed at the photo, saying, "She'd have done better to threaten to reveal it about him."

Yet now that he looked back, that was when King's interest in Ida Jessup had increased dramatically. And his instincts had told him that King knew a lot about her that he wasn't telling his pet cop. That was part of the reason why he had agreed to go to Matlock with King, to talk to her.

The man had said, dismissively, "She's a stupid bitch. Harmless though. If we both go, she'll be more likely to talk." A talk, supposedly about the missing shares, but King had not confided why he thought she knew something.

He had intended to keep the talk civilised, but the silly bitch had panicked, possibly thinking she was going to be arrested.

She had denied knowing anything about any shares, or even of what had happened to his fiancée. Even after King had grabbed her and tied her up, and roughed her up, she denied knowledge. King never even asked her about what happened to the girl – who would have been the most likely person to have the shares.

In hind sight, again, Justin told himself that King probably already knew she was dead, as his hot headed nephew had suggested.

Since Ida Jessup's murder, King had ramped up the threats, "Mention it and you will regret it."

He had told his father anyway. He wasn't sorry about letting the girl go. She was a witness that placed King at the house. King would have killed her. He had been physically sick when he had heard what King had done to her. Now he wanted the bastard put away – even if testifying got him killed.

"Justin."

His father's voice interrupted his ongoing mood slump. "Sir?" He looked up.

"I have a highly confidential side investigation I need you to take on. Not a word of this to anyone but me." Eugene Taylor gestured in the direction of his office.

Justin straightened, and stood up to follow.

With the door firmly shut, and classical music playing on the radio, Eugene Taylor sat at his desk and picked up a folder. He gestured for his son to bring a chair closer.

Without delay, he got to the point. "The Shaw girl managed to trick King and get a set of his prints."

There was an echo in Justin's mind of, "Something you never managed to do."

With the folder opened, a series of photographic prints were revealed. Eugene passed them over for his son to look at. One was of a table tennis bat and the rest of the fingerprints lifted from it.

"Have you had the prints run through the system?"

"Yes, I asked for a rush job, but they don't match the prints of any living convicted criminal," Eugene Taylor revealed. "Which tells us that King has never been convicted."

"So, what do you want of me?"

"This is a long shot. We have no background on King – no birth certificate, no tax records, bank accounts etc. The name King, is probably not his real name."

"How do you think these prints will help us?"

Eugene sat back in his chair and suggested, "What if King does have a record as a juvenile, or was picked up but not charged?"

"Fingerprinted, you mean? Wouldn't we need a court order to look in the juvie files? And aren't incidental fingerprints destroyed?"

"I will arrange access," Taylor waved that concern aside. "And yes, fingerprints used to eliminate people are usually destroyed. However, have a think about what young Jack claims about King and what Stan Jessup claimed."

"That he's a pervert?" Justin confirmed. "So you think he might have been suspected of that but not charged at some point in his life."

The older Taylor nodded. He didn't need to mention that the prints of suspected offenders against children were often kept in the file of the investigation.

"Go back beyond 1940, that's when he was supposedly the proxy for Albert Jessup for the marriage to Adelaide Swan."

"If we are to believe Peg Jessup," Justin pointed out. "Why then?"

"He had to have been in with Costa by then, perhaps just starting. He was using the name 'King' then," Eugene proposed. "That suggests that he was trying to hide some past secret."

"Okay, you get me the access and I will see if I can find anything in those old reports."

"Remember, this is just between you and me for now. Be alert for anyone who gets too interested."

"If anyone asks, I can say I am looking for potential sexual deviants who might have done Blair's daughter in. Close to the truth and I doubt that would worry them since it is so far off what the real truth seems to be."

"Only if you have to say anything," the elder Taylor stressed. "Less is best."

It was a longshot, Justin agreed. Still, sometimes it was such a small detail that broke a case. And it was heartening that his father still trusted his discretion. At least, he could narrow down the masses of old case records and unsolved case investigation reports. He was not a forensics expert, but he had learnt enough about fingerprints to compare the ones he'd been given with any that were in the case files. If he found any likely ones, he'd keep those files aside and let the experts take over.

In the decade between 1930 and 1940 there had not been as many investigations that fitted his criteria as he had feared. Most of the 'persons of interest' in these were older than 18 and could be ruled out, but he checked them anyway. He noted which files were 'restricted' and took details of the basic information – dates, area, file number.

When his father's request for access was granted, he began searching those files first.

He read through reports and statements of incidents where girls had been indecently assaulted by a child not much older than them. In most cases, the child was not charged, as it was considered, 'innocent interest'. One name popped up in three separate reports – one for catching a girl and pulling her pants down, another when the assault went further than that, and the third time was actually an assault on a disabled boy.

In each case, the mother of the accused boy, had claimed, "My son is good boy. He not do such things."

There were no prints in these files, but Taylor took note of the name – Araldo Ricci, as well as his address in Port Melbourne, his mother's name and the dates of the reports. There was no mention of a father's name.

There were two other unrelated reports that Taylor put on his list, but the first one seemed to demand his attention. He found two more references to the Ricci boy. The first from when the boy was 12, when he was questioned in relation to an attack on a 10 year old girl, and the later one when he was 13, and a girl was left bleeding and terrified. That time, nothing could be proved, but the Ricci boy had a reputation. The officers had fingerprinted him and warned him that should he try such things, he would be sent to jail. The fingerprinting was to drive home a point.

Now, comparing the Ricci boy's prints with King's, Justin felt a surge of excitement. Even he could see the similarities. It gave a reason why the boy might have changed his name. And if he hadn't changed his diversions, he had been more careful, or terrified his victims so much they dared not tell anyone of their ordeal.

Justin Taylor put all the files away, except for the selected few, and sat back to consider. He did not want to think that the boy had gone a step further and actually killed his victims. Yet it was a possibility. By 14, the Ricci boy had already been tall and solidly built. If he victimised younger children…

With sudden determination, he went to where the historical missing persons' files were stored. He flicked through those from late in the same era, 1937-1940, looking for children missing from the Port Melbourne or surrounding areas. Ricci had always picked victims within walking distance of his mother's home. He found five, all girls under 10 years old. In two of the case files, he found mention of the Ricci boy being interviewed, and released for lack of evidence. Neither of those victims could or would identify their attacker. The other three were still missing.

"Araldo Ricci," Eugene Taylor considered the name. "I don't recall any older criminals with that name, at that time. Suggestive though, Araldo being Italian for Harold. Has the fingerprint team compared them yet?"

"No, I came to you first."

"Get Senior Sergeant Deakin to come here. He's the best one to look at them. And get those names and dates to Mike Scott to look up in the records. "

"Yes, Sir," Justin agreed.

"Well done. I think we are on the right track here."

Mike Scott was staying with Ian since Jack was still in Matlock. He didn't mind, since it was giving him time to get to know his father better. Another reason to stay there was because old Jack Casey was a frequent visitor. The old miner was also his go between to Eugene Taylor, who had decided it best to distance him and Jack Daws from the OCTF investigation.

He was still checking records, but the last list of people he'd been checking had given him nothing.

When he let himself into Ian's house, he was greeted by Casey arrived and asked, "How was your day, lad?"

"Zip," he summarised. "Nothing at all on any of the names. Not even death listings."

Casey, who knew which names he had been checking, said, "Even nothing, tells us something."

"Huh! They still might have gone out of the state to die. Getting into the records in other states isn't easy."

"There is that, but we can worry about that later if it seems important. Write up where you looked and the years, and I will pass it on," Casey directed.

"Then what?" Mike asked. Tedious though the work was, it stopped him getting bored.

"More names," Casey said neutrally. "These ones need the works – births, marriages, deaths, electoral rolls, old telephone books—"

"Land transfers, divorces, etc," Mike went on. "Will they be checking for criminal records, tax records, bank accounts?"

"That will be done. These ones though, are hush hush. For now, only four people will know what if anything you find. In fact, it would be better if you memorise the names, and don't have them written down on any papers you carry."

"Okay…," Mike agreed. "I don't suppose you are going to tell me why?"

"Sorry, lad. We don't want a hint of this to get out."

"Fair enough. It sounds important. Is there anything you can tell me?"

"Actually, there is. Don't try to ring your friends. They have been moved."

Mike was quick to catch on. "What happened?"

"They had an unauthorised visitor. Avery went up to Matlock and spoke to Jack."

"Is that the guy who got bashed the other day?"

Casey nodded. "Fortunately, Megan was out looking through Ida Jessup's stuff at the time and Jack was with Les. She didn't correct him when he called her Jessup."

"So, if he is getting paid off by the other side, they will believe she is there. How is that fortunate?"

"Oh, they needed to move," Casey agreed. "But I suggested that Megan goes back to join Carson and his manager. If they say she has been back with them for some days already, it is perfect misdirection."

Ian chose that time to emerge from the back of the house. One look told Mike that his father had been drinking again. The slightly slurred voice confirmed it.

"Ya don't wanna let anyone try anything on her again," Ian proclaimed. "She's got talent, that one."

"It has all been thought of, old friend," Casey said gently. "There'll be more security, overt and covert, and I think that young woman has learnt a valuable lesson."

Mike coughed, so that he wouldn't laugh. "I hope so. Will Jack be with her?

"Yes, and Les Shaw. Seems like that young woman has made looking after your friend a crusade."

"Am I missing something here?" Ian asked as he almost missed the chair he was teetering towards. "You talking about Peg Jessup or that girl in Tamworth."

Mike didn't know what to answer, so he looked at Casey, who said to Ian, "Who do you think?"

It took five minutes for the connection to be made. "They're the same!" He seemed to sober up. "That's why she kept avoiding me up there. I'd heard her sing before, with you." Ian pointed at Casey who merely nodded. Then Ian began to laugh, although the sound had a hint of hysteria.

"What's with him today?" Mike asked Casey in a low whisper.

"Later, lad. You go see about getting some tea ready."

By the time that Mike had prepared a basic meal of vegetables and lamb chops, Ian had managed to get himself in hand, even if it was doubtful that the effect of the alcohol had diminished by much.

Ian broached the subject of his depression. "Why didn't you tell me about that motel, boy?"

Mike wasn't prepared for that questions. "Ah, Jack and I had to report to his grandfather. He had to do more investigating."

"My Megan died there!" Ian banged weakly on the table.

"We couldn't be sure," Mike protested. "But yeah, we think she did."

"What about her kid? She must have had it," Ian demanded, but his voice lacked power.

"We found no mention of a child," Mike said helplessly.

Casey studied his friend and made a decision. "Ian, some of us think that Ida Jessup took the baby home to raise it – after her friend died."

"After she dumped her in the dam," Ian corrected. "Why'd she do that?"

Ian sat at the table, and slumped over it.

Neither Mike nor Casey answered him. Finally Ian raised his head. "But she's a Jessup."

"Ian, she is not. We think that Bertie Jessup was dead before that sham of a wedding. Two of her brothers are King's get and Stan's father is Costa. Peg's father could have been anyone."

Although Casey had to stress that point, he added quickly, "Perhaps you have not lost everything of your love. I have seen Peg's birth certificate. Your Megan Pearl was David Blair's daughter Margaret. Peg is Megan Blair. No father is recorded on the birth certificate, probably because Ida registered the birth and didn't know who it was."

Mike wasn't sure if he should mention the letters found at Ida Jessup's house. Some he was sure were from Ian to his Megan, and others that had never been posted, were possibly written to him. He would ask Jack Casey's advice – later.

Chapter 11

"What is this place?" Les asked when the shack came in sight.

"Belongs to an old miner, but the guy is actually a consultant for the OCTF," Jack explained.

"You mean that old guy Church Boy brought with him when he came to get the stuff I had?"

"Ah, yeah, probably."

He didn't need to say more, because as soon as the car stopped and Steve got out, the hut door opened and Peg raced out.

"Is this where you used to hide out, kid? I didn't think it'd be so small. How can anyone live in it?"

Jack let he girls go inside to argue the merits of the place. He watched Steve leave, and then decided to do a scout around, and agreed that the new gravel was an excellent early warning set up. All the same, he hoped they would not be there long. They were too far away from help.

He went inside to hear Les say, "Ask Lover boy."

"What?" he queried.

"How come we had to cut and run?" Peg repeated her question.

Jack summarised his meeting with Avery, and the talk with his grandfather and Maddern.

"The police here are going to run interference."

Les added her bit. "The jerk was on about some keys you had. Lover boy said they'd been sent to Melbourne. He also said your place had been emptied."

"And he asked about those five properties," Jack added. "I implied I hadn't the clearance to find those."

"What's with all that?" Les asked.

"I have been finding out details about people. Finding that Costa still owned those five places really pleased my grandfather."

"He must be trying to draw the guy out," Les decided with a feral grin. "I reckon that must be the fat guy I saw talking to Stan."

"Gianni Costa is fat," Peg agreed. She changed the subject. "Do you know when Steve might be back?"

"No. However, I think we should make it seem like this place is empty. Put our stuff out of sight of the door and windows for a start."

He also insisted that they didn't talk, but just sitting gave them all too much time to think. And with the wind outside starting to increase in strength, making the trees sway and rustle, it was harder to hear nearby sounds outside.

"That change they were talking about must be coming through," Peg said. "I hope we don't get stuck here if it starts to rain."

Jack got up and started to pace. "No, that track didn't look like it would hold up well in the wet."

Before the next hour was past, they began to hear thunder, and the interior of the shack was almost as dark as night time – except for the lightning flashes.

Les wasn't talking, just sitting in Casey's chair, chewing her nails.

They all jumped when the heavy rain began drumming on the metal roof.

"If this lasts for very long, they won't get an ordinary car up here," Peg said. "Looks like were stuck here for a bit. And I certainly don't want to start walking down."

"Great!" Les finally blurted. "You know there's only one bed in here?"

"I won't be sleeping," Jack said.

"I can use the chair," Peg offered. "Though it's not night time yet."

"Close enough," Les growled. "It's dark."

"You can try to sleep if you want," Jack invited. He was surprised when she did go off to the shelf bed and pull a blanket over herself.

Peg and Jack took turns pacing the shack. In any direction, it was at most eight steps across.

The rain was hitting the back of the shack, which meant that the little overhang at the door provided some small protection when Peg opened the door to listen to the outside noises. She was more familiar with the sounds there, and not worried that the shack would leak.

A trickle of cold air forced its way in when she opened the door slightly. Peg sniffed, getting the smell of wet earth, wet eucalypts, and a trace of smoke.

That was one thing that worried her. And after the week of hot days, lightning might well spark a fire. She knew from Jack Casey that his refuge was the mine, and she knew the way there, but getting there would be tricky in the wet. If a fire started, she hoped the rain would quickly douse it. Still, she hadn't heard the fire siren. Up there, they usually did hear the relay siren.

She felt Jack come up beside her.

"This isn't how I imagined spending tonight," he murmured.

"Yeah. I hadn't expected this rain, but then I hadn't expected to be anywhere to need to worry about the weather. Are you getting twitchy?"

"Uh huh. We are on our own her, no phone, no—"

"Shh!"

"What?"

"Listen. I can hear a 4WD coming up the track."

"Do the police have one?" Jack asked.

Peg shrugged as an answer. She was still listening, and the sound was getting more distinct.

"It has to be coming here. And it has to be someone who knows this track."

"Still, we don't show ourselves until we know who it is and that we can trust them," Jack told her.

Peg continued to listen, and sniff the air as Jack went to wake Les and move their bags nearer the door.

Headlights shining through the trees, along with the audible groaning of the engine, heralded the arrival. The 4WD had stopped short of the shack, in the one place that a car could turn around. A figure in a drizabone coat stepped out of the vehicle, and ran towards the shack. He had a torch with him.

"Jack? You there? It's Jed Owens. Vic Maddern asked me to come."

When he didn't get an answer, he rapped on the door.

Inside, Peg told Jack. "I trust him. I am sure he recognised me that day at the races." She heard his okay, and opened the door.

"Hello Mr Owens. Come in."

He didn't seem surprised to see her, or the other two, and accepted the offer.

"Are you back in town to live?" Owens asked Peg. He sounded hopeful.

Peg shook her head. "Afraid not. I have to keep moving or the wrong people will keep finding me. That was why Steve York stashed us here. Where did Mr Maddern tell you to bring us?"

"He is waiting down on the main road. There was a small fire started, not that far from here. Before the rain began, it might have come up this way."

"Are your horses okay?" Peg asked.

"They're fine. I only have three at the moment," Owens admitted. "Are you all ready to head down?"

"Yes, sir," Peg confirmed.

"It's good of you to come," Jack added his thanks.

"Yeah, it'll be good to get out of this dump," Les gave her opinion.

It was still teeming, but the first fury of the storm front had passed. None of them complained of the soaking though, because it meant they were going somewhere civilised. Peg chose to sit in the back with Les, and let Jack take the front seat. Her friend had found the door handles and her knuckles were showing white from the desperation of her grip.

"He's used to these roads," Peg told Les, as the back end of the 4WD slid about on the muddy track.

Soon after, Owens stopped on a level stretch of road, got out and locked the hubs, and put the car into 4WD. After that, although the going was slower, they didn't slide around so much.

As soon as they reached the level, paved road, Les released her grip, and pretended she was brushing crumbs from her jeans. "Well, that was fun."

Owens stopped again to unlock the hubs and they started off again in 2WD. He turned away from Matlock, and just around a bend, they saw the flashing lights from two fire trucks. The police car had its blue flashing light going as well. Owen's drew up next to it. Maddern called up from his window, to have his passengers cross to his car.

Peg opened her door, and while Les slid across the seat to the door, spoke to Owens.

"Thanks for helping us. And tell Blackie from me, to keep his nose in front."

"You are welcome, Miss Jessup, and I might just take your advice. It must have worked in Mildura."

Jack collected their three packs and put them in the back of Maddern's police station wagon. He was relieved to see Peg's guitar case already in there. Maddern drove off once they were all settled, and drove to the North East motel where a dark limo was parked. They were told to transfer into it.

"Now this is more like it," Les said, ogling the interior of the hired limo.

The driver came over and spoke to Maddern, nodded, then approached Peg.

"Miss Arthur?"

"Yes, that's me. Were you also expecting my partner, Jack Dawes, and friend, Leslie Shaw.?"

"Three people, yes. Are you ready?"

Peg glanced at Jack who was taking the last of their stuff from Maddern's car.

"Yes, although I must apologise for our appearance. We were caught out in the storm. I feel like a drowned rat."

The faintest of grins on the driver's face, betrayed his agreement.

"I am to take you to Albury, where there is a motel room booked for the night. Tomorrow we will be going on to Canberra. My name is Jason, by the way."

Les was already eyeing the man, who was probably in his early forties. Peg settled for a nod, and allowed Jason to open the door for her and Les. Jack was again transferring their gear, this time to the boot that Jason had opened for him. He again took the front passenger seat.

By the time they reached Albury, Peg and Les were both dozing, and Jack was chatting to the driver to stop himself doing the same.

Before leaving Albury the next day, Jack suggested that they all go shopping for more acceptable attire.

"Don't expect me to get in a dress," Les stated right away. "Anyway, you paying, Lover boy?"

"No," Peg corrected her. "I am, and he didn't mention dresses. When we arrive, we need to present a better impression than soaked rats."

"Not going all fancy, either."

"Neat and clean," Peg assured her. "That's all. Will you let me help you find something?"

"Maybe, kid. Just maybe."

Peg knew Les well enough to know what she'd be happy with. She suggested new jeans, a two tone shirt, and a casual jacket. For herself, she went a little fancier – slacks, not jeans, a plain shirt, and a mauve twin set."

"You sure you can afford all this?" Les asked her. She was wriggling to settle the new clothes, but wasn't scowling.

"Yes. I have been earning a bit, and haven't had much need to spend it. Are the clothes rubbing?"

"No. I just haven't ever had anything so nice."

This new, almost gentle sounding Les, was new to Peg. She leant over and whispered into her friend's ear. Les snorted in reply and sounded more like her usual self.

"What's the joke?" Jack asked, meeting them after Peg had paid for the new clothes that she and Les now had on. He was in a new pair of black pants, with a dark shirt and woollen jumper.

"Ah, not for polite company," she grinned at Jack. What she had said to Les had been deliberately crude.

Les did a translation that wasn't quite the full comment. "Said I shouldn't get too used to the new togs as I may have to kick butt."

Chapter 12

Les felt out of place in the company of Wayne Carson, his manager and wife. The singer had greeted her as if she were an old friend, and there had seemed no insincerity. McMasters looked at her bleached hair and merely said, "I don't think I like this new trend in hairstyle."

Claire McMasters was more intense, as if she didn't trust this newcomer.

In answer to her manager's comment, Peg said, "Sometimes it is fun to shock people. Besides, Les is my best friend, so much so that I think I will adopt her as a sister."

"You're balmy, kid. I'm no stray mutt. And just you remember, I know all your tricky ways."

McMasters grinned widely then. "Excellent, I think I will make you Megan's chief bodyguard."

"What will that make me?" Jack asked.

Les got in first with a snicker. "You, Lover Boy, are her chief distraction."

"Well, now that we have all that sorted," Wayne Carson said from his position leaning against a chair, "Megan and I need to practice. We have two days and then we'll be flying to Sydney to do some recording."

Tom Avery, when he finally located the place where Peg Jessup had been staying, discovered that the girl had done a flit. He wanted to blame the local detectives for spiriting her away. However, he had been only too aware of the fire sirens going off, and the police needing to go out and warn people. Then of course, there was the storm. It might have killed the fire, but it had also caused localised flooding.

Avery challenged Maddern when he caught up with him the following day.

"They were not under house arrest, Sir," Maddern explained respectfully. "We simply kept the place under observation in case of trouble."

Thanks to the talk he'd had with the senior OCTF officers, Maddern knew he did not need to discuss any of what he learnt from the erstwhile Peg Jessup. When Avery asked about keys and places where safe deposits were made, Maddern was able to seem open and helpful, while actually revealing nothing new.

"There was a box at the Commonwealth Bank. Ida Jessup removed the contents before she died."

"I know about that one. There has to be others," Avery growled.

"If there is, we need to wait under the court grants us permission to go through client lists," Maddern explained.

Avery persisted for a while longer, but he really did not think these rural detectives would be in the confidence of the OCTF. He finally took himself away.

Once he was gone, Maddern put a call through to Eugene Taylor.

Jack called Mike late on their first day in Canberra, to reassure him they were all well. In turn, Mike mentioned the cause of Ian's latest bout of drinking.

"I wondered if he should read over the letters that we think were written to him by Peg's mother but never sent. I was going to ask Jack Casey, but what do you think?"

"Might make him more maudlin," was Jacks opinion. "How does he feel about Peg being the child of his lost love?"

"I don't know. All he said was don't let anything happen to her – she's got too much talent. I am not game to suggest that she might be his kid."

"No, not unless we can get some corroborative information," Jack decided. "Any chance of you checking some of the letters at random?"

"What about the letters to or from other people?" Mike asked.

"I think Peg should read those. Anyway, wait a bit. The main important thing is helping the OCTF get their targets."

"Actually, about that," Mike came back. "I was given some names to check out. I don't know how they fit into things, but one of them I have a feeling about."

"My grandfather gagged you has he?"

"Yeah."

"Okay, go on."

"This person, on his birth certificate, there is a familiar paternal name."

After a moment of thought, Jack asked, "English or Italian?"

"The latter. Child used mother's last name."

"Aha! What else did you find?"

"Not much. The mother died years ago, but the person hasn't shown up in the usual records. Has no record, I suspect."

"Wonder how they got onto that if there is no records?" Jack asked.

"Can't say, but your uncle was sent to the old records yesterday, then I was given these names to memorise, not write down."

"I understand," Jack assured Mike. "Good work."

The satisfied feeling he had, believing he knew who Mike was being cryptic about, was increased when he returned to the suite and began to read the evening paper. He managed to tell Peg what he thought and that Les's present to the police, may have borne fruit, and that an article in the paper revealed that both Blair Holdings and Costigan Consolidated were to be audited. Something about looking for illegal activity during the takeover business.

"My supposed grandparent will be ranting," Peg concluded. "Too bad.'

"Personally, I think he is being included so Costigan can't claim he has been singled out," Jack decided.

"If Costigan is who we think he is, then I reckon he won't have his illegal books where they can be found."

"They must expect to find something," Jack suggested.

"If nothing else, it's one more annoyance."

Peg noticed the extra security around Carson and herself, but didn't make an issue of it. The most visible pair were Jack and Les. The former had adopted a uniform of dark blue suit, shirt and tie, with dark sunglasses. Les, enjoying her role, adopted dark blue, long sleeve coveralls, and sunglasses like Jack's. She had a knack for keeping the love struck pre-teen girls away and the older ones seemed to recognise that she knew how to handle trouble.

Less obvious were the casually dressed duo who were never really close, but always around when the stars were out of their suite. At such times, two other suitably muscled and suited escorts were visible.

Les and Claire McMasters developed a cautious relationship. Claire knew some of Les's background, but trusted the recommendation of both Carson and her husband. Her main trouble was trying not to wince when Les came out with something unexpectedly crude. No one actually rebuffed Les for her language, as sometimes it was the only effective way to get opportunistic strangers to leave.

After a while, during which Les felt particularly powerful in the plumb job, she gradually toned down her language within the suite. Peg noticed, guessing that this period of time, was possibly the first time Les had experienced anything close to a normal group or family relationship.

When Carson and Peg flew to Sydney for the recording session, Les and Jack were sent to have 'bodyguard' lessons, so they would be even more effective in their roles.

When the two week gig in Canberra finished, they headed for Albury. It was the following booking that had Peg becoming anxious. They were booked to appear at the Matlock RSL and she was torn between wanting to stay unrecognised and wanting to have all her old tormentors get their noses rubbed in her new fame.

Jack insisted that keeping her identity secret was better, as they didn't want her location to become generally known. He himself had started to get very edgy the moment they crossed back into Victoria.

McMasters drew him aside. "If you know something that might endanger my people, Jack, I need to know."

"It's nothing specific. Paranoia probably."

"There must be a basis. I have great respect for your instincts. Especially after you averted that incident last week without your wife being aware."

Jack glanced to where Peg and Carson were softly strumming a new arrangement. He gestured with his head to move further away.

"I have heard that the OCTF are set to move in on one of their major targets. So far, the guy believes he is inviolable, but Peg Jessup's evidence could see him jailed for a long time. If he gets a hint of the move, he will come after her. The task force want him out of the way before they go for his boss."

"Does she know about this?" McMasters asked.

"That her evidence could convict him, yes. Not about the raid."

"Tell her! Every extra pair of eyes on her, the better." McMasters held Jack's gaze until he nodded. Then he asked, "Do you think, if the guy runs, he will look for her in Matlock?"

"He might think she is there, even if he hasn't figured out who Megan Arthur is."

"Should we cancel the Matlock booking?" McMasters was concerned indeed if he considered that.

"She's been looking forward to shoving her new status in the faces of all the locals," Jack admitted. "Even if they don't know who she really is. Hopefully by then, we won't need to worry."

"Okay then. Just you keep me advised of anything you hear from your sources."

Jack nodded, hoping that the raid would end in an arrest.

Chapter 13

After the sold out premiere performance at the Matlock RSL, the media, selected town dignitaries and invited guests attended a private function in the restaurant. The invited guests were winners of a local competition. They were all chosen by Peg herself, and were people she liked, or had no issue with. Few people would know of any connection between Mike's landlady, the café owner and her daughter, Jed Owens and the others she picked. No one was surprised to see the elderly Grace Falconer, the mayor, or Vic Maddern.

While this was, in theory, a chance for the locals to mingle with the famous Wayne Carson and his protégé Megan Arthur, the dark suited men standing nearby, eyeing anyone who approached, kept them at a suitable distance.

For this occasion, Les dressed more like the other younger guests, even if in slacks instead of a dress. Her task was to move among the guests, trying to spot anyone who didn't belong. She eventually moved next to Mike Scott and began a casual conversation that quietened down to a hissed, "Have they got that Bastard, King, yet?"

"No."

"What happened?"

"He had to have been tipped off," Mike said. "No one has seen him since just before the raid."

"Reckon he'll come here?" Les asked.

"They have road blocks everywhere," Mike told her. "And I don't know how well he knows this area."

"We're going to be down in the city next," Les reminded him. "That's a more likely place, if not here."

Mike agreed. "Keep alert," he said as he too moved to mingle.

Some kind of scuffle began near the door. Les looked, didn't recognise either of the two men involved, and went back towards Peg. Mike did recognise one of the men – Jed Owens. The other looked like him, but Maddern was moving that way. He turned his attention back to Peg and Carson, and so missed the moment when the canister was thrown. He turned again as Maddern bellowed, "Sydney Owens!"

Something struck the table where the finger foods and drinks were laid out. There was a small explosion, and the room began to fill with acrid, burning fumes. His eyes began to water, and he couldn't see. The guests were all trying to get outside, but were stumbling into each other.

Mike felt around. He was near one of the smaller tables. Someone had left a drink there. He grabbed it and splashed it in his eyes, not caring that it was alcohol. It cleared his eyes for a moment, enough to see one of the dark suited blokes carrying someone towards the door. It had looked like Peg. He couldn't tell if it was Jack or one of the others. Carson was being hustled out towards the kitchen by his manager and another of the guards.

Over the babble of screams and people calling out, Mike heard Maddern's voice calling out, "Open all the windows and doors."

His first reaction was to do that but he needed to know if Peg was okay. Les could look after herself, so could Ian. He pushed his way through the stumbling figures in the direction Peg had gone.

Outside, he was astonished to find a dozen uniformed police. Four were taking prisoners to the cars, handcuffing them to the door frame. Two had a struggling Sydney Owens on the ground and were handcuffing him. He saw Maddern trotting over to where two women had a man struggling on the ground. He went that way when he heard, "A little help here, please?"

The victim was wearing a dark suit, and was currently in a very painful position. Les had his arm forced high up behind his back, and Peg had her foot on his backside. Maddern produced handcuffs and rolled the man over.

Peg said, quite calmly, despite her eyes still streaming tears, "Ed Brownley was never one of our security team."

"How are you, Miss Arthur," Maddern asked, using her performing name, as Brownley was listening.

"Furious. He is lucky you arrived so promptly. I was considering redesigning his delicates – permanently."

Two ambulances and a string of five cars were converging on the venue.

"Get back to where it is lit," Maddern told the two women as he hefted Brownley to his feet. "Where is Jack?"

"I don't know. He pushed me down, and then I was picked up. I thought it was one of the regular guys at first. That was until he called out, 'I have her'. Then I put plan B into action."

Maddern queried that.

"Get him in the balls," Les said at once. "The kid was amazing."

"I had a score to settle with him," Peg said in a lower voice.

Steve York came trotting out of the darkness, slightly out of breath. "The other guy got away. I didn't get a good look at him."

"Take this one to join the rest," Maddern told him. "Whoever planned this seems to have recruited from amongst the local malcontents."

"Brownley," York identified, as he took the man by his arm to drag him to where uniformed officers were minding the prisoners.

Madden summoned one of the newly arrived first-aiders, and insisted that Megan was attended to.

"Fix your hair, kid," Les advised.

Peg felt how her wig had slipped, and tried to fix it, but most of the pins had dropped out. It was too late. The woman who came over was already staring at her in shock. The recognition was mutual, so Peg stopped trying to fix her hair.

"You…you're…you're Peg Jessup!" Mrs Harvey, a resident of Ridge Road, managed to stammer out.

"It doesn't matter if she is the cat's mother," Les said tartly. "Are you going to help us or will I tell the media guys that you refused to help Wayne Carson's singing partner?"

The woman gestured them to sit where chairs had been positioned, and started to rinse Peg's eyes with saline. Les helped herself to another vial of saline and began to wash her own eyes. They both took mugs full of the water to try to ease the effects of the tear gas in their throats.

"Your friend York is hovering," Les commented. "I'll go look for Lover Boy."

Les found Mike helping a groggy, almost helpless, Jack out into the fresh air. He noticed Carson sitting in the open back of one of the ambulances, with McMasters hovering. She changed her direction to let him know that Megan was okay, then went to Mike.

"Get him to the first aiders, will you? I need to go look for Ian."

"Some damn body guard you are," she chided Jack, as she helped him walk the short distance. "Should make you plan C. Peg and I found out that plan B works much better."

"She's okay then?" Jack croaked.

"Natch, you idiot. She did what we taught her. Relished it. Said she had a score to settle with the guy."

"Who was it?" Jack asked.

"Name of Brownley."

"Local guy. He should have learnt from the first time, but then, he probably didn't know who he was dealing with."

The talking made Jack cough.

"Quit yakking, Lover Boy."

The fire truck rolled up and the crew went on to check the restaurant. The initial fire had been quickly doused, but the fumes were still strong. The team leader went out and directed his men and several other men to bring in four huge fans. These were plugged into a generator that had just been started. The power cables were long enough to reach inside.

Mike found Ian getting up from under a table, not too badly affected by the fumes. Perhaps, like in smoke, there was fresher air down lower.

"What were you doing down there?" Mike demanded.

"Best place in a panic. Even so, I got kicked a few times. The girl got out. I saw her picked up."

"Yeah, Dad. Megan's fine." He decide not to mention all the details. "Come outside and get looked over before you rush off to phone in a report of this explosive record release."

"Yeah! This is great publicity," Ian enthused.

"What? Come see Wayne Carson and Megan Arthur and experience the thrill of being tear-gassed."

"Most people won't think like that," Ian said, as he shook his head. "In their minds, they will assume it won't happen again. They will want to be in the audience and maybe be seen on the TV."

"They're nuts," Mike summarised.

"Don't forget you were going to get me in to see the girl."

"I haven't forgotten, but it may not be tonight – after all this. Anyway, she's got a name."

Mike went off to see if anyone else needed help, but it seemed that the less affected kitchen workers had been busy. The important locals and guests were all in two huddles being tended. He went to where his landlady and boss were standing.

"You ladies okay now?" he asked. They still had reddened, irritated eyes and he probably looked the same.

"Better," Mrs Brewster from the café admitted. "When I was a winner in that competition, I didn't expect all this extra excitement."

"Nor did I," Mrs Church agreed.

"Personally, I think the competition was rigged," Mike claimed, and both women stared at him. "Well, all the people who won were some of the nicest people in town."

"Oh you!" Mrs Brewster retorted. "What is going to happen now? Are Wayne Carson and Megan Arthur okay?"

"How come you are back here anyway?" Mrs Castle asked.

"The stars are fine," Mike answered that first. "And I came up with my Dad. He writes music stuff for the city papers."

"Then you'd be staying with him then?" Mrs Castle asked.

"Actually, we had been planning to go back tonight so he could file his story. We might need to stay, after this."

Mrs Brewster had looked over at the ambulances and saw Carson being helped into one. She saw the figure that followed and commented, "I didn't realise that Megan Arthur wears a wig while performing."

Mike glanced where she was looking but missed seeing Peg. He was aware that Les had crept up behind him.

"CB you're wanted," she told him. "The town snobocracy has just made an astounding discovery!"

"What's that?" he asked, glad that Les had abbreviated her usual nickname for him.

"That the marvellously talented Megan Arthur was once the least appreciated resident of this place."

"She came clean, did she?" Mike asked.

Les snickered. "By the time we finished with that fake guard, the wig had slipped. The lady first aider that helped up is apparently quite a gossip."

"Who are you talking about, Mike Scott?" Mrs Brewster demanded.

"It will be all over town by opening time tomorrow," Mike said, sighing. He told them, and enjoyed the stunned looks on both faces.

Les summarised her sentiments. "The kid was right about this place. No one ever gave her a chance. Well, guess what?"

She didn't answer her question, just let the women think on it as she pulled Mike away. "These yokels really jerk my chain, you know."

"Who wanted me?" Mike asked.

"Oh, Lover Boy said to get you. He is arguing with your old man,"

Mike stalked off. Les followed, still with an eye on the current activity. She wasn't worried about Peg now, since the York guy had driven off after the ambulance. She paused near various gossiping groups and decided that Mike had underestimated the speed of gossip.

"What are you on about now," Mike demanded, when he reached conversational distance of Jack and Ian.

"I told him not to mention Megan Arthur's previous name," Jack stated.

"Why not? It's going to be all over town by morning," Mike queried. "It's going to reach Melbourne soon after."

"Exactly," Ian seconded.

Jack seemed to be counting to ten. "I doubt that. Sensational rumours are one thing, blurting it out as truth to the rest of Australia is quite another."

"I still can't see it, boy," Ian argued.

"In this town, we will get those who believe it and those who will staunchly deny its possibility. The same kind of confusion that Les caused the first time she was here," Jack explained patiently. "We have been trying to give the idea that Peg and Megan are two different people. Confusion here can play into that."

"Those bastards in Melbourne will be—" Ian began, then stopped himself. "Ok, you're right. They will believe what they like, but if they don't already believe the two are the same, why the attack here tonight? Or was it against Carson?"

"If you have to mention all this you would have to think the target is Carson, because Arthur is just starting out and is relatively unknown," Jack suggested. "The fact that Megan helped Jimmy Blair was kept from the media, but the bastards knew about it. I just don't want them to be totally, absolutely sure the two women are the same."

"Alright, boy, keep your pants on," Ian capitulated. "This premiere and album launch is going to be a sensation."

"Yeah, unfortunately," Jack agreed.

"Should sell more tickets," Ian suggested.

"Ticket sales have been good already," Jack growled.

"You might need to put on extra shows," Ian persisted.

"More opportunities for trouble," Jack growled.

"How come the police were here in force when the trouble started?" Mike asked Jack, to change the subject.

"Probably McMasters' doing."

"Did you expect trouble?" Ian asked.

"He always does," Mike answered that.

The crowd was dispersing, and the cars leaving the carpark.

"Jack, who was that Brownley guy replacing?" Mike had a sudden thought.

Jack's head jerked up, and he was thoughtful for a moment. "No one I was told about. However, come to think of it, I didn't see Andy Jefferson about. He is a local guy we hired."

"Could he have been involved?" Mike suggested.

"I wouldn't have thought so. We need to find him."

"Indeed," Maddern agreed, having walked over in time to hear the discussion. "Once the fumes have cleared form inside, we will be checking there. Steve saw someone run off, but didn't get a good look. How did you get onto Jefferson?"

"Local agency, I think. His credentials checked out."

"I will get people checking around outside," Maddern told them. "I think all of you should be checked out at the hospital."

"The first aid guy said I would live," Jack argued. "Anyway, how come they got here so fast?"

"Yeah, and all the uniforms outside?" Mike added. Ian just listened intently.

Maddern considered before answering. "We had a tip off that the after party would be disrupted. We were not expecting the tear gas grenade. Young Owens will be questioned about that."

"Should this gig continue?" Jack asked the detective. "I wouldn't want another incident like this."

Maddern merely said, "I doubt they will try the same thing again. I do have extra uniformed officers up here in case King shows his face."

"So, Megan is bait?" Jack demanded.

"We won't be taking any chances," Maddern assured him. "And I heard how Megan and Les took down Brownley."

"She didn't do so bad the first time that guy tried something on her," Mike recalled. He nodded at Ian who was gesturing that he was going to the restaurant.

"I will need a statement from both of you, anything you might have noticed," Maddern went on. "Tomorrow will do. After the doctor looks at you, Jack. You will need all your wits about you."

After Ian was ensconced at the Castles' boarding house for the night, Mike drove Jack to the hospital, and then went back to the hotel with him. Megan immediately took him into her room.

Les, sitting out of the way, smirked, but made no move to join him. Carson and McMasters had moved two chairs into a corner and were in a huddle, talking. Claire McMasters was seated by herself, but she stood up and asked, "Do you want coffee?"

"Water, I think, my throat is still like a desert."

She gave him a sympathetic smile. She returned and asked, "Where will you be staying tonight?"

Mike told her. "I left Ian there, intending to wake up the newspaper editor and phone his report through. He's hoping it will make the front pages, not just the entertainment section. He reckons it will be good publicity, as in making people flock to your gigs."

Claire stifled something that might have been a laugh. "You are not wrong, you know. When we got back, the booking agent had left a message. He'd had fifty messages on the booking line in two hours. Those two," she gestured to her husband and Carson, "are discussing how to do more shows here."

Mike sighed. "They may as well. I doubt the people behind this will try here again. Everyone will be too alert. I'm more worried about when you get to Melbourne."

"You going to stick around, CB?" Les called over.

"Wish I could, but I doubt I will be able to do anymore than you and Jack are already. Down in the city, I might get wind of stuff."

"Then what say I walk you back to your digs?" Les suggested.

"I've got the car," he told her.

"That'll do," she said.

Next morning, when Mike thought he and Ian would be leaving, he had a surprise.

"We ain't going, yet, boy! Carson's manager had the idea to get you and me doing an act."

"What?"

Ian chuckled. "A little bird told me that you don't have a bad voice. And I heard you once, remember? Probably all that choir stuff your Mum's folks forced on you. And I can still play a mean guitar. Won't be anything complicated. So what CW stuff do you know?"

"Ah…" Finally, his mind began to work and he suggested two songs.

"Let's give it a go. I want us to be better than the kids from the high school song club. Carson has them lined up too. It's to give him and the girl a break, so they don't start sounding like squawking chickens."

Put that way, Mike agreed although he wondered if he was going to have to borrow some of Ian's retro clothing to perform in.

Chapter 14

For a week, the regular haunts of Harry King were under notable surveillance, but no sign of him was reported. Yet the police had informants in a number of those places and these were reporting overhead conversations.

During the same period, Stan Jessup was staying with Reg Costigan. His father was supposedly, 'travelling for business'. No mention was made of the ongoing audit of the Costigan Consolidated books.

Reg's fiancée, spent a lot of her time at the mansion, barely acknowledging Stan's existence.

After a few days, she began to eye him off, calculatingly. Stan, however, was sticking to the part he had been told to play, as one of Reg's friends, but he was noticing everything.

The mansion was unlike anything he had ever seen, and the idea of having servants at his beck and call was completely foreign. Yet, he aped Reg, and noticed him smirk when he began ringing down to the kitchen for snacks and drinks as if he belonged to the house.

Playing the yokel wasn't hard. If it kept Reg feeling superior, well and good. Stan knew he wasn't dumb, merely uneducated. He hid how much he was learning. Even in prison, he had been learning, and there he had honed his senses and his reactions to be alert for trouble.

As now, when Reg and the girl would be chatting and go silent when he was near.

The first time Reg's fiancée, Louisa, had climbed into his bed, he had not expected her. He knew what he was meant to do, but Reg must have made it seem like her idea. She was either drunk, or drugged at the time. He let her be the one to start things, and had worked to make the time enjoyable for her even as it eased a need of his own. When she fell asleep, he left her alone and chose to get partway dressed again.

He wondered if Reg was going to check on them, and went to his door, opening it slightly. His host had not been around when he had gone to bed, but now he heard Reg's voice and another that sounded like Harry King in a fury.

He hoped they thought him well occupied, even asleep. Perhaps if he drank as much of the beer Reg had provided as the girl had, he would be. Those he listened to were not making an effort to keep their voices down.

He learnt three things. One, the police were out to bring King in. Two, the only evidence they could possibly have was from Ida's brat. Three, he was going to fix 'her' when they brought her to him.

Stan froze in place, wondering how he could help Peg. She was like a kid sister, and had proved to be more than that when she helped him. She had forgiven him.

He shut the door quietly and looked about the room. The second beer bottle caught his eye. He opened it, and poured most of it down the basin in the fancy en-suite. He quickly shucked his trousers again, and slipped into the bed. He arranged himself so his hand cupped the girl's breast. Sleep wasn't on his mind. He needed to think and this way, if Reg thought him drugged, he might find an excuse to check on him.

His paranoia proved correct. Half an hour later, he heard the supposedly locked door, open. Just before it closed a few minutes later, Reg spoke to someone and chuckled.

Stan left the girl again and went to the window that looked out over the front drive. In a while, Reg went out to his Mercedes convertible. That suggested that King was staying at the mansion. A complication to the nebulous plan he had made. While he showered and half-dressed again, he considered what he had heard and observed. His memory for details hadn't dulled. He recalled the tour he'd been given of the mansion, and how there had been a second wing that was all locked up. If King was hiding here, would he want Stan to know? That wasn't easy to answer. King thought he had the upper hand, making Stan himself too scared to say anything. However, there were other people around – the servants – so, perhaps he was staying in that hidden wing. It might be safe to wander out to look for a phone. If seen, he'd ask for a pencil and some paper for drawing on.

They'd think him hooked if he sketched the sleeping girl in the nude. King and Reg were both warped in their attitude to women. He could be crude about them too. He'd heard enough talk inside.

The mansion was almost silent. The chiming of a clock somewhere, made him jump. Surely some servants were around? Yet it seemed not.

"What are you up to, Jessup?" King drawled from just behind him.

The man was like a cat, Stan thought.

"Where is everyone? I want another beer and some paper and pencils." Stan said after turning casually.

"Paper, Jessup?" King challenged.

Stan imitated his leer. "Yeah, for a bit of still life drawing."

King caught on at once, and laughed. "Beer's in the kitchen fridge – help yourself. I think I can find paper. Be interesting to see how good you are."

"Haven't tried it for a while," Stan admitted. "But the subject is…begging to be drawn."

"She awake?"

"Nah, mate. Whatever you gave her put her right out. Once she'd conked, I got to have more fun."

King's alarm faded, and he went into the room that was Costigan's home office – out of bounds to him. He returned with a blank pad, and several pencils, just as they heard the loud booming of the front door bell.

"No one is here," King hissed, pushing the pad at Stan. "You'd better stay in your room."

"Gone, mate," Stan agreed, putting action to words, but only until he heard King's footsteps fading in the direction of the other wing. Then he reversed his steps and went into Costigan's office.

Before leaving Pentridge, when he had been talking to Casey, he had been given a phone number to memorise. A message drop. Now he dialled it, a machine clicked on at the other end, a voice said a random number, and said to leave a message.

Stan spoke quickly. "They are going to try to grab the kid." Then he hung up, and quickly returned to his room and locked the door.

The girl was still out to it. He uncovered her, and positioned her to display her lower body and began to sketch. It was perverted, he knew, but this was to make King and Reg think he was more like them. The girl was like a floppy doll, and he changed her position several times and sketched the new poses. He found himself rousing again as he touched her, and told himself to forget it. He wouldn't use her when she was asleep, no matter that he implied he had.

When she began to rouse, he was drawing just her face and shoulders while the rest of her was demurely covered. He had put the more pornographic sketches out of sight.

"God, you're beautiful," he told her when he saw her eyes on him. It was true, even as it was something the whore who had been tutoring him had told him to say.

"What are you doing?" Louisa asked with a yawn.

He stood and showed her the last picture.

"Wow! That's good. Did you do any others?"

He allowed her to see the previous one that revealed a bit more of her breasts.

"They're good. Wouldn't want my folks seeing them though."

"You can have them if you like," Stan offered.

Louisa rose from the bed and didn't make an effort to cover herself. "You know, Stan. You're not like I expected."

"I'm sorry. I haven't had much experience lately."

"No, I don't mean I didn't enjoy it. I did. More than with Reg…never mind. You made sure I enjoyed it, didn't you?"

Stan nodded.

"He said that he can't get all the way because he had mumps," Louisa confided. "I think I will let him think I believe that if he will keep you as my sex toy."

She laughed when Stan blushed a deep red. "I need a shower. I will let you join me. Come on."

After Louisa proved that she was more experienced than she had let on, she admitted in a quiet voice, "We will have to do this for a while. I haven't gone off the pill yet and it's the wrong time of my cycle."

Putting aside his misgivings, Stan smiled. If the girl wanted him, and her fiancée wanted him to do it with her, it wasn't rape.

King took the other sketches he had made, once the girl had retreated to her room. He smirked and showed Reg.

"You're not bad with a pencil, Jessup," Reg admitted. "Just don't get attached to my fiancée."

"No way. These are just mementos for when I am snug in the USA or Mexico or wherever I go."

"How did she take it? She's a demanding bitch in bed."

"You had her nice and mellow for the first time. And those lessons from your fat friend came in handy. The second time, I had her begging for it. I kinda hope she don't get pregnant too soon. How will you know?"

"If she misses her next period, I'll know you're a stud, Jessup."

Stan wasn't surprised when Louisa ignored him and hung off Reg. She belittled him, but Reg's faint smirk was because he believed his scheme was working. As for the girl, he wasn't convinced she was fully in accord with the idea. He was sure that Reg, or someone, was drugging her and planting ideas in her head.

The morning after their first tryst, she had returned to being a shrew, and talking of her father in a dismissive way.

Reg had asked her, "How do you think your father will react when you say you are pregnant?"

"He'll get the shotgun out and insist we get married."

"Then we will elope first. I will show him I am man enough to do the right thing."

"Won't he want a big fancy wedding?" Stan asked, idly.

"The old miser will probably be glad he doesn't have to fork out for it. Jenny's wedding cost her Dad twenty grand."

Stan tuned out and went back to reading the morning's paper. He didn't need to feign shock when he read the page three headline. He stood and glared at King who was listening to the talk between Reg and Louise.

"Did you send someone after the kid again?" Stan demanded.

"Wasn't me, Jessup. I haven't left here for the past two weeks."

"The fat guy who reckons he sired me - did he do it then?"

King just shrugged.

"What could she know about you?" Stan demanded, pretending he didn't know.

"Are you really that dumb, Jessup?" King turned on him.

Stan said nothing for a moment, then, "You mean that life lesson a few years ago? If she was going to dob you in, she'd have done it by now."

"The little bitch has got a lot more spine lately," King's tone went low, and menacing. "I think your lush of a mother talked too much. She should have let the little bitch die when she was whelped. She has the shares that your old man wanted. I was meant to get them, and she wouldn't tell me where they were, so I fixed her, and I will finish the job."

Stan didn't know what to say.

"And if you try to interfere, Jessup, I will fix you as well. Your little holiday here will be cut short, and you'll be back in prison. I know people who are inside and they will make your life hell."

"I'll talk to her," Stan tried.

"Do you think that'll work?" King snarled. "No. I will get her and teach her a lesson she won't forget, and I will do the same to you. So, what's it to be?"

Stan merely turned and left the room. King muttered something that sounded like 'faggot'. That was a compliment when compared to what he thought of himself.

If King thought he had scared him into mindless obedience, the reverse was true. He gloated inwardly that the Matlock attempt had been such a fiasco, and prayed that his sister would stay safe. It seemed that Casey was right when he said she could look out for herself. Meanwhile, he would say little, keep to himself, and they would think nothing of it. They would never even suspect that he could have warned anyone.

The most obvious of the watchers on Harry King's haunts had gone, but the more discreet watchers were still present, and these were reported to King. So when he decided that he had to meet with his lieutenants, he sent Reg to arrange a meeting that was well away from any place he usually frequented. He had to keep on top of the organisation, as Costa couldn't show himself at the moment.

King still wondered how Costa's scam of thirty years had never been found out. He had been damn clever and damn careful. A trait he had taught his front man. Only someone who had known Costa back then, might figure it out. Someone like Ida Jessup, but she had been a particularly dumb bitch, and never questioned the reason why she had been moved out of the way. So long as she had as many men as she wanted, she was satisfied. Certainly she was like a bitch in heat whenever Costa visited her. Almost as bad when he himself made use of her.

He'd done something similar himself, he'd made himself a new identity. With his own mother dead and buried, there were no links to his origin. No legal traces either. No one who knew him years ago would know him now.

He recalled that Costa, in his legitimate guise, had seen Ida unexpectedly. He knew she had recognised him, but after that he had her minding stolen stuff and drugs for him, so he had a hold over her. That time when he had last visited his whore, he hadn't realised the kid was back from the girl's training place.

It hadn't mattered, the girl had stayed away. One sight of himself hanging around would have been enough. He had taught her to keep her mouth shut.

Driving in a rented limo with darkened windows, King's driver finally turned into a service road behind a sports club building. Once there, King wasted no time getting inside. He considered that he was being careful, not furtive. His trusted lieutenants would have ensured the building was secure.

Inside the private meeting room, his lieutenants reported that mostly, things were going along as usual. One of the men reported that his police informant had discovered where 'the person of interest' was going to be next. King gestured for that man to wait to give the details in private.

When all reports were given, he demanded, "How did Devlin get found?" His attention was on the two men who had seated themselves furthest from him.

"He must have been spotted when he went out," was the reply. "They nabbed him just as he was about to come back in."

King continued to stare but the two men did not look away. Devlin had promise, but he had not been privy to any of the big stuff yet. He'd been a liability any way – since he was on the run, and had the arrogance of the young to think he could do things better than the trusted ways.

"Okay then, what happened in that hick town? Why didn't they get the girl?" His glare had turned on another of his men.

"Your latest bitch was up there. She helped the singer bitch get free."

"How much help," King demanded.

"Well, to be honest, the singer did most of it. Did something to make the yokel drop her."

"I told Les to get scarce. She's a smart bitch – hooking up with the ex of someone else I want. I will need to get a message to her, but for now, she can wait. If she is getting chummy with the singer's minders, that's a bonus."

He didn't betray any doubts, he had to seem to be in control of everything. That report did worry him, but at the same time it strengthened his conviction that the singer and the Jessup brat were the same person. When he finally got his hands on her, he'd find out the truth.

"What is happening at those five places, Macca?"

"Cops are still going over the buildings with dogs and architects."

"What about the gardens?"

"Apparently dragged the dogs all over, but never got a nose twitch."

"Keep watching. I want to know if they find anything, and if they do, who planted it."

When all the major things were covered, and orders given relating to three defaulters who owed protection money, King dismissed the meeting. Most of the men went downstairs, and would leave in ones or twos by as many different ways. Some might join the betting crowd, some leaving by the front, others by the back or side entrances. The last of the men gave his information, and left as well.

When he was alone, King called Costa at his interstate hideout. The place was, fortunately, far enough away that the impotent fury his boss expressed lost some intensity. He was partly mollified by the fact that his son was finally 'manning up'.

Before he left, King rang down to the floor manager of the betting hall, and held the line open until all three outside watchers reported, "All clear." Only then did he return to the back alley to find his hired car ready to sprint him away.

Even then, he kept checking behind for any car that might be following. He had lasted thirty years as Costa's front man, unsuspected, unarrested, by taking no chances.

The ambush caught the driver by surprise. It came at the quietest part of the route back to the Heidelberg mansion. Six police cars screeched from cover to form a barrier around the limo. Armoured police ran from each, guns held ready.

King's expletive was only heard by the driver, who was on King's payroll as well as that of the hire company.

"Play it cool, Roddy. I'm just a client. Anyway, this is just a shakedown. They have nothing on me."

He could play the outraged citizen to perfection and he also had lawyers on his payroll, for just such a situation. Now was the time they would earn their fee, tie the police in knots and have him free in no time.

King kept his face impassive as his arms were pressed behind him and handcuffed.

"What is it that I am supposed to have done? Spat on the sidewalk?" He aimed a glob of spittle at the boots of the policeman who held his right arm.

He wasn't answered. Just hustled to a dark van with no windows in the back. He kept outwardly cool, controlled, and anticipated the frustration of the police.

At the police station he was searched, and taken to an interview room. At least he had not been found to be carrying a gun, or other weapon. If they were found in the car, he could deny they were his. He had, as always, skin tight black gloves.

Already he was thinking of his defence – they had not yet said what they had brought him in for. He broke his stride, deliberately when he saw the men waiting to question him. He knew who most of them were. He smiled, not with mirth, but to intimidate.

Justin Taylor, Tom Avery - two of his moles who both had secrets they'd not want revealed. The old man, the retired Eugene Taylor, and two others of the OCTF.

Before he was even allowed to sit, or they could ask the first question, he said, "I do not know why you have brought me here, illegally and with force, and I will not tell you anything without my lawyer being present."

"That is no more than I expected, Mr Ricci," Eugene Taylor remarked.

His almost forgotten childhood name caught him by surprise, and he tensed for a moment, then laughed.

"Who? Do you think that is my name? You have the wrong person."

"Do we?" Eugene Taylor asked casually. "Do you have identification on you?"

"Your mates took my wallet before I came in," King pointed out, and he glared as Justin Taylor handed his father the expensive leather wallet that King recognised as his own.

The older man carefully pulled out all items from the wallet.

"Quite a lot of money," Taylor remarked. "Driver's licence…we will have the details checked. They are, unfortunately, easily forged. You reside at the Docker's pub, I see. They didn't have you in their register."

"Of course not. I am not a guest," King stated, forgetting he was not going to answer questions.

"Where do you work, Mr Ricci?" Taylor continued.

"I have independent means," King snapped.

"I see. I will need you to authorise your lawyer to provide proof of income, and its source. Your man should be here soon. George Hanson of Baker and Frederick's isn't it?"

After a terse, "Yes," King snapped his mouth shut. He had the first stirring of alarm. It wasn't impossible that they had found something, or someone to talk. If it was that turncoat Justin Taylor, he'd be dead within a week. If it was Ida's brat, ditto. However, what was beginning to really worry him was the reference to his birth name. They couldn't have found the bodies of the girls he'd killed. That was so long ago. The memory of being fingerprinted back then, suddenly surfaced. How, and where had they got hold of his fingerprints to compare? Again, his mind rocketed the answer – Devlin's whore. It had to be. But he had removed the things she had provided. The bitch had drugged herself to sleep.

No. The cops were just pushing him to get him to incriminate himself.

<h1 style="text-align:center">Chapter 15</h1>

Mike only learnt of King's arrest when he visited Eugene Taylor's house to see if the old man had another job for him. When he'd rung, he'd merely been told to come around.

"We have enough to hold him on a rape charge on Peg Jessup," Taylor told him. "And we are investigating other events with the intent of adding extra charges. However, he has a cadre of high priced lawyers acting for him. They are pushing his so far impeccable record."

"He can't be that clever," Mike said, sitting down in the chair across from Taylor.

"I am intending to prove that he isn't untouchable," the older man agreed. "However, I do have some checking for you to do. More crumbs on a possibly useful paper trail that I hope will link to King."

Mike made a note of what was wanted, and was preparing to leave when Taylor asked, "What happened yesterday evening? You were up in Matlock weren't you?"

"Yes, I went with Ian to cover Carson's record release gig."

Taylor tossed the previous morning's paper across his desk. "Did you see that?"

Mike unfolded the paper and saw Carson's picture on page 1. Ian's by-line was under the title. He scan read the article and relaxed. Ian had focussed on Carson and only mentioned Megan Arthur in passing.

"Maddern sent through your statement. Is there anything else you wish to add? How's my grandson?"

"Jack? He was refusing to admit to a headache, and seeing the sense in removing the sunglasses from the hired security. He is sticking to Megan like glue."

Mike went on to say how things were when he left and added, "I don't think they will try anything in Matlock again. Particularly if King is behind it. However, they will be performing down here next."

Taylor made an admission. "I would rather keep that girl in protective custody, but we don't have the manpower, the budget, or a safe place. However, you go off and see if you find anything. That is something we can do."

Mike went out to the old VW Beetle Ian had helped him to buy. It made it easier to get around now that Jack was with Megan.

Even though the connection hadn't been stated, Mike was sure that the Ricci character was Harry King. The other names he had checked were more of long shots. Today he had to look for land registry data on the block of land where Ricci's mother had lived. He had hoped, that like the birth certificate, the block would have been owned by Luigi Costa back then. It wasn't. The owner of the land had been Maria Ricci. Probate records had it as passing to the son, Araldo Ricci. There was no later record of it being sold. He tried to figure out where to look next. His first idea was to drive out to view the property. Maybe he could talk to whoever was living in the place now. It might be being rented, and if that were so, and he could get the owner's name, proper police could follow up from there.

He went out to Port Melbourne and found the block to have a pre 1930s style weatherboard house occupying most of the width of the block. A narrow path, blocked by a wooden gate, ran down the side to the rear. It had a small front verandah that was edged by the footpath. It was desperately in need of a new coat of paint. He dared to ascend the three crumbling brick steps, and knock on the door. He had no answer, so moved to try to see in the windows, where the blinds were not fully down.

"Can I help you?"

Mike turned to the woman standing on the footpath. She looked to be in her sixties.

"I don't know," Mike said immediately as his mind raced for a suitable story. Then he thought of his recent search. "I have been hunting for my father. He separated from my mother 20 years ago. The last address I have been able to find was here. Do you happen to know who lives here now?"

The name meant nothing to him. It was Italian he thought, but he made a mental note of it.

"Well, it was a long shot," Mike said aloud. "Do you know who actually owns this house?"

"No, it's been a rental place as long as we have been here. That's, oh, twenty years. The agent is Hooker's if that is any help."

Mike slouched a bit. "I doubt they will tell me. Looks like another dead end." He thanked the lady and moved back to his car.

The lady spoke an afterthought. "I haven't seen anyone here for a while. They might have moved out. Are you looking for a place to stay?"

"Me? No. I still have six months lease on the place I have. Why did you ask?"

"You seem like a nice young man. My husband and I are tired of the scruffy types that have been staying here these past few years. The place has been left to run down and the back yard is full of junk that the past tenants haven't wanted."

"Can't the council do anything?" Mike suggested. "The first place I stayed was a dump. I was told that the owners had obligations to keep the place clean and tidy."

The woman snorted, "The council don't listen. Did they do anything about the place you mentioned?"

"Nuh!" Mike admitted. "I ended up ending my lease."

As Mike began to drive back to the city, he thought on the interesting details provided by the woman. As a result, he changed his destination to the main area of Port Melbourne.

He created a fictional brother, recently off the dole, and with a wife and three kids to support and went into the first estate agent he spotted.

In that place, all the properties for rent, or would soon be available for rent, were in the better part of the area. On the grounds that his brother didn't have enough money saved yet for a bond, he asked if there were other agents who handled cheaper places. He was given the addresses of three other agents.

The second place was a Hooker's agency. His question relating to places that might become available soon, got the result he wanted. The tenants at the place he went to see had indeed ducked out, owing three months' rent. However, the owner usually sent prospective tenants to see them, but the agent was willing to mention his interest to the owner, and to call if the owner was interested. Mike gave a fake name and the phone number of Jack's flat. He said he would call himself if he'd heard nothing after a few days.

Mike contemplated leaving things at that, and to get some food before he went back to work. As he set off on foot to find food, he noticed one of the staff from the estate agent seemingly following him – which might have been coincidence, but lately, some of Jack's paranoia was affecting him. So when he found a fish and chip shop, he bought their minimum and ate chips from a hole in the paper wrapping, while looking for the third agency he had been told of.

He went through the same charade there, aware that his follower had entered after him. When this agency had been unable to help him, Mike asked for other agencies he could try – just to make it seem he was a legitimate rental property seeker. By then, his newly roused paranoia was telling him to become scarce. He walked back to the train station, where he had parked his car. He was followed until he went to the ticket window and purchased a ticket to the city. From the platform, he saw the man heading back down the street. He left the platform, telling the ticket collector that he had to make a call and would be back.

Eugene Taylor's expression grew more intent when he heard that the property was still in the name of Araldo Ricci. Since no tax records existed on for that name, Mike wondered if Taylor was considering having that property confiscated too. After Taylor had considered all the details for a while, he dared the question.

"No, that would trip our interest in it. You need to stay right away from there now. From what you have told me, you are the wrong sort of tenant. I will have someone else check out previous tenants. I think, since you mentioned the yard full of junk, that the tenants are short term, transient or not in a position to complain."

"Are you saying that the junk is there for a reason?" Mike asked, although he could not think of one.

Taylor's grim smile told him that the old man agreed. "It could be. What I also find interesting is that the agency managing that place, is a branch of the company that manages the five other properties of interest to us."

"Have you found anything in those places?" Mike asked.

"No. However, our activities are being watched."

Mike made a soundless, "Oh!" and then said, "Are you checking the gardens?"

"Not yet. The sniffer dogs showed interest in a couple of places, and we will have people from the parks and gardens department to go over the area to see if they can see where the ground may have been disturbed in the past. We are looking under the houses as well."

Mike wanted to help more, but nothing else came to mind. He recalled what he had seen of the places that he and Jack had scouted. Before censoring his thoughts, he blurted, "Two of those places had paved over patios out the back."

Taylor chuckled. "You and Jack make a good team. Those are the two areas that the dogs were interested in."

"Oh. So do you think these people repeat successful ideas?"

Taylor merely said, "Not a word about any of this, even to your friends. Phones can be tapped."

After the recent events, Mike realised that the gang they were after, might be aware of him and Jack. Taylor's oblique warning was timely.

Chapter 16

The reaction to the failed attack on Carson and herself had been mixed. Peg had decided that people who were either more open minded, or hadn't really known Peg Jessup, were flooding to the extra shows. Something about basking in the reflected glory of a star in the making. One who had grown up in Matlock. Or as Jack had said, "Ian said it's basking in the reflected notoriety of Carson's narrow escape."

Her view was confirmed when the people who had known her – like her classmates and others from the school, came to the shows, but only to jeer and heckle. If they hoped to frighten, or embarrass her into giving up, they were totally wrong.

After the show the night following the attack, Peg had returned to the suite, disappeared into her room, ignored interruptions about eating and begun to write.

A new song had sprung into her mind, that had her impatient to set it down and put music to it. She wasn't that great at writing music yet, but she had a rhythm in mind, and needed to tune her words to it.

When she hadn't emerged after three hours, Jack went in again.

"What is it with you? You don't have to listen to the hecklers you know."

"Them? They are just plain jealous, that's all," Peg told him without turning to face him.

"So, what's the deal? What are you doing?"

"Do you know that song, 99 bottles of beer on the wall?"

"Yeah, so?"

"Don't interrupt me. I may not reach 99 verses, but I plan to have one for each of those snobby brats that tried to disrupt the show. And some others."

"Peg…"

"Sweet revenge, couched as a mild warning, no names will be mentioned in the song."

"Carson is worried about you."

"Tell him that I have been inspired."

"I am not going to tell them how—"

"Coward! Ok, tell you what, I will also write some nice ones for nice people I know around here. Maybe I will title it, Everybody's Someone. Yes! Now shoo, Jack."

Jack retreated and was immediately quizzed by McMasters.

"No, Mac, she is not upset. I am to tell you she has been inspired. Not sure if you are going to like it though."

Carson glanced at the closed door.

"Am I going to need lawyers looking over this new song?" McMasters demanded.

"Um, she said no names would be mentioned," Jack added.

"Inspired by the hecklers, was it?" Carson asked. "She is a master of allusion."

"And she has suddenly received a chance for some payback," Jack warned them. "You may end up not having to do all those extra shows. You might get booted out of town."

When they began to hear strumming coming from the room, Carson picked up his guitar and went to knock on her door.

"I hope you weren't wanting to sleep anytime soon," McMasters commented when the door was pulled almost closed. "It is likely you will need to use the pull out bed, or a chair."

He spared Jack a wry grin before adding, "Life has certainly been interesting lately."

McMasters and his wife had gone to bed and the practice was still ongoing. Jack decided that Carson must have agreed to her musical intentions. He began to pace, having nothing in particular to occupy his mind. When the suite door was opened, he turned reflexively, relaxing when he saw it was Les.

"Where's everyone?"

Jack shrugged in the direction the music was coming from.

"I guess if they are both strumming wooden objects, they ain't doing anything else, Lover boy, huh?"

"You getting horny for Mike?" Jack accused and she grinned.

"I could have got me a banquet, had I wanted," Les retorted. "This town only breeds yokels, so I passed on it."

"So what have you been up to?" Jack asked, deciding to stop needling her.

"I copied one of the kid's tricks and put a wig on and then went to hang out with those juvenile jerks."

Jack knew she meant the hecklers. "Don't know what jerked their jocks or knotted their knickers, or what the kid ever did to them. They are all set to get more of their friends to come tomorrow evening."

"You tell Maddern or York?"

"Not them, this time. I saw the bike jock and chatted him up. He's even more prim and proper than Church Boy ever was. He'll pass the warning on."

"Garry Hogan is okay," Jack told her.

"Yeah! Yeah! I just don't like the breed, okay?"

"Yeah! Yeah! Lighten up, okay?" Jack teased back.

"So what's going on? Another new song?"

"Something like that. She asked me if I knew the song 99 bottles of beer on the wall."

Les burst out laughing. "Oh, this I have to hear. I've heard how she set up some real twits at Meredan. Might be more than 99 people to do here. Wicked!"

"Did you ring Mike while you were out?"

"Yeah, but he's not allowed to say much. They got his majesty though, yesterday. Had him being grilled."

"Did he tell you that?"

"No, I heard that from the guy who runs the pub. He's sweating because he doesn't want to face the fat guy."

Jack just nodded.

"Church Boy did say he had a message for you. Some guy Stuart called. Wants you or the kid to ring him."

"Thanks, I will do that tomorrow."

"Well, I'm for bed," Les said, eyeing Jack with a smirk. "You're welcome to join me if you get too cold out here."

He didn't have to. Carson and Peg emerged a short time later. Peg was grinning.

"Well, do I get a preview?" Jack asked.

"Mac gone to bed?" Carson asked. Jack nodded and was gestured to a seat.

Peg still had her guitar hung by its strap. She sat on the arm of another chair.

"Okay, this is dedicated to Dennis, Wally, George, Sammy and Tony," Peg said, straight faced. Then she began to strum. When she began to sing, her voice was low.

He began to grin, and Les emerged in tee-shirt and shorts and began to clap the rhythm quietly.

Carson said in a low voice to Jack, "We have the idea of dedicating verses to five people each show. Not just the hecklers, that's for the first night. We will have a variety of people for each show after that."

Jack nodded and then said, "This is the happiest that I have ever seen her."

"I hope she can stay like that," Carson said. "You and she are good for each other."

The memory of the hit on the head and the near abduction soured Jack's mood. It made him all the more determined to protect her.

Peg had thought she had her aunt figured out. However, what Jack told her had her lost for words. He had contacted their financial advisor, Stuart, who was responding to an earlier request from them. She had asked Stuart about the possibility of purchasing the Lomax place, and Jack had provided the data needed. Their conscientious advisor had discovered that the Lomax farm had been sold, nearly thirty years ago, along with a house and land plot nearer town. Sylvia Lomax's will had specified that the two properties could only be sold together. Following up on the sale, Stuart discovered that the property owner had recently died and both properties were under probate.

"Shit!" was Peg's immediate comment when Jack had confirmed that Ida Jessup had indeed been the owner.

"And I never thought to look and see if your aunt owned any other places," Jack admitted. "Or if the Lomax of the farm was related to the Lomax your aunt brought her place from."

"I asked Maddern to pass onto Aunt Ida's solicitor the request for him to attend to the probate stuff. After this, I need to talk to that guy. The aunt never, ever, mentioned that place, and it certainly wasn't mentioned in her will. That is unless it came under the heading of, 'other things'."

"That Theo guy must know about it now. Stuart probably spoke to him," Jack suggested. "But I wonder why that old woman wanted the two properties to stay tied together?"

"May be the lawyer can find out," Peg said. "The question is, are they still tied together? Aunt left the house to the boys. I assume that means they own the Lomax place now."

"I'm no lawyer," Jack told her.

"Okay – if that condition is still enforceable – and if I still want that place – to get it, I would have to buy the house and it off Stan, Ned and Jasper."

"That's one idea," Jack agreed. "If the rider can be ignored now, then you could just buy the farm. There might be extra charges for taking it on. I doubt that your brothers could afford them."

"This is complicated," Peg complained. "I don't want to take anything the boys get. I do want a way for them to start making a living for themselves. Assuming they like the idea. The Lomax farm will need a lot of work put into it to get it viable. My reason for wanting it was to get it ready for them."

"As a farm for what?" Jack was curious to know.

"Horses?" Peg suggested, watching his reaction. He just nodded.

"What do your brothers know about horses?"

"Ah…they like roaming around?"

"The horses or your brothers?" Jack retorted.

"Okay, I said it's what I wanted to do. Do you have a better idea?"

"Something else that you mentioned a while back," Jack said slowly. "Buy the place Owens rents. That way, you will get some return – ie the rent – while your brothers are away. When they get back, you can invest in them, to help them get the place in order, and in theory, get a return from them once they start getting ahead."

"Hmm. I like that idea. I like Mr Owens, and I don't like how the Falconers can push him around. I had the idea of asking him to employ Ned and Jasper, to teach them about horses. Trouble is, the Falconers might want too much for it."

"Or not," Jack mused. "Let me put a few feelers out. I have overheard a few odd comments. Too bad Mike isn't here. That café is a good place to hear rumours, so is the pub."

"Put the idea to Stuart," Peg said. "The main thing is that it does not become common knowledge who the potential buyer is. Anyway, see what Stuart says. I will arrange to actually see Aunt Ida's lawyer and find out about the Lomax farm."

"Won't whatever you do use up a lot of what you have?" Jack thought he should mention.

"Even if we take a chunk of what I got from the share dividends, I have been saving most of what I have been earning, and now that we have extended our stay here by a week, I will be earning more. Two shows a day! It's incredible. It means I get paid for more shows, and get a portion of the profit. Which, here, costs are lower than in the city."

Jack simply shook his head. He hadn't expected her sly digs through the Everybody is Somebody song to have had such a reaction.

The night after the hecklers had started, she and Carson had been ready for them. Peg had got their attention by calling out their names and dedicating the song to them. The twelve young men were torn between anger at being made fun of, chuffed at being singled out for attention, panic that their hidden sins were being hinted at, and annoyance at being marched out of the venue by security guards.

The audience, annoyed by their behaviour, had loved it. Even those who had never thought much of Peg Jessup. It seemed that looking different, made the audience forget who Megan Arthur really was.

The following performance, that afternoon, had been without hecklers. The verses were dedicated to a range of people in the town and surrounds. That is when the Matlock Advertiser had got in on the fun and transcribed the verses, noted the dedications and published them in the paper – letting the readers decide which verse related to each person.

If any of the targeted people disliked the verse, they didn't make a fuss. No doubt they feared that to do so would make the verse stick in people's mind.

After the first two sets of verses were printed, the paper was deluged with letters from people suggesting things to say about people they knew. A lot was gossip, malicious in many cases, but Peg and Carson did find some that were asking for recognition for unheralded volunteers, or others that were doing good for the community. These were easily checked, and include in the pool of verses. Peg asked that these good people received a complimentary ticket to the show where they were being recognised.

Theo Archibald, the lawyer handling Ida's Jessup's will, put Peg's instructions into play and organised contact with Ned and Jasper at the low security prison farm. They liked her idea and were amused that she could do what she was proposing. Not unexpectedly, he could not contact Stan and that stalled proceedings.

He visited Peg one evening, to discuss his activities on her behalf. She couldn't tell him where Stan was or even hint that he might surface soon. In theory, she had been named executor, but she had no clue as to what that involved.

"There was one other thing," Archibald told her after covering the reason for visiting her. "When discussing this estate with my father, who was Mrs Jessup's solicitor when she first moved here, he remembered a box that she had asked him to keep safe. I had not heard of it, and Mrs Jessup never referred to it. It has been in our vault for many years. It is another item that was not referred to in her will."

Peg and Jack exchanged glances before Peg asked, "What kind of box?"

"Oh, just a locked deed box. Metal. We weren't able to find a key. Should we get it opened?"

The shiver that went through Peg was only noticed by Jack who was sitting close to her.

"No. I think I have the key. Aunt Ida gave it to me just before she died."

Jack moved and went to where Peg kept the photo of the key. He showed it to the lawyer.

"That might be it. Can you bring it over to my office?"

Jack asked, "Who would be entitled to that box?"

"Why, if Mrs Jessup gave the key to your wife, I would see that as she intended the box for her."

Peg said, "Please, don't mention that box to anyone. My aunt, when she was a lot younger, was involved with some ruthless people."

"Of course, not a word," Archibald assured her.

Even though Jack wanted to go with her, to protect her, Peg suggested that if she and Les went together, dressed in black like the hotel staff, just with her hair disguised, they would be less noticeable. He wasn't so sure, but he would be going ahead of her, with one of the regular security guys following discretely behind.

Nothing happened, no one stopped them, and Jack had to remind himself not to let his paranoia dissipate.

In Archibald's office, they announced themselves, but not by name, only by saying they had an appointment.

Archibald brought the actual box from the vault to his desk, and Peg stood up and took the key on the chain from around her neck. Les lounged by the door, where she was able to observe proceedings. Jack sat straighter on his chair.

Peg didn't keep them in suspense, she inserted the key, and it opened the box. With the lid up, they could all see the neatly stacked, identically sized journals. Peg eased the left most one out and looked it over.

"1945," she read the year from the cover, then opened it and flicked through the pages, recognising her aunts distinctive, fancy writing. Not all the pages had writing, and the last written page was dated December 31st of that year. Peg read the words there, "I really miss Gianni, but he is right. The country is a much better place to raise children."

"More of the damn things," Jack muttered. "What is the earliest date?"

Peg took the book at the other end out, and read the date. "1930."

"Your aunt kept them all locked away, all this time?" Jack shook his head.

"I haven't gone over the ones I found at the house yet. I think I should. If she went to these lengths to keep these safe…I wonder what she was afraid of people finding out?"

Jack gave her no answer, the question was more rhetorical.

"I'd like to take a few of these to read," Peg told Archibald. "But we need to keep them safe. Can the rest be kept in your vault?"

"Certainly. Perhaps, if you are concerned, I could transfer them to a different box, and store it under…"

"Annie Lomax," Peg suggested.

"Yes, that will do. And I will put this box, empty, back where it was."

"Or just put the deed for the farm in there," Peg suggested. "It would look odd if it were empty, and she kept the ownership of that place secret."

Archibald nodded.

Peg took out the volumes from 1935-1942, as well as the first one. These went into obscure pockets in the jacket jack was wearing.

"Was the box the only think you wanted to show me?" Peg asked.

"Yes. Now, if you discover anything else that might relate to possessions, you will let me know?"

"Sure," Peg agreed.

Back at the hotel, Jack put all but the first book into a bundle in the hotel safe. That one he left with Peg.

"Did you know that she kept journals that far back," he asked Peg.

"Until we found those later ones, I'd had no idea. When I am back in Melbourne, I will have to look at the rest of the stuff Mike put in storage for me."

After spending most of the night reading through the first diary, the 1930 one, Peg had an entirely different view of the woman she had called aunt. The young Annie Simmons had been loved, and pampered, but still lonely. Events that she wrote about, had a great deal of detail, but the woes of the 13 year old Annie, were petty compared to Peg's own recollection of being that age. One thing showed up, Annie had been an intelligent child, who received high marks at school.

The next day, during free times, and again after the second show, Peg moved onto the 1935 journal. It was the year that Annie's parents had died. From her first meeting with Gianni Costa, the young, dashing, Italian, Annie was obviously smitten. Her father had not been so enthralled. Mention was made of his 'vile comments'. Although not recorded, they had probably been about his ancestry and lower class status. Regardless, Annie had slipped out as often as she could to see him.

Events surrounding the crash that killed her parents, had her wondering how it could have happened. She had clipped news items from the paper, and slipped them between pages of the journal. Some things she had written were from conversations she had overheard.

Peg had her own view, which she shared with Jack who was dozing beside her. "I reckon that Costa was after her parent's money, and since they wouldn't have him as a potential son in law, he tried blackmail and when that didn't work, went a step further and made an example of them."

All she got from Jack was a low grunt.

"Oh, boy," she exclaimed a while later.

"What?" Jack asked without opening his eyes.

"Annie has been extoling Gianni's virtues. He is her rock, her saviour and all that. But now, this is reading more like a porno novel. She was a complete innocent, but he obviously wasn't. He was getting her so horny, that she would do whatever he asked, and some things were…exotic, to put it mildly. Anyway, he is already suggesting marrying her when she turns 18."

Jack pushed himself up on one arm. "One thing just occurred to me. If he really was after her parent's money, why keep on with her? I thought her pa had been drinking heavily because he was nearly broke and that was the cause of the accident. There was some talk of it being suicide."

Peg thought on that. "Well, her parents may not have mentioned money worries to her. However, if Gianni was behind some blackmail, or business disasters, maybe they thought they were broke, but actually weren't. I don't see how, but, who knows?"

Before closing his eyes again, Jack suggested, "Maybe he kept her around because she was so good in his bed. I know that idea…"

Peg put the journal aside, snuggled down next to Jack and said in a whisper, "What about now?"

Chapter 17

With the tumultuous ovation still ringing in her ears, Peg slipped out to the car waiting at the back of the building for her. Carson, still chatting to some of the attendees, and keeping most of the attention inside, would leave in another car to return to the hotel. Being the live act on stage at the monthly Matlock dance, was their final performance there. It had been unmarred by any trouble.

Jack and Peg, however, were not going back to the hotel. They were headed for Melbourne, for an early morning appointment with the prosecutor in the case against Harry King. He was charged with rape, from when she was 15. Her original deposition had been enough to have him charged and bound over for trial. This was to be the pre-trial discussion.

Their first stop was a motel in Wilga, where Mike Scott had booked a room. He and Les were waiting there with coffee and snacks to take with them. Here, Peg changed from her performance clothes, and into a short, brown haired wig, and casual clothes. The former would be taken back to the Matlock Hotel and be brought to Melbourne with her guitar by McMasters. Les was going to use the black wig, and be seen returning to the hotel.

"Okay," Mike began, when they were ready to go. "Your grandfather is expecting you to go directly to his place."

"You already told us that," Jack growled.

"Well, drive safely," Mike said.

"And you and Les better not take all night getting back. You want to be seen leaving the dance place before all the crowd is gone."

"Nuh, uh! We just need to be seen getting back to the hotel," Mike corrected. "Get going, alright? Oh, here's the keys to the ford. I'll drive your car down."

Jack remembered to get the keys for his car from his pocket. They got caught on a frayed seam and he yanked them impatiently.

"Relax, Lover boy. His majesty doesn't have a chance."

"It's not that," Jack argued. "It's how they will tear into Peg, cast vile aspersions…"

"Lover boy, he can't get around the fact that she was only 15 and he was old enough to have sired her foster brothers."

"Les, shut up," Peg told her. "I don't want to be thinking about him all the way to Melbourne. I would rather think about you and Mike dancing together like two little doves."

Les made a retching noise. "You have Lover boy. Let me and Church Boy have our fun. Besides, I'd never danced anywhere proper before."

Peg smirked, and let Jack grab her hand to get her out to the hired car. Mike took up the thermos and shoved it at Jack. Peg grabbed the bag of motel made sandwiches from Les.

Jack automatically scanned the area outside the motel unit. Only two other cars besides the ford were parked near units. No light leaked past curtains from any of the rooms. He started the car quietly. Even though King's trial was still two weeks away, and the evidence seemed tight, he was worried about how it would go. The man deserved to be put away.

<h1 style="text-align:center">Chapter 18</h1>

Reg Costigan had received a call that had put him in a state of panic. Louisa, who had been draped over him before hand was told abruptly, "Get off, go home, and don't come back unless I tell you."

She pouted, whinged, yelled at him to no avail. He wouldn't tell her why she had to go. Storming out and heading for the room she used, she caught Stan where he had been eavesdropping. She didn't confront him – just jerked his arm to get him to follow her.

"Do you know what jerked his chain?" she hissed as she pulled him along.

"No. He doesn't confide in me," Stan reminded her. "Has he acted like this before?"

"Only when they took a race win off him for something," she recalled.

As soon as she reached her room, and Stan would have left her, she dragged him in and asked him to fetch her case from the top of the wardrobe.

"Don't go," she invited, as she began dragging clothes out of the wardrobe and drawers and only roughly folding everything. "I heard Reg talking to one of the servants. Harry should have been back by now. I think he might have been picked up for something."

"Good riddance," Stan told her, surprising her.

"I thought you were one of his mates?"

His laugh was strained. "I would strangle him if I had the strength and the guts."

"Then why are you here? Doing what he and Reg want."

"You're smart, you figure it out. I am just wondering why you are."

"Never mind. Why do you hate him then?"

"King? I have known him since I was a kid – back when he was a pervert and a paedophile. He hasn't changed."

Louisa stopped packing to stare at him.

"He came to visit my mother quite often. He's the father of my two brothers. He treated them okay. I was another class."

"He molested you?" Louisa was shocked.

Stan gave a terse nod. "I got over it. My mother was always a whore for

Harry's boss. She allowed King to take the kid when she was only 15."

"Shit!" Louisa exclaimed, going pale. "He has been polite to me, but he makes my skin crawl."

"I think my sister finally got the guts to report him. He tried to have her abducted a week ago. She got away."

Louisa went back to packing and had just finished closing the case when Reg barged in.

"What are you here for, Jessup?"

"To carry my case down," Louisa told him coldly.

"Do it," Reg ordered.

Louisa didn't look at him as he took the case.

Stan was undecided what to do, once he'd put the case beside the door. He fiddled with the luggage tag on it, and realised that it had the girl's address and phone number. Hearing nothing from upstairs, he risked fiddling more and removed the slip with the writing in it. He slipped it into a pants pocket.

Reg and Louisa came down the stairs together. She seemed to have got over her bad mood. She carried a beauty case and a coat over one arm.

"Want me to carry the case out?" Stan asked.

"No, I'll do that," Reg told him. "Go lock yourself into your room."

"What's up?"

"I think the cops have Harry. They picked him up about a mile from here. It's a precaution."

"Shit! What if they know he was staying here?" Stan feigned panic.

"They shouldn't have a reason to. Go!"

Stan went, but stopped and turned back. He saw Louisa staring at the luggage tab, then glance at him. He patted his pocket and she smiled before turning her attention back to Reg. He hurried onto his room and locked the door. He did wonder if Reg would come up after the girl had gone.

He did. He was one of those who liked to vent his frustrations, loudly. He hammered on the door. "Open up Jessup."

Stan stood aside as Reg stormed in. "The police do have Harry."

"So? You said they'd have no reason to come here."

The way Reg was pacing, the truth might be otherwise. "I know, but if they do, I don't want you caught. You are doing a favour for me."

"Yeah, and this has kind of ruined my fun," Stan complained.

"You'd have had that problem anyway. She told me she just got her period and won't be interested for a few days."

"Was that why she was so pissed off?" Stan asked idly. "I couldn't get a civil word out of her."

"Probably. Anyway, forget her. I came to tell you that I think you need to hide better."

"Where?"

"Down stairs. In the other wing. The one that is shut up now."

"What? In some cellar? I'd rather be back inside."

"No. It is a cellar, but it's not like that. My dad had it made really comfortable. It's got a great bar, a TV, the works. You will have to fix your own food, but there is a full freezer and a camp shower. Grab your stuff."

Intrigued, Stan obeyed – wondering how he could get word out about it. A servant entered, as they were leaving, with new sheets for the bed. Reg wasn't missing a trick. Had he told the servant to polish off any fingerprints?

"King was staying here. Was he?"

"Yeah. Lording it. I have to move his stuff down with you. Or rather, lock it in one of the cupboards. Don't even think of looking in his stuff. He'll be like a match to tinder."

"Don't worry. I don't want to be near anything of his."

If he hadn't seen Reg open the secret door in the floor, he would never have suspected it. It was hidden under a thick rug and the edge of that had a solid desk on it.

"This used to be the old man's library," Reg gestured to the empty shelves behind the desk. "My mother was the book lover, but she only read soppy romances, and boring literary works. The old man got rid of them when she died."

"No matter. I was never a reader. Don't suppose you have any playboy mags here?" Stan suggested. Reg cuffed him in an almost brotherly fashion.

"Look, this is just a precaution. A few days. If the police do suspect Harry was staying here, and I am sure he won't tell them he was, they will come right away."

"How will I know if they do? Or if I need something that's not down here? Does it have a loo?"

"It has everything. Come on. I will show you."

Stan didn't ask what the room had been created for, just muttered his gratitude. It did seem to have everything he could think of that he might need. It also had two securely locked doors leading off it. He didn't refer to them either, just walked over to test the bed. It was the equal in quality to the one he had been using. He threw his case there. He'd needed to borrow it for the new clothes he had been given. He checked the fridge. "No milk for coffee?"

"There's powdered stuff. Use that. Someone will be down with King's stuff. Stay in here and keep the door locked once he is gone."

Stan waved an acknowledgement and went over to the 24 inch TV, turned it on, and then slumped in the nearest chair – but only until Reg had gone. He did a quick survey to see if "everything" included a phone. It didn't, but he had seen one on the shelf in the room above. The way up was still open, he ran up the steps, quietly, grabbed the phone and checked if it had a dial tone. No, but then he discovered that it wasn't plugged in.

He heard voices then, and grabbed the unit, roughly coiled the cable, and hurried downstairs. He shoved it under the bed, and was back in the chair when King's stuff was brought down. The servant had the key for one of the locked doors, and the case and bags went in there. He relocked the room, and retreated from the cellar, ensuring that door locked behind him.

Noises still came through the door. Stan wondered how secure it really was if he could hear stuff being moved around upstairs. It occurred to him that they might have moved the desk onto the trap door. That gave him a moment of panic, thinking that they might leave him to rot in this luxury. Then he laughed at himself. The girl had her period. She wasn't pregnant yet.

He turned the TV volume down. If he could hear sounds coming down, the reverse was probably also true. He would rather have advance warning if anyone was coming. Now, he decided to thoroughly examine his new, luxurious prison. Find exactly where everything was. The bathroom was primitive, and that was in a room off the small kitchen area. It had a toilet, and a shower that could also be a square bath. On a shelf beside it were soap, shampoo, as well as laundry powder. A drying rack pulled down off the wall. Switches on the wall were for a heater, an exhaust fan to remove steam, and the lights.

Coming out, the kitchen had cupboards, drawers – more stuff than he needed. The pantry was stocked with tins and packets that only needed to have water added. Nothing hard to prepare. He could put up with a few days on his own.

He recalled the phone and went looking for a place to plug it in. If the place was supposed to have everything, and it didn't look like a prison, it should have a phone socket.

He found it down at floor level, with the cable running under the lush carpet, out under the door, and probably up to the room above. He plugged the cord in and lifted the receiver carefully. He had a dial tone, and right now, Reg and the servants, of whom he had only ever seen two, would be busy removing evidence. He dialled the number he had memorised, heard it answered with the day's date, and said quickly, "Costigan Mansion, disused wing, cellar in library, two locked rooms. King was here." Then he carefully hung up the phone.

His continuing search of the place was interrupted by the phone ringing. It was muffled by the chair, but he dare not answer it. It stopped, just as he eased it out, and he dared to lift the receiver. He heard the upstairs receiver being put down, probably the servant was going to get Reg. He covered the mouth piece with his hand and just listened. He didn't know who might be calling, but he had a strange feeling when he heard Louisa's voice, sounding upset. "Reggie, daddy has had a fall. They want to put him in hospital, but he flatly refuses to go. I am going to have to help look after him."

"Get a nurse," Reg told her callously.

"The hospital is going to send one but I have to stay here a bit anyway. I might as well keep him sweet. He has been on at me about you, so don't ring for a bit. I will ring you."

"Yeah, okay. But don't ring here for a day or so, yourself."

"Okay. Love you, race jock."

"Same here, Pit lane Louie."

Stan, listening, pulled a face. And waited for them both to hang up before replacing the receiver. Then he unplugged the phone, so it wouldn't ring and betray him.

Chapter 19

Louisa Westcott drove away from the Costigan mansion at a sedate pace. Let Reg think he had placated her with his promise of a week on the Gold Coast…once she was pregnant. He hadn't. His abrupt dismissal, out of the blue, no explanation, was like a slap in the face. It had certainly woken her up.

She had ignored everything her father had told her about Reggie. The racing scene excited her, and as Reggie's girl, she had been in the papers, on TV – people envied her. She had met famous people, from politicians to movie stars. And Reggie was wealthy in his own right as well as being the heir to his filthy rich father. She would inherit her own father's wealth and when she and Reggie married, they would be set for a life of luxury.

Reggie had a way with him. Lots of girls had fallen under his thrall. They had never lasted long, not like her. It couldn't be said that he had never made her feel good, even if he was unable to perform himself. He could do it to her without getting inside her.

Hearing Reggie go from making her horny, to 'Leave! Go home!' had suddenly made her realise that once he had got what he wanted, ie her pregnant, so her father would insist he marry her, he could discard her as soon as her father died and she had her father's money.

He would have control of that money.

Yes, she wanted to marry Reggie, but she was in no rush for Daddy to die. Once she was pregnant, he wouldn't need Stan, either. He wouldn't want him to be able to claim her child was his, not Reggie's.

She felt sick.

Stan looked so like Reggie that it was uncanny. Yet he was totally different – gentle, considerate. He had to be a crook though, or why did he seem to panic at the thought of the cops coming? What he had said about Harry King – was it true? If it was, why did Reggie have him at the mansion? Did his father know that he knew such people?

The questions kept swirling in her mind, provoking new thoughts, memories of things she had ignored or disbelieved. She was so preoccupied that she didn't even wonder whose car was parked in the drive where she usually parked hers.

"Is that you, Louisa?" her father's voice called from the lounge.

"Yes, Daddy."

"Come in when you can, please."

The polite tone gave her pause. Had he forgiven her for the argument they'd had before she had stormed out? She recalled the car. Did he have a visitor? Was it the doctor?

She left her case in the hall and went into the lounge. The visitor, was a stranger.

"Hello, dear," Phil Westcott greeted. "I would like you to meet Eugene Taylor."

"Hello," Louisa said warily.

"Oh do sit down, girl," Westcott said, irritably, sounding more like his usual self.

She did, but felt her body freeze when the stranger remarked, "I hear that you are Reg Costigan's current girlfriend."

"Did Daddy—"

"I would advise you to listen to me, Miss Westcott."

"Who are you?"

She took the ID folder he slid across the coffee table to her. "Eugene Taylor, Consultant, OCTF," she read aloud as the blood drained from her face. This, on top of her cogitations on the way home, increased her nausea. She forced the question, "Do you think Reggie has done something?"

"Do you?" Taylor asked neutrally.

Before she had left home this last time, she would have instantly denied it. Now though, she wasn't sure.

"I wouldn't have thought so. I mean, I know the papers talk about drinking, drugs and stuff, but I haven't seen any of that when I am with him. Then some of the girls he used to date got nasty when he dropped them, but that is all in the past. He's treated me okay, and I have never seen him drunk."

"Why did you come back?" Westcott demanded. "You have been cheapening yourself at his mansion, haven't you?"

"I was there," Louisa admitted, controlling her desire to snap at her father with the visitor there to hear it.

"Was his father there?" Taylor asked. "I had heard that his companies and some others were being investigated. It can't be an easy time."

"By you?" Louisa blurted, but Taylor gave no indication of whether the answer was yes or no. "No, he wasn't."

"Did you see anyone else there?" Taylor continued.

"Only servants." She felt herself blushing. Stan could technically be considered a servant. She didn't want to mention Harry King.

"Phil tells me that you have your heart set on marrying the young Costigan. How does he feel about that?" Taylor continued to probe, in a casual way.

"He has already asked me," Louisa proclaimed. Then she looked and saw the frown on her father's face. "Though Daddy doesn't like him."

Westcott butted in. "I told her I wanted to see her married and settled before I go. I want her to be happy."

Louisa couldn't bring herself to say, "Reggie and I will be happy." When she didn't, her father's frown became more pronounced.

"Did you two have an argument? Is that why you came back?" Westcott demanded.

"No we didn't. He was worried about things. Probably what you said about his father. He didn't say."

She looked down at the table as she said that, but then she looked up. "He promised me a week on the Gold Coast later in the year."

Taylor spoke again, "You've met John Costigan, have you?"

"Quite a few times. He's polite, doesn't push his nose in our affairs. He likes me." Louisa couldn't help the defiance. Her argument with her father was haunting her now.

"Perhaps I could get your opinion on a photograph," Taylor asked. He lifted a case from the floor, and once it was on the low table, he opened it. He flicked through manilla folders until pulled one out that contained photographs. He selected one and slid it over to her.

"Have you seen that man before?"

Completely unsuspecting, Louisa frowned at it. "It looks like Mr Costigan, but I have never seen him with a beard. Who is it?"

"We are trying to identify him," Taylor said smoothly.

"Could something have happened to Mr Costigan?" Louisa asked. Her mind had gone back to the phone call Reggie had received. No, that had been about Harry King.

"Ah, what?" Louisa realised she had been asked another question.

"I asked you when you would be seeing Reg Costigan next."

"Ah, I said I wasn't feeling very well. He said to take it easy for a few days. Why?"

Westcott answered, "I am going to have my solicitor over to make some changes to my will."

Louisa looked at her father, her pale face, now flushing red. "Why?

Because of Reggie?"

"Well, yes. But I want you to listen before storming out again."

When he didn't get an instant argument, he went on. "When I am gone, I truly want you to be happy. I don't want you marrying Reggie, if you are so dead set on it, and finding out too late that he only wanted your money."

"Daddy, Reggie is rich. So is his father. He doesn't need my money."

"That may well be, my dear. However, let's not refer to him. Maybe, you might decide you're tired of him. There will be other young blokes, who will see you, a rich heiress, and make a play for your affections. All I want to do is to set up a trust, to last at least until you are twenty-five, so that you remain in control of your money and other things I leave you."

"What does that mean? I won't be able to spend it?"

"Are you that eager to see me off?" Westcott asked pointedly.

"Daddy, no! I don't want you to die for ages yet."

Westcott smiled at her. "It will mean that you may have to justify expenditures with the trustees, and if you spend money on, say, a fancy convertible, it will belong to the trust."

Louisa considered that. "So you don't want any husband of mine, taking control of my money the instant we get married."

"Yes."

"Are you going to stop me marrying Reggie?"

Westcott was about to speak, but Taylor intervened.

"Miss Westcott, there are some things that I would like to tell you. I want you to think these things over very carefully before you see young Mr Costigan again. Perhaps you might telephone him and give him a reason for being away longer than a few days."

"Okay." Irrationally, Louisa had a sinking feeling in the pit of her stomach. She wondered what had brought on that sense of dread. The idea that she might have made a dreadful mistake? She had told Reggie that she had her period, but in fact, it was two days late, and she was never late.

She walked to the phone and made the call, inventing a reason to need to stay away. When she came back she challenged, "Will that do you?"

Taylor nodded and found another file in his case. "Everything I have here has been properly verified. I am asking that you consider these facts in an unbiased a manner as possible. I am making no accusations against Reg Costigan. I have always thought of him as the spoilt, indulged, only son of a very rich man. There are a lot of men like that around."

"Did Daddy ask you to investigate him?"

"No, our interest in him stems from other sources."

"Oh, all right."

Louisa tried to keep her expression neutral, and didn't realise how completely she failed. Some of what she heard, she knew about from people who knew Reggie, but she had only heard one side of it. The rest, well, it was stuff that his mates wouldn't mention in front of her. They were probably as bad. And if people learnt of it, it hadn't made it to the media, or had been suppressed. The emotionless recitation left her chilled.

Taylor paused. "Are you alright, Miss Westcott?"

"Yes. Yes I am fine. Was there more?"

"There is, but it is something that I feel uncomfortable bringing up." Taylor was unexpectedly reticent. "It is also privileged information. But I feel I should mention it since you are thinking of marrying young Costigan."

"What is it?"

"Some years ago, he contracted a STD. He was treated, cured, but it is possible that it made him infertile."

Louisa thought, "STD? Isn't that related to syphilis?" Then the rest of it sank in.

"He said that he had contracted the mumps, and might be. Said that if we really wanted kids, we could adopt one. But you said he was cured?"

"That is the information I have. I would advise that you both get checked over before getting married."

"Tactful," Louisa murmured. She had always heard that whores were likely to get such things, and some of Reggie's exes were little better than that. And with that shock numbing her mind, she wasn't expecting to be tricked, so when Taylor slid another photo across the table and asked her if she knew that man, her face completely betrayed her.

"Miss Westcott?" Taylor prompted.

She fought a battle in her mind and finally nodded.

"Where did you meet him?"

"At Reggie's place."

"Was he staying there?"

Louisa nodded.

"How long had he been there?"

"I don't know, but all of this past week for sure."

"Do you know who he is?"

"I only know him by name. I figured he had to be a mate of Reggie."

"Harry King?"

She nodded again.

"King was arrested today on a rape charge."

Louisa felt hot and then cold. "He never said or did anything that I could object to."

"Apart from Reg, King and the servants, did you see anyone else at the mansion?"

Louisa stared at Taylor, not wanting to answer. Another photo was slid across the table. She looked down and saw the police mugshot of Stan Jessup. Stan! Her world went black.

She came to, lying on the couch with her feet elevated and her father sponging her face. She began to sob. "Daddy, I've been such a fool."

"I guess that's the prerogative of the young, my dear," Westcott said gently. "So, I guess you did see Stan Jessup there. What did he do?"

"Nothing. No, not nothing."

"Did he hurt you?"

"No."

"Do you know why he was there?" Taylor asked from where he was still sitting.

"I think so."

"Do you want to talk about it?" Taylor invited, but the girl didn't answer. He glanced at Westcott who only shook his head.

"If I asked a policewoman to come around, would you be more comfortable talking to her?"

"Okay," Louisa found herself saying.

Taylor stood up and Westcott came over.

"You have been a great help, Miss Westcott. I appreciate your honesty and integrity."

A muffled sob, preceded the question of, "Are you going to raid the mansion?"

"We will put a watch on it," was Taylor's only reply.

"Reggie said that you'd have no reason to, but I don't think he believed that. He told Stan to lock himself in his room. Stan didn't want to be found."

"No," Taylor murmured. "Do you think that he might take Jessup away?"

"He might."

"Let us worry about that. The person I really want to talk to is John

Costigan, but he seems to have gone away. Phil, I will see myself out."

Eugene Taylor was very satisfied with the interview. The girl, coming back just then, had been fortuitous. Yes, he'd need to get the police woman there as soon as he could. Someone from the local station. He would go there in person to arrange it. He didn't want any of this going over the radio. What else might the girl know? If King had been there, he was pretty certain that he knew why Stan was there, but why was the girl protecting Jessup? She called him by his first name, and that implied she was friendly with him.

By the time he reached Yarra Central police station, he had a list of questions for the policewoman to ask the girl.

When he left, after requesting that WPC Stewart reported to him at his home, his mind turned to what to do about Stan Jessup. At home, his man, another retired police officer, gave him a message. His brows rose into his receding hairline.

"Get Halford and Harlow here, and the OIC of the Corporate Crime Unit."

His man disappeared and Taylor went to his study to think. Jessup had come through with useful information, again. First warning about the attempt on his sister, and now, with the answer to where certain missing records might be. Would there be value in leaving Jessup there for a time? Would he be safe, particularly if the girl did not go back? Probably. They would be still thinking she would in time. Would raiding the mansion spook Costigan senior any more than he must be already?

Hopefully, Halford and Harlow would help him decide.

Policewoman Stewart rang the bell at the door of the big house and waited for it to be answered. When it opened, she announced, "I am here to speak to Mr Taylor."

"Yes, Miss Stewart, you are expected. Please come in."

She followed the manservant into Taylor's office, and obeyed his earlier instructions to act as if she had not been told why she was wanted.

"Good evening, Sir. How can I help you?"

She heard the door close behind her, and waited to be asked to report. She had only given a passing thought to the man who had been hovering in the hallway.

"Sit, please, Miss Stewart. How did your interview go?"

"The girl was quite forthcoming, and I believe grateful for the information you gave her."

"Tell me the gist of it, and put all the details in your written report. Did the girl agree to sign a statement?"

"She did, Sir. I have the hand written version that she signed."

"Excellent work, Miss Stewart. Go ahead…"

Taylor listened intently, the asked, "Did she say if she still wanted to see Reg Costigan?"

"I think she is still ambivalent. You gave her a lot to think about. She admitted that he could …make her feel really good, and she liked that. She also admitted that Reg suggested that if she was pregnant, her father would make them get married. Or so she thought."

"Go on…"

"Reggie and Harry King introduced her to Stan. They didn't mention his last name. When he came, he was well presented, and shy. She wasn't interested in him until Reggie sold her on his idea. Even then, she wasn't keen, and thinks he drugged her drink to make her very relaxed. When she woke up, she was with Stan, not Reggie. She wasn't put off. Apparently he was gentle, considerate and once she fell asleep he left her alone."

"How many times were they left together?" Taylor asked.

"Quite a few times. The girl actually admitted that she would be happy if Reggie let her keep him as her sex toy."

"Did she hint that she might be pregnant?"

"Surely it would be too early to tell," Margaret Stewart suggested. "Anyway, she had been on the pill, only stopped taking it two days ago. You might need to ask a doctor about the likelihood of conception."

"You are probably right," Taylor conceded. "Was there anything else?"

"No Sir."

"I will have your report and the girl's statement as soon as you can send them."

Stewart took some folded sheets from her handbag, and passed them over.

"My thanks for your help. Please keep the details of this interview to yourself, if you would. Even from your Sergeant."

"Yes, Sir."

"I may need your help again," Taylor warned. "Do you know of any of the local prostitutes?"

"Some, Sir."

"Good. Good night to you."

Summoned by an unobtrusive bell, Taylor's man arrived to escort Stewart out. This time, she noted that the hall was vacant.

Chapter 20

Jack waited only long enough for the judge to leave the court before hustling Peg out a side door. There was no one to see them walk quickly via a laneway to where his car had a permit to park.

Peg was stony faced as she got in the passenger seat. He pulled away from the kerb, and tried to think if there was a way to go that didn't involve going past the front of the court, where, no doubt, Harry King was smirking for reporters.

How could the jury possibly have found King not guilty? No, he knew. All those 'character' witnesses from Matlock. Half a dozen of the rich brats that used to torment Peg. Probably that fact that it had taken her three years to get around to reporting the assault, didn't help.

King must have got at the jury somehow, too. Or why would they believe spoilt brats, more than people like Jack Casey?

Would the same thing have happened if the police had also charged him with nearly killing her after killing her aunt?

He didn't realise he was speeding until Peg finally spoke, more calmly than he had expected.

"Slow down, Jack."

He obeyed, then glanced at her. "Aren't you mad?"

"Mad? No. And angry does not come close to the truth. Let the bastard think himself invincible for a while longer."

"He's had a taste of prison. He won't want to go back," Jack predicted. "I reckon if they had included the assault after he killed your aunt…"

"It may have been the same result," Peg said thoughtfully. "We would have needed Stan available to testify had they done so. But if we had included that and failed, they couldn't try him again on the same charge. They do have other options still, but some of them are too close to the case they are building for the aunt's murder."

"Did they tell you that?" Jack asked.

"No, but I am beginning to see how your grandfather's mind works. Fortunately, he doesn't know me as well as he thinks. I want to get even with those former classmates of mine who perjured themselves. Just because there were six of them all saying the same thing, I, who told the full truth, is to be charged with perjury. It bloody stinks."

"You are not going to do anything stupid?" Jack warned.

"No. This is too important. I do want to talk to Vic Maddern, or Steve. I saw them there, and I saw the expression on their faces. I think they will be going to check the statements of those two faced cherubs, and how they were obtained. I can tell them a few things about each of those rats that will give them places to start."

"So if the statements are proved false, do you think they can declare a mistrial?" Jack asked.

"I have no idea," Peg admitted. "Where are we going?"

"Grandfather's. I want a word with him."

"Don't go in blowing steam. I am going to take a leaf from a friend's book – don't get mad, get even."

"Let me guess? Les?"

"Right in one. Now, as much of shock as that was, and after that totally humiliating question session, I am probably far from being the only girl that was raped and the guy got free. Even if I was only 15 at the time. It has occurred to me that Peg Jessup is just going to have to suck it up. I no longer care what they say about her. It's not me, not my name, anymore."

"Okay…" Jack said slowly, calming down. "What are you thinking?"

"What I said before. Okay so he got away with raping me, but there is still the assault, and the murder of my aunt. If they get Jack Casey, Stan, your uncle to testify – it is a whole separate case. King might feel superior now, and be extra careful, he will still have to wonder what the police will do now they have identified him."

"What if he tries for you again?" Jack admitted to his worst fear.

"I have you to see that he doesn't succeed."

"Jack!" Eugene Taylor's man greeted them with less than his usual aplomb. He was also glancing nervously back along the driveway. "Both of you get around to the back of the house, quick smart. Drive the car into one of the garages."

"What's up?" Jack demanded.

"Get going. Lad. Explanations later."

Peg pulled Jack's arm, catching the urgency. "Come on."

They returned to the car and did as directed, driving along the rest of the driveway at a faster than sedate rate. Another of his grandfather's servants was rolling one of the garage doors aside. He drove in.

"Mr Taylor is aware of your arrival and requests that you wait here until summoned. He is expecting visitors and does not wish them to see either of you," the servant told them.

"Okay, Hank," Jack agreed. "Is there any chance of a drink or two?"

"I will see to it," the man agreed.

Jack and Peg emerged from the car as the door was rolled shut.

"Wonder who is coming," Jack murmured, so his voice wouldn't echo. He walked around to where Peg was leaning forward against the car, with her head on her crossed arms. When he got close, he realised she was shaking.

"Hey, are you okay?" He pulled her around and hugged her. She didn't answer him. "What happened to you don't care what they say, and don't get mad, get even?"

"I haven't got there yet."

"Do you have a show tonight?"

"No. Carson is doing a fund raiser somewhere. Mac got told that as we couldn't be absolutely sure how things would go, not to rely on me."

"He got told what?" Jack almost said loudly.

"Talk to your grandfather. His nickname should be Machiavelli not Squizzy."

"Yeah. So long as he is not planning to use you as bait."

Peg rubbed her eyes with her sleeve. "I don't know. It might be fun fishing for Kingfish with a very, very sharp hook to stick in his—"

"Enough. I get the picture, but don't you dare!"

"Too bad."

The servant, Hank, brought Jack's usual preference and a lemonade for Peg.

"Do you know how long my grandfather intends to test my patience?"

"I am afraid not, Sir. He was not expecting you, apparently."

"He should have."

"If it gets too late, food will be brought out."

"He's so—" Jack began a sarcastic comment.

"A picnic in a garage," Peg interrupted. "A novelty."

Jack waved the servant off.

"We could cuddle up in the car," Peg suggested. "I need cheering up."

They were doing that, after Jack tried unsuccessfully to see anything through the louvre windows at the end of the garage.

A sharp cough interrupted their mutual absorption.

"What are you? The chaperone?" Jack demanded, irritated with himself for not hearing his uncle come in and approach. They separated, but not guiltily.

"I don't want to argue with you, Jack," Justin Taylor said with resignation. "The old man said that you can come in now. I suggest that you don't get argumentative with him either."

Peg adjusted her clothing while Jack glared at his Uncle.

They went in, not to the study but to an elegant dining room, and were invited to sit at the places set for them.

"Sir, it is very good of you, but could we have a few minutes to clean-up first?" Peg asked politely.

Justin Taylor smirked, as his old man agreed. He took his own place at the table.

"How are you Megan?" Eugene Taylor asked, once she had settled into her seat.

"I am okay. I have had lots of experience in forgetting humiliation."

"I expect you have. Though, you might like to know that I have asked your Matlock friends York and Maddern to check the depositions that the young Matlock witnesses presented. Perfectly detailed as they each were, Senior York was able to attest to at least two inconsistencies."

"They were 100% fiction," Peg said flatly. "Are you going to try for a mistrial?"

"It is something to consider. Another is that now King is out again, you particularly, are in danger."

"I am very glad you thought of that, Sir," Jack said with thinly veiled sarcasm.

"King is going to find a long list of unsettling reports waiting for him. For a while, he will be dealing with them," Taylor proposed. "It might even be enough to force Gianni Costa out of hiding - even if only to prove he is still alive."

"Any reaction to having him declared dead?" Jack dared to ask.

"Not noticeably," Taylor admitted. "The tenants at the various properties, except that apartment block, have vacated. Our investigations there have netted us seven of Costa, or King's lesser adherents. Over the past two weeks, while King was incommunicado, we have had excavators in and dug over the four gardens, and had two patio slabs broken up and removed."

"Find anything?" Jack asked, hopefully.

"Ah, now. That's something I can't tell you. Lad."

"I will take that as, yes, you did." Jack got a tight smile in reply.

Taylor went on. "Did your Matlock friend tell you what I have had him doing?"

"Mike? No. Said you'd gagged him."

The smile grew wider. "Your friend found the place where King, as he calls himself now, grew up. Though never charged, when he was still a minor, he was suspected of, accused of, indecent acts with younger girls."

"Too bad that didn't come up at that farce of a trial today," Jack blurted.

"We still have to prove, beyond doubt, that King was previously known by that name, but I am sure. We must be careful, as the fingerprints we used were obtained by deception. It will have to seem that the finding of his priors was unrelated to the rape charge. King is aware that I know that name, but otherwise that information is being kept quiet."

"What good will him knowing you knew who he was do?" Peg asked. "He will just cover it up further."

"King is being watched. The house where he grew up is being watched."

"Still, what will that tell you?" Peg insisted.

"If King or some of his agents go there, it will indicate that there is something there that he doesn't want anyone to know about. He doesn't know that we know about the place, and the back yard had a pile of junk that had been accumulating for years."

"Had," Jack pounced on the word.

"It still has a great deal. The neighbours petitioned the council to have the junk removed. The council issued the writ on the owner via the property manager. As it was meant to be done by last week and wasn't, the council sent in a team to do it. I supplied the team that included forensic pathologists. However, it is not a particularly pleasant subject to discuss at the meal table."

As Taylor spoke, his 'man' was bringing a trolley into the room, and Hank was bringing plates.

Jack took the opportunity to glance at Peg, who returned it and gestured at the array of cutlery set out at her place.

He grinned. Peg might have laid out such place settings, but never eaten at such a fancy table. He lifted the larger knife and fork.

True to his implied statement, Eugene Taylor did not talk 'shop' while eating. It didn't stop the so far taciturn Justin from asking, 'You've reported Avery then?"

"Yes, and I will leave it to the internal affairs team from now on."

"You spoke up for me," Justin said.

"I knew what you were doing and everything you did. Avery was not instructed to do the bidding of the criminals we are investigating."

Jack leant towards Peg and whispered in her ear, "I wonder if that was who he was expecting?"

Eugene Taylor went on, "He will have a chance to prove which side he is on, just as you were given. I have also reported King's lawyer to the law society, and they have revoked his licence to defend cases in court. They will be investigating his work practices, and ethics. Even if his prior record is clean, they will be watching him in the future."

"King has a whole pack of crooked lawyers," Justin growled.

"Who, if they are smart, will be watching their own steps," his father pointed out.

Peg recalled that Justin had opted out of King's 'pay' when he thought King had killed her. "Uncle Justin?" Her voice, calling him that, startled him. "I know that you tried to save me from King by letting me slip away. I want to say thanks."

"For your sake, you should continue hating me."

"Well, so long as you know that I don't. Anyone can make a mistake."

"Or years of them," Jack murmured very quietly, while looking at his grandfather.

"I didn't save your aunt," Justin reminded her.

"The old bitch was on borrowed time, anyway," Peg said. "You know that guy she told you about? The one who came accusing her of blackmail?"

That so surprised him, that his expression confirmed her guess. "Yeah, I saw her in Shep that day. I was helping to take some horses there. Anyway, that bloke wasn't the only one she was doing it to. There were four other photos that I know of, and the one the bitch sent to a reporter and to a rather prominent gentleman. A new print, from an old negative. She had a death wish."

Eugene Taylor pounced on the last snippet of information. "Did you mention that last photo in your statement?"

"Thought I did. Why?"

"Do you know who the gentleman was?"

"I know who I think it was," Peg told him.

"Elucidate, please."

"The bloke she thought was Gianni Costa in public life. It was an old photo from twenty or more years back."

"Did she mention anything else about it?" Taylor probed.

Peg thought back, recalling the conversation. "The bloke was with a girl. Someone she knew. I took that as her being another of Gianni Costa's whores."

"Do you think that photo might be amongst those photos from Albert Jessup?"

Peg shrugged and looked at Jack, who answered, "We didn't look through them all."

Peg added, "She may have taken these particular few from that collection. Anyway, I don't know why the silly bitch needed extra money. Gianni was sending her enough male callers."

Eugene Taylor spoke after a moment. "The post mortem on Ida Jessup showed that her liver and kidneys were badly diseased. She might have died at any time. She was meant to have treatment, but she only attended intermittently. She didn't have health insurance."

Peg suddenly didn't want to say more, and Taylor wasn't finished.

"Her doctor urged her to stop drinking, but she got worse after you were sentenced."

"Stupid old bitch!" Pegs voice was unsteady. Her aunt had faults, lots of them, but she had not given way about the shares. She had looked after them for all these years, so the child of her friend would have her rightful inheritance.

"King may not have meant to kill her," Taylor finished.

"I reckon he did intend to kill me," Peg retorted.

"To remove a witness," Taylor continued.

"Doesn't that put your son in danger too?" Peg asked.

Justin spoke up. "There are still some things that he doesn't think I have told anyone about. He thinks that I have been suspended over a lesser matter. Your aunt's death is still under investigation, as if the police do not have enough evidence. And now, with him being freed, and your reputation in ruins, he will think, that if you accuse him of your aunt's murder, you won't be believed."

Jack merely shook his head. "I hope you both know what you are doing. Peg does not deserve to be King's scapegoat."

"I know, lad," Eugene Taylor agreed. "However, you need to realise that we are investigating activities from over twenty years ago. Many are now outside the limits for prosecution."

"I understand that—"Jack stopped talking when Peg grabbed his arm.

"Sir, did you get that box of journals that I asked Vic Maddern to send to you?"

"Yes, but I haven't looked at them yet."

"I think you should read them. I have more, stored down here, that I haven't read yet. Annie Simmons left very little out of her journals, and kept them very secret. Even I didn't know she kept them until I nicked stuff just before she died. Gianni started on her when she was barely seventeen."

Taylor held up his hand. "Yes, I will read them, and I want you to have the others you just mentioned, brought here. What else did you 'nick' as you put it?"

"Lots of old letters, but most were written by my real mother. A lot were never posted. Letters from various other people. I didn't have a chance to read any."

"Yes, have them brought here too."

"I didn't finish going through everything that Maddern had taken from the house," Peg told him.

"Do you think you will find anything else there?"

"No idea." Peg shrugged. "I found old photos of me and the boys that I didn't know she had, let alone kept. Jasper was already looking a lot like Harry King in the latest of them."

"Those might be of interest too," Taylor mused.

Peg saw that Jack was smirking, and he whispered, "I bet he wants to compare them with whoever he mentioned earlier."

"What years were your brothers born?"

"Stan, 1937. Jasper, 1941. Ned, 1943."

"And your aunt supposedly married Albert Jessup in 1941," Taylor mused. "Suggestive. Trouble is, we don't have a good photo of Jessup."

"He was short, wore thick glasses," Peg blurted. "He was shorter than the aunt."

"Indeed? Is Jasper short?"

"No, he was almost as tall as Stan when I last saw him."

Taylor's man entered and spoke softly to his employer, causing him to place his serviette back on the table and rise. "Please, enjoy the desert course and coffee." He left the room as fast as he could with the help of his cane.

An awkward silence descended. Neither Justin, nor Jack, were into small talk with each other. When the desert was brought in, Peg asked, "Did you really think you might have been my father?"

Justin didn't look at her. "There was that chance."

"Can you tell me about my mother?"

Now, he did look at her. "She meant everything to me. She was intelligent, literate, and had an amazing voice."

Peg encouraged the reminiscences for a time before asking, "What happened?"

"We argued. She had already met that muso, Ian, by then. I felt I was losing her and pushed her to set the wedding date. Pushed too hard, I suppose. She also argued with her father about that and took off. He tried to have her dragged home, but when he found her…I found her…she had already been hooked on drugs, and booze. You know I blamed the muso, and he thought I had made up the charges against him, but at the time, I really believed he was guilty of getting Margaret hooked. I kept trying to help her, but she wasn't listening to me. That is when I discovered that she was prostituting herself for Gianni Costa. I made an 'appointment' with her."

Justin stopped abruptly. Finally, he went on. "That was a month or so after Ian was jailed. I was never sure if she kept away from me then, or Costa made sure she did, but I lost all trace of her."

"I reckon Costa did," Jack offered. "He was after those damn, Blair shares, even back then."

"How do you know?"

Peg answered him. "Something the aunt said, and hindsight. She was babbling about having something Gianni wanted. You probably know that King was after the same thing – the shares."

Justin nodded.

"So why did you slap on that restraining order?" Peg suddenly challenged him. "If you thought I was yours, or might be, you didn't know then."

"No, you are right. I didn't. I wanted to keep Jack out of it."

"Did you know who I was? I hadn't given the cops my real name then."

"At first, I thought that you were just some bimbo off the street. I heard who you were next morning."

"So, is that nonsense still in effect," Jack demanded.

"No."

"Just as well," Jack growled.

Peg had another thought. "Are you sorry that Jack and I got together?"

There was a long silence. "No. With all that has come to light since then, more than I managed to discover by demeaning myself for twenty years… What I am, is relieved. I resented you both, but it didn't matter who provided the evidence, if Costa was nabbed and jailed. King too. I finally believe we are close."

"Do you know everything?" Jack asked. "He has been keeping us out of touch of events."

"I agreed to keep away from the investigations, and not be briefed on progress, so I can't be made to give details. However, I have known my father a very long time and he is acting like a case is about to be cracked wide open."

"I hope you are right, Uncle," Peg said quietly.

Eugene Taylor did not reappear for the rest of the evening, nor until late the next day. Word had come from him that Jack and Peg were to stay at the mansion, but if visitors arrived, to keep out of sight. During the following week, when they were sent out of the way, Jack watched from their window, to try and identify the callers. On the Saturday, Jack came to a conclusion.

"Something is up. Most of the task force are here, along with half a dozen police cars."

Chapter 21

Mike found Steve York at the front counter of the café and greeted him with a grin, expecting good news. "How'd it go?"

York shook his head. "He was acquitted."

The summary made Mike flush, angry for Peg's sake. "That's ridiculous! Whether she did or not lead him on, she was only fifteen. She didn't look old enough, back then."

"You didn't know her back then," York reminded him. "Are you able to tell me a few things?"

"If I can. What?"

"Do you know these girls?" York showed him a list of names.

"Yeah. They often come in here. When they aren't trying to get me in their…clutches. They are always running Peg down, knowing that I was seeing her."

"What else can you tell me about them?"

"Why don't you talk to Mrs B.? My impression will be biased. In fact, in about 20 minutes they will probably come in. If they have heard about the trial result, you can listen to them. It might be enlightening."

"Maybe I will," York decided.

York went through to the manager's office, and Mike went to the phone and rang Jack's place.

"Hello, Church Boy. I guess you heard, huh?"

"Is Jack there?"

"Nah. He probably went to the Old Man's place. I'm hiding out here. When it's safe, I want to come up there and scare the shit out of those lying bitches."

"Don't bother. York is onto it already," Mike assured her. "Listen, any chance of getting Jack a message?"

"He might ring. What is it?"

"Ask him what I can do."

"I can tell you that, Church Boy."

"Les!"

"Okay, okay. Keep your pants on. I'll let you know, okay."

Right on four o'clock, fifteen minutes after the train from Melbourne got in, the first of the girls on York's list came in. Within ten minutes, the group had swelled to twelve. Mike wondered if the boys who had come in were also on York's list. He went out to serve them, ignoring the figure at a nearby table, sitting behind a copy of the afternoon's Matlock Advertiser. A special edition, with a report of the trial, since the victim had been from Matlock.

"Heard your little slut of a girlfriend got her comeuppance," the first nasty comment began.

"Do you know that she is to be arrested for perjury?" a second went on. "They will send her back to jail."

"Then you haven't anything to worry about, have you?" Mike said amiably.

"Why don't you come to my place later, Mikey? We're having a celebration party."

"Can I bring a friend?" Mike asked as if he were considering it.

"Someone from around here?" the girl who had issued the invitation asked.

"No, from New South."

"Why not? She might enjoy herself."

Mike thought he knew what they were thinking. This bunch, together, thought they were the new snobbocracy. Probably thought that any girl he brought would be a mouse and easily overawed.

"Oh, she will. She'd have you all for breakfast. What can I get you all?"

He'd stirred them up, exactly as he had thought. York ought to get an earful now.

They orders came out. Eva, helped him to bring them. The muffled voice from the paper called out something. Eva went over, was given a note for her mother, and told to say nothing.

Five minutes later, Vic Maddern entered and walked directly to the group. They all stopped talking and eyed him, none of them aware of York rising from the table nearby as Maddern addressed them.

"I would like you all to come down to the station."

"Why?"

"What for?"

"I have to ring my mother."

"We've done nothing wrong."

Maddern kept his face grim looking. "You are all over eighteen, so you don't need to call your parents. What this is about, will be discussed at the station. Senior York will take four of you. Four will come with me, and Constable Hogan is outside to take the rest of you."

One of the boys began to edge away, but felt York's hand grip his shoulder. He turned, realised the paper reader was no longer there, and guessed who it had been and that their uncensored talk had been overheard and went pale.

This group were not all of those who had given character witness depositions, and only half of those who had actually appeared in court were here. These though, were not going to have a chance to warn the others, who would be brought in from the neighbouring towns where they now lived.

York indicated the four he thought would crack first. The boy he had grabbed being one of them. Maddern took those back and had them come up to his office first. The rest, when they arrived, would be made to wait downstairs under the watchful eyes of Gary Hogan and Bert Kennedy.

All of the depositions had been included in the evidence of the case. Maddern had all of them faxed through to him, and they were in a folder on his desk.

At first, he made it seem that he was merely confirming their information matched what was in the depositions. He asked, as if uninterested, who had approached them. Had the person explained the purpose of the deposition and the legalities associated with them.

Then he asked, abruptly, "How much did he pay you?"

Four smug expressions suddenly changed to uncertain, and a couple to fear. Maddern was already sure of the answer.

Darlene Archer managed, "Was he meant to?"

"Twenty dollars," one of the boys admitted.

The other three glared at him, then Darlene asserted, "No one paid me."

Two other heads nodded.

Maddern looked at York and said, "Take Jamie Seddon and Andrew Ladner into the other room."

When the two boys had gone, Maddern fixed the girls with his gimlet stare.

"I have a copy of your depositions here. Both are impressively detailed. Now you, Miss Archer, refer to a period in 1970 when Peg Jessup was absent from school for two weeks. Tell me a bit more about that time."

The recitation was almost word for word with what was in the statement, and nothing new was added.

"And where were you at this time, Miss Archer?"

"I was at school."

Maddern turned his attention to Nancy Cartwright, and asked the same questions. The results were the same. She asked the question that he had expected her friend to ask.

"Why are you going over this?"

"I believe that you are aware that Peg Jessup is to be charged with perjury?"

"Well, she lied about stuff in court this morning," Nancy said.

"Do you know the penalty for perjury, Miss Cartwright?"

"No."

"It is a jail term of up to 12 months." Maddern saw two faces lose all colour. "Now, both of you signed a deposition to say that everything in that statement was true. In court today, you swore on the bible that you would be telling the truth. Do either of you wish to change your statement?"

Darleen said, firmly, "We told the truth. Peg Jessup always was a little tramp. She would let any of the boys do what they wanted with her. No wonder she got pregnant, twice."

"Just boys?" Maddern asked.

"That I know of," Darleen claimed.

"I see. Well, today's trial was not because a boy raped her."

"She said she'd do anything to leave Matlock. She probably led that guy on, to get money," Nancy suggested.

"A girl of fifteen and a man three times her age?" Maddern commented. "What if that had been you?"

Neither said a word.

"No matter whether a fifteen year old girl led him on or not, the man should not have done what he did. Peg Jessup could not have passed for eighteen if she wanted to."

"The jury acquitted him. Jessup lied about it. Probably because he wouldn't—" Nancy began.

"Enough! One last chance…Do you wish to change your statements?"

When neither answered, Maddern used the phone to call downstairs. "Oh, Bert, can you bring up the file on the Edith Cressey case?"

Maddern did not miss the shocked look that was shared by both girls.

Bert Kennedy, appeared, dropped the file on the desk and retreated.

Maddern sorted through the pages, taking out two that had been separated from the rest.

"Miss Archer, during the period which you mentioned that Peg Jessup was absent from school, you claim you were there. However, I have checked with the school here and those records show that you were absent at that time. I also have records from a case of an illegal abortionist, Edith Cressey.

She kept very good records. On the dates in question, she did indeed have a girl in her care. A Peg Jessup."

"I told you—" Darleen interrupted.

"Be quiet!" Maddern ordered. "Her patient description was tall, 5 foot 9 inch, blond hair parted in the centre, shoulder length."

Maddern turned his attention to Nancy. "And you, Miss Cartwright, for the period you mention, Edith Cressy also had a patient, as before, Peg Jessup. The description, a black haired, tan skinned girl. Hair, short and very curly, height 5' 3". Quite a change."

The girls were ashen faced, and Nancy's lips were trembling. Maddern wasn't finished.

"At the first of those time periods, the Jessup boys and their sister, were working off some mischief, doing gardening for Olive Glassman. At that time, Peg Jessup was not quite five foot, with long, light brown hair."

Nancy broke first, "Libby told us to do it. The guy told us she had sent him."

Darleen slumped. "That Jessup bitch got us in trouble with our parents. She put playboy mags in our room. Old Hargreaves saw her."

Maddern simply shook her his head. "Josh Hargreaves claims many things when he is drunk and looking for more money to drink away. And I would have thought that you would be wary of obeying Libby Falconer, since she has been sent for psychiatric assessment. Today, you were instrumental in getting a very dangerous man freed, just for the sake of petty revenge on someone who had to put up with a great deal more ill treatment from Libby and her friends, including you, than you even pretend she did to you. Not only that, you have probably given that same dangerous man a reason to kill her. That would make you both accessories to murder."

Maddern used the phone again. "Steve, bring the two boys in and take a new statement from Miss Archer and Miss Cartwright."

The changeover, two frightened young women for two arrogant young men, didn't cause Maddern to falter.

Once again, their claims were almost verbatim from their depositions. He let them elaborate on their lies, until they claimed that they often rode up to Ridge Road and visited her. That they would go out the back with her.

Here Maddern became deliberately misleading. "There was a neighbour, who is known to spend a lot of time in her garden watering, or looking out through her windows watching Ida Jessup's activities. I am surprised that she never mentioned your visits. She would be well aware that Peg was too young, and you unlikely to be visiting her aunt."

"We only ever felt her up," Jamie claimed.

"You rode your bikes there. Why didn't you drive? You had licences then."

"We couldn't pay for the fuel," Jaime answered that.

"Was that your trouble too, Andy?"

"Yeah! So What?"

They didn't even realise what they had admitted.

"Jessup was happy with that, was she?" Maddern asked.

"Of course she was. She begged for it."

"Who put you up to making the deposition?" Maddern barked.

"Some bloke. He said he wanted a character deposition."

"How did he know to come to you?"

"Ed Brownley," Andy said. "Look, we told the truth. Jessup was a tramp, like her aunt."

"Did the man who approached you explain that the document you signed was legally binding?"

Both nodded cautiously.

"And you are sticking by your word?" Maddern insisted,

"Yes."

"Do you know what perjury is?"

"Yeah, what the Jessup tramp was spouting this morning," Andy jeered.

"Do you know that there is a jail sentence for perjury?"

"So, the tramp should be locked up."

"So, you both think that it is alright for a grown up bloke to do more than feel up a fifteen year old girl?"

Maddern saw the moment of realisation.

"Hey, we never actually, you know, went all the way," Jamie said quickly. His voice was unsteady. "We were just kids."

"No. You were both over eighteen. Peg Jessup was under the age of consent. Do you understand what that means? You have admitted to fooling around with a fifteen year old girl, when you were eighteen. There is also a jail sentence for sexual relations with a minor."

Loud protestations followed, but Maddern spoke louder. "Quiet!"

The two boys subsided.

"Now, I want the truth. All of it. Particularly if you wish to have a chance to avoid a charge of perjury and interfering with a minor."

When York had taken their handwritten and signed statements, denying that Peg Jessup had ever led them on but had always cursed them, kicked them away or run off, they had also implicated Ed Brownley, someone with a known grudge towards Peg Jessup. They too were warned that they could be considered accessories to murder if the dangerous man who was freed, went after Peg Jessup.

They joined the two girls in the other room.

Maddern called downstairs to get the duty constable, to type the statements. He was warned that the eight others, waiting downstairs, were getting restless.

"Let their imaginations haunt them," Maddern said. "I will be laying charges of perjury on all of them. And other charges on the lads we had up here. I will come down shortly to get some of the others."

Much later, when Mike had been home from work several hours, York called at the boarding house. He suggested a drive, as he wanted to talk to Mike privately.

When York had pulled into an out of town picnic spot by the river, he began. "This is unofficial. Of those we had in, all have been charged with perjury. Some may get off with a warning, or a bond. The main ones will have a harder time. We picked up the rest of the group – those living outside Matlock. Same basic story. They were paid to give a defamatory deposition. Each was approached by either Ed Brownley or Libby Falconer."

"How did anyone get close to those two? Aren't they both locked up?"

York shrugged. "King has contacts throughout Melbourne underworld, and probably informants where ever those two are."

"As much as I am glad that they have admitted lying, how is this going to help Peg?"

"Well, for a start, we have enough evidence that the perjury accusation against her will be withdrawn. We have identified the agent who spoke to all these –"

"Liars," Mike interrupted. "But King got free!"

"I can't tell you details, but it is likely not for long."

"I hope you are right."

"Now, Vic has a task for you," York distracted him.

"I'm listening."

York explained about the effects that had been impounded from Ida Jessup's house. "Peg started to go through them, but was interrupted. Vic thinks that you will have an idea of what is likely to be important."

"When?" Mike didn't need to think. He was already thinking of Peg as his sister, even if he couldn't positively confirm it.

"I will come and get you tomorrow. Eight o'clock."

Chapter 22

"Jack, what brings you here?" Megane Blair greeted her brother.

"I thought you might be able to help me," Jack Everard, now calling himself Jack Casey, surprised her.

"Me?" she laughed. "Do you need help in your dirty old mine?"

"No, Meg. This is more serious. I am trying to keep your granddaughter alive."

"I don't have…Jack? What are you saying?"

"Margaret's daughter was born alive and survived."

She glanced to where her husband had his home office. "David said—"

"I know what he said," Jack cut her off. "And I don't want to hear it from you."

Jack saw the tears forming in her sister's eyes.

"Is it that chit who was pretending to be her daughter?" Megane then demanded. "Some ex-con running a con job."

"David is a brilliant businessman, but his people skills are abysmal," Jack said bluntly. "And his attempt to have those damned shares confiscated from the young woman, was very quickly denied."

From his jacket pocket, he drew out a birth certificate. "That young woman was born addicted to heroin. No one expected her to survive. She was raised by a whore, but that woman looked after the child for her friend's sake. She looked after those shares in trust for the daughter, and did not use any of the money for herself. The girl grew up in near poverty. The opposite of what we did."

"Why are you telling me this? She is still somebody's bastard."

"Not surprisingly, she is not in the least bit interested in claiming blood relationship with you or David. However, if not for her, David's business empire would be ruined, not just wobbly, and your grandson might be dead. I expected better of you, Meg."

"What is it you want? I don't want anything to do with her."

"Like I said, she'd rather you and David went to hell. What might impress you is that she has been pivotal in bringing to light evidence of who was really responsible for your daughter's debauching and death."

"She ran off—"

"And what did David do to try to compromise?" Jack demanded.

Megane went silent, finally saying, "She was running around with that dope-pushing muso."

"Yes, she had met Ian, and they were in love."

"She was engaged to Justin!"

"She never loved him, Meg. You and David virtually threw her at him. Shhh! Listen."

Megane gestured to the couch and sat herself in a chair.

"Ian was set up. Someone wanted him out of the way. It wasn't Justin. His being the arresting officer was coincidence. He was just doing his duty."

"Jack, Margaret was like a daughter to you too. You are just trying to—"

"I said…Listen! Even back then, someone saw a chance to get at her inheritance. The shares, her jewellery, her trust fund. Once Ian was out of the picture, this person turned her into a whore, by getting her hooked on drugs. She literally, had no one to turn to for help."

Casey ignored his sister's sob.

"That man has been successfully hiding for over thirty years. It was his favourite whore, Adelaide Swan, who befriended Margaret and after she died, looked after her child. She tricked that man for over twenty years. Now, if that child had died, she wouldn't have been in a position to see this man, or to learn things from Adelaide Swan, about him. We now believe that we know who he has been in public life all this time. That is where you could help us. Will you?"

"Will I have to say anything in court?"

"For now, if you know anything, a written statement will suffice."

"What do you want to know?"

"You were friends with Alida Costigan, weren't you?"

"Yes. Are you saying—"

"I'm not saying anything," Jack stressed.

"We were friends all through school. She was my chief Bridesmaid, and I was her matron of honour. We stopped seeing each other when her husband and David started opposing each other in business."

"I recall he and John knew each other from school…" Jack suggested.

"I think so, but John was some years younger."

"So, when he and Alida were going out together, did you and David socialise with them?"

"A few times. John was busy helping his father with things. He was being groomed to take over the family business."

"Can you recall what John was like then?"

"In general, impressions only."

"How long was Alida going with John before they got married?"

"A couple of years."

"Did you see Alida a lot after her marriage?"

"Not as much, but we went out every now and then."

"How was she? Compared to before?"

"Jack, what do you mean?"

"Just tell me what you remember."

Megane relaxed back into the chair. Jack didn't try to hurry her.

After a time, Megane said, "She stopped wanting to go swimming. What she wore changed too. She said that John wasn't one for women wearing skimpy things. He preferred elegance. So instead of low necklines, she wore clothes with collars, or high necklines."

"Did you think that odd?"

"At the time, but Alida said, that John had to be businesslike, sober, mature, now that he was married and running the business. He didn't object to bikinis before that."

Jack was trying not to suggest ideas to his sister, but what he was up to was not easy to prompt.

"Do you know if there was anything distinctive about John Costigan before he was married?"

"He was handsome," Meganne said at once. Then she stopped to think.

"He had a limp. Alida said that he had hurt his hip in an accident at school. They put a pin in it. Why? Have they found a body?"

"Why did you think that?" Jack asked the question as if it had surprised him, and his sister had not just made an unexpected leap of logic.

"Well, when they started doing that audit of David's companies. He said that Costigan had gone into hiding."

"As far as I know, your husband's business rival is still around somewhere. You mentioned a limp."

"Yes. After their honeymoon in France, when they came back, he wasn't limping. Alida said he'd found a great physio."

"Interesting," Jack murmured.

"You know, Jack, it is almost like you are saying that the person Alida married wasn't John Costigan. But it had to be. He looked just the same."

Jack said mildly, "What do you think of that idea?"

"It's preposterous. Who else could it have been? But…" Megane paused, as if something else came back to her. "At the wedding, I remembered thinking that he had aged during the previous week. I recall asking him if he was nervous. He just said that marriage was a big step. Alida said later, that he'd been in bed most of the previous week with a bad stomach bug. It may have been that. I just thought he looked older."

"Did his wedding suit still fit him properly?" Jack asked.

"What?"

"If he had been ill, and lost weight, it might have been loose on him."

"I don't recall that. I still have photos from the wedding somewhere."

"Can you find them up?"

"What for?"

"Meg, find them for me and don't mention our conversation to anyone. Not even to David."

"Will you explain all this one day?"

"Yes, I promise. For now, if anyone learns of what I was asking, young Megan Blair will be in danger. I will see myself out."

Meganne stood quickly, catching Casey before he could move more than a step.

"I want to meet her."

"When this is over," Jack told her. He didn't point out her abrupt change of sentiment.

Chapter 23

Mike brought a small satchel of items with him from Matlock, and turned up at his father's place. When greeted, he made an assessment of Ian's sobriety and made his comment once they were both behind the closed door.

"The bastard thinks he's free, and invincible. It will make his inevitable fall, all the harder."

It seemed to be the right thing to say.

"What've you got there?" Ian noticed the satchel.

"Stuff Old Jack Casey wanted," Mike said, being deliberately misleading. "Is he here?"

"Nah! Off visiting his stuck up relatives."

Mike didn't have to ask who. He joked, "That's the trouble about family. They can sneak up on you without warning."

His father gave a snorting laugh.

Mike went on, "So, what's happening on the music scene?"

"You mean, what's that Megan doing?" Ian guessed. "Don't rightly know. Since the other day, she's not been around. Carson is playing coy, as is that manager of his."

"Aren't they meant to start a week long gig at Festival Hall?" He wasn't letting on that he did know where Megan and Jack were.

"That has been postponed, new date to be advised. People can get a refund or wait for the new dates. So far, most people are hanging on. The first three shows were sold out."

Mike whistled. "That's great. Any idea when Old Casey will be back?"

"When he is sick of his sister's airs and graces, or Blair kicks him out." Ian shrugged. "Want to do some practice together?"

Mike was surprised and pleased. "Yeah, okay."

"Huh! I didn't think you'd be so keen. Thought you'd want to get back to your bird."

Jack Casey arrived back just as they were finishing one of Ian's old songs."

He began clapping. "Well, the next generation has it and the old one hasn't lost it."

145

"How are the unspeakables?" Ian asked.

"Only Megane, and for once, she has been useful. For her sake, I hope she does keep her mouth shut as I asked."

"I don't think she's the one to be worried about. It's Blair who sounds off before engaging his brain," Ian commented accurately.

"So, Mike. What have you got for me?"

"Bag of stuff from Ida's place that might be useful. Have you seen Megan?"

"Ah, no. Not since the trial. Must have been sent somewhere until we see how the wind blows."

"Good idea, I suppose. Probably that's why she won't be performing for a bit."

"Likely," Casey agreed. "Show me what you've got."

"Want a drink, you old joker," Ian asked, going off.

"Later, Ian. I have to go out again." Casey waited for Ian to be out of the room before asking Mike, "How is he?"

"Not too bad," Mike gave his opinion. "Megan still has him obsessed."

"Hmm. Alright. I have a few things for you to do, lad. Taylor started reading some of the old journals of Ida Jessup. I'm told there are more in your stash. He wants them. Also, all the old letters. He suggests that we let Ian read all the ones from his lost love. The ones that never got sent."

Mike frowned.

"What's the matter, lad?"

"I don't know how he will take them."

"Have you read them?"

"No. The few I glanced at, didn't seem to have any useful value," Mike admitted. "At the time, anyway. It's just that I don't know what might be in them. And…I'm losing track of who I have told what about certain matters."

"What in particular, lad? I do know all that's been found."

"The motel?" Mike asked and he saw Casey nod.

"I haven't heard him maundering about it, but he is pretty certain that our Megan is his lost love's child. He is keeping that to himself, because the father could be anyone."

"I know. It is the most likely thing and I had to come out and say it."

"But you don't believe it?"

"Jack, I can't explain it, but from when I first met her, at your place, I have been comfortable about her. I don't mean like a girlfriend. Just a friend. She doesn't try to treat me as a male object."

Casey chuckled faintly. "I shouldn't be telling you this, but Maddern and

York have put the fear of hell into those lying…you know who I mean."

"So, the perjury charge will be withdrawn?" Mike asked. "What about the trial? Will it be made void?"

"That's out of my hands. Let's say, that the police are in no rush to pick her up. When can you get that other stuff?"

Mike checked his watch. "This arvo, if we hurry."

"Good. I'll come with you and you can drop me off at the house afterwards."

Mike collected everything else that might be useful, and repacked those things in one of the packs. Now, only the clothes, and the cases remained. He locked up again, and wondered if he could take the rest to store at Ian's place. No, he decided. If Ian saw and recognised the clothes, it might depress him further.

At the mansion, the door was not opened by Taylor's 'man', but by Justin. "He gestured them both in."

"The Old Man is not here," Justin told them. "He's in at Russel Street for meetings and he wants to visit the forensics lab. Have you brought what he wanted? The journals, photos, letters?"

Mike nodded.

"Have you read any of the stuff?" Justin asked.

"No. I had thought that Megan should read the letters."

"Not until the Old Man gets back."

The phone rang, Justin automatically noted the time, as he went to answer it. His monosyllabic replies, as he wrote the message, were unhelpful to the listeners.

He had time to comment, "At the end of the trial, King ducked out of sight. He brushed past the media, trying to hide his face, and got into a waiting car and went off. There are watchers at various places, in case he turns up there. However, I believe he has places we still don't know about. We may not have traced all his names, either."

"All? How many does he have?" Mike was startled.

"The one he grew up with, the one he uses now, the one for the account where the rent from his mother's house goes, another on the account for what his boss pays him. We also think that there might be another that he uses for official purposes, like tax."

"Right!" Mike shook his head, amazed. "Is Jack here?"

Justin ignored the question. The phone rang again. "Just wait here."

Casey took himself off, but Mike asked to watch TV, and was told to, "Keep the volume low."

Nothing on any of the channels really grabbed his attention, but watching it was better than doing nothing. Every time the phone rang, and it was often enough to be annoying, he started. Then he would strain to hear what Justin was saying into the phone. He had hoped, that if Jack were in the house, he'd come down. But, perhaps, he had been told to stay out of sight.

The late night news flash, woke him from a light doze. Justin heard the distinctive preliminary tones and came at a run catching the announcer's first words. He swore creatively, and when the on-scene reporter came on, Mike recognised the place and began listening as hard as Justin.

"A police raid on a house in Port Melbourne resulted in the arrest of Oswald 'Ozzie' Berry, a man wanted for questioning about a number of recent unexplained explosions. Two policemen narrowly escaped injury when they tripped an explosive device intended to collapse an old cess pit on the property. A second man, seen at the house, escaped.

"How the hell did they find out about that?" Justin asked the air.

"Who?" Mike asked. "The guys they arrested, or the media?"

"The media."

"Well, if there was an explosion, one of the neighbours might have," Mike suggested. "And if the police were preparing a raid…the neighbours might have noticed."

"Yes. That's true. Only those immediately around the property were evacuated. So, no one around will know that we found something."

"What?" Mike asked, but Justin Taylor remained mute. Instead, Mike put together what he did know and guessed. Araldo Ricci, now known as Harry King, owns the place. The junk was probably hiding something…. bodies. That had to be it.

When the news report finished, Justin went back to what he'd been doing and Mike dozed off again until he was woken by the front door opening and the sound of half a dozen voices.

Eugene Taylor spoke over the babble. "We will debrief in my study."

The four officers stopped talking, and Taylor came over to Mike. "Show me what you have."

Mike obeyed, keeping his voice low. Then he watched as Taylor did a flick through the bag. He found the bundled letters and pulled some out at random. "Do you think these are from the girl to your father?"

"The few we glanced at, some were and some were to or from other people."

"Okay, Lad. You get off to wherever you are staying tonight. Come back in the morning. You may have to wait around until I decide what to do with these. First though, I need you to sign a statement of providence. Where you got them, where you kept them, and that you have passed them on to me. I will just get the form and come back."

He waited while Mike wrote and signed the statement. He read it, noting the additional travels of the item.

"Sir, I saw an item on the news...."

Taylor gave him a faint smile. "You did good work, lad. Even though we believe that King was there and got away. I will accept that an attempt made to blow up the evidence, is a sign of a worried conscience. He was, however, three days too late."

"You found something," Mike voiced his guess. "Bodies?"

"We have put an end to six, 35 year old missing child cases. That information will be released when I am ready."

"Won't this put King into hiding?"

"Perhaps, but it is just the first of many nasty surprises. He is going to be on the wrong foot and apt to make mistakes. Now, not a word of this, lad."

Mike hoped that The Old Man knew he was putting Megan in danger. No, he did realise that. It was probably why Jack and Megan were somewhere secret.

<h1 style="text-align:center">Chapter 24</h1>

Louisa Westcott drove slowly towards Reggie Costigan's place. This was the inevitable moment of truth. Now, he wouldn't need Stan anymore, and the truth was, she wasn't sure that she wanted Reggie anymore. The doctor's test had come back positive. She was eight weeks pregnant. Other tests had picked up other things – several illegal drugs.

She had been lectured about how the drugs might affect her child. The woman had not believed her when she had denied ever taking drugs. Thinking on it, if she had been given them, the only possible place was Reggie's.

Stan had tried to tell her, but why hadn't she listened? Why indeed? Stan was a stranger, and she had known Reggie for over two years. Stan was wanting to keep getting the perks he'd been hired for. She had thought he had been playing with her mind, and she had been a bitch when they weren't enjoying sex. He hadn't got angry with her, all he had done was stop her drinking so much of Reggie's expensive plonk. He said it could harm a child, if she got pregnant and might even prevent conception. Reggie kept pushing the wine on her, every time after she'd been with Stan. Then he'd be all over her, doing whatever it was he did to get her so hot for him.

She pulled over to the curb, not far from the Costigan mansion. She needed to think. The week after his mate King had been arrested, when she had kept away from Reggie, she had been feeling dreadful. In fact, when Reggie had called, she had just started feeling better.

Part of her had been thrilled when her period still hadn't come. Part of her was angry because her father was going to make her wait another five years for her inheritance. Actually, no he wasn't. If he lived at least another five years before dying, she wouldn't.

Louisa caught herself…Why was she thinking that Daddy would die soon? She didn't want him to die.

Other things came back to her mind. What the former policeman had told her. She should never have gone back to Reggie. She had been going to break off their engagement – but before she'd had the right moment, he'd pushed more wine at her, and her intentions had flown out the window. Then all he had been interested in was her cycle. Lucky for her, he hadn't asked the right questions to get her to blurt out about her father's trust idea.

On the phone, he had insisted on a celebration, talked of him bringing her to the Gold Coast, announcing their engagement there, during the V8 races. Everything, just as she had wanted it….

What if she was going to have a girl? Would that matter to Reggie? Would he decide to keep Stan around, to try for a boy next time? Without really thinking about it, she started driving again, her body craving Reggie's caresses.

At the gate, she stopped. Normally, they were open and she just had to drive through. This time, she had to get out and push them open, and decided not to bother closing them again.

Everything seemed normal as she parked at the end of the drive and walked back to the front door. A curtain in a window near her parking place twitched. One of the servants, she decided, and expected the door to be opened when she got there.

A moment later, she sensed someone behind her. A hand closed over her mouth and a voice told her, "Police, Miss Westcott. Please make no sound."

She was drawn back to the side of the house and forced to wait in an area of shadow.

The front door opened, spilling light. "Lou? Where are you?" Reggie called out eagerly.

A dozen armed men suddenly erupted from hiding, calling for Reggie to put his hands up. He began yelling his innocence, as he was frisked, and restrained. All but two of the police, clad in bulletproof vests, poured into the house. Reggie was taken out of her sight.

From her vantage, she could tell that lights were going on all over the house. She tried to get free, but she was still being held and the hand was still on her mouth. She wanted to warn Stan, but it was too late. She saw him, being hustled outside, was elated when he broke free and began to run, and wanted to cry when an officer brought him down with a rugby tackle. They weren't gentle with him, yanking his arms behind him, and dragging him to a police divvy van that was just drawing up. They shoved his head down, so he didn't hit it going in.

Guiltily, she wriggled until the officer released her, and tried to see where they had taken Reggie. She glared at the constable.

"Take it easy, Miss. I don't think you will want the media to know you were involved in this."

"Part of what? What is Reggie supposed to have done?"

"I am afraid, that I can't discuss that, Miss. Why don't you come and sit in the sergeant's car?"

What seemed like an hour later, Louisa saw Reggie being escorted to another police car. He wasn't handcuffed. She wondered what was going on, why the house was still lit up everywhere, and wide open. Now she could see that the lights were also on in the wing that was never used.

The van where Stan had been taken had gone off a long time ago. Probably taking him back to jail.

When he had been introduced to her, it had been as Stanley Simmons. She'd had no reason to think that he might be violent. Time had proved him to be gentle, or had Reggie been drugging him, too?

Even when she had been told by that old policeman that he was really Stan Jessup, the penny hadn't dropped. Now it had. She'd heard the police radio, picking up the call being made that they were bringing in the escapee, Stan Jessup. She would bet that the media would speculate that he had been holding Reggie hostage, rather than being shielded by him. It's what Reggie would claim, she was certain.

The sergeant finally returned to his car, told her guard to drive, and didn't acknowledge her until she asked, "Where am I going? I haven't done anything."

"We will need to ask you some questions, Miss Westcott, and have you sign a statement."

"Questions about what?" Louisa persisted.

"When we get to where we are going," she was told. Her stomach began to churn. If they weren't telling her, did they think she had done something illegal? Would they believe that she hadn't?

Even when they turned into the driveway of a big house, she didn't relax. There were as many police cars here as there had been at Reggie's.

The constable helped her from the car. When he heard her moan as her stomach cramped, he asked, "Are you all right, Miss?"

"I feel sick."

"I'll get someone to help you," the constable promised. "As soon as we get inside."

He was as good as his word, he spoke to the servant who opened the door. It was only then, that she recognised where she was.

Eugene Taylor's man saw the pale face, and the beads of sweat on the woman's brow. What was needed was a policewoman, but there had been none included in the raid. No one else had the time to care for her. He used his own judgement. There was only one woman in the house, she was meant to stay out of sight. It was a bit of a risk, but…

"Come through here, we have a guest room. The lady can wait in there and I will fetch someone to assist her. Constable, if you would be so kind as to stay with her?"

When someone knocked on the door, Jack turned from the window to answer it. He gestured to Peg to get out of sight. When Johnson hurried in, something frilly clutched in his hand, asking for Peg, Jack guessed that something unexpected had occurred.

Peg emerged from the en-suite.

"Here, put this on. I need someone to look after a lady guest. The master will have me skinned for this, but I have no choice. Now. You are to pretend to be a maid. Offer the lady whatever help she needs. Ask her no questions about anything else, and tell her nothing, understand."

"Yes. Okay." Peg took the frilly material from him and realised that it was an apron.

"At least, what you have on is neat," Johnson babbled.

Peg glanced at Jack, who shrugged and waved her out. Johnson hurried her downstairs, giving further instructions. "There is a small guest room, down the passage from the lounge. I have the lady there. If she needs to lie down, she can use the bed, and it has an en-suite."

As soon as she arrived, Peg understood, Johnson's haste. The stranger was sitting, but looked to be on the verge of throwing up. Instinct took over, and she relieved the green looking constable, and didn't see his look of recognition.

"Hi, I'm Megan. Come through to the en-suite."

They made it there, just in time. Louisa only made it as far as the basin. Peg let her empty her stomach, while she looked for a face washer and a mug for water.

She filled the mug with water from the tap when she was able to get close, and dampened the face washer. She offered both to the woman, who wasn't much older than she was.

"I'm sorry," Louisa managed to get out.

"These things happen," Peg said neutrally. "Feel better?"

"A little. Can you bring a chair in here?"

"Sure."

When Louisa was sitting, close to the basin, and leaning her head on the cool porcelain, Peg asked, "When did you eat last?"

"This morning. I haven't felt really hungry all day. I really don't want anything, thanks."

"Well, if you change your mind, I am sure that something can be found," Peg told her. "And, you might feel a little better if you give your face a wash."

That suggestion wasn't taken up either, and Peg was running out of ideas. When there was a knock on the outer door of the suite, she studied Louisa for a moment, then went to answer it.

Johnson came in. "We have a police woman coming. She should be here in 10-15 minutes. Do you think that Miss Westcott will be better by then?"

Peg spoke in a normal voice. "I think she is starting to feel better. Will I ask her?"

Johnson shook his head. "I will come back then."

Peg touched his arm and said quietly. "I don't know what caused the nausea, but she's eaten nothing since breakfast."

Jack continued to watch the activity outside the house. He had the idea that his grandfather was orchestrating the movements of the guests, as police cars came and went. He'd seen Reg Costigan emerge from one car that had been sitting there for over five minutes. A young woman, probably the one Peg had gone to help, had come in quite quickly. He wondered if Peg would learn anything from her. Before Costigan had arrived, there had been two men, servants most likely, and the man-handled Stan Jessup.

Haldane and some of the other OCTF officers were probably questioning them. Jack assumed that the questioning was being done here, instead of at Russell Street because the Task Force was headquartered at the mansion. Seeing Stan Jessup though, had surprised him. Surely, he would have gone direct to be returned to prison. Or would he? If he was playing one of his grandfather's games with Reg Costigan. Stan has originally escaped to avoid his father's plan for him – had he agreed to do it to find out what it was? For his grandfather? Interesting.

The activity had settled down, and the cars coming and going were possibly bringing reports or following up other information. Whatever had gone down that evening had been big. He itched to know the details, besides, obviously, a raid on the Costigan mansion.

With nothing else to do, Jack kept watching out the window. He saw another car drive up, but it wasn't a police car. The driver did not get out immediately, and when he did, his manner was furtive. He glanced around, and up at the façade of the mansion, before heading for the side entrance. He passed under some of the exterior lights and Jack saw his face.

"Avery! Why is he here? He was kicked off the task force."

Apart from being told to keep out of sight, it never occurred to Jack to rush down and confront him, for surely he would be spotted and challenged. What worried him was whether Peg was well out of casual sight. He would mention Avery being there later, just in case. He had better not let the man see him. Costa, if that was why Avery had come, probably wanted him as well.

Jack checked his watch again. It wasn't even eight o'clock yet. Another police car. A policewoman emerged and Jack breathed easier. She was surely here to take over from Peg, who would be sent back up here with him. Five minutes passed. Still no Peg, and Avery had not come out. His paranoia was starting to rise. He had been told to leave the phone alone, but now he disobeyed, but on carefully lifting the receiver, he heard voices and lowered it.

Peg decided that Policewoman Stewart, who she recognised, cannot have been well briefed. She had come into the suite and on seeing her had asked, "Peg Jessup, isn't it."

She had immediately replied, "No, I'm Megan. Are you here to look after Miss Westcott?"

Stewart must have decided not to challenge the different name, for she asked, "How is she?"

"I think, feeling better. I left her sipping water. I will take you in."

"No, that's fine. Miss Westcott and I have met. You should go back to your duties."

She had nodded, and turned to go, but actually paused before leaving to hear how the policewoman greeted the other woman. Friendly. Not like the guest was in trouble.

Peg considered ditching the frilly apron, and then ducking around to the stairs to go up. As she emerged, two figures turned into the passage – Eugene Taylor and one of the task force.

"Why are you here?" Taylor demanded, breaking off his conversation.

Peg looked at them, and caught a furtive movement beyond them. "Sir, your regular girl needed time off. I was sent here to help."

Taylor frowned, but only said, "Why wasn't I told?"

"I thought you had been, Sir. I have been relieved by Policewoman Stewart."

"Get back to where you are meant to be. No, go the other way."

"Yes, Sir." Peg recalled that there was another set of stairs at the other end of the passage. Jack had called them the 'servant's stairs'.

The other stairs were near one entrance to the long kitchen, and Peg didn't think twice about seeing a figure standing there. She assumed that the man was on guard, to keep the servants away from the police activity. Or, she amended, in case the dangerous Stan Jessup gave trouble. She caught a glance of her brother being hustled, roughly, out of a room and towards a door leading outside.

For an instant, he looked her way, seemed startled, but was forced to keep moving. Once he was out of sight, she walked back upstairs. At the top, she looked down, but the guard was gone.

Jack, still looking out the window, only glanced her way before returning his attention outside.

"What's so fascinating?" Peg asked as she locked their door.

"I thought I saw Avery."

"Who?"

"Avery. He was on the OCTF until recently. Grandfather had him kicked off it. I don't trust him, but I am sure I saw him go in, quite a while ago."

"Maybe he is back on it?" Peg joined him at the window.

They didn't have any lights on in the room, so it was unlikely they would be noticed looking down on the now lit front paved area.

"No. There he is – coming from around the side." Jack pointed.

"Did you see Stan being brought out?"

"No. Why?"

"I saw that guy, Avery, on guard near the rear kitchen door when I was heading back here. That was while I saw Stan being taken somewhere. They were being really rough with him."

"Did he take notice of you?"

Peg knew he meant Avery. "No idea. I had this silly, frilly apron on, paying a maid. Jack, are you being paranoid again?"

"Yeah. I am. I need to tell grandfather about him, but I can't while everyone is here. I don't trust him not to have us locked up in some watch house if we can't stay here. Anyway, learn anything?"

Peg told him all she had seen and heard, and Jack added his own ideas.

"I reckon they raided Costigan's place, hoping to get Reggie's father. I don't think he was there though, unless he was taken directly to Russell Street."

"Who knows? I am sure we won't be told." Peg removed the apron and went over to flop on the bed.

Chapter 25

Eugene Taylor was an unexpected visitor to their room late that night. Jack hadn't started to get ready for bed, but Peg had changed into the shorts and tee-shirt she usually slept in.

"Sir," Jack greeted. "It's late. What can we do for you?"

"You told Johnson that you had seen Avery," he said once the door was closed again. "What do you know?"

Jack settled his grandfather in a chair, and perched on the arm of another. He repeated what he had earlier told Johnson and Peg added what she had seen.

To Peg, he asked, "Do you think he had a good look at you?"

"I had that frilly apron on so he may have thought me a maid. I don't know if you usually have one or not, and if he knows that. What I can't be sure of, is if he heard WPC Stewart greet me as Peg Jessup. When you saw me earlier, I thought I'd seen someone loitering beyond you. It might have been him. He could have cut through the kitchen to where I saw him later."

Taylor's expression was grim. "I will have to have you moved. I will organise that first thing tomorrow. It is vile luck that fool Avery came here and saw you."

"I hope you weren't too hard on Johnson. Miss Westcott was in a bad way," Peg inserted.

"Johnson is used to my testy ways," Taylor softened enough to admit. "Avery was told to keep away. Obviously, King has a stronger hold on him than I realised."

"So you think King sent him here? To do what?" Jack asked.

"King or his boss," Taylor confirmed. "For whatever reason."

"Were you hoping he'd be at Costigan's place?" Jack asked. "John Costigan, I mean."

"I was not expecting it. The raid was timed with a number of concerns in mind. The company squad is still unable to trace some of the cash flow of Costigan's companies. We had a tip off about a hidden cellar and some locked rooms there."

The grim smile was a give-away that the tip had proved correct. "The other reason was that we knew Stan Jessup was there and it was time we brought him out."

"You knew?" Peg exclaimed. "Was he undercover for you?"

"That is one way to put it."

"Would I be able to talk to him? Where is he now? Pentridge?"

"He will be, later. That is out of my hands. He will be kept in isolation."

"Is he still here?"

"Yes. We made it seem as if he was being taken off. I didn't have time to fully debrief him. And, there is a complication, concerning Miss Westcott. Did you learn anything from her?"

"Johnson said not to ask her questions or tell her anything. Didn't she talk to WPC Stewart?"

"She did, but Miss Stewart thought she was holding back something."

"Okay…do you think I might be able to help somehow?"

Taylor smiled. "Do you feel up to playing the maid again?"

"If that's what you want. Though I doubt that she would confide any secrets to me. She would assume that I would tell you. What are you trying to find out?"

"If she is pregnant," Taylor said bluntly.

"Can't you just call in a police doctor?" Jack asked.

"She seems to be in a fragile emotional state. We couldn't get her to speak out against Reg Costigan, or even to confirm that Stan had been there on her recent visits."

"Are you saying that she knew who he was?" Jack asked. "Surely she'd wonder why Reggie had an escaped prisoner there and not report it."

"I don't know about that, but on the day when King was arrested, Reg turfed her out. I was visiting her father when she came home. After that, yes, she knew who Stan was, and admitted that Reg was throwing them together, hoping to get her pregnant."

"That bastard!" Jack spoke before Peg could. "I bet I know who put him up to that."

"So do I. I think Costa wanted to do that with my mother. He stole Aunt Ida's inheritance, and I think that's what this is about."

"I agree," Taylor said. "I had hoped that I had warned the girl off, but apparently not."

"And you haven't proved that Costigan is Costa?" Jack challenged.

"When we get the man we know as John Costigan, he will be charged with murder," Taylor told them. "And you will keep that to yourself."

"Murder of Costa?" Peg was confused.

"No. The murder of the real John Costigan, who, as you surmised was the Gianni Costa's half-brother. When the patio at the property once owned by Luke Simmons was dug up, we found human remains. I have just received proof that it was John Costigan. At one of the other houses still held in Costa's name, we found more remains. Those, we think, might be of Albert Jessup."

"Shit!" Peg swore. "Are you sure that charge will stick?"

"Leave that to the task force. There are other charges likely too."

"Those bastards like to repeat things," Jack growled. "What's happening with King? Were you after him the other day?"

"We had a tip off, and did the raid. We were not sure if we would get anyone. However, the result was most satisfactory and confirmed the importance of that place."

"It's like pulling teeth," Jack growled. "Mike hinted at something about King, but wouldn't tell me. Was that it?"

"Yes, Lad. Your friend found where King lived as a child. He was Araldo Ricci then. His father was Luigi Costa."

Peg's eyes blazed. "How did you find that out?"

"Didn't the Shaw girl tell you? She tricked King and got his prints."

"He had a juvenile record?" Jack asked.

"No, but his prints were on file as a person of interest in some indecent assault cases on young girls. He either got smarter, or stopped after he was 14."

"He didn't stop," Peg said flatly.

"No. We found the 30 year old remains of six girls in the cess pit at the property."

"I hope you can pin that on the bastard," Peg said "But it sounds circumstantial."

"It is another brick in the wall," Taylor said. "And that information is confidential as well."

Peg returned to the topic of Reggie's girlfriend. "I think you should have the police doctor look at her. If you thought she would drop Reggie, and didn't, it might be that he is drugging her to be compliant."

"Perhaps you should drop in on her before you go to bed?"

"I will. If I can get her to trust me, can I tell her a bit about me?"

"Specifically?" Taylor enquired.

"That I was a whore's brat, born addicted to heroin, and my mother was once an heiress."

"Yes. That might wake her up," Taylor agreed, thoughtfully. "If she asks if you are Peg Jessup, she may open up about Stan."

"I reckon you could go at Reggie for procuring," Jack inserted a snide remark.

"Wouldn't that make her a prostitute, Jack? She's the victim here. Is she still awake?"

Peg got dressed again in the black outfit she had worn earlier, found where she had thrown the frilly apron, and went down to the guest room being used by Louisa Westcott.

She knocked and called out, "It's the maid," and heard a muted, "Come in."

Louisa only had the dim bedside lamp on, and in that light, she looked dreadful. She was shivering, even though the room wasn't cold and she was still fully dressed.

"Can you get anything to make me feel better?" she asked.

"What's the matter?" Peg asked.

When Louisa described how she was feeling, Peg felt herself nodding. She had seen a number of girls at Meredan who were having drug withdrawal symptoms, and decide that her supposition had been right.

"Have you felt like this before?"

"Yes. A couple of weeks ago."

"What helped then?"

"I took something for the aches, but the rest went away after a week."

"I can probably find some aspirin or Panadol. Have you stopped throwing up?"

"No. The little I ate, came back up. I think that is because of everything that happened today."

"Maybe to that," Peg agreed. "I can get you some headache stuff, but if you want my opinion, you ought to see a doctor."

"I saw one today."

"What did he say?"

"It wasn't about this."

"Perhaps you should go back to him."

Louisa just shook her head. "I think she is useless. She did some blood tests and I think the results had got mixed up."

"Go to another doctor and get a second opinion," Peg suggested. "It sounds like she upset you. Did she reckon you were pregnant or something?"

Louisa's shivers got worse.

"She tried to tell me that I'd been taking drugs," Louisa blurted, deliberately not answering Peg's question. "I haven't, so the result is ridiculous."

"If you think that you can't be taking drugs because you didn't choose to take any, then you have lived a bloody sheltered life."

"What do you mean?"

"I mean, I just connected as to who you are. You are Reg Costigan's current girl. My mate likes watching the V8s, and the after race interviews."

"So?"

"Well, wasn't there some hooha about him and drugs and drinking?"

"It wasn't true," was the instant defence of her boyfriend.

"Well, I guess you'd know better than me." Peg shrugged. "So, you reckon that doctor was completely wrong? Then get another test done."

Louisa didn't comment immediately. She might have been thinking.

"I'll go get the aspirin," Peg said.

"No. Will you stay? Talking to someone helps."

"But not talking to WPC types?" Peg inserted casually.

"Did Miss Stewart recognise you?" Louisa asked, "It sounded as if she did."

"Um, well, she thought she did." Peg deliberately tried to imply she was hiding something. "I'm using a different name now."

"Does the cop who lives here know who you are?"

"That I am an ex-con? Yup! But he can't do a thing about it because his grandson and I got married as soon as I was old enough."

"So you are not really a maid?"

"Oh, today I was. Helping out with all the comings and goings. You know, work for idle hands. Are you cold?"

"I can't stop shivering."

"I will see if I can find another blanket in here," Peg offered. She went to check the wardrobe, which gave her some moments to try to think of a way to bring the conversation back to where she wanted it.

After wrapping the blanket around Louisa, she said, "I'll go get the stuff for the headache, and if Johnson is still up, I will ask about a warm drink. I won't be long, and I will come back."

The door to Eugene Taylor's study was shut, and some of the task force officers were lounging in chairs in the formal area. They all saw her, gave her severe looks, but said nothing as she kept heading for the kitchen. Johnson was still up, he had a cup of something next to him, and was sitting by the table, reading a book.

"Does the Old Man know you are out?"

"Yes and no. He asked me to look in on the girl. You can tell him I have had no luck so far, but I have the feeling that she is suffering withdrawal from something. I am not sure if the nausea is related to that or not. However, she also felt this way a few weeks ago. I came for headache stuff and a hot drink for her."

Johnson rose, and went to a cupboard over the fridge. He returned with a small bottle. "Two only. I will bring the drink when it is ready."

"Thanks. If you see the Old Man, tell him that I wonder if she should be allowed to see Stan. I will keep trying to find out about her but all I have learnt so far is evasion."

Peg quickly repeated what Louisa had said to her. Johnson waved her off.

Once back with Louisa, Peg helped her take the tablets, and asked, "Will you be going home in the morning?"

"I don't know why I was even brought here, or why they raided Reggie's place. I want to see him. Is he here?"

Even though she knew the answer, she pretended she didn't. A maid would not be privy to such things. So she said, "I guess the Old Man wanted to talk to you, has he?"

"No. Only Miss Stewart."

"Well, he probably will in the morning. Oh, and Johnson will be bringing you a hot drink."

When the knock came on the door, Peg answered it, expecting Johnson, but it wasn't. Taylor, Stan and two OCTF officers were in the passage. Wordlessly, she opened the door wide, and let them enter. Her eyes stayed on Stan. Her brother recognised her, forced a mirthless grin, but said nothing.

He was handcuffed, with wrists behind him, and held by the officers.

Taylor was apologising to Louisa for disturbing her, but claimed time constraints. He asked how she was, but her eyes had gone to Stan and she probably wasn't even hearing Taylor. She had started to rise, but must have realised he was restrained, and she wouldn't be allowed near him.

It would have been clear to anyone that could read body language that Louisa was in no way frightened by Stan Jessup, even though she demanded,

"Where is Reggie?"

It was late. Taylor was tired, and he didn't soften his words. "Reginald Costigan is being held on charges of aiding and abetting an escaped prisoner, having drugs of dependence in his possession, supplying drugs of dependence. We need to speak to you to decide if we will add procuring girls for the purpose of sex to the charges."

"Reggie wasn't having sex with other girls," Louisa insisted.

Stan, at a nod from Taylor, said gently, "What about you and me, Louisa?"

"I agreed to that."

"Would you have if he had not drugged you that first time?" Stan asked her.

Louisa stared at him with dawning horror.

Taylor added a sharp word. "We warned you of who you had been associating with. I had hoped you would have seen sense."

Louisa gulped, as if about to be sick again, and what little colour she had in her face fled completely.

"I had intended to do that," she remembered. "But somehow, I just kept going back."

Stan spoke again. "I am sure he was drugging you. After that week, when he'd sent you away, you came back and I know you and he had an argument. Did he give you a drink? Because when I saw you next, you were all over him again."

When Louisa burst into tears, Peg would have gone to her, but Taylor's expression said clearly, "Stay where you are." This was the hard, implacable ex Chief Superintendent that Jack had known.

Stan was allowed to speak again. "Lisa-Lou, they are going to be taking me back to prison, but I need to know, did I get you pregnant?"

The tears intensified, and Louisa nodded.

"So, you will be going to marry Reggie, like you wanted."

"I don't want to marry him. I want to marry you!"

Peg saw the shock on her brother's face.

"But, you don't know anything about me. I'm a criminal, an armed robber."

Before she could censor her mouth, Peg blurted. "In a pig's eye! You've never handled a gun in your life."

Taylor glared at her, but Stan gave her a wry grin. "That changes nothing, Peg." Then to Louisa he said, "How can you marry me? You are an heiress, with a good reputation. Think what your father will say."

"I don't know what he will say, but I misjudged him. He was going to let me marry Reggie if I really was set on it. And it seems I would have been just as bad off if I had. I didn't tell him that I was having second thoughts."

Stan glanced at Taylor, who said, "Miss Westcott, you would be very wise indeed to make no hasty decisions."

Somehow, even though she really had never got to know this eldest of her foster brothers, Peg wasn't surprised when he spoke. "Louisa, I will willingly admit to being the father of your child, and support it. But I cannot do much while I am still in prison."

"But I can," Peg blurted. She did not want Louisa to even consider having an abortion.

"Would you marry me?" Louisa asked.

"Willingly," Stan admitted. "And that is not just because you are beautiful, or it's the honourable thing to do. But I don't want you to rush into it. Wait until they let me out, then we can discuss it. If it is what you still want, I will be overjoyed. By then though, you may have changed your mind and decided you still want Reggie, or someone else."

Stan's two escorts gave his arms a tug towards the door. Peg sidled between the men and the door.

"Stan, if they let you, I need to get a temporary POA from you so that I can deal with probate on your mum's stuff. She left the house to you, Ned and Jasper. I'm an executor."

"What about you? Didn't she leave you anything?"

"I'm okay. Jack and I are married. If they let me visit you I will explain things then."

She moved to let the officers take her brother away, and turned to see that Taylor had seated himself in a chair and was waiting for Louisa to stop staring after Stan.

"I think, Miss Westcott, that it would be a good thing to have the police doctor check you over. I also believe that it would be best for your child, if they help you through the symptoms of drug withdrawal."

"I want to go home."

"Your father cannot look after you, Miss Westcott. He is too frail. I think that it would be wise to have you somewhere more protected for a while."

Louisa looked at Peg. "What do you think?"

"He's right. You don't want to have a child that's born an addict – like I was. They reckon that I cried all day for weeks."

"You? How do you fit into all this?"

"Well, I'm hiding out. I don't know if you read in the papers about a guy called Harry King being absolved of rape. Well, I was his victim and I don't think he is going to forgive me for having him charged and having to go to court."

Louisa began to add more facts together as Peg went on. "I was 15 the first time, and he is the father of two of my brothers, for all that they are officially called Jessup."

"Stan?"

"No. His father was some other bastard. So, like I said, I'd take up the offer of the clinic."

"So, you were a Jessup. I didn't quite hear what Miss Stewart called you."

"Were, yes. I now know who my real mother was before someone turned her into a drug addict and a whore."

Taylor then suggested to Peg, "Go and see if Johnson has the hot drinks ready, Megan. I think Miss Westcott has taken in all she can today."

Peg went off, returning with Johnson who had a tray with two mugs, a jug, a dish of marshmallows and a small jug of cream. In the short time that she had been away, Louisa must have agreed to Taylor's suggestion. For he asked Peg to stay with her until the ambulance arrived.

Once they were alone, Peg poured them both a drink, added cream and marshmallows. She noticed that Louisa had stopped shivering, and guessed that her headache had abated.

"Tell me about Stan."

Peg had to admit that she really didn't know him well, but recalled the times he'd been home and how gentle he had been with her. She mentioned his drawings too, Then she finished with, "Don't start thinking he is violent, because he is in jail for armed robbery. That was all the glib-tongued Mick Devlin's doing, and us dumb Jessups were all in his thrall. Stan has never touched a gun, not even to hunt rabbits. We didn't even know that Mick had a gun."

When Peg finally returned to her room, Jack moved from the window and gestured to the bed. It was an invitation she was more than ready for, and wasted no time getting there.

"Some of the task force must be staying here tonight," Jack told her. "There's still three police cars outside."

"I'm glad of that. I'm just surprised that all the detainees from the raid came here. I thought they would go to Russell Street."

"I think it's because this is the HQ of the Task Force," Jack reminded her, as she yawned hugely. "Did you learn anything?"

Peg had just enough energy to give him the bare facts before falling asleep.

Chapter 26

"Follow that guy in the brown shirt," she told Mike. "If you lose him, head for High Street. The State Bank."

There was a vacant parking space just past the bank and Mike pulled in. The publican had already reached the bank, so Les hopped out and went in after him. Not wanting him to feel threatened, she waited until he had deposited the previous 24 hours takings, and was walking back towards the door.

"What do you want," he demanded as Les walked towards him.

"I need to talk to you," she said in a low voice.

"Don't expect me to help you," he responded, looking like he wanted to brush past her and run. "He's right angry with you."

"He's an insane bastard," Les agreed. "He should've been put away. Must have bribed the jury, or frightened them."

"Yeah, he did. Or rather, the fat man, Costa, did. But you don't want to light his fuse just now. Be glad he's off after the bitch who accused him."

Les didn't let on that the statement worried her. "Look, can we talk?"

"What about?"

"Getting that bastard what he deserves. Wouldn't you rather he wasn't around?"

"You won't get me ratting on him to the police."

"Not asking that. Come out to my car, okay?"

The barman was as tough as they came, well able to deal with the rowdy drunks and other trouble. Yet Les had seen his dislike of King in his expression when King went off. She was sure he had been made to do illegal things.

"I won't be telling his majesty anything, nor the cops." Les assured him, and she told herself, that was technically correct. Mike would talk to the cops, if this guy knew anything useful.

Before the barman knew it, he was beside Mike's car and the door was opening.

"What's this?" The barman baulked at getting in.

"Sir, we, don't intend to hurt you," Mike said quietly. "But we don't want to talk where you might be seen."

He gave Les a head to foot glance and realised that the tight fitting top and jeans could not conceal a hidden weapon. He ducked his head and slid into the car. Les followed.

Mike drove away from the curb and took random turnings while checking in his rear vision mirror.

"I think it's okay, CB," Les said. "Nothing came out to follow us. Take the next left and pull in where you can."

The side street led down to residential houses but wasn't a main road. After five minutes, at the kerb, with no other cars going past, Mike turned the motor off.

"So, what do you want?" the barman demanded.

"I want to know where the fat man hangs out," Les told him. "I don't expect you to know, but answer this – how often did he call the pub and ask to talk to King?"

"Never whilst King was being held."

"Since then?" Mike asked. "Did he ring today or yesterday?"

The barman nodded, but sweat was beginning to run down his face.

"About what time?" Mike persisted.

"What use is that?"

"It is info that I can work on, that they won't expect to have come from you."

"About four o'clock today." The man's voice had taken on a higher pitch.

"Sir, what is making you so frightened?" Mike asked. "Did you hear something?"

Les gripped the man's arm before he could dash out of the car. He wiped his forehead with his sleeve and muttered, "It's like I said. King is to get that bitch and bring her to the fat man. She had to be alive. Able to talk."

"The police will be looking out for her," Mike assured the barman. He was certain that his friends were staying with Jack's grandfather.

"How often did the fat man ring before King's holiday?" Les asked. "I saw the fat guy at the pub before King got hauled off."

The barman was relaxing a bit. "Useta be only every now and then. Since around that time, it's been every week. I had to keep track of reports for him, and pass messages onto people."

"Did he call from a phone box?" Mike asked.

"No, at least it didn't sound like it."

"Did he call at any particular time?"

"Usually in the evening when King was around. Between six and eight."

"Local or STD?" was Mike's next question.

"Ah! Last few times, it was STD. Not today's though."

"Do you happen to recall any of the dates he called?" Mike suggested. "Les reckons your memory is amazing."

The barman recalled a couple of dates, due to other events that occurred on those days. "My memory is really only good for numbers, like who owes me what, you understand."

Les patted his arm. "Of course we do. Now, let us give you a ride back nearer the pub."

While watching the man move off like a vindictive wife was after him, Mike asked, "Do you think he knows more?"

"He's sure to," Les guessed. "But King has him terrified, and he has a wife and two kids. Will what he said help?"

"It might. We can pass all that on to Jack's grandfather in the morning."

"You will, CB. You heard me say that I don't talk to cops. Don't like the idea of that bastard going after the kid."

"Jack is with her and they have police protection," Mike assured her. "Who else do you think might know something?"

"Only a couple of the regulars," Les considered. "I overheard them commenting about the fat guy when he was there that time."

"When are they normally there?"

"Anytime from factory knock off to closing time."

"So they will be at the pub now. I don't think it is a good idea to go there."

"You sure ain't stupid, CB," Les told him. "Let's grab a newspaper and get back to your place."

"Ian only has one spare bed," Mike protested.

"We only need one. Or we could go to lover boy's place."

"No. Jack suggested that certain people might go there."

"Yeah. Right again, CB. So where will we go tonight? Your car or a motel?"

"I'll find somewhere," Mike told her.

"You gonna ring Lover Boy?"

"No. I was told to keep away. Jack said he thought something was about to go down. Let's head east and find somewhere."

The evening paper had tantalising hints to the day's police raids, but statements from Russell Street, Police HQ, were not forthcoming. All that seemed clear was that the raids were carried out by the OCTF. Mike could, in places, read between the lines, since he knew a lot of what the task force was looking at, but he revealed none of that to Les.

"Says here that they found Stan Jessup," Les told Mike. "No mention of Reg Costigan. I told you what they wanted Jessup for. Wonder if the rich bitch got pregnant?"

Mike shrugged, and used the excuse of spotting a motel, as a reason not to comment.

Despite the exercise he'd had before trying to sleep, Mike found that he couldn't because of all the 'what ifs'. The main one was 'what if Harry King got his hands on Peg?'. He hadn't told Les that he thought Peg might be his half-sister. He hadn't any proof. The only reason why he hadn't tried to go see Jack and Peg was that if he was followed, unlikely as it might be, he would lead the wrong people to them. Surely though, they would be kept safe.

He considered the Old Man, Eugene Taylor. Jack had not had much good to say about him at first, but over time, he had gained respect for the Old Man. It sounded as if Taylor had become even cannier since his official retirement. That he had been made head of the OCTF, also said a great deal.

On the verge of sleep again, Mike's mind was turning over all sorts of details, but some were sticking with him. One was that the task force HQ was Taylor's place, the second was that was most likely where Jack and Peg were and third, did they keep the records of all their investigations there?

What would happen if that place was raided and the records taken? King surely knew where the HQ was. He had Jack's uncle as a source, and that other one…Avery.

Sleep and any thought of it fled and Mike eased himself out of the bed and pulled his shorts on.

Les spoke sleepily, "What's up CB?"

"Can't sleep."

"What's bugging your brain?"

He outlined his ideas and saw Les quickly becoming alert. "Want to go and watch the place?"

"What could we do?"

"Make a ruckus if we see King."

"He'll kill us if he saw us," Mike protested, but he was reaching for the rest of his clothes.

"Only if he sees us," Les suggested slyly.

Peg woke abruptly. Jack was shaking her shoulder. "Get dressed! Fast!"

"What's up?"

"I don't know. We need to hide."

Then Peg heard a series of thuds, and quickly dragged a track suit over her sleeping shorts and t-shirt. As she put the strap of her small shoulder bag over her head, the door to their room was kicked in.

Two figures, with faces hidden by stocking masks, rushed in. One went for her even as Jack charged the other. Neither of them had time to prepare a defence. Peg struggled fiercely, twisted and tried to hit her attacker, but something hard hit her head. It didn't quite make her unconscious, and she saw Jack go down, and heard the warning, "Move or come after us and you're a dead man."

Seeing the determined look in Jack's eyes, Peg tried to struggle again, knowing that Jack would be after her the moment these men were out the door. Once again, something hit her head, she had just one glimpse of the butt of a silenced pistol. As blackness finally overcame her, she had no time to wonder why the police who were to the house, had not acted.

Jack couldn't recognise the squashed looking faces of the intruders, so he studied their clothing. One wore well used, slightly grubby jeans and black tennis shoes. The other had on a suit that looked like it had been worn for several days and slept in. It had been the other that spoke, and Jack thought he knew why. The one with the suit kept the gun on him – the same type as the police used. The suit was familiar.

"Avery, let me go, damn it!"

"I don't want to hurt you," the muffled voice warned. "Just stay there." The speaker backed out into the passage and glanced along it.

"Why are you doing this?" Jack demanded.

"I have to go. They have my wife. They will kill her."

"Bastard! You've let your mate take my wife and they will do more to her than just kill her."

The gun aimed at him wavered, and lowered. Jack sprung up and pushed past the corrupted policeman, racing for the stairs. He hardly noticed the two bodies in the hall, his focus was on the man carrying his wife. He forced himself to go faster. The man went out the door, trotted towards the nearest police car. Its boot was open, and the man forced his weakly struggling burden into it.

Before Jack could get close enough, the man saw him and fired his gun as he went to the driver's seat.

Delayed reaction caused Jack to fall. There was burning agony in his leg. He rolled, saw the blood and tried to put pressure on it. The car sprayed gravel as it took off. It barely missed a small car that had just entered the gate. Belatedly, he recognised Mike Scott's VW and hope eased some of his fury, fear and frustration. He tried to stand to go and meet him.

It was dark, with dawn still two hours away. Mike drove back towards the city and the home of Eugene Taylor. Les was uncharacteristically quiet, but Mike didn't feel like talking either.

Mike drove past the big house, noticing police cars parked on the driveway in front of the house. He saw an unmarked car parked in the street, and drove further along and pulled in.

"They have the place covered," Mike said, feeling foolish. "Perhaps we should just call the old man and tell him what we got from the publican."

"They'd still be asleep," Les countered. "Let's just watch from here."

Not having a guilty conscience, Mike twisted to watch the driveway, and Les kept her attention alternating between both sides of the street.

After a while, she said, quietly, "Company coming, CB."

A casually dressed figure came and knocked on his window. Mike wound the glass down.

"Put your hands on the steering wheel, Sir."

Startled by the request, Mike straightened in his seat and obeyed. A second man opened the passenger door and requested, "Please step out of the car, Miss."

Les smothered a smirk, and when she was out, submitted to being patted down.

"What is your business here, Sir?"

Mike told him, adding, "We saw the place was okay and decided to wait until morning." He went on to explain his concern and was invited to step out of the car. As a precaution, he too was patted down.

"All has been quiet," the officer reassured Mike, having seen his police aide ID. "The last check was routine. Half an hour ago."

"Can I head in then?" Mike asked.

"Go ahead, we will alert the gate guards."

The man walked back to his car and his partner moved to follow, just as the roar of a V8 engine startled them. Next moment, a brown Monaro squealed tyres around a corner.

"Hey! That's King's car," Les exclaimed, her eyes following it. The two detectives raced to their car and took off after it.

"They probably haven't called the gate guards," Mike said. "I'll go and talk to them, can you drive the car to the gate?"

"All's quiet," the guard at the gate confirmed.

"Can you call up and tell them what I said," Mike asked as Les slowed his VW just outside the gate. His gaze went to the house as the guard dialled. He was hearing voices – not loud, but urgent – coming from that direction. No one answered the guard's phone call, so he reached for the portable radio. This time, a terse voice answered the query. "All's green here!"

The voice cut off, but sound still filtered through the radio's speaker. It was as if the person was keeping the microphone on.

"Hurry up! We've been rumbled." Then a muffled shot.

The guard immediately dialled triple zero for back up. Before he could stop him, Mike began to run towards the house, keeping to the edge of the drive. Someone had just run from the house, towards one of the parked police cars, carrying someone. Another figure ran out, pursing the first. The figure dropped at the sound of another muffled shot.

The police car did a gravel spewing take off and sped for the gate. Mike saw Les backing his car out of the way, and then taking off after the car. He forced concern for Les out of his mind as he raced to where a figure was trying to get up from the ground.

Mike recognised the voice that was cursing fluently.

"Jack! What happened?"

"Help me up!"

"You are in no state," Mike said, seeing the dark stain on his friend's track suit. He also saw blood on Jack's face from a scalp wound.

"Some bastard took Peg. She's in the boot of the police car that just took off."

"It's long gone, mate. Stay here. I'll tell the cops that have just arrived."

Jack was still trying to stand when Mike returned after some initial suspicious questions were answered and he passed on what Jack had told him, and his friend's condition.

"Let me do something about that leg wound," Mike said, pushing Jack back down. "You are losing a lot of blood."

"But Peg…"

"The police will find the car and Les took off in my car after it."

"She'll never keep up in that!" Jacks voice was getting weaker.

"And you won't help her if you pass out from blood loss. What happened?"

Jack didn't answer, managing only a stifled gasp of pain as Mike placed a folded handkerchief over the wound and pressed down.

Sirens were getting closer, but headlights were turning in at the gate and cars, probably the nearby stakeout cars, were racing up the driveway.

A voice above the asked sharply, "What happened here?"

Jack looked up at the uniformed constable. "Four masked blokes with semi-automatics – maybe more. I heard the front door kicked in. My wife and I were going to hide, but two of them barged into our room, one grabbed her. I went after them, saw her being put in the boot of a car, and he shot me."

"How many others were inside?" was the next urgent question.

"Don't know for sure. Four of the task force guys were staying the night. Damn Avery was one of the masked guys."

Jack's attention seemed to be slipping so Mike added, "Usually, the ex-chief super, his man servant and Justin Taylor are there overnight. Sometimes another one or two servants."

Several shots sounded from inside. Mike and the constable both looked that way.

"Is the ex-chief super inside?" the constable demanded.

Jack managed to answer, "He was when I went to bed, but I didn't see him. Is his car out the front? It's a grey merc."

The constable glanced around, but only said, "I'll get an ambulance."

As much as Mike wanted to know what was happening inside, the sound of more muffled shots from inside reminded him that he was unarmed, untrained and really had no place being in there. Besides, Jack needed him.

"I think Uncle Justin had the right of it," Jack said weakly. "He never married. Avery said they'd grabbed his wife, but he let me go after the other guy."

Moaning, that didn't come from Jack, seemed to be coming from somewhere close by. Mike removed his jumper and used one sleeve to form a crude tourniquet on the place where his handkerchief was soaking up blood. Then he stood and trotted over to one of the hedge borders of the ornamental front garden.

He had thought that Jack's injury was bad enough. However, the whole front of Inspector Ed Brown's jumper was dark with blood. It seemed impossible that he was still alive, but his breathing was a bubbling whistle.

Mike only had his shirt to use, and he stripped it off, ignoring the morning chill breeze on his skin. He wadded the shirt and placed pressure on the centre of the blood.

"Here! Help! I need an ambulance," he found himself yelling.

The approaching sirens sounded like ambulances and he hoped they would hurry. Someone crouched beside him.

"I'll take over here. You go back to your friend."

It was the constable who had questioned him, and Mike heard the sympathy there and only then realised that the distressed breathing had stopped. Nausea rose from his stomach, and he managed to stumble a few feet away before being sick. He was shaking from shock and the cold. When he finished retching, he remembered Jack and went back and slumped beside him. His friend was still okay, unconscious, but breathing.

When the ambulance men came over, Mike moved to give them room. He told them where the wound was, and watched them remove his jumper, place a thick pad over his blood soaked handkerchief, and wrap a bandage around them. Another pad was placed on a head wound and secured before they lifted Jack onto a gurney.

The constable approached, spoke quietly to the ambulance men. A second gurney was brought from the ambulance and wheeled over to the dead man. When they returned, the body was covered in a sheet.

"Where will you be taking Jack?" Mike asked.

"Royal Melbourne," was the terse answer.

"How is he?"

"His vitals are not too bad. He has lost a lot of blood, but your first aid helped minimise that."

"Thanks," Mike told them, although they had not really told him how bad Jack was.

He felt someone put a blanket around him as the ambulance drove off. He glanced at the constable, grateful for the warmth. "Thanks, Constable… ah…"

"It's Kev Dawson," the man said. "How do you fit into this mess?"

"I'm Mike Scott, Jack's friend." He was watching the ambulance turning into the street and saw a small car come in once it had gone. "I have been helping Jack do grunt work for his grandfather. Has anyone told him about this?"

"He is on his way here," Dawson said as exterior lights came on and figures emerged from the house.

Two prisoners were being herded towards one of the still present police cars.

"Will you be all right waiting out here, Mike?"

Thinking of what he might see inside, Mike nodded. He guessed that the law had won out, but the other medics were wheeling gurneys inside.

Someone was running along the drive towards the lighted front door, seemingly focussed on it. Mike recognised him and forgot his nausea.

"Dad!" When he got no response, he called louder. "Ian! Wait up!"

The man turned, teetered, but came over.

"Why are you here?" Ian demanded.

"Why are you? They won't let you in."

"I gotta see the Old Man. Gotta tell him something."

"He's not here. What's so important?"

"That girl. He's gotta keep her safe," Ian blurted.

"He knows that!" Mike said, reluctant to tell him what had happened.

"But he doesn't know something."

"What?"

"The girl's my daughter!" Ian revealed with a drunks earnest intensity. "My Megan said so. In a letter. I want to see her."

Mike gripped his father's arm. "She's not inside. The bastards that broke in here, took her."

"Took her? No! They can't!" Ian tried to get free and continue into the house.

"They won't let you in! There has been shooting and the police have prisoners. We'll be in the way."

Ian subsided, and recalled his question. "Why're you here?"

"I heard the bastards were going to try something and came here to warn them. I was too damned late. Didn't think they would be ready to act so quickly."

"Who took her?"

"King, or rather, he was hanging around, but took off just after I got here. Cops went after him. Les took the VW off after the car that took Peg. They put her in one of the cop cars that had been here."

Ian slumped, dropping abruptly to sit on the ground. Mike sat down beside him, mutely. He had known that there was a chance that Peg was his sister. Ian had found proof. He should have been elated, but all he could think of was, 'King's going to kill her'.

Then another thought occurred to him. That made Jack his brother-in-law. He had always wondered what it would have been like to have a sibling, now his sister was missing and his new brother badly hurt. He sent a prayer skyward, hoping that the God his grandparents had taught him about would listen, even if he had not thought of the deity in years.

Ian had fallen into another bout of melancholy, and Mike tried to forget the images of violent death and injury that he'd seen close up. Neither of them were aware of the continued activity around them. The car that stopped on the drive near them, might as well not have existed. The radio voice of the police dispatcher hardly registered. The voice that addressed them had to repeat a question three times.

Mike finally looked up to see Johnson, and to his question of, "Are you all right?" answered, "Ed Brown is dead."

Ian blurted, "The bastards took my girl!" He saw Eugene Taylor hobbling towards the house and stood up to follow. He took off, calling out, "Taylor, you've got to find her. They took my girl."

"What do you know of what happened?" Johnson asked as he offered Mike a hand to help him up.

Mike passed on what he had seen and Jack had told him.

"Where's Jack?"

For a moment, Mike was confused. He thought the man would already know. "He's gone to hospital. He was shot in the leg."

Johnson drew in a deep breath and exhaled. "We hadn't heard that. How bad was he?"

"He'd lost a lot of blood." As an afterthought, he added, "The ambulance went off without sirens." It cheered him, since one of the other ambulances had gone off with lights and sirens.

"Come into the house, Lad, I think you need a hot drink."

Mike didn't argue. He still felt cold in spite of the blanket.

At the front door, Eugene Taylor was talking to one of the officers who had stormed the house. He broke off to say, "I've sent for a forensic team. Keep out of the front rooms."

Johnson nodded and diverged into a side passage that skirted the formal front room, Taylor's study and the two downstairs bedrooms. The various rooms could be reached from the passage, and Mike had a glimpse in one of blood spattered furniture. He decided he was not ready to find out all that had happened. In another room, the sitting area near Taylor's study, he saw Avery sitting in a chair, but being guarded by another of the task force.

Ian was already in the kitchen, hands around a steaming mug of coffee. A middle aged woman had the kettle boiling and more mugs ready. Mike accepted the offer of hot chocolate and when it arrived, he found it had been liberally laced with sugar. He declined the suggestion of a dash of brandy.

"I found her and I have lost her," Ian was muttering as Mike sat opposite him.

"No you haven't, damn it!" Mike hissed. "Don't give up on Peg yet. She's tough!"

Ian subsided, and Mike began sipping his drink.

Finally, Eugene Taylor joined them. "I was going to move Jack and his wife this morning. Everything was arranged." The old man sounded defeated. "King tried to silence Justin. The fool went out…Now Jack."

Johnson brought coffee to his employer. Mike had seen him add brandy before he had.

"Sir, it must mean that King is frightened," Mike offered.

"Yes. He knows that Justin can put him in Matlock for Ida Jessup's murder. So can young Peg…Megan, I mean."

"She can finger him for more than that," Mike added. "Peg is tough. I know. But I really wonder what they took her for. I am glad they didn't just kill her, but…" He didn't want to think of them torturing her first.

"S'right, Taylor," Ian blurted. "My little girl is tough. King tried twice to kill her. Couldn't. Had to be him that dumped my Megan Pearl too."

Taylor suddenly straightened, returning to his usual intentness. "How do you figure that, Sinclair?"

"Ol' Ida Jessup wouldn't have dumped her in that dam. She'd the kid to look after. Musta tricked that bastard into thinking the kid had died already. Look how she kept her a secret all these years."

"She was hardly a secret," Mike retorted.

"Didn't know she was Megan's daughter, did they?" Ian shot back.

"If they suspect, or know it now," Mike thought aloud, "They might think she can help them get those damn shares. Maybe twist Blair on that basis."

Taylor stood abruptly, muttering, "I'm getting old!"

"What did I say?" Mike asked the hovering Johnson.

"Maybe that's a reason for keeping her alive?"

"But…Blair won't have anything to do with her. Not even if he had proof she's his granddaughter."

"Maybe not, but if they think he might, and Blair agrees to play along…"

"Gods!" Mike swore. Let it be so! It will give us a chance to find Peg.

He sipped his drink, silently praying to the deity his grandparents had taught him about. He hoped he would be forgiven for being less than pious since his adoptive parents had died.

"Am I needed here?" Mike finally asked. "Can I be of any use?"

"You can stay if you want," Johnson invited. "We will have the forensic team giving the place the once over."

"What else happened," Mike finally ventured to ask. "Jack mentioned Avery."

"Tom is still here. He called the old man and rung for the ambulances. He turned on the man who was going to force the safe – so we have him in custody."

"They were after the files kept here?" Mike asked with alarm.

"Relax, lad. They didn't get anything and Avery didn't mention the cellar strongroom, just the office safe. Besides, most of the files, evidence and sensitive statements here are just copies. The originals are at Russell Street."

Mike couldn't seem to get motivated. He didn't know where to start looking for Peg. "Did they put out a call for that car they stole?"

"It's been done," Johnson assured him. "But it was found abandoned in Kew Cemetery."

"Damn! No Peg, I guess?"

Johnson just shook his head.

"Les went off after it. In my car. I wonder if she saw the switch." Or if she got lost. I don't even know how well she can drive. He glanced at the clock. Not even an hour had passed since he'd arrived.

The telephone rang and Johnson went to answer it. He returned saying,

"The call is for you, Mike."

His immediate thought was, it has to be Les.

"Hi CB," Les sounded dispirited. "I lost the bastards."

"Where are you?"

"Someplace. Kangaroo something. Your car ran out of gas."

"How'd you know this number?"

"Found it on some card on the floor."

"So how come you went there? Did you see them change cars?"

"Yeah. They got into a brown Kombi, rego JXE 2 something. Didn't get close enough to try to stop them. Saw them go into the graveyard but by the time I got there they were about to come out."

"You sure it was that car?"

"CB, I'm sure. The driver was that sicko Vince Todd. He hangs out at the pub. Tell the Old Man, huh?"

"I will. What will you do?"

"Hitch back, unless you can come and get me?"

"Hang on. Where are you calling from?"

"The garage. But I reversed charges." Les chuckled.

"Ok, stay on the line."

Mike covered the mouthpiece and asked, "Did Jack have his car here?"

When Johnson nodded, Mike decided, "I'll borrow it. Jack won't need it for a bit. Les followed a brown kombi." He passed on what Les had said, then added, "I'll need to go and fill up my car."

Eugene Taylor heard the report. "You do that, Lad. Call me when you are there. I might need someone to check around up that way."

Mike told Les his plans and hung up after getting the name of the garage.

Eugene Taylor murmured, "I wonder why he headed that way?"

Mike recalled his drink and sipped. "King will want to kill her," he said. He recalled the comment by the barkeeper, that King wanted her able to talk. It didn't help. He had seen what King had done to her before.

He did wonder why they had taken her, what they wanted to know. Apart from getting her, it seemed the intruders had been after the files from the OCTF investigations. They had been too late. The Old Man had taken the latest reports to Russell Street, and Jack's Uncle had been out somewhere when the men had come in. However, it seemed that Justin Taylor had been ambushed too, for he had been taken to hospital, and the Old Man had been summoned from there.

Mike said, thoughtfully, "I don't know how well King knows Matlock and that area. I suspect he has been there fairly often."

"Why Matlock?" Eugene Taylor asked, even though he had been thinking along similar lines.

"I don't know – just that Jack suggested he repeats actions and he might decide to dump--"

"That bastard better not try!" Ian blurted, coming out of a morose silence.

"There is a lot of country up that way," Taylor inserted. "I will alert our people to watch for the van"

"I'll get going," Mike decided.

"I'm coming with you," Ian declared. "You can pick up my mate Jack Casey on the way. He knows those hills better than any city hoodlum."

"You call him then. If he can't come now, he can follow and meet us," Mike told his father. "I will bring Jack's car around to the front."

Chapter 27

Peg felt her head throbbing as she roused and tried to move a hand to the sore spot. Knowledge of being tied up coincided with the question of, 'What happened?'

She kept her eyes closed as her mind struggled to remember. Someone gripped her shoulder and shook her, but she couldn't have said anything even if she had wanted to. She gave no sign of being awake. If she was trussed up and gagged with tape, whoever was with her was not a friend.

"She's coming round," an accented voice announced.

The voice came from behind her, so Peg risked opening her eyes, just a slit. Her eyes took a while to focus, and when they did, the flat grey metallic surface in front of her was uninformative. She quickly shut her eyes when she felt a hand on her face, turning it, then opening her eyelid. Her head was moved back and the hand withdrew.

"You going to keep her in here?" the accented voice demanded.

"Is there a reason you want to leave here?"

That voice was familiar, Peg realised. It wasn't King. Gianni? Shit!

"I just don't want to be here still if the cops come by to check again," the accented voice explained.

"They found nothing before," Gianni Costa's more cultured voice pointed out.

"That was just a routine check. Normal inconvenience, checking logbooks. Haven't you been hearing the CB radio? The cops are stopping all cars and trucks out this way. Igloo Two mentioned hearing the cop radio saying to look out for a brown kombi."

"Vince won't talk. The police have no reason to connect him to this truck. If they come by, you are here for your mandatory rest period. You will have more trouble if they find you driving. Was that not the reason why we stopped here? It is a regular truck stop."

Faint rocking movements coincided with the sound of pacing boots.

"Are you this edgy when you carry other special loads?" Costa asked.

"Those loads aren't likely to make a noise!"

"You have a point. However, she won't be able to do much. Go get yourself some food and coffee and listen to the gossip."

"You want anything, boss?"

"No. It would look odd if you were to bring food for two."

"Yeah! It would."

The truck door was opened, and slammed shut.

The other speaker didn't move, but it felt like his eyes were boring a hole in her back.

Overconfident bastard! You might have fooled everyone for this long but not anymore and not me!

Peg decided to pretend to be asleep as she might hear more. Like your mention of special loads. Stolen stuff or drugs, no doubt.

She might have thought she was alone, except for the strong smell of aftershave. Gianni Costa, if was he who had spoken earlier, wasn't one for talking to himself, or needless pacing. Perhaps he was listening to the CB radio as intently as she was. The truckies were like a flock of birds at sunset – non-stop chattering.

The driver returned with some news, names or nicknames of half a dozen drivers whose rigs had been stopped and searched.

He'd been told, "We stay here until your rest period is up. No one will be expecting us to be sitting in plain view. Then we keep heading north-west. I will tell you when to diverge from your itinerary. You just make sure there is nothing to indicate we are here."

"There's nothing," the accented voice stated.

Now, in the brief respites from the radio chatter, Peg heard snores from the other side of the metal partition. It slowly occurred to her that she was in a truck, one of the big ones – but she had the sense of being in a small area. The voices hadn't echoed, but she couldn't see to figure out why. If she dared, she would try to roll over, but that would tell her minder that she was awake.

Light was coming into the space from a small high window. A faint breeze was stirring the dust in the air as well. Opening her eyes a slit, it seemed like the sun was shining in – more than it had earlier. What time did that make it? It had been dark still when the bastards had grabbed her. Had Jack seen where they had taken her?"

Unexpectedly, Peg felt hands rolling her from her left side to her back. Then a hand gripped her chin and held her head still.

"I know you are awake," Gianni Costa said in a low voice. "So listen, and listen well. Make any noise to attract attention and I will kill you. Only one thing is keeping you alive right now and if that plan falls through, you will quickly go from asset to liability."

Peg opened her eyes, but didn't try to talk. Even without the tape it would be impossible for her mouth was like a desert. Nor did she react to his face – as far as he knew, she had never seen him before

"Do you understand me?"

Peg made a faint sound, but her mind was not thinking, "Yes".

"Good. Because soon, you and I will be having a talk and you will be answering my questions. Cooperate and your existence will be less unpleasant."

As Peg could only stare at him he went on, "I found it hard to believe that my darling Adelaide could have been lying to me all these years. Telling me you were hers, by Harry. Now I find out you weren't hers, but the child of Blair's daughter. Had she still been alive now, I would punish her for that deceit. And now, you get to redeem yourself for interfering with my plans for Blair's grandson."

Shit! He knows! Peg's mind froze, not even able to consider all the implications. Only one thought came to mind – Blair won't want anything to do with me.

The conversational tone continued with Costa's eyes boring into hers. "And you will tell me all the lies you have been telling the police about me, and how you even came to think they would believe you."

Peg tried to shake her head free, but the hand gripped more tightly.

"How else could they have found out so much?"

Tremors began to shake her limbs and Costa laughed.

"Don't think that you can be stubborn and not talk. I have other ways besides pain and humiliation to achieve that. In fact, when I finish with you, you'll be begging to be my whore, just like your slut of a mother."

His low laugh stopped abruptly as someone banged on the truck's cabin. The truck rocked as the sleeping driver came abruptly awake and sat up.

"What is it?" the accented voice growled.

"Police. Open up and step out."

Costa's hand moved to Peg's neck. A tacit threat.

While only her eyes dared move, Peg studied what she could see. She guessed that the bench where she lay was right behind the driver's cabin, and the roof over her seemed to be wood and was fairly low. Across where Costa had been sitting was another bench, but there the roof was the full height of the load space. A wooden partition blocked her view of that, but there was a door shape visible from this side. The driver, when he had been there, must have left that way.

As she listened to the sleepy, yawn filled conversation between the driver and the police, Peg wondered how such a space as she was in, no doubt used often for special loads, had gone unnoticed.

The truck rattled as the rear door was unlocked and opened. The floor juddered as someone entered and walked along the load bed. She heard the questions.

"What's in the boxes?"

"What's on the pallets?"

"Where are you headed?"

It wasn't long before the police retreated, and the driver returned to his cab. Costa released Peg, and quietly knocked on the metal above her. A panel slid open from the other side.

"All's green," the driver confirmed. "I'll just go off for a shower and then we can move on."

The driver returned with coffee and a takeaway box of sandwiches for Costa. Peg didn't expect anything, but Costa took out a sharp knife, made a small hole in the tape over her mouth and forced a straw through it. The other end went into a bottle of water that looked to have been unopened, so she thought it was safe to drink.

She thought wrong.

Peg woke again to realise that she was no longer lying down, but tied to a chair. Her surroundings were more spacious – about as big as her aunt's bathroom at the Ridge Road house. It had a tiled floor with a drain, and the walls and ceiling were padded. There was no window, the light came from a globe in the ceiling, somewhere behind her.

Her mouth was free, but the skin around it felt like it was burning, so likely the tape had been ripped off. She tried to moisten her lips, and hoped her head would stop spinning. She had her eyes closed when she felt a breath of cooler air. She heard voices, one was Harry King. She wanted to be sick.

"You should have died," King told her when he came around where she could see him. When she didn't react, he went on. "No matter. I get to indulge my preferences, unless of course you give me a satisfactory answer to my questions. Do you understand?"

"I want a drink!"

Someone handed King a bottle with a straw. "No truth drug, this time," he remarked.

"What do you mean?"

"You've already told us a lot." The look Harry gave Peg sent shivers down her spine. "But we need you awake to get more details."

What? He's got to be lying. Playing with my mind.

"Oh, and don't expect your…husband… to come to your rescue. Todd shot him. Left him bleeding to death outside the Old Man's house."

Peg felt as if King had punched her in the chest. Jack? Dead?

"And that traitorous rat, Justin Taylor? He will wish I had killed him. He'll be a cripple for the rest of his life. What? Don't you care?"

"I don't believe you."

King's chuckle was pure malice. "Disbelieve me all you like. The more stubborn you try to be, the more fun I will have. Besides, I owe you for setting me up to be arrested. Whose idea was that? Old Man Taylor?"

When she didn't answer, King slapped her face. "Too bad he didn't keep a better eye on you. Now, you won't have a chance to make more false allegations. Not that a court will believe you now."

In your dreams, bastard! "I told them what you did."

"I know, but without you to testify, that's nothing but a hollow accusation."

Peg felt a sudden chill. Could he wriggle out of a murder charge?

The questions King asked, seemed to confirm his earlier claim that she had been made to talk already, and some voice in her head seemed to say, "What harm can it do to say more?"

However, that voice didn't win over the deeper rooted voice that said, "Tell him nothing."

Silence got her hurt, but she sensed that he believed some of her lies. It also seemed that he only knew some things – so if she had babbled under some drug, he can't have asked the right questions. Most of what he asked about, he could have learnt from his crooked cops.

Later, hurting, hungry and thirsty, Peg could only sit in the chair and listen to a conversation taking place outside the room.

"We should kill her and be done with it," King proposed.

Then Costa countered, "Not yet. She still might be more useful alive. She will do as we say, even if she doesn't want to and Blair, well he's in a state thinking that the secrets he covered up are going to rise up and bite him."

"You had better be right! That little bitch knows too much. If she is put on the stand, and they believe her, even you will be history."

"And I know it. However I was only ever with Adelaide once when she was around, and you were there too. Did you see her?"

"The little bitch wouldn't come anywhere near if she saw me."

Peg picked up on the anger in each voice and wondered if things were not going well for those two bastards. Were the police onto them? Had Jack…

Grief overwhelmed her. No! They had to be lying. He had to be alive still. Had to!

Someone returned, but she was not facing the door. A hand gripped the nape of her neck.

"I don't think it a good idea to keep you alive, bitch, but as long as you are, I get to enjoy myself. Now what's this about you being some singer?"

Did I tell him that? "Not!"

"Don't lie to me! The media will go to town when I let out that Carson's new singer is a whore's brat."

"Not! She's just covering for me."

"How? It was you who ruined things for us in Bathurst. The police said it was the singer."

"Megan is from Meredan too. She got me a job as a roadie for Carson."

"Liar!"

"Not! She knew people were after me and we did a deal to confuse them."

Kings fist came around and hit her hard in the ribs.

"If Ida Jessup wasn't already dead, I would kill her a hundred times over! Keeping you a secret all these years then spilling secrets for you to blab about."

Peg expected another punch, but it didn't come.

"You are going to withdraw every statement that you have made, bitch!"

As Peg was thinking, "No, bloody way!" a phone rang and King retreated. With the door shut, she heard no outside sounds.

Chapter 28

"We can't just sit around, CB. We have to do something." Les leant back in a chair outside the local pub, discarding the can of coke she had finished, by tossing it three feet and into a bin.

Mike knew how Les felt. "Ian is off quizzing the locals. He's good at that. I'll be calling the Old Man again in ten minutes. Last time, he said he thought that King or Costa might have a place up this way. He was having enquiries made. If he gets a hint that it's true, he will let us go looking."

"That might be dangerous."

"I know, but I feel like you. And, well, Ian was reading some letters Peg found, and he believes that Peg is my sister."

"For real?"

"He is sure, and from what Jack and I found out, it is very possible."

"Well now... Hey, he's on his way back."

Ian slumped into a chair beside them.

"Learn anything, Music man?"

"Nothing helpful," he summarised. Then to Mike he said, "Get me a beer will you?"

Mike rose without comment. He had the idea Les was about to try and shock his father. If she did, it might jerk him out of his mood slump. She could try, and he did need to go in and make a call to Melbourne as well.

He returned outside with Ian's drink, and had a thoughtful look on his face.

"Did anyone mention trucks going through here? Costigan trucks?"

"Trucks?" Ian snorted, as he took the first sip of beer. "There's been a coupla dozen trucks through here since we arrived. We are on a main road. What's the point, anyway?"

"Apparently, just before they knocked him out to fix his leg, Jack muttered something about Costigan trucks like in Bathurst."

"Why them, CB?"

"Didn't you get to hear Jack's theory? Costa is Costigan?" Mike asked Les.

"Nah, missed that. So, is Jack's Old Man onto that?"

Mike nodded.

"Truckies get all over the air about police checking them," Ian contributed. "But they'd need to look see if them trucks are on the littler roads."

"The police aren't stupid," Mike told him.

"I wouldn't bet either way, but if those bastards do have a hideout up this way, I don't reckon they'd be on the main road. They'd want out of the way."

"What colour are those trucks?" Les asked.

"Brown and blue," Mike said. "Peg saw one in Bathurst that time she saw Devlin and found the kid."

"I saw a couple of them go past here while waiting for Music Man to get back."

"So, the bastards might use them," Ian agreed, dismissively. "How is that going to help? The company has hundreds of trucks."

"Maddern has organised a charter flight to overfly his area and the abutting ones."

"Bit late for that, Boy. A truck, if one was used, could have dropped its passengers hours ago and be across the border by now."

"Or it might not be!" Mike argued. "They might keep it close in case they have to make a quick getaway."

"Stop being a wet sock, Music Man," Les said suddenly. "Peg isn't some rich bloke's spoilt daughter. She'll be ready for the main chance and we will be ready to back her up."

"You don't understand," Ian argued.

Mike saw Jack Casey returning along the footpath and gave a sigh of relief. When he was close, Les blurted, "Can you convince Music Man here that Peg is not going to roll over and die?"

Casey obliged. "Ian, my niece might have been delicate, like her mother, but Megan, or Peg – whatever you want to call her, has a double dose of your stubborn intransigence."

"What are you saying?" Ian demanded.

"What I am saying is that I agree with my young namesake. These animals repeat what has worked for them before. Now, I know you were in prison when they got Margaret into their clutches, but I also know that you were driven to find out what happened. When you sober up, I want you to recall all you learnt. Then adding that to what I know and what Justin Taylor told me, we should have a start on knowing what they might do now."

"Torture, rape, drugs," Ian began. "Then they'll kill her."

"Nah, you bleeding pessimist," Les agued. "She was born drugged and survived. His majesty tried the rest and she survived. I reckon she has another seven lives left."

"Unless it's third time lucky for King," Ian objected, sounding less addled.

"Nah, more like third time unlucky for them."

Casey inserted his opinion. "They thought they owned Ida Jessup completely. Now we know how well she managed to keep secrets from them. That might have been self-preservation, but it seems that your Megan Pearl, even addicted as she was, still outsmarted them. If Costa ever had those shares, her jewellery and bank account details in his keeping, she somehow managed to get them back. Or she might have kept them from him in the first place."

"Ida might have helped her."

"She probably did. I believe that she decided to run away to have her child. The way I reckon things, if Ida hadn't hidden the baby, King would have killed her. Your Megan Pearl, didn't want that – she believed that child was yours."

"Damn it, old man, you'd better be right."

After listening to Ian and Casey recalling a time long past, Mike finally interrupted. "That's all very well, Casey, but it will take more than a day to get her addicted. How does it help us find her?"

"Lad, think about it. They will have gone to ground somewhere. They will think they have time to do as they like. They will feel safe."

"And that's where we started." Mike's worry was as great as his father's, but he knew Peg better. "Did your damn brother-in-law agree to play along if they contact him?"

Casey merely nodded. "Stubborn ass is scared that the family scandal will ruin him. My sister, bless her, finally grew a spine and told him the only scandal was how he had behaved back then. He didn't corrupt her and cause her death. So now he is playing along, pretending to be in a panic, but actually thinking that any announcement about where his daughter disappeared to is a chance to get closure and understand how it was that she ended up in a dam up this way. The news of the finding of her body was reported sympathetically in the press. If he sticks to his new viewpoint, he will survive this slur on his name. He will help us buy time and enjoy thwarting those who thought to benefit from disgracing his daughter."

"Yay for the Rich Man," Les summarised. "Does that mean he wants to get to know Peg? Or does he secretly hope he won't have to? She doesn't care two hoots for him, ya know."

"I told him that," Casey admitted with a faint grin. "Only I put it as she didn't think he was good enough to deserve her. I may have put a slow leak in his ego."

"Well then, what are we going to do? Stay here or go onto Matlock?" Les asked, looking at the others.

Mike was getting tired of Ian's pacing. Since arriving in Matlock, he'd not touched anything alcoholic. Now though, he seemed as twitchy as a druggy needing a fix – or a drunk needing a drink. They had not heard anything from the police, only that they had a light plane up looking for trucks parked in unusual places. Casey had gone into town, he too wanted something to do.

"Come on CB," Les suggested. "Let's go outside, huh?"

"I should call the hospital. See how Jack is. Maybe he has heard something?"

"If he hasn't discharged himself already."

"Yeah, there's that. Reckon they will have had to tie him to the bed."

Chapter 29

From the moment Jack woke after his operation, he wanted out of the hospital. The last thing he recalled from before going under the anaesthetic, was that fact that Peg was missing. It was the first thing he remembered. The trouble was, he was still too woozy to ask the questions he had and make them understandable.

When he was finally wheeled into a ward, it took him a while to realise who his roommate was. The privacy curtains had been around the second bed. He woke from a doze, hearing voices that he recognised. His Uncle Justin, and his Grandfather having a low voiced disagreement. His uncle, seemed equally keen to leave the hospital.

"Uncle? Grandfather?" he called in a voice that felt strained.

"Back with us, Lad?" His grandfather poked his head through a gap in the curtain. "How are you?"

"Have you found Peg?" Jack had no patience for the social niceties.

Eugene Taylor pushed back the curtain between the two beds, and admitted the scant information that was known. Then, before Jack could erupt, suggested, "You won't want to put weight on your leg until it has had a chance to start healing. So, instead of trying to steal crutches and run off, why don't you and Justin try to work out how to find where King or Costa have hidden hideouts?"

"What makes you think we can succeed at finding something the police have failed at for twenty or more years?"

"Your fresh viewpoint and plenty of time to think on it."

Jack growled as his grandfather left. "Which hospital is this anyway?" he asked his uncle.

"The police hospital. They had you transferred from the Royal Melbourne once they had you stable."

"So the old man pulled strings to get us put together?"

"I expect so. And it means only one place to guard."

"To stop us leaving?"

"And anyone that might try to get at us."

"What happened to you, anyway?" Jack wondered if his uncle would answer.

Justin Taylor was not Jack's favourite relative, but simply due to the fact that they were stuck in the same small room, brooding over events that were related, they began talking. The remaining traces of animosity between them, inspired a kind of argument as each aired their personal views about people or recent events.

Jack was worried about Peg, and sure King was behind her abduction.

"No one has seen him," Justin countered.

"What about at that pub?"

"They've checked there."

"Someone must know! The bastard is Costa's front man – overseeing all his rackets. Is there any indication that the little men are getting above themselves?"

"Not that I've heard," Justin admitted. "Do you think someone else is relaying orders?"

"Could be," Jack decided.

"Who?"

"I dunno. Les thought the barman was scared silly of King. So I don't think him, but a lot of suspicious types hang out there."

"The barman has a record of petty crimes. Nothing recent though. He's the one who answers the phones, most times."

"If he was King's mouthpiece, he wouldn't be such a wuss."

"If he was running some game of his own on the side, he wouldn't want King suspecting. Being a wuss is good camouflage."

"I can't see it," Jack argued, then went quiet. Finally, he said, "On one point, all that would be irrelevant. If King or Costa was calling in with orders for people, the barman would answer and give it to whoever was relevant. He may not know the content of the calls, but they come in there."

"Yes…"Taylor considered. "Didn't your friend the Shaw girl say something about Costa calling STD?"

"I think the bar guy suggested interstate."

"I think I might see if the Old Man can get hold of the phone records for the pub – calls in and out. Those who took your wife, headed up country. The STD might not be interstate. Would you recognise numbers from up Matlock way?"

"I might," Jack considered. "But if we see frequent calls to an STD number, it would be worth checking. The phone exchange people might know the source."

A call to the ex-Chief Super resulted in the pair having a visitor several hours later. CS Haldane from the OCTF arrived with two thick loose leaf binders. He grinned as he passed one to each patient. "To keep your minds occupied so you don't think of running off before your wounds have healed enough."

Jack growled at the reminder of what he wanted to do. It was only the realisation that he had no idea where to go, that had kept him abed.

"What's this?" Justin demanded.

"Phone records from the North Melbourne pub, and from the one the Dockers union use. I have requested a list of area code prefixes from the phone people. I will have it sent in when it's ready."

"This will take ages," Jack said.

Justin gave a quiet snort. "Do you have some paper and pens, Sir?"

With a grin, and like a magician, Haldane took two pens and two notebooks from an inside pocket of his jacket. "Ring if you find any hot prospects."

When Haldane had gone, Justin muttered, "There is a reason why I liked to give this sort of work to you!"

The records began twelve months before, and after scanning columns of numbers for half an hour, Jack paused to consider. The earlier records might give a clue to Costa's location, but King wouldn't have needed to call there often. Perhaps though, when King was hiding out before his earlier arrest, he may have called the pub. Recalling those dates, Jack skipped ahead. One number appeared frequently, and he mentioned it to his uncle.

"That's the Costigan mansion number. King was hiding there before his arrest."

"Damn," Jack muttered. Then he skipped to the most recent records, from between King's acquittal and before the assault on his Grandfather's place. That raid needed planning.

Several numbers were repeated, two were local. One was STD. He would need to check the geographical prefix to be sure, but the STD number was, he thought, for an area near Matlock.

"I might have something?" He repeated the number to his uncle.

"I have that too. Any others?"

Jack mentioned them.

"I have them as well. Let me make a call."

Justin waited to be answered, then identified himself, asked some questions about the numbers and thanked the person on the line before hanging up."

"All those numbers are unlisted, or rather they are unassigned."

"Interesting," Jack agreed. "Where would you look next?"

"Find out what exchange they came out of," was the quick reply. "Though I don't think King will be in the local places. If he took your wife – he went bush."

"You could get people to watch the places," Jack suggested.

"If we find them. We still need to trace that country number, which might be more difficult."

"Would the Consorting Squad know of any bent telephone linesmen?"

"You are too smart for your boots, you know," Justin flashed a rare smile at his nephew. "Any other smart ideas?"

"Yeah. What about cross checking numbers with those from Costigan's place?"

"They looked at those and found them all to be legitimate."

"So apparently is Costigan's trucking company," Jack insinuated. "One might be a front."

"Well, it may be worth checking them further, and with this list. Meanwhile, look for those numbers in the earlier records."

Chapter 30

"I'm surprised they let us do this," Les said as she and Mike set off in the VW. The police had asked them to drive by a number of properties on the outer edges of the Matlock district.

"Obviously, these places are unlikely but need checking. The police will check the most likely ones."

Mike agreed with Les's sentiment though. "Still it is better than sitting around all day with Ian getting maudlin, and we know King and you might recognise people who are helping him."

"The old Miner Guy had better keep a leash on your old man if he see's King," Les predicted.

Mike sighed. "It's just as well that Jack is not here."

"So, where to first, CB?"

"The old Watson place on the Boryallock Road."

"You know this country stuff is getting to me," Les admitted. "So how do we tell if the bastards are hiding someplace?"

"We will drive past first, find somewhere to park and sneak back closer," Mike proposed.

The first place was only a shell, with no roof, and part had been burnt. The second location had an intact house, but on close inspection, was empty with windblown rubbish in most rooms, broken windows and holes in the roof.

They drove past the third place, pulled over and checked his map. A windbreak of ancient pine trees shielded the car from being seen from the farmhouse.

"Someone with cash to spare must live there," Les said.

"Hmm. Certainly a bigger spread than I expected," Mike agreed. He opened the car door to get out. "I'm just going for a better look."

Mike studied what he saw, as he kept most of his body behind one of the pine trees. There was a ring of eucalyptus trees around the house, providing shade, as well as paddocks around the house, including between the house and the road. Except for a few horses dozing in the sun, there was no sign

197

of life. He took out a small pair of binoculars to get a closer look. Les joined him a few minutes later.

"What do you think," he asked, handing her the binoculars.

"Couldn't see King in any of the other places even if they were okay. But this…they could hide a truck in that barn, and they have all this open ground around to see if anyone is coming. There's power going in."

Mike took the glasses back and looked at the line of poles. "Telephone too."

"Want me to sneak closer?" Les asked.

"Maddern said not to," Mike began, then said, "Here, quick, look near the front door."

Les took the glasses back and swore. "Bloody Vince Todd. This must be where they have Peg."

Mike grabbed her before she ran off. "We will go back to that last town, and call Maddern."

"Alright, damn you, CB."

"Shh, Get down."

Mike had heard the slight sound of someone moving over dried pine needles. He pulled Les after him as he moved to where there was a dip beside the road. What kept them from being seen was that their car had been the focus of the man's attention, and they were 50 yards from it.

They heard the man reporting via a walkie-talkie but could not understand the garbled reply. Afterwards, the man emerged from the trees and headed for the car. Once there, he stuck his head in the open window, and then walked all around the car.

"I have seen that guy too," Les whispered.

Mike gestured for them to move along the road, further from the car. When the man wasn't looking, they dashed across the road and into the cover of a growth of scrubby bushes. After a short while, he emerged, pretending to be adjusting his jeans. He headed back to his car, noticing that the man was no longer in sight. Les caught up to him, and moved in front of him, turning to face him and walk backwards.

"You'll fall over," Mike warned.

"If I do, you will too," Les snickered as she put her arms around him. "If that guy knows me, I don't want him to see my face, and I will be blocking yours, huh?"

Mike didn't mind the pretence and had to laugh. They guy might think they'd been….rolling in the scrub.

Even though the man wasn't visible, Mike felt sure they were still being observed, so he gave Les a long kiss before shoving her towards the passenger side of the car.

As soon as he got in, he smelt an acrid whiff of cigarette smoke. He gave the interior of the car a quick glance, but saw nothing to alarm him. He drove off slowly, noticing that Les was looking behind.

"CB, that bloke just dashed back across the road."

Making no comment, Mike continued until they were around a bend before pulling up. He looked around before getting out.

"What you doing, CB?"

"Looking to see if the guy fiddled with the car. Keep a look out."

"You saying he knows who we are?"

"Or saw us watching the house," Mike said as he tried to get as far as he could under the car.

"Do you know anything about cars?"

"Not much. But there is something dripping under here and that can't be good. Open up the boot at the front. Ian said he put some tools in there. I hope he put some kind of tape too."

The rattling and rustling sounds ended and Les came and crouched beside him. "Just some electrical tape was there."

"Will have to do. Keep alert."

Somewhere nearby, a sound like the motor of a muscle car, started up. He thought of the brown Monaro from the night before last. He tried to hurry, but the leak was right at the extreme of his reach. However, if King had been at the farmhouse, he might now be getting away. If the car came this way, he and Les were sitting ducks.

The sound came closer, but then began to move away.

"Can't you hurry, CB?"

"I won't be able to catch him," Mike grunted. "I think that guy damaged the brake line. We are going to have to go carefully, and stick to the main road."

"What about the radio the cop gave you?"

"You can try it, but in amongst the hills we can't get a signal. That's why I had to ring up before."

"Hey! This is mobile 7. Can anyone hear me?"

Mike moved his head. "You have to press the button at the side when you talk, and then release it."

Les repeated her non-regulation call, but no one answered. She was just about to chuck the radio back in the car when she heard, "Solo One to Mobile 7. Gary here."

Mike said quickly. "Tell him we have broken down, but saw some friends on the Mill Creek road. Ask him to relay for us."

They heard Gary's end of the onward relay, and then Gary spoke to them. "Your message was understood. Do you need assistance?"

Mike emerged from under the car and took the radio. "We can probably get back to Mill Creek, but a V8 left the place five minutes ago, but must have turned off on a fire track just past the place."

Gary relayed again, and after a pause came back. "Ring when you get there. We will get Thommo from the garage to come and get you."

Chapter 31

Gianni Costa, alias John Costigan, turned when Vince Todd came in.

"There's a VW Beetle parked on the road. Might be someone nosing around. Tippy thought he recognised your effing bird – the bottle blond."

He was directing his report to Harry King, unaware that the fat man was King's boss.

"Tell Tippy to see to that car if it doesn't move on. Tell everyone else to be alert. Shoot anyone that comes onto the property."

Vince trotted out and once the door closed behind him, Costa swore.

"I knew you coming here was a mistake. How else would that bitch know about this place?"

"I don't know, but she has been sleeping around with some mate of Taylor's nephew. Him and the nephew have been real nuisances. I reckon they were the ones who found out about your five old properties. Maybe they discovered this one too?"

"That could have been from something Ida's brat leant. However, this place is not owned under my name, and I did not have it until a few years ago."

"We ought to have killed the girl already!"

"She has a use while Blair is desperate to get her."

King laughed unpleasantly. "I would have thought that he'd be relieved if we killed her. It would hide the scandal that his daughter caused."

"Don't forget, she has his damn shares," Costa reminded him. "If we can get her to sign them over to us, we won't need her."

"How will you make her take you to them? We would need the actual shares too."

"Leave that to me," Costa promised.

"What about what she has told the cops?"

"After that farce of a trial, her credibility must be zero. Wasn't she charged with perjury?"

"I haven't been able to confirm that. Look, if I have to keep that trash alive, it had better not be here," King decided.

"You said you had nowhere else to go."

"I know a place. And you should leave too. I think I can hear a plane circling."

"If the police come here, it will only be that take over business they can be on me about. I have that under control."

"Heard from Reggie?" King asked.

"Not since I got here, but he told me the girl was pregnant. You go if you must. Just don't let them find that bitch with you. They can't have anything else against you. If they had evidence, they would have added extra charges when they had you."

King stalked from the room. He hadn't admitted certain things to his half-brother, but the matters were old and would be hard to prove. The only things that he had to worry about were what the girl could say. He needed to leave, now, and he'd need to keep the girl quiet. Before he returned to where he had left her, he collected a syringe and a bottle of the addictive sedative that he had been using on her. He filled the syringe, and went to where she was tied up. He made no effort to be gentle when he grabbed her arm and jabbed the syringe into muscle and pushed the drug in. He quickly cut the bindings and dragged her up.

"Come on!"

He moved at a pace that Peg had no hope of keeping up with. Her legs were stiff, and so he was dragging her by the time he reached his car. The car was parked under trees, and before he had emerged from the cover of the house he listened for the plane. It must have moved on.

Peg had collapsed when he stopped to open the boot of his car. He tossed her in and ran for the driver's door. He didn't even stop to consider how his prisoner would fare in the airless boot, on a day when the temperature was meant to reach 100 degrees or 38 degrees in the damn silly new Celsius scale. He simply gunned his engine and took off. Mindful of the car Todd had mentioned, he checked the road before emerging. He turned right, alert for other cars, but he only went a mile, until he turned off the main road onto one of the fire access tracks that would take him over the ridge towards Matlock. It had the advantage of keeping his car from being sighted by the police or the plane.

King thought Costa foolish to stay, even if they were not sure if the place had been discovered. Smarter to leave and watch what happened. Costa, his elder half-brother, was smugly arrogant, thinking that since no one had twigged to his public identity in thirty years that he was invincible.

No one was, not even himself – although Costa's advice had worked all these years for him too.

How the hell had the police found out his birth name? He had never told that to anybody, not even Costa. He had thought it might have been Mick's whore, but how? He had taken all the evidence. Besides, she hated the police, and it was no act. And way back, he had never been charged. The police had never been able to prove anything against him.

Still, the police could not know everything about him. He still had his last ditch hideout – like his brother - he had bought it through layers of deception and it wasn't even in his name. It was where he cached all his trophies. If need be he could hide there for several years.

Anger made him plant his foot harder on the accelerator, and he raced along the graded track at a faster rate. Tippy should have fixed the VW – the nosy driver would either crash or roll with no brakes on twisty hilly road past the farm. Even if they survived, they would have to walk to the town to call for help. The folk there were insular, and would be their usual obstructive selves.

King did a wheel squealing turn onto a second track, leaving dry dust drifting back to the ground. As the ground rose, he slowed, but kept the revs up. The dust still rose behind him, but he believed the trees would hide it from above.

Back at the farm, Costa yelled for Vince. "Any sign of that plane?"

"Went off before King did."

"I hope he knows what he's doing. Go tell Eddie to warm the truck up. I will be leaving in ten minutes."

Costa had very little to take. What was vital, went into a briefcase. This place may or not be compromised, but he had two other hideouts that were, like this one, not connected to him. When he went out, the truck was waiting. He gave it a look over. Eddie had sprayed brown paint over the blue Costigan logo. He had also blown dust onto it, giving it a more rustic, anonymous look. It now also had different licence plates.

Eddie opened the rear door of the furniture van sized truck for Costa to climb in.

"Where to, boss?"

"Head towards Benalla and then turn north."

From the moment that Gary had relayed the message from Mike, the police had swung into action. He was told to head towards Mill Creek and take up a watching position. Maddern tightened the ring of road blocks around the district. If the fugitives were to leave, they would still have to get back on the main road. The reconnaissance plane reported seeing a brown car turning onto the Donnington fire road, and travelling towards Matlock. Gary reported seeing a brown van leave the suspect farm and turn onto the main highway.

A car from Wilga was heading towards the farm to interview anyone there. Cars from surrounding major towns were alerted to watch for the suspects.

Maddern had to make a call. If they had taken Peg from that farmhouse, if she had been there, which vehicle would they use? He decided on the truck, for that had to have been how they took her from Melbourne. He and Steve were heading to Mill Creek.

<h1 style="text-align:center">Chapter 32</h1>

It was well after dark before Mike had his car back in Matlock and had walked back to Mrs Church's place. He found Jack Casey waiting there.

"The man greeted him with, "Good work."

"Huh?" At first he was too tired to understand, but then, "They caught them? Did they have Peg? How is she?"

"Sorry, Lad. Peg is still missing. She is probably with King. However, the police found the van that Costa was in. They think he was trying to get interstate."

"What about King then? I heard his Monaro go off."

"He took to the hill tracks," Casey told him. "He is still in the district."

Mike moved forwards and slumped into a chair. Les muttered, "You hope," as she went to sit on the arm of the same chair. "Are the coppers going to announce that they have the fat man?" Les asked louder.

Casey shook his head. "They will make is seem like they are still looking. King won't know unless he expects to hear from Costa when he goes to ground. The police don't think that he has another bolt hole up here. Likely he will hold up in an old mine, deserted shack or farm."

"Or invade someone's home," Les added. "Likes his comfort, does his majesty."

"Warnings are going out over the radio and television," Casey assured them. Then he had a sudden feeling of disquiet. "Why did you ask if Costa's arrest would be announced?"

"His Majesty hates the kid. He'd probably prefer her dead. So if they took her alive, it had to be at the fat man's direction. Reckon if his majesty knows the fat guy is a stuck pig, he'll do Peg in."

"He hasn't managed it yet," Mike said, trying to be positive. "You heard how Jack is yet?"

Casey managed a faint chuckle. "Stitched up and thinking he's good to go. Changed his mind when the painkillers wore off. Give him a call. Don't say anything about Costa though, in case the local exchange is listening in."

"He'll want to come up here."

"He is sharing a ward with his uncle," Casey revealed.

It was Les's turn to snicker, but she didn't elucidate her thoughts.

"Did they find anything at that farm?"

"All I know is that they arrested the couple who usually live there and one other. Two men got away. The couple know Costa as John Louis. Oh, and they found young Megan's handbag – seemingly untouched."

"The kid is sneaky clever," Les applauded. "Must have managed to shove it out of sight."

"Go ring the hospital, Mike," Casey urged. "They took him to the police hospital, once they had patched him up. The number is by the phone."

"Will they let me talk to him this late?"

"Tell them you are ringing on my behalf," Casey suggested.

Mike pushed himself up and went to the phone extension. The suggested ruse worked, and his call was transferred. A sleepy voice answered, "Hello?"

"That you, new found bro?" Mike asked, and he grinned at Les, who had come to listen in. Her brows rose in surprise.

"Mike? Have they found her?" Jack's voice became stronger.

"Not yet, but they found where they had been. The bastards got away just before the police got there."

"Damn it! I spent all day yesterday ogling phone numbers. Found a hot prospect up that way. Where was the place they found?"

"Near Millbank. Know where that is?"

"No."

"Over a ridge or so from Matlock. Did you find other prospects?"

"Not near there, but all the numbers were unlisted and supposedly unassigned."

"Maddern got some telephone linesmen to help trace them. He got me to check that place. I don't think he expected that to be the one. The others he gave me were run down places. I feel really bad. We must have been seen and recognised. While we were away from the VW, someone did the brakes. Lucky I wasn't going fast, and we had a police radio."

"They have to be running out of places to hide," Jack growled. "If they have to act quickly, they might make mistakes."

"I hope so. The police have roadblocks everywhere."

"The task force is heading up there," Jack revealed. "Uncle is foaming at the mouth to go with them. Reckons he knows most about the bastards. Working on the idea that they repeat successful tricks, I told the Old Man they'd better stake out all waterholes, old mines, tips and such in the district. I got told not to try to teach the police their business. They have already contacted the Department of Mines, the Rural Water Board and local rescue volunteers."

"I hadn't heard that," Mike admitted, but he was relieved.

"Call me as soon as you hear anything, okay?" Jack urged.

"I will if you do," Mike agreed. "I am trying to figure out where they might hide around here."

Mike hung up, and went to tell Casey and Les what Jack had said.

"I had better go and prise Ian off the seat at the police station." Casey stood and stretched. Before he left, he said, "We'll find her."

Peg was barely conscious when she felt herself lifted out of the boot. The cooler, but not cool, evening breeze revived her enough to be aware of voices.

"Go on! Get her inside!"

The hands that had lifted her were gentle, and trembling. Some poor sod that King was terrorising, no doubt. She needed a drink. Her mouth was parched, and she had a vicious headache. Her clothes were damp from sweat that soon evaporated in the hot air.

Inside the house, cooler than outside, her Samaritan put her in a chair, not daring to untie her hands first. She had no time to enjoy the softness, before King yanked her off it, so she fell to the floor.

"You got a cold beer, old man?"

"The woman needs water."

Peg felt she should know that voice.

"Oh, that's right. You're one of those god-taken sorts who'll forgive criminals. Well, I want a beer. Then you can coddle the trash. Though she probably won't be awake for hours yet."

"Just get his beer," Peg murmured in an almost inaudible whisper, and not realising that she wasn't just thinking the advice.

The presence beside her moved away, and something pointed kicked her ribs.

"How can you be stirring? I gave you enough stuff to drop a horse."

Peg, who thought she was in a dream, knew, even in that state to stay mute.

King kept moving about, even when the other presence returned with a bottle of water and a straw.

"Try to sip this," the gentle voice urged. He put the straw to lips that were reddened and swollen.

There was no response, only the lips opening slightly. He withdrew the straw and carefully tipped a few drops of water into the mouth, and when the mouth moved more, he replaced the straw and saw a few tentative swallows.

"Who else lives here?" King demanded.

Peg heard the other say, "I gave the housekeeper the weekend off. My son and daughter are in Melbourne until Tuesday."

"You better not be lying, old man. And the bitch has had enough water. Anymore and she will piddle on your fancy carpet."

"Why are you doing this?"

"None of your business. You sit in that chair, and keep your hands where I can see them."

Jed Owens silently cursed the man he knew to be Harry King. The man had caused him more than enough grief by encouraging Sidney to gamble recklessly, and all the ensuing events. Now, though, his callousness towards his prisoner, Ida Jessup's girl, was beyond his understanding. He felt old and useless.

King's pacing was terrifying in itself. Every time he moved out of view, Owens felt the hairs on his neck try to rise. He felt like a stalked deer. The radio suddenly came on, but the chamber music on the ABC was not to King's taste. He turned the tuner, but finally left it on the local Matlock station.

The time beeps went through and the music theme preceded the news.

The first item was a warning to all residents in the district.

Too late, Owens thought, recalling how King had ambushed him on his return from checking the lower paddock. Now, King's car was hidden in the barn like stable, the spotter plane wouldn't see it.

While the news was on, King stopped pacing. Owens watched the girl on the floor surreptitiously testing the rope tying her hands. He couldn't see her face, but he was sure she was awake and watching King. She stopped when King began to move again.

The phone rang, but King had his gun out, a warning for Owens to stay where he was.

"Who would call you?"

Owens decided to be truthful. "Likely the feed merchant after his money, or the Falconers after their rent."

When the ringing stopped, King yanked the phone plug from its socket.

"If they decide to come visit, I will do you a favour and shoot them," King stated before he went over to the window to look out towards the gate he had come in through.

Movement on the floor distracted Owens, and he saw that the girls had kicked off a shoe somehow and was pushing it towards him. She was moving her legs slowly and silently. He leant back in the chair and stretched his own legs in her direction. His foot touched the shoe as King glanced over at him. When he looked away again, Owens moved the shoe closer to him, and gradually pushed it under his chair. Was the girl trying to leave a clue here? Why?

"Give the bitch some more water," King directed abruptly. "I still need her alive."

Owens was relieved to comply. He had formed a good opinion of Peg Jessup, and didn't think she deserved King's attention. He had to kneel down to help her suck on the straw. She was swallowing more easily now, but not gulping it. Even so, King didn't allow her much, before insisting she had had enough. The silent regard of the girl's eyes signalled her appreciation of his concern and help.

While replacing the bottle on the table, and seeing that King was watching outside, Owens slipped a hand into his pocket. He took out the sharp folding knife he usually carried, and slipped it quickly into the girl's pocket. As he stood awkwardly, the girl gave him a faint grin before closing her eyes.

He hoped she could make use of it. He hoped her grin meant that she thought she could.

When he heard the sound of a car driving up the gravelled driveway, King moved from the window and went to reduce the volume of the radio. When he returned to the chair, he had a knife in his hand.

A sharp rapping on the door was followed by a voice that called out to ask if he was home. It wasn't the voice of anyone he knew.

"Make a sound, and you and the girl will be dead," King warned before he moved soundlessly to the rear of the house.

Owens watched him until he was out of sight, then quickly knelt to try to loosen the ropes on the girl.

"That's enough," an almost inaudible voice warned him. "Just do what he wants. He is not ready to kill me yet."

Even though he couldn't understand the girl's apparent calmness, he took the hint to sit back in his chair.

The radio, even at the lower volume, was still audible. The news bulletin warned people again, and mentioned a property to property search for two wanted men and a missing woman. Owens wondered if the unexpected callers were police or volunteers. Would they notice anything unusual? Would they question the locked stable door?

When the callers gave up and returned to their car, King collected the card they had slipped under the door. He seemed to be muttering under his breath and edgy. He paced the room until it was fully dark, then announced, "Get up! You're going to drive me."

"What about her?" Owens protested.

"She won't be going anywhere. You got some shovels?"

"Yes."

"Get them, and no heroics, old man."

Shivers of dread ran up and down Owens' spine as he went out to the tool shed near the stables. King watched him from just outside the door until he returned.

"Put them in your 4WD and go lock the house."

Thinking of the girl's advice, he considered that the girl must know the man. He already knew King was ruthless, and cunning. When Sidney had failed to get his gambling debts paid off, someone had caused two of his horses to die. The only good thing - neither of the two was Black Diamond, although both horses had been brown.

"Get in! Drive towards Matlock."

Owens didn't question the destination, just hoped and prayed that the girl could get free and escape before they returned.

Owens had already decided that obedience was prudent, but he could not understand why King wanted him to dig into an old cess pit. It seemed that he didn't realise that when the district was converted to a proper system, these old pits were meant to have been filled in. Still, that would soon become obvious, and he was used to hard work. Though why King was digging a ditch down from the house to where he reckoned the pit inspection hatch was, was another question he dared not ask.

They were like two grave robbers, digging in the moonlight. That thought sent shivers down his spine.

"What the hell do you expect to find here?" Owens finally asked, hoping the maniac wanted something other than a burial place for something.

"Keep your mouth shut! Old Ida Jessup had stuff down here – once the pit wasn't used. And she had stuff she stole from me."

Owens quietened, still not reassured. He paused to wipe sweat from his forehead. The night was still oppressively hot, like the day had been. He hadn't heard the weather forecast, but there was no hint of rain in the air.

From nearby, a dog began yapping. A light went on in the next house. King began to swear under his breath.

"Found the hatch yet?" King demanded, coming down to check.

"I think so. I just hit something hard."

"Clear it."

A door opened in the neighbour's house and a torch shone towards them.

"Get down," King ordered as he shoved Owens. Then before the older man realised what he intended, his ankles were tied to one of the shovels.

"Not a sound," King warned, drawing a gun that glinted in the moonlight.

Owens wanted to call a warning, but he had no doubt that King would kill him and dump him in the pit. That wouldn't help the girl. If the person went back in the house, maybe they would be safe. If he could get his feet free, maybe he could run for help. The thin rope that tied his feet was hard to get a grip on, had he still kept his knife it wouldn't have held very long. He listened for sounds from the other house. If King used his gun, the report would echo and be heard for miles, but he also had a knife.

The yapping grew more frantic, then there was one yelp, and silence. The light went off in the house and soon after, Owens heard someone walking back along the road. He kept trying to free himself, until King was back at the house.

"Good thing you didn't run off," King said when he realised the bindings were loose. "Though you saved me wasting rope. I can reuse this. Get back to clearing the hatch."

Owens kept digging until the whole of the wooden door of the hatch was exposed. Then King pushed him aside, and yanked on the handle, lifting the cover. He had a torch now, and he shone it down.

The land sloped, and some of the dirt had slipped, so the way in was a slope, not straight down. King snapped off the torch.

"That will do for tonight."

"Aren't you going to look for your stuff?"

"That is what Ida's brat is for. She reckons what I want is down there.

She's going to find it."

"She won't be able to see much in the dark."

"She'll have a torch," King sneered.

"What if it isn't there?"

"If it's not, I ought to leave her there. The trash is more trouble than use. No, if she wants out, she will find it. If not, I'll have some fun with her. I'll let you watch if you like."

Owens turned away and King laughed. "Drive us back to your place."

Any hope that the earlier callers had sensed something wrong and decided to return were dashed. His house was quiet, no cars were parked awaiting his return. No doubt the searchers had regrouped in town when dark fell.

"Open the door."

Owens fumbled for his door key, and hoped the girl had got free. As soon as the door was unlocked, King shoved him in and turned on the lights. He swore when he saw the girl was not where she had been. He quickly slammed the door shut and turned the lock.

"You had better hope she is still here."

Owens saw the broken glass bottle, and the pieces of rope and felt a surge of elation. He eyed the door, and was about to make a dash for outside when he heard a scuffle, and loud curses coming from further in his house.

King re-emerged, dragging a struggling figure. "Look what I found, hiding in the bathroom."

"Peg!" Owens exclaimed involuntarily.

"He's not as smart as he thinks he is," Peg said aloud. It earned her more pain as her arm was forced up behind her back. "My mate Jack has him all figured out."

"Too bad the dead can't talk!" King laughed. "Vince got him in the leg. Left him pumping out blood. I heard on the radio that three people died. No loss, any of them. Heard too that his uncle is likely to be a vegetable for the rest of his life."

"Him? Yeah, well, he deserves it for helping you," Peg claimed.

"Get some paper and a pen," King ordered Owens.

"You going to write your confession," Peg retorted.

"No, you are. You are going to tie up some loose ends before I take you back to the fat man."

"I reckon he and you are a pair of queers."

Her arm was wrenched again, but with some of his drug still in her, the pain was still bearable.

"You're on borrowed time, bitch. The only reason you are still alive is because the fat man has your grandfather in a bother about you."

"Nah, the faceless man just don't want to kill me and make Blair happy."

"No, the fool still wants the shares that you and your dead con artist mate are hanging onto."

"If you think I can give then to you, you're wrong. I told you, the cops have them. Confiscated, they said. Blair is going to have to go to court about them. He won't win though."

"Maybe so, but you are going to sign them over to me."

"In your dreams."

King laughed. "You are also going to sign a confession, admitting that you killed your aunt."

"They don't think that –"

"Haven't you learnt that the police are devious? They are just letting you have enough rope to hang yourself. Your little scam with the shares, is reason enough to have done the old whore in."

"Nothing I write will be legal," Peg tried.

"I think it will. You see, Owens here is a JP. He can witness it and see it delivered to the police."

Peg glanced at Owens, saw him regarding her with an expression that was both of pity for her, and fearful. She had tried not to blurt out too much, but odds on, King planned to kill him before he left. She had to warn him.

Peg's first attempt was torn up. "No one can read that scrawl, make it legible," King snarled.

"Your fault. My hand is still in spasm from how you had my arm."

"Write what I told you again!"

With a look of contempt at King, Peg began to write slowly in capitals.

"Better." King let her finish, reading what she wrote over her shoulder and snorting at her bad grammar.

"Okay, old man, add your signature, and the date as witness.

Owens read through the 'confession' and didn't comment on the double negative, 'I didn't write this under no pressure from anyone'. He simply stayed silent and signed the page.

Similarly, with the will, written to assign the disputed shares over to King, lacked certain elements to be legal, particularly if the girl already had a legal will. King seemed to be assuming that Peg, being an uneducated yokel, and young, would not have thought of making a will yet.

As soon as Peg finished, and before Owens could protest, King grabbed her and knocked her out with a violent fist to her head. He dropped her and glared at Owens.

"Back in the chair or I will do the same to you."

Owens let himself be tied to the chair and gagged. He wasn't convinced that King would keep him alive if he had to flee again. He was almost sure that King had no intention of keeping the girl alive. In which case, his knowing where King had been digging was a death sentence. Maybe it would be a blessing, his life was in ruins now. He would be evicted from the farm soon, overwhelmed in debt, too old to learn any other job.

<h1 style="text-align:center">Chapter 33</h1>

Peg awoke to absolute darkness; a stale, putrid smell, and a renewal of the vile headache. Where ever she was, was stuffy and airless, and she was on some kind of wooden floor. She tried to move and realised that she was tied up again. Her breathing became ragged, even as her heart seemed to be beating way too fast.

Fearing that the place was sealed off, she forced herself to take deep even breaths, but she didn't feel any calmer. She tried swearing aloud, and realised that King hadn't gagged her.

Did he even intend to come back and get her?

Did he really believe her aunt had what he wanted down here?

If he was still after those damn shares, who had told him that the police didn't have them? Jack's uncle?

She had been trying not to think of Jack. Was he dead? King was more likely to lie, to make her feel even more helpless. But how could Jack find her – even if he were alive? She knew where she was. In a cesspit that hadn't been used all her life. The boys had dared each other to come down in there, but they said that the hole had been boarded over. Did King realise that?

Come to think of that, how could she look around down here if she were tied up? She couldn't exactly recall what he had said before pushing her down the opening. She'd been well out of it.

No, he wasn't going to come back and let her out – if he came at all it would be to gloat at her helplessness. He'd only let her out if Gianni insisted. If he was caught…damn it!

She wanted that fat bastard caught as much as she wanted King hung. What would happen if she died down in the smelly pit? Why was she thinking like that? She didn't want to die. She wanted to get free, like before with the broken glass.

A laugh escaped her. King hadn't checked her pockets. He had found her hiding, but not the piece of glass she had hidden in a face washer, or the knife Owens had slipped her. She had only just got free when she had heard the car returning. Maybe if she had gone straight out the back door, she might got away, but probably not.

She had more time now – but how to get the things from her pocket? If she could wriggle out of her track pants, or twist them, then maybe…

It took longer this time, because she had to fight off attacks of giddiness, and force away the sensation of the earth closing in on her. Finally though, her hands were free and she set to work to free her feet.

"There you bastard, I'm free!" Now to get out.

Recalling things that Ned and Jasper had said, steadied her. They'd gone down a ladder – one that was used by the people who'd pumped out the pit when it needed it. Stan, on one of his infrequent visits, had told the other two that the liquid stuff seeped away – down towards the creek and the earth filtered it. That had been enough to rid the others of their last qualms. Stan had agreed that his mother had stashed stuff – rubbish – down there, but he had not been specific. Ned and Jasper had found an old pram, and used the wheels for a billy-cart. She didn't recall anything else.

"OK, find the ladder," Peg said aloud. Hearing her own voice, steadied her.

Crawling, rather than trying to stand, she inched in one direction until she came to the concrete wall, and then stood to feel along it. She came to a vertical bar, and her next movement brought her to a place where the earth had slipped down. Deciding that door to the inspection entrance was above, she tried to climb up it. There was no room to put her feet on the mostly covered rungs, and her feet soon slipped. The dirt was more like mud.

That caused her more shivers. The past several days had been hot, and that increased the likelihood of a storm. What if it teemed again, like the night she'd left Matlock last time? She tried climbing again, pulling herself up using what she could of the ladder. This time, her head reached something solid, but she could not push it up, no matter where she put her hand. Giving up, she eased herself down to the wooden floor.

Around the landslip, the floor was getting wetter, and a rivulet was flowing towards a lower area of the pit. Peg wished she had a way of catching some of it. She was parched enough to consider drinking it.

Her manic energy evaporated, and she lay on the wood – tired, but not wanting to sleep. The dark, dank stuffiness closed around her.

Chapter 34

Jack woke, hearing the sound of someone moving around beyond the curtain around his bed.

"Uncle?" he called softly.

The movement stopped and the curtain was pulled back.

"Where are you going?" Jack asked when he saw that his uncle was dressed.

"You stay here. I'm going after King."

"Take me with you!"

"You can't move far on that leg, boy!"

"They gave me crutches. If you are going after King, I am going with you. The bastard has Peg. Has had her for two days now."

"Don't you mean Megan?" Justin taunted.

"I'm sure you know damn well who I mean."

"What could you do?"

"Help you to out-think that bastard. I haven't done badly, so far."

"True enough. Do you have clothes? They probably cut off what you were wearing."

"No," Jack said with frustration.

"Let me look. I should be able to lend you something."

They left the hospital, unchallenged. It was almost as if Justin Taylor had ordered the staff to ignore them. Someone must have been helping him for when they were outside, Justin went straight to a silver falcon hire car. The keys were on top of the rear kerbside wheel. Jack asked no questions, just let his uncle drive.

By the time they reached Matlock, Jack's leg was throbbing, but he refused to complain. His wife was in danger, he hoped not dead, and he was not going to sit out doing nothing any longer. His uncle pulled up outside a house Jack recognised. It was the one he and Peg had stayed at previously. While Justin strode up to the door and rang the bell, Jack moved more slowly on his crutches. A light came on and the door opened.

"Sir," came the greeting, and Jack recognised York's voice. "Jack? Should you be here?"

Justin answered, "No. Nor am I, so forget the 'Sir' for now and get this young fool some water."

"Water?" Jack queried, but his eyes widened when he saw the medicine vial his uncle took from his pocket.

"You look like hell, boy. Take two of these then get off your feet and rest."

"Thanks. How come you had them?"

Justin chuckled softly. "If you hadn't wanted to come, I would have been disappointed in you. You and your wife have as much right as I do to be in on King's capture."

"So, he's not been found yet?" Jack asked as he juggled crutches, pills and the water York handed him.

"No," Steve York told him. "We have the area bottled up and people visiting all the farms, houses, shacks. He can't get away and he is without his usual ability to call on others to help him."

"What about the sods who perjured themselves? Or the others who attacked us on the opening night?"

"He hasn't tried to get in contact with the first group and everyone in the second is either under remand, or being held incommunicado in Melbourne. We are doing everything possible, and watching all the places he might try to hide evidence."

"Hide Peg, you mean," Jack retorted.

York didn't confirm his meaning. "There are two beds made up. Nothing more can be done until morning. I will let Mike and Les know you are here, and they can come around. You all know King better than we do, so any thoughts will be welcome. Sir, Vic Maddern would like to see you in the morning."

Not long after York left, Jack was settled on one of the beds, more than ready to sleep, but his mind was still too active. Only when the heavy rain began, and he couldn't hear himself think, did he slip into sleep.

The pain in his leg woke him before dawn, but he didn't feel like getting up. Instead, he reached for the pillowslip he had borrowed to carry the few things he had bought with him from the hospital. His grandfather had sent Johnson to visit, with the journals he had been reading. He had grabbed them first, even before the few necessities he'd been given. He glanced at the end few entries for 1954, around the time Peg had been born, but it seemed that once Ida Jessup had got home with the baby, she had been too busy to write. All she had put in were her reasons for protecting the baby and how she had tricked King. He had been reading the earlier entries, trying to discover how events had played out to get to that point. He switched on the bedside lamp and found where he had inserted a bookmark. He was about to reach for the next journal, when Mike and Les arrived. He blessed their early arrival, for he wanted to know all they knew.

It was little more than York had told them.

"It's only a matter of time," Mike told Jack, quelling his tirade about the lack of success in finding Peg.

"Does she have time?" Jack protested. "I know the area is bottled up, but what if King dumps Peg somewhere and walks out? Ditches his car?"

"Likely places are being watched, Lover Boy," Les inserted. "But you have a point. He don't have to use a dam or a mine. However, they took her alive – so they want her that way."

"What if King is cornered?" Jack persisted.

"He'd use her as a shield or a hostage," Les decided. "He'd know we want her alive."

"All the more reason for him to kill her," Jack insisted.

"One thing though," Mike interrupted the glaring session between his friends. "King doesn't know the police have Costa – who is still claiming to be Costigan, of course."

"Ah," Jack breathed. "I gather there is a media blackout on that?"

Mike grinned. "And King called David Blair, trying to extort a ransom."

"Could they tell where he called from?"

Mike shook his head. "He didn't stay on the line long enough."

"So, what's happening today? My Uncle went off to see Maddern."

"Everyone will keep searching," Mike said. "I will see what Maddern wants Les and I to do, later."

"I'm coming with you," Jack insisted.

"You are a sucker for punishment, Lover Boy. Maddern had us checking out of the way places and talking to certain people."

"Yeah, the little charmers who got off with a warning after the fracas at the RSL," Mike explained. I checked where they are all living, and Les has a really neat way off –"

"Scaring the shit from them," Les finished. "None of that lot have admitted seeing him, and know that if they do, helping him will put them in prison."

Jack got dressed while Mike found food in the kitchen for breakfast. They ate before driving to the police station. Once there, they were aware of a constant coming and going. When they had slipped in, they heard Sergeant Kennedy issuing instructions for one team leader, then to another. While they waited for a lull, Steve York and Justin Taylor went off together.

York abruptly turned back, gestured to Mike and asked, "You've your car here?"

"Yes."

"Okay, follow me. I'm heading out to check Jed Owen's place. I will get you to watch from the back road before we go in."

"Right! I know the road you mean, and there are a few good spots to hide the car."

"You've still got the radio?"

Mike nodded.

York pulled up before turning into the long drive leading to the horse stud. Mike stopped his car next to his and had Les wind the window down.

"I will give you ten minutes to get into position where you can watch the back road. If we flush anyone, report only. Don't go off after them."

"Do they really think King is there?" Jack asked as Mike drove off.

"I doubt they can be sure, but they need to check," Mike explained. "I did over hear some comments. One of the teams went out there. The first time, his car was there but he wasn't. The second time the car was gone. They left a message, but he hasn't called in."

"I heard that he might have gone down to Melbourne," Les added.

Jack considered, "So, if the place is empty, he might be there. I know he got Sidney Owens in trouble."

Mike drove slowly off the road until he was behind a fallen tree limb. It mostly obscured the car, and although they couldn't see the house, they were probably closer to it than York had intended. He reported tersely, and sat back to wait to hear if York and Taylor found anything.

Two shots, reverberating around the hills, had them all on edge. Then they heard revving.

"That sounds like a V8,"Jack said.

"King's got a Monaro," Mike reminded him. "If he's getting away, he'd've been smarter to take Owen's 4WD. These roads are still muddy from the rain over the past two days."

"We should have blocked the road," Les suggested.

"Is the car coming this way?" Jack asked.

Mike listened, but decided, "Hard to tell." Moments later, they heard on the radio, "Message to all units. Suspect is driving a brown Monaro, registration…heading east towards the highway."

When the message was passed on, Mike used the portable radio to ask, "Was he alone?"

Taylor relayed for York, "Unit 7, proceed to house and investigate. Do not assume that suspect was alone at the house."

Mike acknowledged, and started his car.

"The sod is still trying to teach us the business," Jack muttered. "He can't talk."

"Stow it, Lover Boy. Let's see if the kid's at the house."

The stable door was hanging off its hinges, and a double rut went from it, across the muddy yard, to the driveway.

"It doesn't look like Owens has any horses here," Mike remarked, after a careful look around. He had pulled up a short distance from the house. "Les, check the stable, and then around the back. I'll check the front." He fiddled with something under his dash, then told Jack to stay with the car.

The huge house seemed to be unoccupied, but Mike was careful as he peeked in each of the front windows in turn. None were open. He approached the front door and jumped back when it opened from inside.

"CB, Lover Boy! Get in here."

Mike went right in, Jack cursed his slow progress as he awkwardly got from the car, reached for his crutches, and hobbled to the house. When he arrived, he heard Mike on the radio requesting a doctor and ambulance.

"Is it Peg?" Jack demanded of Les.

"No. Some old bloke. He's pretty bad. But the kid was here. I found a shoe pushed under the old guy's chair."

"York and my damn uncle had better catch that Monaro," Jack swore. "He must have put her in there."

"They were right behind him," Mike said. "They will get him."

"This time?" Jack muttered.

"Jack, help me untie Mr Owens. Les, see if you can find a first aid kit anywhere. Try near the back door where they come in from the yard, or the kitchen."

Being careful not to jolt the man, they freed his hands from the arms of the chair and found a towel to wad over the bleeding scalp wound. Jack felt for a pulse. It was there but weak. Owen's breathing was shallow.

"Why'd he bash the guy?" Jack asked aloud. "He was tied up, hardly in a position to stop him or chase him."

"He might have seen something or heard something that King wouldn't want people to know," Les proposed. "There's broken glass under that table, and scraps of rope. I reckon the kid got herself free."

"Then where is she? Peg knows this area."

"I'll check this place," Les said, dashing off.

"Watch for the ambulance, will you Jack?"

On his way back to the door, Jack saw the phone, tried it, and when he realised there was no dial tone, saw the damaged wall plug. He muttered more curses. He hoped that Owens would live. He might know something of Peg.

A car drew up, Jack thought it was the doctor, but the man had no bag. Before he could open the door, the new arrival hammered on it. Jack opened the door, but blocked the way in. The man, about to charge in, stopped at the sight of the crutches.

"Are you the doctor?"

"No. Who are you? You're not one of Owen's boys."

"I am not. Will you be kind enough to tell me who you are?"

"Henry Falconer. I own this place, or rather my mother does."

"Sir, you would be advised not to come in. We are waiting on a doctor and ambulance. After that, the police will want to check over the house."

"What's happened here? You are in there, trampling mud everywhere."

"I came across the gravel to get here, so if the mud is from the man the police are hunting, you do not want any of it on you."

The man took a step backward.

Jack, keeping his voice even, went on, "The man, who I presume is your tenant, is inside, badly hurt. As I mentioned, we have called for medical help."

"Who gave you authority to stop me coming in?" Falconer demanded. "Owens was going to pay me the rent today. It is already late."

"If you are that hard up, Sir, I am sorry. The man we found here is unconscious. He was bashed. If you have to come in, you will need to talk to the police. I think I hear a police siren as well as the ambulance bells."

Another car arrived first. This time it was the doctor. Jack forced Falconer further from the door by hopping out and allowing only the doctor to pass. "First door on the left, Sir."

Maddern and Hogan arrived after the ambulance, and while the senior detective went in, Hogan greeted Falconer.

Jack, still keeping his voice even, remarked, "Mr Falconer came to visit. He was lucky not to arrive a few minutes earlier. He might have met King's Monaro head on." He had the satisfaction of seeing the man's ruddy face turn pale.

Without seeming to be interested, Jack listened to Hogan's conversation with Falconer. He heard enough to guess that Owens was just about broke, and likely to be evicted. He would tell Peg when they found her. His impression of Falconer was 'arrogant jerk'.

Jack also tried to hear the conversation between Maddern and the doctor. From the snippets he caught, the prognosis for the old man was not favourable. He tied not to picture Peg laying somewhere, bashed, or worse.

The marks on the cream carpet, mentioned by Falconer, now took Jack's attention. It looked like clay mud, not the darker mud around the house. Who had tramped that muck in, and from where?

The ambulance men were summoned and they brought the waiting gurney in. Les and Mike appeared.

"Maddern said to come to the station," Mike told his friend, as he glanced at the stranger. "It's getting crowded in there. Hello, Gary. Any word on the chase Senior York went on?"

Hogan shook his head. "No, not yet."

Jack hadn't heard anything on the portable radio, so he guessed the pursuit was being monitored on another frequency.

After Mike and Les gave a report of what they had found in Owens' house, and put it in a signed statement, they collected Jack from downstairs. He had made notes of things he'd noticed, for Sergeant Kennedy to give Maddern.

"We're to hang around," Mike told Jack. "But not here. Let's go to the café."

Jack waited until they were outside before demanding, "Any word on King?"

He wasn't answered until they were away from a small group of men hanging around outside.

"Lover Boy, I'm betting they got him, and that is why they don't want us hanging around too close."

"As we went up, I heard the Task Force guy, Haldane, organising a secure transport vehicle to come here," Mike added.

"No mention of Peg, then," Jack said with anger and worry changing his voice. "Did they check his car? Did you check everywhere in the house?"

"Yes," Mike assured him.

"I reckon his majesty was only worried about himself when he took off. He must have stashed Peg somewhere else."

"Where?"

"All the likely places have been staked out for the past two days," Mike pointed out.

"Then they missed somewhere," Jack retorted.

"Let's eat and think on it," Mike suggested. "They won't stop looking for her. She is still a vital witness against King."

"If the old guy doesn't die," Les put in, "he might know something or why did his majesty try to finish him?"

Once they were at a window table, with coffee and sandwiches, Jack lapsed into silence. After a while, Casey and Ian joined them. The latter was as silent as Jack.

"They caught King," Casey told them. "He tried to ram one of the police road blocks and when that didn't work, tried to run for it. He didn't have anyone in the car with him, or in the boot."

"Bastard wouldn't say what he did to my little girl," Ian said abruptly. "Just laughed, he did. Said he left her alive, safe and dry."

"Safe and dry?" Jack echoed. "I know that bastard. He wouldn't care if she died. He tried to drown her before and failed. But it has teemed since she went missing. He's put her somewhere that he expects will flood, and where she can't get out of. Where around here might it flood after such a cloud burst?"

All eyes went to Casey who was considering the question. "There have been watchers on all the waterholes and all the old mines shown on the geological maps of this area. I will suggest a new check. I do not think King would know of any unmarked mines – he's a city person. The creeks and the river might come up…there might be caves or holes…I'll talk to Vic Maddern."

"Can the kid swim?" Les asked.

Casey smiled faintly. "She followed her brothers everywhere. I reckon she's good enough in the water."

"What if she's tied up? He wouldn't want her escaping," Ian stated their worst fear.

"While near a creek is an option, most of them are overgrown. I doubt King would force his way through the brush."

"Nah! Not his majesty."

"We are missing something," Mike said.

"Great observation, CB."

"Shh. I'm thinking. We know Peg was at the Owens farm, at least for a bit. He'd probably learnt of the place from Sidney Owens, and went there when he left Mill Creek. We know when that was. If he reckons she was 'safe and dry' he must have taken her somewhere before the rain began. Can we use that to estimate how far he might have gone? If he ditched Peg somewhere? Did anyone recheck Ida Jessup's place? Peg used to walk from there to the Owen's farm."

"There was clay mud on the carpets near the front door out there," Jack said. "I don't know if you noticed. Where can we find that around here?"

Casey dampened their hopes. "All the ridges, and wherever the topsoil has been washed away."

"Ridge Road?" Jack asked pointedly.

"Any water would run straight downhill," Mike pointed out.

"Maybe water isn't the issue?" Jack decided. "Let's go look around there. King and Costa have hidden bodies in places where people wouldn't think to look."

Ian made a sound like a sob.

"Dad! We're not saying she's dead. She'd never give in against them," Mike said bluntly. "Just that Jack said once that those bastards repeat things that have worked before."

"And your little girl, Ian, is tough." Casey met Ian's eyes until he nodded. Then he turned to the three younger people. "I think you should check around Ida's place. That neighbour might have seen something. Older people often don't sleep as much."

"Yes, and that little dog usually barks at shadows," Mike recalled.

Mike drove them up to Ridge Road and stopped outside the Jessup house. When they walked around, it showed even more signs of unauthorised visitors that he'd noticed the last time he was up there. Now, most of the windows were broken, and a section of the metal roof had fallen off at the back. They also saw the hole in the rain tank and the pipes fallen down to the ground, that had once fed the tank.

"Ain't heard the yappity dog," Les commented, causing Mike to glance at the neighbour's house.

"No, and the old woman hasn't come out."

"If there have been a lot of vandals, she might be too scared to," Jack suggested. "Her car is there."

Without further discussion, they headed down the road. When they entered the front yard, they began to hear a high pitched keening. Les moved off, looking for the dog. Jack tried the front door. It was locked.

"I'll check the back," Mike said, going off at a trot down the driveway. He come back quickly. "Locked, like all the windows, but I saw someone lying on the floor. Can you unlock the door?"

Jack nodded. "I guess this time, my uncle and grandfather won't have my hide."

Les returned, crooning to something she had wrapped in the jumper she'd had tied to her waist. "Poor little mutt. Reckon it got kicked around. Must have run off and hid. I found it behind a potted tree."

It didn't take Jack long to force the old lock. He stepped aside to let Mike go in first. He hopped in more slowly, but stopped when he saw Mike squatting down beside an elderly woman.

"She's alive," he said with relief. "Can one of you find a rug? She's icy cold."

The dog in Les's arms was trying to get down, in spite of its hurts.

"Let it down and go and see if there's a phone."

Jack returned with the rug from the woman's bed. "Peg said she doesn't have a phone. The nearest one is at the house nearest the main road."

"Do you still have the police radio, CB?"

"It's in the car."

Les ran to fetch it while the little dog snuggled into its mistress. Mike draped the rug and tucked it close, all the while speaking gently, to reassure the woman if she roused.

"I reckon I know who did this," Jack said quietly. "She has probably been lying here several days."

"Yes, and Peg has probably been missing that long. If King was here, he must have been doing something at Peg's old place. There is clay there."

Jack and Mike stared at each other. The same deep fear occurring to both of them.

Les returned with the radio, giving it to Mike, and then went to find a bowl of water for the dog.

"What's with you both? Did the lady cark it?"

Jack announced, "I'm going back to Peg's to look around."

As Mike took the radio, he shoulder shrugged at Les, and glanced at Jack. She picked up his meaning quickly. She put the water near the dog, and stood up.

"Not so fast, Lover Boy. You don't want to end up sitting on a muddy backside."

The police and the ambulance arrived together, Maddern striding in first. "How is she?"

Mike stood. "Pretty bad. Weak pulse and she was cold. I didn't want to move her. The dog has been badly treated too." He glanced to where the dog had been. It wasn't there.

"What made you come here?" Maddern asked. He stepped back to let the ambulance men lift Elvira Bernstein onto the gurney.

"Something Jack said." Mike outlined his friend's reasoning. "And someone has been digging in the back yard of the Jessup place. I thought it was more vandals, but…"

Maddern caught on to what Mike didn't say. "Come on." He gestured for Mike to leave, and they went to his car and drove the short distance to Peg's old home.

Jack was systematically looking over the yard. Les stood where Mrs Bernstein's dog was persisting in digging near a concrete slab.

"The whole damn area looks to have been dug over," Jack exploded. "And that last lot of rain didn't help."

"The council had the overgrowth cleared," Maddern said. Then he looked at the dog. "Is that Elvira Bernstein's dog?"

"Yes. The silly mutt must be able to smell the chooks, a decade on," Les proposed. "And it's doing it even though it's been hurt."

"I will see if I can get Frank Levin's dog out here," Maddern said, turning to walk back to his car.

Jack, Les and Mike looked at each other.

"The kid's not dead! She promised me –"

"She's tough!"

"Stubborn too," Jack added.

"Hey! Where did the mutt go?"

Jack hopped over and prodded the small hole with his crutch. More dirt fell as the hole got bigger.

"Mr Maddern! Over here," Jack yelled.

Maddern trotted back. "You'd best keep back. I'd say that's the old cess pit. They were meant to have been filled in, but the filling might have subsided."

"Peg's in there! I know it," Jack insisted. He saw Maddern frown.

"The dog went in there," Les backed him. "It likes the kid."

"And the channels someone dug lead there, and the spouting from the tank…" Mike pointed out.

"Okay, I'll organise a rescue team."

Oblivious to becoming wet and muddy, Jack lay on the ground so that he could call down the hole.

"Peg! Can you hear me?" He could only hear the dog yapping excitedly.

Chapter 35

The dog's yapping aroused Peg from a feverish stupor. Sometime during a period of sleep or deep unconsciousness, she had rolled from the wooden false floor, down into the muddy residue at the base of the pit. She realised that most of her was in water. The ground sloped, so her head was out of it, even if her clothing was soaked.

It took her a while to realise what her ears were hearing.

"Dog rat?" The barking took on a higher pitch. "Are you dead too?"

In the next instant, she felt the dog land on her chest and move to start licking her face.

"You brainless mutt," Peg told it. "How will you be able to boast that you found me? Even I can't climb back up to that wooden floor."

Peg forced herself to stand, to ignore her headache and the feeling of vertigo. "Shut up a minute, dog."

The little Chihuahua did so, and Peg thought she heard Jack's voice. Her eyes began to water. It brought back memories of her dreams. Dreams that had convinced her that she was dead. She had been talking to her mother, and her aunt. They had been trying to tell her something. Proof of who she was, but she already knew that. Her mother had apologised for dying. Her aunt had said it was King. He'd been there, and told her to remove all traces. She'd done what she could. Removed the bloody sheets and towels.

Now, if she could hear Jack, he had to be dead too. He was still calling, waiting for a reply. She tried to yell, "About time you got here." But only a whisper came out.

"Dog rat, if I lift you up, can you take something and get out?" She felt in her pocket, she'd put the face washer in there, but could the dog manage it?

"Here, boy?" The dog grabbed the fabric and allowed itself to be lifted. It sprang from her hands, onto the wood.

Please, let Jack be real. If not, bring his ghost down here.

Minutes passed. Jack's ghost didn't appear and the dog didn't return.

"Damn! He isn't there. No one is."

Jack grabbed the dog when it reappeared dragging the muddy scrap of cloth. Les took it as he pushed himself to his knees.

"She's got to be down here, alive."

"Jack," Maddern began, not wanting to raise hopes.

"Copper! The mutt's excited, not whining," Les pointed out.

"Can we get it to take the portable radio down?" Mike suggested. "I can go look and see if Peg's aunt had string in her house."

"Alright," Maddern agreed. "And look for something to wrap the radio in."

While Mike was in the house, two more cars drove up. One held Steve York, and the other man wore overalls and donned a hard hat. He reached back into his car for some rolled up maps, then strode over.

"Sergeant, you were correct. There is an old pit on this property. Along here, they weren't filled in, but a wooden floor was inserted. There should still be an inspection hatch."

"Good of you to come, Mitch. It looks like a concrete slab was poured over the area," Maddern commented.

"Yes, yes, the lady applied to put a chook shed there and to use the pit for shovelling the muck from the hens into. Not what I would recommend, but this was before I took over as chief."

"Where might the hatch be?" Maddern prompted.

Mitch unrolled his charts, selected one to place on top, eyed the area and moved into a line between the house and the slab.

"About there," Mitch estimated. He pointed to where the three younger people were looking at a hole. . "Let me get a crowbar and shovel."

Maddern studied the signs of digging, the channel from the tank to the hole, and hid his apprehension.

Mike ran back. "Plastic bag and string." He took the bulky radio from his car and began to tie it into the bag, and then unravel the rest of the ball of string. Les handed him the muddy cloth.

"Tie it to that, CB. Hopefully, the mutt will take it to the kid."

"I will have to feed the string in after it," Mike thought aloud.

"Hurry up then," Jack urged.

Peg was listening in the darkness and only the muffled whine told her that the dog had returned. She moved until the sound was overhead.

"Couldn't you find anyone?" she asked in a quiet voice. "Damn!"

The dog yipped, then growled, and seemed to be waiting for her to do or say something.

"What's with you, dog? I can't see anything from down here."

The dog yipped again.

"I can't lift you down!"

She heard something scraping on the wood, then something hard struck her shoulder. One end of the object, now on the muck at her feet, glowed faintly. She picked up the almost exhausted torch. She shone it up. The dog's eyes gleamed, and she could just make out that it had something in its mouth.

"Just what I needed, a muddy cloth back."

The dog dropped the cloth over the edge of the wood. When it didn't drop, Peg reached up, but she still needed to jump to reach it. Not an easy task on the unstable footing. When she finally grasped it, she felt the string. That hadn't been on it before! Her hopes rose.

"You could've brought me a rope," she told the dog. "Then I could have climbed out of here."

As she was talking, she gently tugged on the line, and began to feel resistance. She gave a gentle tug on the line, heard something hit the wood above her. She kept pulling, and heard something scraping across the floor. She was ready to catch whatever it was, once the object was straight above her.

She was surprised by the solid weight, but even with the faint torch light, she had no idea what it was. Her fingers felt over the plastic, seemingly causing the thing to vibrate. Then she heard a muffled voice.

"Peg? Can you hear me?"

Jack?

She felt over the package, felt a coiled cord and a handpiece.

"Jack?" she tried to shout as she pressed the microphone switch.

She heard, "It's Steve York." The voice was clearer that time.

"Oh! I didn't invite you to hell, did I?"

She couldn't help the feeling of disappointment. Her mind wasn't being logical. All she could think was that if York was dead too, she wouldn't need a radio to talk to him. And if Jack was dead, why hadn't he appeared, like her aunt and mother had.

"How are you?" the voice asked.

"Huh! Burning up. I'm in hell!"

"Are you hurt?"

Her laugh was strained. "Ghosts can't get hurt."

"We are organising a rescue team," Steve's voice said. "We'll have you out soon."

"Oh! Ok! I fell though the floor."

Outside, Mitch was already removing a neat sod that had been put back over the hatch cover. The hole had been right on the edge of the sod. Now the wooden door was revealed, and with a little more digging, opened.

"Let me go down," Les insisted.

"No," Maddern said immediately. "It's dangerous."

Les gave the two policeman and the rotund Mitch a raking head to foot gaze. "I don't give a shit if I get dirty." She eyed York and Maddern in their suits. "And I am leaner than the rest of you. I can take a rope down and some water. The kid's raving sick. Can't you understand that?"

After persisting in her demand, Maddern finally agreed. Mitch warned her what to expect and provided her with a torch.

"The ladder seems to have been covered by an earth slippage. We will need to lower you down."

"Nah! I'll be right," Les asserted. "Where's the rope? Let's hope I don't land on the mutt."

Once she had started to crawl feet first into the hole, Les began a sub-audible conversation berating herself for voluntarily going into a dark, dark, hole. She had only ever admitted it to one person, but she hated dark enclosed places. It reminded her of how her old man had kept her locked up – on many occasions – so that he could do what he wanted with her. If it had been anyone else down the hole, sick and injured, she would have said nothing. But it was the kid. The first person who had been a friend, and didn't care that she had done all sorts of crook things. And the kid had promised to help her get a new start.

The dog heard her and yipped.

"Dopey mutt! Why don't you get out of here before you get buried in this pit?"

It came over and twined around her feet. She scooped it up and put it on the slope of the earth slippage. "Shoo! Get out!" She gently shoved it until it got the hint.

Les shone the torch around, and edged to where the floor had collapsed.

She looked down.

"Where the hell are you kid?"

"Hey! Don't go!"

"What are you on about? I'm not going anywhere. Not without you, you silly idiot."

"Les? Did he kill you too?"

"Of course bloody not! Who do you think he killed?"

"My mother, my aunt, Jack…"

"You're delusional kid. Lover Boy would be down here with bells on if he didn't have to use those damn crutches."

"Huh? King said he killed him."

"And you believed him? His majesty is not so bloody lucky and I intend to make sure it isn't third time lucky for him with you."

"Okay."

"Kid! Will you concentrate? I'm coming down to you."

"Okay."

Les used the one end of the rope to tie around her waist. Then she moved back to call up through the hole, "Keep tension on the rope and lower me slowly, okay?"

She smiled grimly when she felt the tension. Good feeling, telling cops what to do.

Peg wasn't directly below, Les saw as she used her torch. There was water below, and Les hoped it wasn't deep. Finally, her feet felt the water, and the underlying sludge. As she tugged the rope to tell those above she was down, she heard rustling – like of plastic. In the torchlight, she saw a shadow on something pale - trying to dig something from the muck with her hands.

"Kid? What are you doing?"

"Gotta take this with me."

"What for? It's rubbish."

"No! Aunt Ida said it would crucify King."

Les shone the torch, there were several plastic bags, already exposed. She felt one and guessed the soft stuff inside was fabric."

"Your cop mates are up above. We will tell them about the bags. They can make sure it comes up carefully. It will be awkward enough, getting just you up."

In fact, Les had expected Peg to be on the wood floor, not right in the old cess pit. She grabbed Peg's hand and pulled her from the plastic bags.

"Hang onto me. I'll get them to pull us both up. We'll have to climb over the edge of the floor, though."

Les grabbed the radio first and caught it in a fold of her jumper, then tugged the rope. When she felt the tension on it, she caught Peg in a hug, and very slowly, they were both lifted to where she could begin to climb over the edge of the broken floor. Les managed to heft Peg up, before climbing up herself. She tugged the line to get them to stop pulling. Then she found the small kids drink bottle of water in her pocket and gave it to Peg.

"Here kid, drink. You're a bloody furnace. You need water."

Peg made no move to take the bottle, so Les nudged her. "Keep awake, Kid. We're almost out. They can drag us or you can get up and move your butt."

When that didn't seem to have any effect, she added, "Jack is waiting for you out there."

That worked. With Les to help her, and provide a shoulder to support her, they walked to where the ladder was part buried. "Okay, climb up. I push from here. Go on!"

As soon as her head and shoulders were clear, York and Maddern helped Peg the rest of the way out, and let her collapse onto the ground. Jack began to hobble over as fast as he could. When he reached her he heard a very soft, "Took you long enough."

Not knowing how to reply, Jack settled for, "Glad you waited. Next time don't go off without me."

Mike went to help Les out, and noticeably sniffed.

"Not a word, CB. It positively reeks down there." Les moved Mike aside and fronted Maddern. "The kid is convinced that you have to get some plastic bags of stuff from down there. Reckons it'll crucify King. Maybe you'd better do it, even if I think the kid was hallucinating or something."

The ambulance had arrived, and Maddern gestured for them to take Peg to the hospital. When they tried to move Jack out of the way, Peg hung onto him.

"They have to get that stuff. My aunt told me."

"Your aunt is dead."

"She was down there with me! She wrote about it in her notebook. My mother was there too."

Jack took a calming breath, and asked, "What stuff is it?"

"From the motel. When I was born."

Jack stared at her. It sounded like she was raving or had been hallucinating. He turned his gaze to Maddern.

"We will bring it out," Maddern promised. "We will have it looked at, but after so many years, it may not tell us much."

"It will!" Peg insisted. She described what the ghostly form of her aunt had told her that she'd done eighteen years before, ending with. "King killed my mother. She might have been dying already, but he made sure. He would have killed me too, but my aunt had hidden me, saying I was born dead."

Jack merely shook his head, and decided to check the journals he was reading. He'd past the entries for the birth, and none of that was mentioned.

"You go with her, Jack. We will be along after the doctor has checked her," Maddern directed.

"What about the pooch. The little hero deserves a treat."

From the gurney, as she was being carried to the ambulance, Peg said, "It likes cheese."

Maddern smiled. "The vet is in Main Street. I will let him know to expect you. He can look after it until Elvira Bernstein is able to come home."

Mike saw another car arrive. It was Jack's, but being used by Casey. "Uh Oh!"

Maddern looked over as Ian rocketed out of the car. Jack and Mike moved to intercept.

"Where is she? Where's my little girl?"

"Dad! She's okay!" Mike gestured to Jack to get go join Peg. "She's going to the hospital to be checked over."

"Why? What's wrong?"

"Dad, she was down a pit for over a day or more. But she said she found something that will finish King. Maddern is going to have it brought up. If it is what Peg said, you might be needed to see if you can identify anything."

Ian turned to the policeman. "You better make sure that bastard and his boss don't get away, and don't wriggle out of a charge of taking my little girl."

"The task force has taken control of them and both are on the way to Melbourne. They won't be allowed contact with each other, and there is enough evidence to hold them both."

"Bastard got off last time!" Ian commented, but he was standing a little straighter.

Maddern turned to the three younger people. "You all deserve credit for your actions today. Can I ask you to come to the station tomorrow to add to your statements?"

York, who had been organising for a forensic team to come from Melbourne, and advising the SAR team who had arrived that they were no longer needed to rescue Peg, but would be needed to bring up some potential evidence, now came over.

"The forensic guys should arrive about five," York told his superior. "They said to wait until they were here to bring anything out."

"Then I'm going to the hospital," Ian announced. Mike just shrugged and said, "Let's get the dog to the vet and go there too. We can't do any more here."

Chapter 36

Jack was decidedly twitchy once Peg had been wheeled into one cubicle, and he was firmly directed to another.

"Your wife is in excellent hands, Mr Dawes," the Indian doctor assured him. "It is my job to check your injury. A bullet wound, I was told."

"Yeah," Jack confirmed, having a good idea who had sent the information. He watched as the man carefully unwound the bandage from the dressing. It had absorbed some muddy water from his jeans. This was the first time he had seen the damage the bullet had done, and he winced. The doctor back in Melbourne had assured him that with physio, the damage to the muscle would heal. Right now though, his leg looked a mess."

"You have been doing too much," the doctor told him.

"I was using crutches," Jack assured him.

"You should be resting it. Keeping it elevated. See, the stitches are straining against the swelling, and the area is red. I will give you a shot of antibiotics and a prescription for more, which you will take each day for a week."

"I should be able to rest it more now," Jack said, meekly.

"When you wash. Put a plastic bag around the bandage. It is not to get wet."

When the new dressing and bandage were in place, Jack asked, "Can I go and be with my wife?"

"That should be allowable."

Steve York entered the private ward later in the afternoon. He grinned when he saw Jack had his leg resting on a stool. "I thought you could use a lift, to go and change before dinner."

"I hoped she'd wake up before I had to go."

"What was the doctor's verdict?"

"Dehydration, lack of food, probably some lingering drug effects, grazes and bruises, and some kind of infection. The test results haven't come back yet, but they have glucose in the drip, as well as antibiotics."

"She's in good hands here. Let her sleep."

Jack reached for the crutches and stood up. "Mike said you were paying for dinner."

"Only for half of it." York grinned. "CI Taylor is shouting the other half."

Jack's jaw dropped. "You're kidding!"

"No, the three of you did good work, and he said you deserved a good meal before his father caught up with you."

"He's not up here is he?" Jack asked quickly.

"No, but he insisted that I made sure you had your leg checked over. What did you do to it?"

Jack explained, ending with, "King's flunkey probably thought he killed me."

"I guess he is in for some unpleasant surprises," York concluded. "Anyway, Vic still wants a word with you about Megan's insistent suggestion."

Jack slapped his forehead, "Yes, but I need to check something before I see him."

"And clean up?"

"Yeah, I probably should."

On the way out, Jack noticed a constable on duty outside the door.

"We're keeping an eye on Megan as well as the other two you helped," York commented. "All could be witnesses against King."

"Yeah," Jack said heavily.

"Do you think Megan will be put off testifying?"

"No damn way! I just hope the damn lawyers don't get away with bringing in a bunch of perjurers again."

When he returned to the house, Jack's first action was to avoid the lounge room where he could hear Casey and Ian talking. He went to the room he was using and found Ida Jessup's 1955 journal still locked in a drawer. He quickly scanned the earliest entries and finally came to where Ida Jessup told of registering the birth, and wandered on to recalling the outcome at the motel.

"Yes!" Jack breathed out, as he read how Ida had removed the bedding, the clothing her friend had worn, and anything either of them had touched. She was brutal in her condemnation of King's callous smothering of the new mother, and admitted to herself that she was terrified of being accused of being an accessory but dared not go against King.

After changing into cleaner clothes, borrowed from Mike, he put the journal into his pocket. He would show it to Maddern, and indicate the entry that mentioned hiding the bags Peg had found.

Had she really talked to the ghosts of her mother and aunt?

Chapter 37

Peg, known at the hospital by her real name of Megan Dawes, felt immensely better the following morning after a breakfast of Weetabix and milk, followed by a poached egg on toast. She still had to have the drip in, but was allowed to make her own way to the shower and toilet. She wanted to look the best she could for when Jack returned. The nurse had told her that he would be in late morning. The same girl had casually mentioned the other two patients brought in through the emergency department were in rooms adjoining hers. Peg had got her talking and when the names Owens and Bernstein were mentioned, some of her good mood had vanished. Because of her, King had hurt them too. It had to have been him.

No one had said that she couldn't go visiting other patients, so she decided that she should.

Mrs Bernstein looked old and frail, lying in the hospital bed. Any residual animosity towards the busybody, drained away. When she rolled her drip stand into the room, Elvira Bernstein opened her eyes.

"You! Why are you here?"

"To make sure you were okay. You see, even though I wasn't in a position to do anything, I feel partly responsible for King roughing you and the pooch up. You had seen that bastard before, at my aunt's, hadn't you?"

A frail hand reached from under the covers for the button to call the nurse. "You leave me alone!"

"I'm not going to hurt you. I hate the bastard worse than you. He intended for me to stay buried alive and if your little pooch, who is a real hero, hadn't come digging, I would still be in my aunt's old cess pit."

The woman's expression didn't change. "What happened to Pepi?"

"I don't know. But I can ask Jack and have him come and tell you."

"Hmm!" was the only reply as Peg saw her former neighbour glaring at her.

Peg guessed the problem. "I didn't kill my aunt! When I got back from hiding some stuff, King was there with another bloke. I managed to get free, and was running to the nearest phone when a third bloke got me.

King killed my aunt, then tried to get me to tell him things, then left me for dead."

"I know what I saw and heard that day!"

"Fair enough. What about the other night? Do you remember that?"

The old woman nodded stiffly. Since she didn't volunteer the information, Peg sighed inwardly and suggested, "Make sure you tell Vic Maddern all you saw. You must have seen King, or he wouldn't have been worried enough to visit you. This time, I hope that bastard will be jailed for life. Anyway, I do hope you get better quickly."

The constable on duty relaxed enough to grin at her. He'd heard her conversation with the old woman and knew she wasn't a risk. "Where are you off to now?"

"To see Mr Owens. He was the first guy in this town to give me a go."

Owens didn't stir when she entered, but he wasn't alone. Neville and Cecily, two of his children, were with him.

"What do you want?" Cecily demanded in a low voice. "Haven't you done enough?"

"Enough what?" Peg said without heat. "If you mean done enough to fix the bastard who did the injuries to your dad, then the heck I haven't. I have an even bigger score to settle with Harry King."

"This wasn't her fault, Cec," Neville said. "If anything, I blame Sidney. He had to spout off about Black Diamond, and how rich dad was, to King when he got in too deep gambling."

"And now Mr Falconer wants to evict us," Cecily hissed. "It will finish Dad. Even if Nev and I were working, we couldn't keep the place."

"Well, I'm sad to hear that," Peg admitted. "I respect you father, because he gave me a chance. That's why I came to see how he was. I wanted to wish him well. Will you tell him that?"

Neville nodded.

"Are either of you working?"

"What's it to you?" Cecily demanded.

"Dad was teaching me about training," Neville admitted. "Cecily is training to be a secretary."

"Then there might be others you could work for," Peg suggested, ideas coming into her mind.

Neville shrugged. "Not around here."

Peg shrugged in turn and turned to leave, only to run into Jack as he poked his head into the room.

"There you are, you idiot. You're meant to be resting." He hopped fully into the doorway.

"I was just catching up with Neville and Cecily Owens. Mr Owens is still unconscious."

"Oh, I'm sorry to hear that. Mike and I did what we could until the ambulance came."

"You were one of the people who found him," Neville asked. He came over and held out his hand. "The doctors said that you probably kept him alive."

Jack took the proffered hand and shook it.

"Are you a friend of Peg?" Neville asked.

"He's my mate," Peg said quickly.

"More like your keeper," Jack retorted, resting on the crutches. He went on, "Come on, Carson is waiting to see you."

"Wayne Carson?" Cecily asked, wide-eyed. "He's here? So it is true that you are Megan Arthur? Darlene said you were pulling a giant scam."

"And you believed that snob?" Neville snorted. "She's just a jealous bitch. I'd not listen to her if I were you. She's likely to drop you anyway, once she hears Dad's practically broke."

Peg had a thought. "Want to meet him?"

Cecily turned back. "Wayne Carson? I'd die!"

"He's not an ogre. His manager is the real dragon." Cecily's star struck expression was answer enough. "Come on, then."

Peg's introduction of Cecily, clued Carson to the fact that she was trying to befriend her. He was, as usual, the consummate gentleman, and easily engaged her in conversation. Peg took the chance then to give Jack a longed for hug and kiss.

"Saw Mrs Bernstein," Peg whispered to Jack. "She's worried about her dog. Can you go and reassure her?"

Cecily left when Carson suggested that he needed to talk to Megan, and she actually gave Peg a smile when she left.

"One of your former school mates?" Carson queried that part of the introduction.

"Well, not a mate as you guessed, but she wasn't one of the worst of the snobocracy. More of a follower. Besides, her father was the guy that gave me a chance. So, how did you find out that I was incarcerated here?"

Carson glanced at Jack, and she needed no vocal answer.

"For someone who reckons I should be resting, he's doing too damn much himself," Peg directed at Jack. Then to Carson she asked, "I take it, that since you came to visit, that you are not about to tell me to get lost again."

Carson merely grinned, and reached for a flat wrapped parcel. "Not while we, as a team, can get this…"

Peg took the parcel and unwrapped it. She was speechless as she gazed at the gold record with Carson's name and hers, along with the title of the record, clearly engraved.

"As soon as you are fit to be seen," Carson grinned, because Peg had instinctively closed the gown she wore over the white backless hospital gown. "Mac will be organising a photo session and some publicity."

"How soon will I be wanted to perform?"

"You let Mac know when you are ready."

"Which isn't right now," Jack inserted.

"No. My chief body guard needs to get over his shot in the leg, and I don't know when I will be wanted for other things."

"And how is that other matter going?" Carson asked with concern.

Jack answered that. "The police haven't let the media know yet, but Harry King and Gianni Costa were both caught. And soon will be in shock over the number of charges they are facing. We should have some warning of when they will be appearing in court, and if we are needed."

"I will tell Mac that you will soon be fit to work. Have you anymore new songs underway?"

"Maybe," Peg admitted. "You'll be amongst the first to find out."

Once Jack came back from reassuring Elvira Bernstein about the disposition of her little Pepi, Peg had him ring Vic Maddern and let him know she was up to talking to him. He sent Steve York to get her statement, and he confirmed her claim of being drugged, from the results of her blood tests.

When asked, Steve told her how he and Justin Taylor had caught King. He had crashed his Monaro, and taken off on foot. The prisoner had refused to tell where he had stashed her, and since she had still been missing then, she hoped King thought her still buried. He could have a really nasty shock when she appeared in court to testify against her. Steve had no idea when that might be, but Jack promised to confront his grandfather on that matter.

Finally though, Peg and Jack had time to themselves.

"Ian is itching to meet you again," Jack warned her. "So expect him this afternoon."

"I still don't believe it. How odd is it that I meet my half-brother, who finds his father, and he's the same as mine?"

"Truth can be stranger than fiction," Jack remarked. "It makes Mike my brother-in-law, and we've both felt we'd have liked to have a brother."

"And if he and Les ever hook up permanently, it will make her my sister-in-law," Peg grinned. "I told her already I had adopted her as one, but well…"

"However," Jack went on, "that other relative of yours is another story. He's still dead set against you."

"Blair? What's his damn problem?"

"Well, in his favour, he co-operated with the police, and that kept certain people needing you alive, but it messed up his cash flow again."

"Too bad." Peg fell abruptly silent.

"What's the matter?"

"I…I don't know if I am imagining things or not, but I think King made me write something so those shares would be transferred to him."

"Uh, but would it be legal if it was under duress?"

"I don't know. Maybe he didn't get a chance to do anything about it?"

"We should mention it to Steve, and see if he had such a letter on him. I don't know what's involved to transfer shares. Did King tell you what to write?"

"Yes, and if I am remembering right, he got Mr Owens to witness it. He's a JP or something. Maybe though, I might have used my old name, not the name they are under now…at least I hope I did. If I didn't, old Blair will really hate me."

"You don't need him," Jack told her.

"I know. But, I will like to keep knowing my great uncle Jack Casey, and my cousin Jimmy and reserve judgement about the rest."

"I expect Blair will want to see you," Jack considered.

"Not until I am out of here," Peg decided. "Then, as far as I am concerned, he has got five minutes to convince me that I should admit to knowing him. I am everything that he disliked in his daughter, and more. I don't think he will ever acknowledge me, and personally, I don't want to admit any blood relationship to him. He is probably wondering what he did to deserve me. And if he can't figure it out by now, he never will. What he is probably too self-centred to realise is that he doesn't deserve me."

Jack's smile turned to a malicious grin when he took in her meaning.

Peg went on, "He had better not try to make me do anything I don't want to do."

"If he does, he won't be the first to regret trying," Jack chuckled, thinking that King and Costa would come to regret that soon.

"Now, I have been thinking," Peg grabbed Jack's arm to ensure that she had his attention. "I want you to contact Stuart and get him to buy the Lomax farm as cheaply as possible. Then, I need to know how much money I have left, because I want to buy the farm that Mr Owens is renting. Falconer, I think that's Henry, not his Mother, wants to evict him. I want to know if the Falconers are having money trouble, because if they are, maybe we can buy that land dirt cheap too."

"That will probably use up all that you got from the trust from the shares," Jack guessed.

"I am hoping not, because the Lomax place will need a lot of work but I am hoping Ned and Jasper will do most of it. Stan too, when he gets out. Don't forget what I am earning as a performer. I intend to save and invest most of that, and live off what you earn. Mine being a buffer against hard times."

"What about the Owen's place? If he can't pay the rent now, you won't be making anything from it for a while."

"I know. And that's something I need to find out. It might mean getting Stuart to talk to Mr Owens when he is better, to discover why his place went downhill. I think he used up all he had, trying to bail Sidney out of trouble."

"Well, if King was behind that, he is now out of the picture. Hopefully Sidney Owens will have learnt his lesson after he finishes his sentence for various things," Jack considered.

"Yes, that's assuming my assumption is right. I think Owens was doing okay until then. If so, all he might need is a loan to get started again. Maybe, instead of charging him interest, I ask him to let Ned and Jasper work for him and learn about horses and training them. Then, when he is back on his feet, and the boys have fixed up the Lomax place, the two farms can work together. I think we can have places for training horses, a place to agist them, or they can come to stud. Maybe even have a horse riding camp, or a holiday farm."

Jack just shook his head at the plans. "Are you sure that your brothers, the original ones, will be in this?"

"They will need a job and it is a chance for them to settle down. I am pretty sure it will suit them."

"What about your Aunt's place?"

"She left that to the boys. They can decide if they keep it or sell it. They can either live there or at the Lomax place once it is habitable again."

"Okay, I will put all that to Stuart. No doubt he will have questions, particularly about the no interest loan. Will you be charging rent?"

"If he likes it better, yes, but I will be putting the rent back into building the horse business back up. At least at first. Oh, and right now, I want to pay what Owens is owing on his rent. I don't want him worrying about having to move out."

"Okay. Anything else your ladyship?"

"Yeah, Jack. I need some decent clothes if I am to meet my Dad for the first time."

"Performance style?" Jack queried.

"Yeah, why not."

After the way his father had been carrying on while Peg was missing, Mike expected him to have been kicking down the hospital doors to get to her. He wasn't. Nor was he drunk. If he had to guess, Mike would have said he was scared.

"What if she doesn't like me? Doesn't want anything to do with me?"

"Dad! Can I tell you a few things? One, she has never had a father figure, and she is just damn glad that it wasn't King or Costa who sired her. Also, you and she have a lot in common. Best of all..." Mike paused for effect. "Your name isn't Blair!"

"But I have been in prison."

"So has she."

"I never did anything for her."

"You didn't even know about her. She knows that."

"I can't just march in and announce that I'm her father."

"Then just ask to be friends. Peg, I mean Megan, isn't a child anymore. It will be fine. You will just have to put up with two of us telling you what to do."

Ian scowled, and then laughed. "Boy, I'm sure glad we found each other again, even if you are an old hen at times."

Ian dressed very carefully in a conservative suit and tie before going to the hospital. Jack had arranged to meet them on the ground floor and show them to the room where Peg was. When he saw what Ian was wearing, his eyes went to Mike, who only rolled his in return.

When Mike was next to him, he whispered to Jack, "First date clothes!"

Jack murmured, "I told Peg about the letter he found, and the references her aunt had made in her journal. She is not going to give Ian a chance to be shy."

Peg, dressed and sitting on her bed, greeted Ian with, "What's with the suit?"

It startled Ian so much that he forgot the speech he had prepared, and the stress he felt at meeting with his grown daughter. He just laughed.

"I wanted to impress you."

"What's changed since I last ran off from you? I liked you when I first met you up at Jack Casey's place. Even more when Mike said you were his dad. And now, wow! It seems that you are mine too."

"There is a very good chance," Ian admitted. "But even if I am not, you are the daughter of someone that I loved deeply."

"And my damn aunt kept any clue to that, hidden all these years," Peg said bluntly. "Why didn't she take those letters to you?"

"When I got out of prison, I moved a lot. Maybe she couldn't find me?"

"Well, do you know what I think?" Peg asked him.

"No," Ian said cautiously.

"Well, apart from the fact that my mother died, if she hadn't I reckon she would have chosen you to be my father regardless. So, I reckon I will adopt you as my father anyway. That makes Mike my brother, Jack gets him as a brother-in-law, and will probably ensure that my maternal grandfather keeps away from me."

Ian moved from where he had been standing, closer to the bed. "Do you really feel that way?"

"Yes! So do I get a hug or something to seal the deal?"

Ian didn't need a second invitation, and Peg saw his eyes glistening in the moment before his arms closed around her. She didn't try to pull away too soon, for she felt how the older man was trembling and sensed that it was a bitter sweet moment for him.

She finally said, "I do wish my aunt had found you sooner."

"Well, now we have all the soppy stuff over," Jack said when Ian had composed himself. "My wife has a secret to share with you."

"Yeah, and it is to stay a secret until I am out of here," Peg preceded her announcement. Then she said quietly, "You know that record I did with Carson? Well, it went Gold!"

Ian hugged her again, and this time, Mike did as well. Jack hadn't even hinted the news to him.

Then Peg proposed something else. "And I want to write some songs for the three of us. I heard you two singing and liked the retro/modern sound of it. I want to make a record, without Carson, to see if I am good with you two as well. So, Ian, if you have any recordings from way back, I'd like to hear them."

"I…I will see what I can find," Ian promised, flushing in pleasure.

"Oh, and one other thing…" Peg paused for effect. "Lose the suit before you take me out to a sumptuous dinner to welcome me to your family."

Peg was glad to lie back and rest after her busy and emotional day. She had been too distracted to feel the unpleasant effects of withdrawing from the drugs King had been giving her during the days she had been his prisoner. She hadn't asked what the drug was, and the doctor had merely said it was highly addictive, and it was well that she hadn't been having it very long. Since she didn't want to be given more drugs to counter the withdrawal symptoms, she said nothing to the doctor or nurses. When she began to shiver and feel cold, she wrapped herself back in her borrowed gown, drew her knees up to her chest and hugged them.

Les slipped in without her noticing, until she was right beside the bed.

"You really alright, kid?"

"I am no longer starving or dehydrated," Peg told her. "How come you didn't come earlier?"

"Didn't want to intrude," Les said with unusual reticence. "What with you meeting your dad and all."

"Actually, I had met him once already, but I didn't know about him then."

"Go alright?"

"Yeah, he's okay. I decided to adopt him anyway."

"You're nuts, kid. You make him sound like a stray mutt."

"He kinda looked like one when he came in, in a suit and all. But he really loved my mother, and if things had been different, he would've been my dad."

Les shrugged. "Do you wish it were like that?"

"It wasn't. So I figure I get to choose who I call family. You, Mike, Ian, Mr Casey, and my brothers."

"Aren't you forgetting someone?" Les smirked.

Peg reached out and squeezed Les's hand. "No, he's –"

She didn't finish what she was about to say, because her door opened and a well-dressed couple walked in.

Instead, in a very low voice said, "And ditch some who are. Give me five minutes, will you?"

Les glanced at the couple, and returned a hand sign that they had once used for 'five'. She took herself out of the room, but only to the passage outside, where she could listen.

Peg had a very good idea who her visitors were, but she didn't let on. She really didn't feel like dealing with them either, for she was feeling the unpleasant symptoms of the drug withdrawal, though maybe a good argument would distract her.

"Who are you?" she asked bluntly.

"You know very well –" the man began.

"Megan, we are your mother's parents," the woman interrupted her husband, but she wasn't being aggressive.

"Really?" Peg maintained a touch of belligerence. "Seems I have relatives coming from everywhere now that I am becoming famous. Took you long enough to look me up."

"You refused to come and see me when I requested it," David Blair glowered.

"Too right," Peg asserted. "Why should I have? When I don't know you from Adam, and you made no secret of saying I had stolen those shares from you. They are legally mine. I inherited them from my mother. And since you chucked her out into the streets, I don't think you deserve to have any claim to her, or me."

"Megan, that was a different time." The woman was trying to keep the conversation civil.

"So, if I was your daughter now, you'd not cast me out because I had been in prison? Not to mention, raped twice, almost killed twice – all because of some damn shares?"

The blank looks on both faces told her she had succeeded in shocking them. "I met the guy who is my father today. The guy you didn't think was a fit husband for your daughter. But he loved my mother, and for over 18 years, he has lived with the knowledge that he wasn't able to look after her.

248

You two could have, and did nothing when she needed you most. He never knew about me until recently."

"And neither had we," Megane Blair said quietly.

"No offence, Grandmother – whose name I don't even know – even before you discovered that your dead daughter had given birth before her death, my Grandfather has considered me some kind of thief, con artist and who knows what. By all accounts, I am even worse than my mother ever was when you disowned her. So I can only assume that you don't care about me, and the only reason you bothered to come here is those damn shares."

"You never went slumming with doped up musos…"

"Enough!" Peg raised her voice, as her patience vanished. "Your five minutes is up. You can go, or I will call the nurse to evict you." She moved her hand to the bell push to emphasize her point.

"There's no need to be like that," Blair insisted.

"Megan, please, we would like to get to know you," Megane Blair tried.

Peg stared at Blair when she said, "You are a petty minded, close-minded, ungrateful bastard who does not deserve to be related to me. Do you even care why I ended up here? Do you know?"

From the reddening in Blair's face, she suspected that he didn't. "I was abducted by someone working for Gianni Costa and Harry King. I was drugged unconscious with a drug I was told was highly addictive. Those bastards are still after those damn shares, and when the police were close to finding where they had me, King had me buried in an old cess pit and when caught refused to say where. It was a good thing my friends were a damn sight smarter. Do you think I invited all that?"

Blair seemed unable to answer.

"No, Megan, of course we don't," Megane said quickly.

Blair's face had taken on a new expression. It suggested that something she had said had struck a chord.

"Gianni Costa hasn't been seen for twenty years," Blair blurted. "What would someone claiming to work for him, want with those shares?"

"You're the businessman, go figure it. My money is on Costa being in cahoots with John Costigan."

Peg thought it prudent not to mention her conviction that Costigan was Costa.

"Do you mean that John is being coerced by him?" Blair challenged.

"Are you chummy with Costigan?" Peg asked, instead of accusing him of being thick witted.

"Not these days."

"Well, let me tell you something that I can personally attest to. I know damn well that Costa is still around. He visited my aunt and I saw him. I also know that Harry King is his usual front man. I believe that Costa contrived to financially ruin Aunt Ida's parents, or convince them they were, so they committed suicide, and he could turn up and be Ida's saviour, marry her and get control of her inheritance. Based on that, I believe he was trying to do the same thing with my mother – get control of her inheritance by getting her addicted and relying on him. Even without your help, she was too smart for him. Costa has probably tried the same tricks on other young rich women, and still is."

"That's a rather tall tale, young woman."

"Is it? I will tell you something else I personally know, and maybe the police of the OCTF will give you confirmation. Eugene Taylor knows this. Aunt Ida's oldest son was fathered by Gianni Costa. Stan is a near twin to Reg Costigan, son of John. Stan was forced to participate in a scheme to get Reg Costigan's girlfriend pregnant. Reg, it seems is sterile. The idea was that the girl's father would insist she marry Reg. That girl was, I know, being drugged over a period of time."

Peg wondered why all the colour slowly left Blair's face. Was he getting the point or was it something else?

"If you want collaboration of this claim, you might discuss it with your brother in law, Jack Casey. You might also consider telling him what ancient hold Costa has on you."

Blair stumbled to a chair and practically fell into it.

Peg gave him a last dismissive glance, and turned to his wife. She was frowning at her husband, probably worried by his look and manner.

"The real reason why King tried to bury me, is because I know too damn much from my aunt and I intend to see they are put in prison until they die in there. I am not so image conscious as to be scared off."

Megane turned to her.

"Now, just for the record, I am glad your son was found well. And I find my young cousin Jimmy a truly delightful and talented young man. Please pass on a message that his cousin said hello."

By the door, just inside the room, was a grinning Les Shaw. Actually, smirking might have been a more accurate description. She began a slow handclap. Peg glanced at her, but kept a neutral expression, for Les had riffed up her hair to give it an unkempt look, and was posing with the come hither slouch of a street walker.

"You said five minutes, kid, but I gave you a bit longer since you were doing so well."

Her attitude was sufficiently disconcerting that David Blair stood up and gestured to his wife to leave.

Les watched them walk along the passage and out of sight before coming back in and closing the door.

"That sure put a kink in his tail," Les approved.

"Yeah. And I hope they let me out of here soon."

"Not too soon, kid. I call tell you are still hurting."

"I can do that anywhere. It should ease off in a few days, right?"

"Yeah, but they can help you more here?"

"I am too damn easy to find, here."

Jack was dozing in a chair beside Peg's bed. She had fallen asleep soon after her meal, and he hadn't wanted to disturb her. He woke when the nurse came in to check the drip and to add the next dose of antibiotics to it. The woman, not one of the nurses he had seen before, managed to check Peg's pulse and temperature without waking Peg.

"How is she?" Jack asked.

"Oh, you startled me," the nurse admitted. "All visitors should have left, you know."

"I have permission to stay," Jack told her. "So, how is she?"

"Pulse is fine. Temperature still mildly above normal. The antibiotics seem to be killing the infection."

"Thanks." Jack watched her fill in the patient sheet, and add the antibiotics to the drip.

She gave him a smile and picked up the kidney bowl used to bring in the medicine and left the ward.

Jack stood up to stretch and to go to the visitor's toilet. When he returned, he spoke briefly to the duty constable before slipping into the ward. Before sitting again, he took his wife's hand, and feeling how hot it was, moved his hand to her forehead and cheek. They were burning, not just 'mildly hotter than normal'. Alarmed, he went at a trot out of the ward and towards the nurse's station. Peg's initial fever had responded well to the antibiotics, and her temperature had been near normal since the previous day.

"Who is in charge of the patient in room 5?" Jack demanded.

"Room 5? I am. I'm due to take obs shortly. What is the problem?"

"My wife is burning hot, yet when obs were taken half an hour ago, her temperature was only just higher than normal."

"Obs aren't due until 8pm. Who took them?"

"Whoever was on before you, I expect. I hadn't seen that nurse before."

"I have been on since six. I took obs just before tea."

The nurse was already moving, and Jack had to trot to keep up with her. "Is your wife awake?"

"No. She fell asleep soon after eating her tea."

Within moments of arriving, the nurse was taking fresh observations and comparing them with the chart.

"Tell me what you saw," the nurse insisted, urgently.

Jack reported in detail, and something about what he said had the nurse looking at the drip and then removing the tape at the needle, to remove it.

She held her finger over the insertion site and directed Jack to bring a swab and tape from a drawer in the bedside table. Her free hand held the needle up above the level of the fluid filled bag on the drip stand.

"Hold this up for a moment," the nurse directed. When Jack took it, she taped the swab in place, then turned off the tap on the drip bag and took it and the tubing from Jack.

In that brief moment, Jack saw two things. The tubing near the needle was clouded and the liquid in the tubing was yellowish, not clear.

Before leaving the room, the nurse used the room's phone to page the doctor and then summoned the constable from the passage. "Do not let anyone else in this room, except for myself or the doctor."

Jack kept near Peg's bed until the doctor arrived with an emergency team.

An hour later, with Peg surrounded by sealed plastic bags of icy water, her temperature was slowly coming down.

The doctor finally came over to talk.

"I have had blood samples taken and sent the drip and tubing to the lab. I don't know what was injected, but whatever it was, wasn't miscible with the saline and glucose solution. It is possible that some entered your wife's bloodstream, but most did not since the tube soon became clogged. I will be reporting this incident."

"I will add what I saw," Jack promised. "How is she?"

"We will be watching her very closely, but I believe we caught this in time. I will know more when we get the lab report."

Jack let the nurse take the chair he had been using, since he was too tense to sit still. He wasn't going to admit that his leg was throbbing. He berated himself for slacking off his paranoia, because Costa and King had been caught. He jerked around every time the door opened.

When he saw Maddern and York enter, he relaxed marginally.

"What can you tell us, Jack?" Maddern asked. "We have spoken to the doctor."

After telling all he knew and describing the mystery nurse, York asked, "Who did you tell about Megan being here?"

"No one that didn't already know. Mike and Les knew, as well as that Inspector you brought along. Mike or someone told Ian, because he was here. And somehow Blair found out, because he came too. Les said Peg sent him off with a flea in his ear."

"Would he want Megan out of the picture?" York asked.

"Why don't you ask him? He has been hostile to her ever since he found out she had the shares that once belonged to his daughter."

"We will talk to him," Maddern promised, then said, "We have arranged with your grandfather to have Megan transferred to Melbourne as soon as she is stable."

"Costa and King are still safely locked up?" Jack asked.

Maddern nodded. "They are being kept apart, but messages may be being passed via their lawyers."

Jack just growled wordlessly.

"Megan is tough," York reminded Jack. "Do you think these tries at her will deter her from testifying?"

"No damn way! The opposite if anything."

"Well, as I see it, she has one hell of a reason to stay around," York pointed out.

"Have you heard from the doctor if they have the lab report?" Jack asked.

"Only a preliminary one," Maddern admitted. "He believes that there must have been a sedative in her meal, judging from the levels. He thinks that should wear off by midnight. The substance is still unknown, but it is likely that the nurse made a mistake by injecting it into the drip. Likely if she had injected it directly into a vein, Megan would have died."

"Shit!" Jack said, swaying with shock. The nurse stood and directed him to a second chair.

"Seems some guardian angel is looking out for her," York commented.

"She reckoned she was talking to her mother and aunt while she was down that pit. I assumed she had been hallucinating or something."

"Maybe not," York remarked, but he didn't explain that cryptic comment.

Maddern ended the visit with, "We'll be in touch."

The hospital did not protest when Mike and Les came in to relieve Jack. He had told them what had happened, and that they were now running a new drip at a fast rate. His theory was that it was to flush out any last traces of the inimical solvent, and the frequent changes of the catheter bag was to have the contents tested.

Jack only slept for a few hours, and was back early. By then, Peg was stirring although still drowsy from the fever. She was well enough to recognise those around her.

The doctor came in later to check on her, and reported that the substance injected was a concentrated form of the pathogen that had caused the original infection.

"So we would think she merely had a relapse?" Jack proposed.

"Possibly," the doctor agreed.

"Then why the earlier sedative?"

"So she would not feel the symptoms and ring for help, perhaps," the doctor suggested.

Les, who was still around suggested, "Or recognise the fake nurse."

"That is certainly an idea to pass onto Vic Maddern."

"I will," Jack promised.

The doctor continued. "He has arranged for a medivac helicopter. "If her condition is stable this evening, they will transfer her to the police hospital."

"I know the place. They will likely incarcerate me there again if I show my face."

"So I believe," the doctor smiled faintly. "So while your friends are still here, why don't you come with me and I will check you out?"

With a faint grin of his own, Jack agreed. "Fair enough, thanks."

Chapter 38

Once Peg was feeling normal again, she was moved to a safe house and told to stay inside. It reminded her of being at Meredan, but she really did not want any more friends of Harry King of Gianni Costa to find her. Her friends were allowed to come and go, and Jack was there more often than not.

His grandfather had introduced him to several former policemen who were now working as private investigators. They felt Jack had a knack for the business, but he still had to decide. He knew that Peg had plans for business in Matlock, but he wasn't sure where he would fit in that. So, he was studying material the private investigators had given him, and that was preventing him from being twitchy with inactivity.

Another guest at the house was Louisa Westcott. She had been delighted to have company, and even got along with Les when she was visiting. She had her own amusements, particularly sewing and needlework. Both pastimes that were mysteries to Peg and Les. The latter allowed Louisa to try to teach her knitting, but generally she spoke more curses than knitted stitches.

Peg's guitar had followed her again, and she often went off into her own little world, strumming chords, and writing down notes and lyrics as they came to her. Her audience rarely complained of the music. Jack was content to let her compose, even if it meant she was ignoring him, as he knew it meant that all the bad things she had endured, hadn't soured her.

One evening, she gave a preview of one of the half a dozen songs she had been working on. Her working title for it was 'Vengeance', but likely when it was finished, the title would be a more subtle idea of the theme. Jack decided he would suggest, 'Unrepentant'.

Periodically, the prosecution lawyers would come and talk to her to clarify her understanding of various points, since she had known Ida Jessup quite well. It seemed that excerpts from her journals were being used to correlate with other evidence. The men were close lipped about the cases against the two long term criminals, but had mentioned some of the other charges against both. Peg had to hope that the defence lawyers could not negate everything.

Jack Casey, when he visited, was able to tell them a little more, mainly that the evidence on some charges was very tight. One thing that had particularly delighted the old miner, came as a surprising snippet to Peg.

"They found some odd things in those bundles you unearthed. In short, it provides the missing link between your mother alive, giving birth to you, and her death."

"Stuff from the motel," Jack guessed, from his listening position perched on the arm of a chair.

"Indeed," Casey confirmed. "Bloodstained sheets, clothing and towels – all with your mother's blood type. It is my thought that while King went off to dispose of the body, your aunt was told to clean out the room. It seems that she took it literally, ensuring that she got everything that she or King might have touched that was portable. That included two glasses, an empty beer can, and empty lemonade can and one of a pair of fine leather gloves."

Peg was leaning forward in her chair, knowing that Casey had yet to get to the cause of his glee.

"The glasses had the motel name stamped on them, and the bedding and towels had cleaner's marks that were traced to the motel. The cans…had King's prints on them, and the glove, when shone with UV light and some chemical, had prints on too."

"Yes!" Jack shouted. "I bet he took the gloves off so that he wouldn't get blood on them."

"And expected Aunt Ida to be so scared herself that she would leave no trace of them," Peg guessed.

"She probably was," Casey concurred. "However, if you read between the lines in her journal, I think King expected her to dump the stuff at the local tip or someplace like that. I think that she thought the cess pit at her place was the safest place."

"Huh!" Peg said, as she considered. "I have probably been misjudging the bitch. I know Costa conditioned her to think herself dumb, and most people would think disposing the stuff where she did was dumb, but I think she had moments of smart thinking."

"How much did you learn from her," Jack asked, looking thoughtfully at his wife. "After all, she was the one who nurtured you."

He kept his thought to himself, that it was the nurture and neglect of her upbringing that had made Peg particularly resilient and resourceful and self-reliant. She was a contrast to Louisa Wescott with her privileged upbringing, who even now thought that the only future she had was to get married. He had seen a different side of her, the side that had listened to her father talking business. She wasn't unintelligent, she just hadn't learn her true worth yet.

Jack didn't try to influence her thoughts, just let her take in the details of Peg's plans. She had made some astute comments about potential pitfalls. Even though Mike and Les knew about the plans, Jack and Peg only discussed them when no one else was around. Louisa was the exception.

The NSW financial advisor, Stuart, had succeeded in purchasing the Lomax farm – buildings and all – and at a very satisfactory price. He was still working on getting the farm that Jed Owens was renting, and making discreet investigations of the Falconer family finances. He'd had a particularly satisfying discussion with Jed Owens, who was grateful for his rent being paid up to date, and open to the idea of a short term loan at modest interest to get back on his feet. He had even proposed a kind of trust arrangement so that it would not be possible for his son to drain money from his business again. Stuart had a great deal of respect for Jed Owens.

"Do you like horses?" Louisa had asked, as that aspect had caught her attention.

"Well, I never really had anything to do with them until I met Horse," Peg admitted.

Louisa laughed. "Horse?"

"I didn't know his real name." Peg explained how she had encountered the misnamed Black Diamond. "But the real thing is, Mr Owens gave me a job, and a fair go when I was just out of Meredan. And I am pretty sure he recognised me in Mildura when I was hiding from the police and everyone and working at the race course, and he didn't tell anyone."

"Do you ride?" Louisa persisted.

"Uh, no."

"Then why are you going to start a business with horses?"

"Horse never looked down on me like people did. He only did because he was taller than me."

Louisa laughed again. "So, if this Owens guy trains horses, will you be in competition?"

"No…I thought of having placid horses for people to come and ride, or have a holiday horse farm for people, or trail rides."

"All by yourself?"

"No. I am going to ask Mr Owens to take on Ned and Jasper – my other brothers – and teach them about horses. I already know how to muck out stables and groom a horse."

"You amaze me!" Louisa admitted. "You are going to be a great singer and yet you are willing to muck out stables."

"Well, my aunt never taught me to be a proper lady so I muddle along. Can you ride?"

"Oh yes! I love horse riding," Louisa exclaimed. She told of her experience and awards for dressage and other events.

A huge grin appeared on Peg's face and she suggested, "You could always agree to join the business. It would add class to it."

Louisa fell silent, and grew thoughtful. "I wonder what my dad would think of the idea?"

"The idea is one thing. Working with a pack of Jessup idiots is another. But I feel sure the idea will appeal to Ned and Jasper who are due out in less than a month. I think it would suit Stan too, whenever they let him out."

Peg was watching Louisa's face as she mentioned her eldest brother. However it was the hand that went to her vaguely bulging stomach that was most telling. All she said was, "I will certainly consider your offer. When will you have a more detailed business plan? And have you thought of a place for Les?"

"I promised to help her get a new start and I have a few ideas. I will need a manager for when I am doing singing stuff, and Les is good at ending nonsense. And if Mike wants in, I will set him up with his own café."

Jack snickered. "You'd better hire a cook. I don't think Mike is up to cooking."

Peg merely waved that problem aside. "Anyway, whichever way you decide, Lou, I would be interested in picking your brains about horses and horse people and all those events you mentioned."

Later, Jack twitted her in private. "Are you matchmaking?"

"Not really. I already know that Stan made an impact on her – in a good way. The problem is her upper crust upbringing and Stan's supposedly violent criminal record."

"What was it you said about her father?"

"That he's pretty sick, and he wanted her married off with an heir on the way before he kicked off. He'd reluctantly decided to let her and Reg marry, until that scam of Reg et al came to light. I think if she had got pregnant to some less disgraceful rich son, he'd have got the shotgun out to make them marry."

"Does her father know what she thinks of your brother?"

Peg shrugged. "I think she is still thinking of what I told her. She was all set to insist on marrying Stan before they took him back to Pentridge. I told her to wait until he came out – give her time to be sure."

Jack's mind switched tracks. "Is Stan still in Pentridge?"

"No, he went back to Goulburn. Devlin went to Long Bay to finish his time and the extra time."

"I thought they would want him to testify," Jack said.

"Either way, he's probably safer up there."

"What about the special consideration for his help?"

"I don't know what was agreed to, but that decision might have to wait until after the trials."

"Yeah! After them. Did you know that the Task Force received kudos from the Chief Commissioner for catching Costa?"

"Let them take the glory. I know I have helped a lot, but the bad guys don't have to know exactly how much and I want all this behind me."

"I guess, while we wait, I can distract you for a while," Jack suggested.

Chapter 39

Ned and Jasper Jessup walked out of the training centre and were surprised to see a car waiting for them. They were even more surprised to see their 'kid' sister racing towards them.

"Hey, you aren't little anymore," Ned grinned as she hugged him with one arm.

"Didn't expect to see you," Jasper admitted. "I thought we'd have to hitch a ride home."

"I couldn't have that," Peg said with a huge grin. "You might have got lost on the way and I have plans for you guys."

"Oh no! We wanted to bum around for a bit," Ned complained.

"On what money?" Peg retorted. "And even though the house now belongs to you two and Stan, it needs some fixing up."

"So, what are your dastardly ideas, sis?" Jasper asked.

"You are going into business with me. What do you know about horses?"

"Ah, they have four legs," Ned joked.

"I didn't think you were into horses like those rich girls," Jasper teased.

"I wasn't, but Jed Owens gave me a job at his place and I learned about mucking out stables and grooming horses. I kinda fell in love with one of them."

Jasper had glanced at the car and noticed Jack leaning against it. "He don't look like a horse to me, sis."

"What? Oh, that's Jack. We're married. No, I am talking about a horse. The one stupid slimy Sidney tried to abduct and sell. I reckon your unpleasant daddy put him up to it."

"I heard he got caught," Ned grinned maliciously.

Peg copied his grin. "Yeah, he did. The bastard killed Aunt Ida, you know and I reckon they have him tied up for that."

Jasper hissed. "I hope they hang him."

"He tried to kill me twice, so I agree with you. Only they don't hang people anymore."

Ned looked her over. "You don't look like death warmed up."

"Not going to give him the satisfaction. Anyway, I can't discuss all that as his trial is still ongoing. I've had to testify at various times, and this time they can't claim I am lying. But back to business. Do you want to come into business with me? You will need a job of some kind."

"With you as our boss?" Ned asked, his eyes betraying both interest and disbelief.

"In a way. Come back to the car. I want you to meet Jack, and I can tell you my ideas as we drive back to Matlock."

"That went well," Jack murmured as he and Peg were driving back to Melbourne.

"I think so too," Peg agreed. "They never really had any direction when we were growing up and by the sounds of it they made the most of their opportunities to learn stuff while they were away. We were all more used to being outdoors, and those two must have been doing a lot of physical work, since they have both filled out and muscled up."

"Jasper does look awfully like King," Jack admitted. "But he is nothing like him."

"You do like them, don't you?" Peg asked.

"They'll do okay. They will soon realise that hard work now is for them, not for domineering officialdom. What's more, I think that Owens will think them saints compared to Sidney."

"He was rather taken aback when Jasper suggested he do less of the heavy work because he was a special commodity. A guy that gives ex-cons a go," Peg commented. "And I noticed that Neville made the effort to be friendly."

"Still, Owens was shocked when he saw Jasper and realised who their father was," Jack put in.

"Ah, but when Jasper told Owens the situation and their hatred of him, I think that sealed the deal."

Peg fell silent for a while, recalling that King's trial continued in the morning and she would still be needed at some stage.

It seemed as if Jack read her mind.

"The Task Force have accumulated so much evidence against King and Costa, more than I realised. The jury may not accept some of it, and some charges may not be proved, but they will both definitely go down for murder and if their lawyers try to prove you are a proven perjurer, they will be in for a shock."

"I am glad I have you, Jack. You straighten out my mind when it goes into a spiral."

"Happy to distract you whenever I can," Jack suggested.

Chapter 40

Peg slipped out of the court once the judge had left, keeping just ahead of the crowd who had been present to hear the sentence. The experience had brought home to her the knowledge that she was by far, not the only person King had made to suffer. Perhaps though, she had been the luckiest. He hadn't been able to break her like the seven other girls he had abducted, held prisoner and raped repeatedly. Four of those had committed suicide, and the other three were barely existing.

The mothers of the six little girls he had killed when younger, now had closure. That huddled group looked little happier than she felt. The life sentence was fitting, but it did little to pay back the misery he had inflicted. The charges for what he had done to her, to all the other girls and all the things he had done for Costa, deserved the penance of several lifetimes.

At that moment, Peg just wanted to be alone. The tally of his crimes had been so long, it was sickening. The murder of her aunt was one of the crimes there was the most evidence for, but the twenty year old murder at a Mansfield motel had, at first, seemed to invoke little reaction from King or his lawyers. Her confidence in the outcome had hit rock bottom. Yet it had been that old case that had been the first nail in the final outcome.

When the prosecution had presented the evidence, the bloody fabric had not worried King. However, his fingerprints on a can that could be traced to its date of manufacture, having the same blood on it, had for a moment provoked an expression of shock. She had been far enough around in the seated onlookers to see it as he turned to talk to his lawyer. They had tried to discredit the corroborating evidence in Ida Jessup's journal, but the details had matched too well. Other quoted excerpts had added more nails to the case.

While the moment of sentencing had reminded her of when she had been sentenced, she felt as she had on the moment of her release, with a fresh start waiting for her. It wasn't quite that time yet, for she might still have to appear and testify at Costa's trial. However that was a minor matter compared to King's trial.

"It's over, kid," Les said quietly in her ear. Peg turned, and smiled at her friend. "It isn't enough. If I had my way he would be neutered as well."

Les snickered. "He might pretend to be strong and macho, but I would like it if the other prisoners got to hear about his perverted ways with little kids. I hear that blokes like him are not liked. Maybe someone will stick a knife in him."

"Huh! I can't see that happening. He will be in high security."

"Who knows?" Les shrugged. "Come on. Jack said to meet him down the street."

"Okay, but I need to use the ladies room first."

When Peg re-joined Les, she looked very different. She had exchanged the pant suit she had worn in the court for a dress and let her hair out of its ponytail. It had been Jack's suggestion, for the crowd of media waiting outside the court never gave her a second glance. She was happy to let them bother the other witnesses. When Costa's soon to start trial was over, Peg Jessup would finally fade away and Megan Dawes, nee Blair, would come into her own.

Jack was waiting for them outside a small café. He gestured them inside. Peg was not surprised to see Casey, Mike, Ian and Justin Taylor already there. They had been her other stalwarts during the trial. They had all left before the sentence was announced, but Justin had his own way of hearing the result.

"My father said 'well done' and he will talk to you later," Justin greeted before ordering afternoon tea for the group.

During that interlude, the talk was, by mutual consent, about the future.

"Does it always feel a bit of a letdown after the criminal is finally convicted?" Peg asked Justin.

She received a considered answer. "You have the sense of a job well done, and the knowledge that the next day you will be starting again with another crook, another case. This isn't the end. We have the head of this gang, and the task force has a lot of lesser members to go after. The trouble is, now there is a power void. Some other gangster will move in. However, your part is nearly over and you deserve much credit. Not many women would be able to take the humiliation King's lawyers put you through and come back for a rematch."

That did cause Peg to smile faintly. "Wasn't that part of the plan to get King's lawyers over confident? Why King was initially only charged with that old case?"

Justin gave a wry grin. "The intention was to get him put away while we gathered more evidence, but still, it established a precedent."

Peg shook her head, not understanding. Justin didn't explain, it wasn't the place for that. All he said was, "The crowd of media should be gone by now. Time to go home."

The result of the trial had been the top item on the TV news and Louisa Westcott was full of the details when Peg and Jack returned to the house with Mike and Les. She went immediately to Peg and hugged her.

"Thank you so much for waking me up to what was happening to me." There was no trace left of reserve due to their different social status. She had not expected the shudder that shook Peg, but she quickly understood.

She gestured to Les and said to the others, "You guys get up to something else. We are going to have some girl time."

In Louisa's room, with the door shut, Peg was free to let out the last of the tension she felt. Neither Les, nor Louisa told her that tears were stupid. They just sat close and let their presence comfort her.

After the tears eased, Louisa told them, "My dad called earlier. He has been following the trial too. I don't know if you saw him there or not, he really shouldn't have gone at all. He said he hadn't realised how truly evil that man was, and far he might have made Reggie go. You impressed him. I had told him about you and how you had helped me."

Peg wiped her eyes with a borrowed hanky and asked her, "Does he know about Stan?"

"Some," Louisa admitted. "I think he is gleeful that Reggie isn't the father of my baby, and is not related to criminals as bad as King. He has heard rumours about Reggie's father too."

"But Stan is still a criminal," Peg reminded her.

"Yes, he knows that, but I think Old Man Taylor had a word to him about how Stan was working with the police."

Les inserted, "Stan isn't a vicious person, although everyone probably thinks he is. I can attest to that."

Peg laughed wryly. "Us Jessups were a pack of sheep ready to be led astray." She decided not to mention who had sired Stan, if she didn't know.

"You still thinking of marrying Stan?" Les asked in her usual blunt fashion.

Louisa pushed away the question by asking, "How long does he still have to serve?"

"I don't know," Peg admitted. "I think the police did a deal with him, so I hope that will be a reduction in his time. He has been treated like Mick was, but he did little more than Ned or Jasper during that damn robbery. My other brothers got out a couple of months ago. However, I don't think anything will be decided until after Costa's trial."

Louisa sighed. "I told Dad about how you plan to run a horse ranch, and set your brothers up to join the business. I think that got him thinking. He was going to let me marry Reggie, if I had my heart set on him, but he was glad when I changed my mind. His real problem is that he has quaint old fashioned ideas, and is proud of his public image. Having his daughter become an unmarried mother is bothering him."

"At least your old man is a decent bloke," Les countered. "If I had've got myself pregnant, mine would have told me to go and get rid of it."

"And my mother ended up kicked out and pregnant," Peg said. "And it was another like her that cared for me. She had lots of faults, but even so, she didn't have to take me in. But it is because of her caring about her friend's child, that today's outcome came about. So, if you still want Stan, your dad will need to realise that poor people, basically good people, can make mistakes. He will need to form his own opinion of Stan, but I think his main concern is that you will be happy and well cared for. You don't have to be filthy rich for that."

On the day that John Costigan, aka Gianni Costa was sentenced to life imprisonment, Peg felt as if a great weight had been lifted off her, or a dark cloud that had been around all her life had been blown away.

Already, words were in her mind, describing the experience and waiting to be put to music. In the past month, as her mood had swung from hopeful to fearful and back, the ideas for songs had matched. Now she could see how to combine two songs to match that mood swing. She had eight new songs to show Carson, who was sure to be in touch soon.

That evening, the celebration had been at Eugene Taylor's place. An early tea for the task force members and their wives, then a late supper for the non-police helpers. He gave commendations to Jack and Mike for their assiduous 'grunt' work, and to Peg, Les and Louisa for standing up and speaking out.

Once again, the media had been full of details, and many people were still in shock from all the crimes perpetrated by John Costigan. Many unsolved cases had been closed. The public had been shocked to learn that

Gianni Costa had murdered his brother and taken on his identity.

Jack, Peg and Louisa had been dropped back at the house where they had been staying, but they were all still too wound up to sleep.

Peg went straight to her guitar and the file of music and lyrics she was working on. The two songs that she was intending to merge had been playing in her mind, and just needed to be written down. She was hearing it as a duet between male and female voices. She hummed as she played, sometimes singing softly.

"Is she often like this?" Louisa asked. She was curled up on the couch and Jack was in one of the chairs.

"When the mood strikes," Jack admitted. "It's good to hear her like this."

"She is good," Louisa said after a while.

"I know. She has been performing under the name Megan Arthur, since early this year. The album she did with Wayne Carson went Gold in just under two months."

"Megan Arthur! Are you kidding? How did she hook up with him?"

"Let her tell you," Jack suggested. "But she is living proof of what a nobody can do when given a chance."

"And the horse farm idea?"

"We'll give it a go. She has her foster brothers involved already. You might like to meet them. Being in prison hasn't soured them. They took every chance they were offered to learn new skills."

"Have you met Stan?"

"Briefly."

"Like him?"

"I am deeply grateful that he was around when Peg…I am going to have to call her Megan now…needed help. He was more concerned for her than himself."

At that point the phone rang. Jack rose to answer it. He hoped that the media had not found them.

"It's Jack, Mr Carson," he said after the caller asked for Megan. "She is in fine form…can you hear?"

There was a silence through the phone until Carson asked, "Will you still be there tomorrow?"

"We can be," Jack confirmed.

Carson then said, "Good. I will be there to see her. Has she any other songs?"

"Oh, six or seven. No, make that six. She is in the process of combining two of them."

"Tell her I want to hear them all," Carson directed.

"I will if she will hear me," Jack promised, and heard a chuckle over the line.

"Wow!" Louisa exclaimed when Jack had put down the phone. "Was that him?"

"He will be visiting tomorrow. Will you still be here?"

"No one had better suggest I go," Louisa challenged.

Jack laughed. "Just don't start acting like swooning teens and pre-teens. Les and I have got very adept at keeping them at bay."

Louisa rubbed her belly and said, "I think I have more sense than that now."

The speed at which Carson's manager organised a series of gigs, now that Megan Arthur was back on the scene, impressed Jack. Though that did make him wonder when his wife would have time to work on her business plans.

He had already accepted that he was her 'secretary' in addition to a body guard and bed partner, but he had no idea of business, nor had Mike and Les. At least she didn't have to oversee her brothers, just send through their wages and keep abreast of how Owens' business was recovering. Stuart was helping there, and happy with progress. However, he had not yet been able to broach the idea of buying the property Owens rented from the Falconers. Megan did have an idea about that but it meant she would have to go to Matlock. With the number of gigs she had lined up, though, that might be months away.

The first performance was a huge charity event to raise money for the Red Cross. Carson was a huge draw card but not the only performer on the program. It seemed that adding Megan Arthur to the program had not been a problem, even though the programs had already been circulated. Jack assumed that was because she would mostly be doing duets, not solos.

On that night at the MCG, two days after Gianni Costa was sentenced to life, and a month after Harry King had been sent to oblivion, the audience cheered when Carson took the stage, and louder still two songs later when he was joined by Megan Arthur.

The duet, 'From Darkness to Light', and dedicated to the work of the Red Cross, brought a standing ovation and calls for an encore. For that, Carson took a backup role and let Megan sing solo. That song, 'Flying Free', hit the Top 40 list within the following week, and stayed there for nearly a record time.

MacMasters arranged a celebration when her new song reached the top five on the Hit List. He booked a room of tables at a swank city restaurant. Accepting suggestions from Carson and Jack, some unexpected people were added to the guest list.

Megan, having put her life as Peg Jessup behind her, did not recognise the two tall men who entered the room. It was only seeing a recovered Jed Owens entering behind them, that she took a second look at the figures in evening dress suits. She had never seen her brothers looking so fine.

"Hey, Sis. I could get used to all this," Ned grinned hugely, and gesturing around the room.

"Yeah, but not the penguin suits," Jasper agreed in part.

Megan hugged them both before looking at a smiling Jed Owens. "Have these two louts been behaving?"

"I don't know where they get all their damned energy," he admitted.

The three new comers from Matlock joined the table near Jack Casey, and accepted a sardonic grin from Les who sat opposite with Mike Scott.

Jack directed his wife's attention to more people entering. Of them, she only recognised Jimmy Blair. He wore a suit that was a match for his father's. She greeted him as a friend, and he grinned hugely.

"So, you really are my cousin!"

"Guilty," Megan admitted. "Not my fault though. Um, why don't you introduce your escorts?"

With aplomb, the teenager did so, and meeting her maternal uncle for the first time, decided he was nothing like his father.

"I am more than pleased to meet you," Richard Blair admitted. "You were an enormous surprise and a delight. Jimmy made me go to the concert last week, not expecting to see you, but because Carson has become his idol. You are so very like how I remember my sister and I wonder now how high she might have flown."

"Times were different then," Megan said quietly. "But I am really glad to meet you. Were your parents not invited?"

Now Richard Blair looked apologetic. "They were. However, my father said he was having a bilious attack and to bring his apologies, and my mother's."

His wife, Catherine added, "Actually, he might well be. He has been celebrating since last week. I still don't know what was between him and Costigan, but he was ecstatic about the trial result."

"It probably doesn't help that he finds my existence odious, and I told him what I thought of him," Megan admitted. "He is probably too old to change his spots anyway, and I intend to show him that I don't need him. However, since the cream of my maternal relatives are here, I am delighted. Why don't you go and sit near your uncle?"

There were still three empty seats and Megan wondered who else had been invited. Jack simply shrugged.

"Must be last minute additions. I thought everyone was here now."

Yet there was the faintest of smiles on his face, and when she glanced at Les and Mike, sitting beside Ian, they both had smothered grins. Megan turned to the door in time to see the pregnant Louisa Westcott followed by an old man, who was probably her father. A tall man followed and she gave a squeal of delight and trotted to meet the group. She gave Louisa a quick hug and felt the baby kick from within her friend, welcomed her father and then launched herself at the other man.

"Stan!"

His grin was self-conscious as he hugged her back. "Thank you, Sis," he whispered in her ear, his voice wavering a little.

She defused the emotion she sensed by saying, "Jasper doesn't like the penguin suit either. So, when did they let you out?"

"Two days ago. Not in time to go to your concert but after I had started hearing you on the radio." He gave her a half grin. "I had enough time to start spreading word in various ears about certain people and their perverted ways. Like how he treated young girls, and how he couldn't even kill a baby like he thought. It will spread to where those certain people are."

Megan chuckled. "Come on. You already know a lot of the people here, but Louisa and her father don't."

The evening was summed up when Jack Casey proposed a toast. "To Megan, from unregarded child, to the unsuspected holder of secrets and unrepentant nemesis who is now unshackled and flying free. May you prosper amongst those you have chosen as family and friends."

The End

Other Books by Margaret Gregory

WANDA: FROM BAD TO WORSE

If she was going to die young, like her mother, Gwen Willard was determined to die rich and she had very few years to do it. Her first step was to leave home. She met Hooch, who taught her some exciting and illegal skills. She was the Draco's lucky mascot until she came to the attention of the police. Then her uncanny knack for predicting trouble, warned her to flee to the city and change her name.

Life wasn't easy. She was 15, had little money and no regular job, but her new skills came in handy. Then she crossed the path of an evil and unscrupulous man and she didn't want him to have his way.

WANDA: CHOOSING CRIME

Wanda was free. She was never going back to jail. But she was homeless, almost penniless and Harrison Franklin had a long and vengeful memory.

Jim Phillips had a long memory too, and Wanda had saved his life. Could he save her from Franklin?

WANDA: RISKING LIFE TO LIVE

The euphoria of successful heists were what kept Wanda Dean alive. At 23, she was crime boss Harrison Franklin's top agent – well paid for absolute obedience. That's all that mattered. Until she met Mike Johnston and her boss ordered him killed. For that, the Franklins were going to pay. In Risking Life to Live, justice conflicts with loyalty and the penalty for betrayal is death.

WANDA: A NEW LIFE - HIDDEN SECRETS

Even before beginning as a covert agent for the US Government, Wanda is abducted by a foreign operative. After being rescued, there are signs that she had been subjected to hypnosis. With an important government gathering imminent, her handler must ensure she is not a security risk.

Can Wanda's psychic extra senses help her recognize and resist the implanted commands and clear her for secret work?

WANDA: A NEW LIFE - FIRST MISSION

On her first covert mission for the US Government, Wanda calls on the skills that made her a skilled thief to convince a revolutionary general that she's an ideal recruit. When her team mates' covers are blown, it is up to her to ensure that two missing scientists and confidential Government documents are not smuggled out of the US.

WANDA: FULL CIRCLE

Three generations after the alien Kumatan left Earth, their own world is suffering from alien invaders. In desperate hope, one returns to Earth seeking help - little knowing they had left one of their own behind.

Wanda, a child of the third generation, answers the call.

ERIN: THE FORCING OF WISDOM

For years, Erin has used the intricacies of cyberspace to banish unwanted emotions. Others call what she does hacking, and her manipulations criminal, but now her skill was exceptional - in, out, traceless. She was wrong. Someone betrayed her.

Travis has dangerous plans. He needs an electronics expert – one he can coerce through fear. Erin was perfect.

With the inescapable threat of prison looming, Erin accepts his offer of sanctuary. When she realises his intentions, she is in too deep. But the terrifying of innocents is unforgivable. She cannot walk away. She is an empath and shares their distress. She has to help them, even if it means prison, and insanity…

ERIN: THE CALL including
ELISABETH AND TANYA: BLOOD CALLS TO BLOOD.

Elisabeth's sister, Wanda, had been missing for half a year. Multiple authorities had found no trace of her, or her two colleagues. Yet she knew her sister was still alive and had answered a call for help from an alien who had once lived on Earth.

Elisabeth, along with her newly found cousin Tanya, have started to sense things from her missing sister. Enough to know that she is in dire trouble, but not enough to help her.

While looking for traces of the aliens, Elisabeth makes some unexpected discoveries about her family. Yet even with the help of a second newly discovered cousin, she fears she is not strong enough to help her sister and the others to return.

ERIN: THE CALL

Convicted cyber-criminal, Erin Mason, is startled into awareness in an unfamiliar place, with no memory of escaping and only vague memories of getting there. Voices in her head were urging her to go west, and they were getting more urgent. After a chance meeting with covert agent, Jim Phillips, when she helped save his mission, he realised that she might be the key to another, more personal quest – to find three missing state department agents.

All he must do is keep Erin safe, and hide her from an intense police search, until he can introduce her to cousins she was unaware of.

However her uncontrolled psychic gifts conflict with a logical mind that prefers the ordered intricacies of computers and electronics. She only wants to shut out the voices and the madness she sees looming.

Can Phillips convince her to help him, before the forces of the law find her?

KORVU: THE BEGINNING - The prequel to The Wild One

Jai Ansuni was the first female Atapi sorcerer for thousands of years, but she dare not reveal it. However, when tribal sorcerer, Stacion Ansuni escalates the enmity between Atapi and Kumatan to an ominous level. Jai and her womb mate, Con, try to mitigate his atrocities but can two young Atapi, not even a score of years old, win against the powerful sorcerer?

THE WILD ONE

Sixteen year old Jai Cassidy thought she was finally free of her family until she is discovered by her other relatives…the ones that aren't human. Jai uses her natural perversity and cunning to escape their control, but catapults herself into the middle of a deadly feud between two alien races.

ATAPI SORCERESS - The sequel to The Wild One

Jai Cassidy is beginning her mission of reversing the decline of the non-humanoid Atapi. As a sorceress and an Atapi-Human hybrid, she is vehemently disliked by the male Atapi sorcerers and the humanoid rulers of Korvu. Her task is complicated by the treachery of a group of alien engineers, who are inciting insurrection and harsh reprisals.

THE TYMOREAN TRUST BOOK 1 - POWER RISING

The Tymorean Trust - When peace rules Tymorea - Peace reigns in the universe. Chosen to be the Advocates of the mystical and incorporeal Guardians of Peace, twins Tymos and Kryslie must first learn to control and use the power rising in them - or it will destroy them.

On Tymorea, only the ruling Triumvirate Governors are powerful enough to guide the strong-willed alien-bred twins until they have mastered their power.

THE TYMOREAN TRUST BOOK 2 - GREAT ONES

The peace of the Guardian Planet, Tymorea, is in deadly peril. War there will create ripples of unrest and destruction throughout the settled universe. Tymos and Kryslie, still adolescents, have barely mastered their power and Llaimos is still less than a year old, but they are the three chosen to be Advocates of the mystical Guardians of Peace, to safeguard the Tymorean Trust.

THE TYMOREAN TRUST BOOK 3 - RETURN TO EARTH

Even before the war on Tymorea, the Elders foresaw that Great Ones Tymos and Kryslie would have an imperative mission on Earth.

But as the Tymoreans prepare to build an Earthbase to support them, they discover that specifications for two vital protective shields are missing.

Now, nearly a century later, Tymos and Kryslie must find his work and build the generator before the base is found.

THE TYMOREAN TRUST BOOK 4 - EARTH MISSION

Just before their graduation from the prestigious WSRA Washington University, Tymos and Kryslie Ward deliberately disappear.

The Great Ones have foreseen the capture and death of the new Tymorean missionaries and discovered that the leader of the Eastern Imperium plans to undermine the United World Nations.

Tymos and Kryslie must protect their kin and prevent a potentially devastating world war.

THE TYMOREAN TRUST BOOK 5 – ALIEN CONTACT

Tymos and Kryslie Ward, hide their Tymorean intelligence and abilities while working as low ranked technicians at the WSRA's lunar base. When an alien ship arrives at Lunar One, pursued by a powerful enemy who will stop at nothing to get what he wants, only the two Tymorean Great Ones have the knowledge and abilities to overcome him, but to do so they must risk their sanity, and their souls.

THE TYMOREAN TRUST BOOK 6 – INVASION

Great Ones Tymos and Kryslie go to rescue the crew of Earth's first deep space mission – and discover that Ciriot space pirates have discovered Earth's location. When the Ciriot invade in force, the Great Ones reveal themselves so that Earth can gain vital help. However, Kryslie becomes the victim of Ciriot, who want to control her mind and make her betray the people of Earth.

TRICKS

Tom and Jo Dwyer had a reputation for playing tricks – and getting detention. They didn't seem to care about that, so long as they made their class laugh. That was until someone began to turn their tricks against them, and it was no longer funny.